THE FIRST LIAR

MC RISING

RUNNING WILD

To late nights and the people who got me through them.

CHAPTER ONE

Director James MacGillivray was almost twenty minutes late. They couldn't start without him. Tori Jaecar groaned, smashing random letters on her keyboard. She couldn't concentrate in this environment. Not with Maena and Dick gossiping nonstop about who had and hadn't brought home cooked food to the last company potluck. Normally she wouldn't mind, but she really had to focus if she wanted to go to bed tonight. She had a deadline.

Five minutes later, James waltzed in like he owned the place. He did whatever he wanted, and usually he wanted to nap in his office while Tori slaved over his projects.

He plopped down next to her. It took him another five minutes to adjust his chair.

"Good morning, James." Tori hoped announcing his presence would help kick things off.

"Mornin' Victoria." He retrieved a meatball sub from his backpack. Slowly, he unwrapped it. He tasted the marinara sauce, smacking his lips in delight.

Richard "Dick" Mercer, James' favorite sales rep, chimed in. "Have you lost weight, James?" He had not.

James beamed, wiping his mustache. "You can tell? I'm trying that new sandwich diet."

Now that Tori could smell food, she was starving. Great.

"You should smile more, Victoria." James took a bite. Still chewing, he added, "You would be pretty if you smiled. Like Maena here."

Maena Dixon, a project manager who had nothing to do with this project, giggled. "Stop it, you'll make me blush!" Her grin didn't quite reach her eyes. Tori couldn't detect any trace of embarrassment on her dark skin. What a fraud.

Tori managed to smile by imagining James' sandwich growing teeth and eating him.

"Much better!" He patted her on the back—a solid six inches lower than he needed to. He booted up the conference room monitor. "Alrighty. Let's talk about cutting costs."

The meeting dragged well into lunch. Dick had never heard the term "software infrastructure" before and constantly interrupted with questions. After another grueling half hour, James stopped talking to refill his soda.

Tori seized her chance. "Why don't we migrate our apps to the cloud?"

Three sets of eyes bored down on her.

Her heart dropped into her stomach.

She rarely drew attention to herself. Not that she was shy. It was simply smarter to stay quiet and disappear into the gray of her chair. James hated letting anyone else talk. She knew that. She knew that, yet each tick of the clock, pointless project, and wasted heartbeat cut into her soul. If nothing changed, she would never amount to more than dollars on a spreadsheet. She had to try.

"Like—" She swallowed. Her throat was as dry as Interstate 75 on a summer afternoon. "Like I was saying. The cloud. I've been working on a proof of concept. We could finish the migration by the end of the year." She'd lost a lot of sleep over this new technology.

Well, new to her and her company. The rest of the world had been using it for decades. For Tori, who'd been stuck in the same routine since college, it was the future.

With her pulse pounding in her ears, she shared her laptop's screen. The numbers told a clear story. Even James had to understand. "The monthly charge would be pretty low. We could save thousands." This was a good idea. He didn't like her ideas, but he liked money, right?

"Tori." James crumpled up his trash. "If you have enough time to play around in the cloud, shouldn't you be working on that new feature I asked for?" He laughed. "Or making me more sandwiches. Women are good at that, right?"

"Value add," Dick stated. "This company is all about value add. Not proof of concepts. Get your head out of the clouds, Victoria."

The vulture never missed an opportunity to pick at Tori's bones. If not because of work, then because of her off-brand sneakers, her rebellious curls, or her swarm of freckles that made it look like she constantly had chocolate stuck on her lips.

Sympathy flickered across Maena's face. "Oh, don't be so hard on her. She's trying."

"Fine, fine." James cleaned the grease off his fingers with a napkin. "Finish my new feature first. We can talk about it next year." He slipped his arm around Tori's shoulders. He reeked of oil and crushed dreams. "No hard feelings, eh?"

Hard feelings? Tori had nothing but hard feelings. Every few months she worked herself up like this. She suggested a new project. She fixed something important. She grasped for hope. And every few months that hope was crushed all over again.

James was a dirtwad and Dick was a suck up. But Tori couldn't blame them for her daily suffering. She'd chosen this life. She'd wanted this. She'd traded her tiny hometown for the big city and her life savings for student debt. Currently, she was trading her youth, her vision, and her social life for a paycheck large enough to cover said student debt.

It was a good deal. Almost no one could afford college anymore —time in a classroom was time teens could be helping pay for groceries and rent. She had independence, an apartment to herself, and a respectable career. She had it made. This was success.

Tori accepted her fate. "No. No hard feelings." She stopped counting the minutes.

The meeting adjourned with no action plan. There would be another one tomorrow.

Tori no longer cared. Denial, anger, bargaining, and depression would wait for her at her desk. Right now, she could only think about food. She tucked her computer into her bag and fled into the stairwell.

Work sucked, but life still had simple pleasures. Hot Georgia sun welcomed her at the bottom of her building. Tori closed her eyes. She soaked it in. Slowly, gently, it melted the tension in her shoulders. The aroma of cooking meat soothed her soul. She crossed the street into a park full of food trucks and bought herself lunch. She selected a clean, private bench. Six-foot azaleas exploding with pink flowers hid her away from the world.

A stray cat leapt into her lap.

She yelped. She shooed him to the ground.

He was hungry for a free meal and would not be defeated so easily.

The hunter stalked around her legs. He peered up from between her ankles.

A large white spot marked his gray fur. A cloud.

Tori broke. She doubled over, cradling her face in her hands. Tears fell freely into her sesame fries.

She hated James. She hated her tiny apartment in Midtown. She hated that she was the last junior developer in a department of senior software engineers, despite having worked there longer than anyone else. What was the point in trying so hard? What was the point in trying at all? She would always be trapped in this thankless job. A part of her would always be missing.

"Dear." A gentle voice calmed the tempest. "It's gonna be okay, dear."

With her mind reeling from heartache and hunger, Tori hadn't noticed that she and the cloud cat were no longer alone.

Before her stood an elderly woman wearing a turquoise jumpsuit. Her wild hair had been tamed with a ponytail. She carried a brown paper bag full of cans. It was the resident cat lady. Rumor had it her dementia was so severe that she could no longer tell the difference between people and animals. She wandered this park, feeding strays, chatting with pigeons, and playing with squirrels.

"I don't... I mean I..." Tori had to pull herself together. The last thing she wanted was to involve a stranger in her problems.

Straightening, she met the woman's sharp eyes. She managed a smile. "Thank you, but... I'm fine." Her face was still swollen and puffy. She had never been a good liar.

Dementia or not, the woman wasn't fooled. "You don't have to act tough. Not with me. What's your name, dear?" She settled on the bench. She smelled faintly of the cabin Tori's parents once rented up in Nantahala, all pine needles and earth.

"It's Tori," Tori wasn't in the mood for introductions. But there was something about this woman that lured her in.

"Tori is a lovely name." The woman sifted through her bag. "Means 'bird' across the ocean. But you're no dove or chickadee, are you?" She offered Tori a handkerchief. Hand stitched lions, leopards, and cheetahs pranced along its edges.

Meekly, Tori accepted the handkerchief. She blew her nose.

"There, there. You can call me Dee. It's short for Diana." The woman pressed a candy into Tori's palm. "Go on, eat something. You'll feel better."

Guilt squirmed in Tori's belly. Dee owed her nothing. They'd never spoken before. Yet here she was, doing her best to help, a doting grandmother calming a lost child.

Tori unwrapped the candy and popped it into her mouth. Shame pinned her gaze to the ground. How many times had she walked past this woman without a second glance? How many lunches had she listened quietly while her coworkers complained on and on about the crazy lady in the park like she wasn't even human?

Dee didn't hold it against her. Beaming, she helped herself to a candy of her own. "See? You're stronger than you think. You'll get through this."

She tapped the seat of the park bench.

The cloud cat hopped between them.

Instinctively Tori stroked his back.

Purring, he curled into her lap. The little ball of fur warmed her in ways talking never could.

Silence lingered between them. Dee chased it off with a clenched fist. "It breaks my heart that young girls still have to suffer so much."

Suffer? Did she know about James and Dick?

"Men will never change." The doting grandmother disappeared. In her place sat a wizened woman, full of bitterness and far too tired. "You shouldn't have to fight just to be taken seriously." Her "you" sounded like she meant to say "we". She definitely wasn't talking about office politics.

"What if I told you"—her tone fell to a whisper—"that you don't have to fight by yourself anymore?"

Tori didn't like where this was going.

"Give this to HR." Dee pressed a photograph into her palm.

The photograph pictured the patch of grass across from them. It was late at night. Clothes littered the sidewalk. The red glow of the lamp posts kissed naked skin. An older man embraced a young woman in a rather, uh, compromising position. Tori recognized that facial hair immediately. It was James! That meant... Oh no. Oh god. His lover was their secretary!

She dropped the photograph as if it'd shocked her. She leapt to her feet. This image was too dangerous for a mere mortal like her— she had to escape.

The cloud cat meowed in protest and bounded off.

She squeezed her eyes shut. For good measure, she also covered them with her hands. But no matter how hard she tried to forget, James and the secretary burned in her memory.

"Don't back away! Move forward!" Dee grasped her arm. "Make him suffer." Her grip tightened. "Like he makes you suffer." A predatory purr lurked in her tone. She wasn't a cat lady. She was a lioness.

This photograph could ruin James in a million ways. Fraternization was against company policy; if his boss saw it, he would be fired. If the secretary used it to claim sexual harassment, he could be sued. If his wife saw it, she would take their children and leave him. On top of all of that, he was one of those religious types. Tori was pretty sure his church did not condone trysts in a public park... or lying... or adultery... What a stupid hypocrite.

It was a weapon of mass destruction. If Tori used it, it would wipe all traces of James MacGillivray from her life. The mere thought of being freed forever from his pointless meetings, his complaints about her unique choices in clothing, and his backhanded compliments about how logical she was *for a woman,* filled her with hope.

She opened her eyes. She felt powerful.

She knew better.

Weapons of mass destruction always had collateral damage.

"No," Tori replied immediately, firmly. She pulled her arm away from Dee. "No. Find someone else!"

"He deserves it."

Tori hesitated. She was right. James had earned the hell the photograph would unleash upon him. And he deserved SO much worse.

"Do it for the others," Dee bent to retrieve the photograph. "You can protect them from those unfunny jokes... Those passed over promotions... Those wandering hands..."

Tori hadn't thought about it that way. Women around their office quickly learned to avoid James. He was forward. He was pushy. Their secretary was young, like fresh out of college young. What if she was being manipulated? What if she was being coerced?

"Take it, dear." Dee tucked the photograph into the front pocket of Tori's hoodie. With a two-finger salute, she sent her soldier to battle. "You know what to do."

Tori had no idea what to do. But one way or another, tomorrow James was going to have a very bad day.

CHAPTER TWO

Thank God, Gandhi, and Buddha—the elevator was empty! As soon as its double doors closed, Tori dropped to her hands and knees. Her mind raced. It practically ran a marathon through all her thoughts, hopes, and fears.

She ought to mind her own business. But she couldn't help but think of James' poor wife and the secretary. How terrified would she feel if she was trapped between losing her job and losing her dignity? She had to do something.

Taking care not to make eye contact with anyone, especially not James or the secretary, she hurried to her desk. She collapsed in her chair. Safe! There was no reason she had to use the photograph right now. This was a big decision. She had all day to weigh wrong against *really* wrong.

An email notification lit up her laptop's screen. Subject: Cloud Migration. It was from James. She clicked it immediately. It announced his new plan to cut infrastructure spending in half by moving their apps to the cloud. Her plan. Yet he failed to mention her anywhere.

Betrayal kicked Tori in the chest. Hot blood surged through her veins.

Her eyes had been opened. She was powerful. She would never be James' victim again.

Without processing what she was doing, she pushed back her chair. She stormed down the corridor. She'd almost reached HR when a coworker stopped her.

"Hey. Tori." It was Zach Godfrey, a software engineer who'd joined her team last August. He was a good kid. Kinda short. Usually kept to himself. "You get that email?"

The question brought her back to her senses. "Yeah," she mumbled.

"I, um." He adjusted his glasses. "Thanks."

She blinked. "For what?"

"The migration. That's really going to help us out."

"But James didn't give me—" Credit? She hadn't realized how childish she sounded until she said it out loud.

Zach shrugged. "Doesn't matter. We all know it was you."

James wasn't Tori's only coworker. She had allies in this war.

Suddenly she knew what to do. She retreated into the women's restroom. Hiding in a stall, she peered at the photograph. Dee had misled her. Using it to hurt James would not be justice, it would be selfish, ugly vengeance.

Tori tore the photograph in half and flushed it down the toilet. She didn't need it.

In the morning, she'd write his wife an anonymous letter about his infidelity. Then she'd invite the secretary to lunch, far from the office. She would bring up James. It would be awkward as all get out, but she needed the other woman to know that she had support if something wasn't right about their relationship. Just in case.

And as for James? Forget sabotage. The next time he stole one of her plans, or slacked off on a project, or blew office budget on his personal snack fridge, she would document it. Make pretty charts.

Take them all the way to Tianyi, the conglomerate that owned her company, in New York City. She could convince those higher ups that she was better. She would beat him at his own game.

Taking a deep breath, Tori returned to work. She felt like she'd aged twenty years.

* * *

The next day, Director James MacGillivray resigned.

When Tori arrived at eight o'clock sharp, those cake donuts with fancy toppings welcomed her from the middle of the break-room. At nine, James called everyone over to celebrate. He was done with software. He was headed back to St. Louis. He wanted to go home to his family and reconnect with God.

It made no sense. James had started a new project yesterday. Why would he quit with no notice?

Snakes slithered in Tori's stomach. She couldn't enjoy her donut.

Even though James feigned happiness, he was off. His movements were stiff. His palms were clammy. It was freezing inside, yet his pits sweated through his collared shirt. He barely touched his breakfast.

Tori watched him select a trinket—a business card, a best-employee award, a tee from some famous golf course—from his desk, sigh, then drop it into a sad cardboard box over and over again. It was so pathetic she almost felt sorry for him.

No, this wasn't sorry. This was guilt.

Anxiety buzzed in her head like a swarm of mosquitoes. Maybe a coworker had seen her photograph. Maybe a piece of it had fallen out in the bathroom. Maybe someone else had blackmailed him with their own evidence.

Tori had to know what had gone wrong. She had to investigate.

James locked himself in his office all morning. At lunch, he vanished. When Tori failed to find him in the cafeteria, the break room, and the smoker's balcony, she decided to check the food truck park.

Tori had barely made it outside her building when a hand clasped her shoulder.

"You didn't do it," Dee observed.

How could Dee possibly know that? There had to be more to her. A grudge against James, perhaps? A disgruntled relative? She probably handed out copies of that picture to everyone who would listen to her.

Wariness pricked up Tori's spine. "What did you do!?"

"Nothing." A whisper of a smile curled Dee's lips. She gazed up at the sky. "Sometimes Fate tests us, Tori. Our choices don't actually make a difference."

Tires screeched. A man shouted. Tori wheeled around just in time to see an oversized SUV barreling through a red light. It skidded to a halt, having narrowly missed a pedestrian.

The stunned pedestrian cowered in a crosswalk.

She gasped. It was James!

Tori sprinted to James' side. She checked him over. He was shaken, but otherwise he looked fine. No scrapes or bruises. "James!" He didn't respond. "James?" It was like he couldn't hear her. The emptiness in his eyes filled her with dread.

"You can't help him," Dee called after her. "Not anymore!"

The SUV from hell revved its engine. It rolled forward.

Tori reeled. "What is wrong with you!?" Atlanta drivers were the worst. Only a psychopath would drive off after almost killing a man.

A gear grinded. The vehicle flew backwards, straight at them.

Something thunked into Tori's chest. She couldn't breathe. Gasping, she looked down. A silver arrow protruded from her heart.

Seconds later, she was flat on her back. No arrow. Totally fine.

Fog swirled in her head. She sat up on her elbows.

The SUV was parked behind James. He sprawled out, face down. Awful lumps covered his body. He wasn't moving.

Shock and horror cut through Tori, clearing the fog. Murder. She'd witnessed a murder!

A giant of a man—so tall he could turn off a light and jump into bed before the room got dark—eclipsed the sunlight. Sunglasses sat on his nose. He was a professional, equipped with all kinds of gadgets, a red-plaid shirt, and leather gloves. Thick leather belts strapped a compound bow and an ax to his back. He gave off a distinct Paul Bunyan vibe. Like something straight out of a childhood fable.

Whistling an upbeat song, he rifled through James' pockets. He stole his wallet. Tucking it into his jacket, he climbed back into his car. Or rather, he tried.

Tori grabbed his ankle.

"Let go." He kicked at her. "You're not my target."

With the ferocity of an alligator, she clamped down and pulled. Her strength surprised them both. Somehow she, an office worker who'd never seen the inside of a gym, dragged legendary Paul Bunyan's muscular leg out from under him. His butt hit the concrete with a satisfying thud.

What on God's green earth was she doing? She'd lost her damn mind! First, she'd hallucinated being shot to death. Now she was picking a fight with a murderer.

"You harpy!" Paul Bunyan snatched her wrist. "I told you to let go!"

Her body knew what to do. As soon as his hand closed around her, Tori yanked with all her might. He fell forward. Tackling his back, she hooked her arm around his neck and her legs around his hips. All she had to do was stall him until the police showed up.

Wild barking broke her concentration. She looked up just in

time to see a massive mastiff lunging from the SUV. Its eyes glowed, twin drops of hellfire. It chomped on her bicep. Hard.

Blood streaked down her bronze skin. Pain knotted up her arm. She lost her grip.

Paul Bunyan rolled her onto her back, straddling her. He lifted his ax.

Tori stared Death in the face. She should've been afraid. She should've screamed. She felt nothing. Those crimson eyes held her captive.

Faded memories flurried around her like snow. Snow was so rare in the flat parts of Georgia that it would always remind her of him. Of the teeth marks. Of the demon-eyed silhouette that disappeared into dark.

An animal attack, the police had told her.

Animals hunted for food. They didn't turn their prey into Rorschach ink tests in red.

Somewhere nearby, a siren screeched. Colorful lights bounced between the skyscrapers.

The disconnect jerked Tori back into the present, disoriented. There was no snow. There would never be snow in safe, sunny spring.

Paul Bunyan swore in a language Tori couldn't place. He and his dog fled down an alley.

The thrill of the hunt possessed Tori. She couldn't let go. She scrambled to her feet and chased after them, adrenaline fueling each step.

She knew these streets better than they did. She gained on them.

Despite the agony, despite the warm scarlet staining her shirt, despite brushing against death twice, she'd never felt more alive. She was taking action. She was making a difference. Determination, not resignation, burned in her soul.

The photograph had been a placebo. This was what power *really* felt like.

He turned a corner. She followed him. Diving forward, she seized his collar.

A steel cable pressed into her shin. It tightened around her legs, launching her upside down. The next thing she knew she was hanging between two streetlamps. No amount of struggling helped. How soon had her power abandoned her.

Paul Bunyan sauntered towards her. He removed his shades, revealing harsh gray eyes. Under different circumstances, he would've been crazy attractive. He was the kind of man you'd find on the cover of an outdoor magazine—dark curls, broad shoulders, five o'clock shadow across a square jaw, and a scar for character. He was her age, too.

"I'm not used to being the one who gets chased. Not gonna lie," he purred. "It's pretty hot."

What a creep. She spat at him.

He punched her in the jaw.

"Don't think I'll go easy on you because you're a girl. I believe in gender equality."

He swung again.

Easy? She'd show him easy.

Before his fist made contact, she sank her teeth into his arm.

More cursing. He smashed his elbow into the back of her head. "We're gonna have to do something about that attitude of yours."

An old blue muscle car roared into the alley.

A bullet tore through the steel cable restraining Tori. She dropped to the ground.

Stars danced at the edge of her vision. One by one they winked away.

"You again?" Paul Bunyan groaned. "Give me a break!"

Another gunshot shattered the bricks to their left.

Paul Bunyan retreated into a side street, his hound at his heels.

Tori lacked the energy to stand, much less follow him. Her courage softened alongside his retreating footsteps. Confusion beat at her brow. She'd attacked an assassin. She had attacked a *literal* assassin. She'd chased him down, she'd taunted him, and she'd even bitten him!

A man emerged from the muscle car. "Hey Lady. You okay?" An old-fashioned revolver smoked in his hand.

Oh no. Another criminal! These days it was pretty much impossible to own a firearm. Most police officers didn't even carry them.

Tori gave him a once over.

Her muscle-car-hero had a strong jawline, an olive complexion, and the build of a fitness influencer. Short but thick, wavy hair framed his face. Everything he wore, from his band t-shirt to his jeans to his laced boots, was smudged with dirt. There was something vaguely off about him, and it wasn't his twice-broken nose, his chipped front tooth, or the defiance in his eyes. She couldn't quite place it.

He couldn't be older than a college student. Practically a baby. That eased her nerves.

"Yeah. I'm okay." Mostly. "It's Tori, not Lady."

"Sure. Whatever." He seemed distracted. "So this is gonna sound strange..." Searching the alley high and low, he sifted through trash bags. Whatever he was looking for, he didn't find it. "Did that guy happen to, uh. Breathe fire. Make lights flicker. Y'know, that sorta thing?"

He was right. It sounded strange. Tori wondered if she was hallucinating again. "He had an ax." After a pause, she added, "And a dog."

"Damn." Kicking a trash can, he gave up. He tucked his revolver into his waistband. He fished a cigarette out of his pocket and shoved it between his teeth. "I could've used a lead."

Dude completely ignored James' wallet. It sat in the middle of the pavement like a quest drop from a video game. Tori scooped it up. "Would this work?"

She shook it. A small plastic bag tumbled out into her palm.

He walked to her. He pinched open the bag. It contained sweet scented golden powder.

"Hmm... poison?" He chewed his lower lip. "Magic gunpowder?" He dipped his finger in and tried to stick it in his mouth.

Tori slapped the powder off his hand. "Are you stupid!?" He was definitely stupid. "You don't know what that is. It's probably a drug!"

"Trust me." He instructed her like a schoolkid. "It's never just a drug."

"Well excuse me, mister... mister..."

"Vincent Lenoir," he finished her sentence. "Call me Vince."

Tori eased into a sitting position. Now that her adrenaline had stopped flowing, pain flooded in to take its place. A bruise swelled on her jaw. Nausea carved at her ribcage. Her shoulder wept hot misery down her arm, all the way to her fingertips. None of it compared to the murder of questions clawing at her like crows.

"Forget the drug, Vince. What just happened? What are you doing here? Why did you ask me about fire breathing?"

"Slow down, Usain Bolt. Please. One question at a time."

He shouldn't have talked down to her if he didn't want to play teacher.

Ever the diligent student, she ordered her questions in a bulleted list in her mind.

First things first. "Thank you for saving me."

"All in a day's work." He offered her a hand.

She took it. She stood. "What kind of work?"

"It's... complicated."

Those two words came out so reluctantly Tori figured she wouldn't get much more information from that bullet point. She crossed it off the list. On to the next.

Paul Bunyan and Vince Lenoir clearly knew each other, and not in a friendly met-at-a-concert sort of way. There was history there. History she needed to study. "Who was that"—the term "wicked" didn't seem strong enough—"incorrigible murderer?"

"What does incorrigible—" Frustration rumbled in Vince's throat. "You know what? I don't have time for this."

He retreated. He couldn't get back to his car fast enough. "Go home. Take a nice long nap. Pretend this was all a bad dream." He settled into the driver's seat. "Twenty years from now, you'll thank me for not getting you involved. If I'm still around. Which I probably won't be." He turned the ignition. "Sooo, if you'll excuse me, I've got an incorrigible murderer to catch—"

She opened the passenger-side door.

The color drained from his face. "What are you doing."

It wasn't a question. It was a statement. Leave. You're not welcome. Go away.

Tori was all too familiar with those kinds of statements. She had learned to ignore them in her very first computer science class, as one of four women in a lecture hall of two hundred people. She wouldn't have made it far in life if she didn't trespass where she wasn't wanted every now and then.

She plopped into the cracked leather passenger seat.

Vince gaped at her, slack jawed. "Get out."

"I can't."

It was the truth.

Today, Tori had chased down, taunted, and bitten an assassin. Now she'd locked herself in a closed space with the most suspicious man she'd ever met.

The excitement and insanity had gotten under her skin, worked its way through her body, and infected her down to her core. For the very first time since that night in the snow, she felt like herself. Like she was whole. Like she had a purpose. If she went home, took a nap, and pretended this was all just a dream, she might never feel this way again.

"Yo, seriously. Get out."

"Not until I know why Paul-Bunyan-Gone-Wild killed James."

Unlike Paul Bunyan, Vince wouldn't put a hand on her. They were stuck in a stalemate.

"Look Lady—"

"Tori," she interrupted.

"Tori. Please, get out. If I show up at our base with you, Roy will tease me about it until the day I die. Those twenty years will feel like eternity!"

Roy? Yet another new name for Tori's mental bullet points. Judging from Vince's tone, Roy was either his father, his boss, or a fire breathing dragon.

"Don't worry. I'll talk to him for you," she promised.

He groaned. He smacked the steering wheel with both hands.

That was it. That was the sound of him giving up.

"Fine. You win."

He shifted his car into drive. "I don't care if you tag along, but I'm warning you. You might not be able to tag back out."

Tori buckled her seat belt.

CHAPTER THREE

Tori didn't know what to expect when Vince mentioned a base, but it wasn't this.

Vince's old blue muscle car squealed as he pulled into a condo complex. Scenic buildings towered atop a granite bluff, looking down on the roaring Vickery Creek. Manicured trees and flowers framed the road. Tori counted at least four luxury cars in the parking lot. What business could a gun-toting cigarette-smoking bad boy possibly have all the way out here in Roswell, Georgia?

Roswell was one of the oldest suburbs of Atlanta, full of old plantation houses, ruined cotton mills, and historic cemeteries. Maybe fifty years ago—recent enough for Tori's ma to have seen it, but not her—it mostly consisted of tiny affordable houses. Now any green space near the big city sold for a premium. Mansions dominated every avenue. All the people like her parents had been shooed south of Interstate 20.

Tori would've been uncomfortable here, even if Vince hadn't refused to talk for the entire twenty-minute drive from Midtown.

With a pop, Vince's car unlocked. They climbed outside.

"Ladies first," he gestured towards the only condo without a welcome mat.

Tori rang the doorbell. She could barely hear its melody over the anticipation pounding in her ears.

A god answered the door.

Okay, not really. But he was still the most handsome man Tori had ever laid eyes on. She placed him somewhere between Vince's and her pa's age, maybe early thirties, in the prime of his life. A worn traveler's hat hung at his neck, giving him an Indiana-Jones-raids-a-tomb sort of vibe. But he wasn't rugged at all. His sleek strawberry-blonde hair pulled into a neat ponytail without a strand out of place. His tanned skin glowed with youthful energy. His body looked as if it had been lovingly sculpted from Grecian marble.

He gasped. "Wow Vincent. You look different!"

Vince had slipped behind Tori without her noticing.

What in the world was he hiding for? Wasn't she the outsider?

Indiana Jones dropped the act. "Please, come in. Any friend of Vincent's is a friend of mine." He pushed the door aside. If he was concerned about the blood dripping from her arm, he didn't show it.

"I'm Roy Angelus," he said with a smile. "Nice to meet you, Miss...?"

"It's Tori." She stepped inside. "Tori Jaecar."

The condo opened into a spacious living area. Light filtered in from a pair of sliding glass doors on the wall.

"Well then, Miss Tori Jaecar," Roy settled in a pin-striped armchair. Its bright colors clashed with everything else in the room, from the white walls and carpet to the coffee-stained tables and shelves. It was also the only piece of furniture not covered in a layer of dust. Were it not for that armchair and the remnants of take out containers scattered over every surface, the place would look abandoned. It had to be a rental. "To what do we owe this honor?"

Vince brushed past Tori. "I can explain—"

A voice as low and smooth as New Orleans jazz interrupted from the hallway. "What's going on in there?"

"Vincent finally brought a girl home!" Roy answered.

Immediately another man burst into the room.

Mystery man number three was the oldest of the trio. He was built like a linebacker, with broad shoulders and staggering stature. A short-cut beard powdered his harsh, square chin. It couldn't conceal the long, gnarly scar that curved his mouth, giving him a permanent frown.

Tori might've been intimidated if he didn't look so tired.

Dark circles smudged under his eyes. Decades of sun, hard work, and misery had worked deep wrinkles into his forehead.

The moment he saw her—and her wound—his suspicion shifted to concern.

"Oh. Oh no! Are you alright?" He rushed to her side and dragged the couch over to her. "Please. Sit down. I'll get you some gauze. And an ice pack."

As quickly as he had appeared, he was gone again.

"She was like this when I found her!" Vince called after him.

"That's Brooks Wyman," Roy explained. "You'll have to forgive him. He's been through a lot."

Tori sat on the couch, wondering what "a lot" meant to people who made bases in expensive condos and chased after confirmed killers.

Roy rested his chin in his palm. "Now Vincent. You were saying?"

"Right. This lady—uh, I mean Tori—was strung up in one of Orion's traps."

Orion. Was that Paul Bunyan's real name? Tori took a mental note of the new vocab word and waited for more.

"She was just an innocent bystander, I think," Vince continued.

"I would've left her for the police to deal with, but she wouldn't get out of my goddamned car."

Roy looked more amused than any man had a right to be by the situation.

Brooks returned with an ice pack in hand. "This should help with the swelling. May I treat your arm?"

Tori didn't love the idea of a strange man putting his hands on her. But the idea of spending this month's grocery budget and eight hours at urgent care was even worse. "Please." She pressed the ice pack against her jaw.

With a nod, Brooks retrieved a bright red case from a coat closet. He settled next to her on the couch and snapped it open, revealing a military grade first aid kit complete with duct tape, surgical scalpels, and so many prescription bottles it could've been a portable pharmacy. "Hold still please. This will sting a little." He cleaned her shoulder with alcohol.

Tori couldn't help but stare. The first aid kit was pretty weird, but it was the least weird thing in that coat closet.

A battered combat shotgun hung from a hook on the wall. Behind it stretched a sniper rifle. Knives, ammunition, a whole hardware store's worth of gadgets and tools stacked in neat, clearly labeled toolboxes. At the center of it all, an honest-to-goodness sword leaned against an umbrella holder.

The sword was out of place among the modern arsenal. With its winged cross guard, intricate snake-entwined grip, and artful wine-bronze sheen, it belonged in a museum.

"Now I'm closing the wound." Brooks threaded a stitch through her dog bite. His touch was so gentle that she barely felt the pinch of his needle. He'd done this before.

The entire time he worked, Tori watched wordlessly. The ice pack soothed her jaw, but it couldn't soothe her growing headache. This was too much information to process at once. Maybe coming here had been a mistake.

This trio was far more suspicious than the dude who murdered James. Vince had faced off against Orion without the faintest sliver of fear. Brooks clearly had some sort of military background. Roy lounged around like a cat in a sunspot without a care in the world. Their coat closet had enough weapons to win a war.

Still, Tori had to give Vince, the loud one, credit for saving her. If he hadn't showed up when he did, she might've been killed. Besides, had they planned to hurt her, surely they would've done so by now.

Brooks tied off the last of her stitches. "There. You should be able to pull them out in a week or so."

"Thanks." Tori smiled weakly at him. He requested permission before he touched her. He explained what he was going to do and why before he did it. Her comfort was his priority. He reminded her of her pa. He was about the same age, too.

"So. What happened to Orion?" Roy asked Vince.

Roy had been friendly so far. But unlike Brooks, he kept his distance.

Tori was grateful for that. People like him made her... uneasy. He was perfect, and he knew it. His gaze cut like light through a window, scattered, colorful, and sharp. From head to toe, with every movement, he shone with confidence. Next to him, she felt like a used glow stick.

"Don't know. That bastard bailed as soon as I showed up. But we did find this." Vince dug the baggie of golden powder out of his pocket. He offered it to Roy. "What do you think it is? Poison? Magic gunpowder?"

Roy dipped his finger in the powder and scooped some onto his tongue. He frowned, disappointed. "It's just a drug."

Tori's eye twitched. Sane people didn't eat mystery chemicals. Were they all crazy?

"How are you so sure? Let me snort it! If I get high, I'll believe you!" Vince grabbed at the baggie.

Roy held it just out of reach.

The more Roy teased Vince, the more gray shone through Brooks' salt-and-pepper hair. "That's enough, Vince," Brooks scolded. "Mercy knows what he's talking about."

Mercy? The fifth name threw Tori for a loop. There were only four people in the room, and they'd already established that the killer's name was Orion, not Mercy.

"Actually," Roy admitted, tapping his chiseled chin. "Drugs aren't really my thing."

Ah. So Roy was Roy, but he was also Mercy. Of course. Why not?

"Then what should we do?" Vince popped open a can of beer.

"We either figure out this clue..." Roy continued, as though it was the simplest task in the world. "...or we find another one."

Brooks sighed. "Preferably both."

"Are you kidding?" Vince complained. "It took us forever to track Orion down. Don't tell me we're not any closer to catching him!"

Roy shrugged. "We would be if you'd caught him."

"Mercy," Brooks breathed. It was both a nickname and a request.

"Vincent." Roy retracted his claws. His tone softened. "We'll get him. He can't have gone far."

Tori felt like she was observing them through a television screen. They seemed to have forgotten her presence. Usually that suited her just fine—she could learn a lot by listening—but not today. Today, she didn't want to be alone with James' ghost. She cleared her throat. "Uh. I'm sorry to interrupt, but..." She didn't know where to begin.

Yesterday, the mere thought of never seeing James again had filled her with euphoria. Now that her dream had come true, she felt hollow. Restless. Guilt itched beneath her skin. His wife would never hear the truth. His children would grow up without their father. She'd practically held him when he died! There was no way she could just go back to... to what? Back to work? To the police station? Home?

There had to be a reason for it all. And if anyone knew that reason, it was these three crazies.

"Tori, was it?" Roy flashed the kind of smile Tori saved for first dates —polite but measured. "Apologies; we're not used to having company."

"Speak for yourself," Vince mumbled.

"I'm sorry you got dragged into all of this." Brooks said with sincere remorse. "How can we help you?"

"Before Vince showed up, the guy y'all're hunting—Orion, right?—ran over my..." Tori swallowed. She couldn't say it out loud. Saying it out loud would make it real. She started over. "Do you know who he is? Why he would do something so horrible?"

"Yes," Roy traced his fingers along a pattern on his armchair. "And no."

"He goes by Orion Treyvon," Vince spat. He gulped down his beer to wash the bad taste from his mouth. "We don't know what he is or who works for. We first crossed paths with him in California. And again in Louisiana, where he, er."

"He killed several people. Tried to kill Vince, too, for that matter." Roy finished casually, without a trace of tension. And yet Tori found that even more ominous. It was like he already knew they would put an end to Orion. He was merely waiting.

"We've been one step behind him ever since," Vince complained.

"I'm sorry, Miss Jaecar." Brooks moved to pat Tori on the shoulder but thought better of it. "I know you're upset about your friend, but you should let us deal with Orion. He's extremely dangerous."

Dangerous was such a strong yet vague word. After everything that had happened, it no longer meant anything to Tori. "Why would someone like that kill James? He was middle management at a finance company." Not a thief. Not a murderer. Not important.

Roy shook the drug baggie between two fingers. "The question and the answer."

Tori fell quiet. This was pointless. That drug baggie was a single corner piece of a puzzle. She really needed all four. And what would the whole picture look like? If she discovered more about this Orion... If she somehow managed to find him, what could she do? Bring him to justice? Risk her life to avenge a man she hated?

Once it became clear she'd run out of questions. The others moved on without her.

Roy straightened. "I'm going home to visit my sister. She'll know exactly what kind of drug we're dealing with." He stuffed the baggie into his jacket. "Brooks, you come with me."

Brooks grimaced.

Tori wondered what kind of woman could make such an imposing man turn so white.

Vince also straightened. "And what about me? You're not leaving me alone again, are you?" He already knew what Roy's response would be.

"You"—Roy prodded Vince in the chest—"still need to find Orion."

"I'm sick of chasing dead ends!" Vince slammed his half-empty beer on the coffee table. "If I have to spend one more day in this goddamn heat, I'm going to blow a gasket. And so will my poor Mustang."

Tori was offended. Atlanta's weather was one of her favorite things about the city.

"You'll survive." Roy stole the can from Vince's fingers. He took a sip. "It's not a dead end until you can't go any further." He made a cheers gesture.

Vince grumbled under his breath.

It was settled, then. The trio would split up. They'd hunt down Orion. They'd put James' ghost to rest. But where did that leave Tori? They didn't need her.

If she went to work in the morning, it would be the end of the story for her. She would never know why James had died. She would never redeem herself for failing to save him. She would never be sure that Orion was gone; that he wasn't still out there hurting more people. All that awaited her was more meetings, more projects, and more frustration.

This was her chance. This was bigger than her. It was bigger than her company, the outdated software that defined her life, and all the office buildings in Atlanta. Instead of logging pointless hours, instead of making rich people richer, she would actually be helping someone. She would matter.

Tori broke the silence. "I have an idea."

Everyone looked at her. Vince with surprise. Brooks with dismay. And Roy as though he'd been expecting her to steal the show from the moment she arrived.

Her heart trembled in her chest. She was afraid. But she'd rather die than go back to half-living. "I know how we can set a trap for Orion." She managed to sound much more confident than she was. "Make him come to us."

"Vincent." Roy smirked. "Why can't you be more like her?"

Vince threw the half-empty can at him.

CHAPTER FOUR

Skyscrapers shattered the morning light. A breeze pierced the gaps between them, sending dust devils spinning in the road. Even though it was springtime, a strange chill hung in the air. It was as though the whole city was holding its breath. Or maybe that was just Tori.

Somewhere, in the window of one of those skyscrapers, Brooks Wyman watched her through the scope of his sniper rifle. Vince's beat up muscle car gathered rust at the edge of a twenty-dollar-an-hour parking lot nearby. She didn't know where Roy had gone off to, but what did it matter? Even if she had a hundred secret service agents protecting her, she wouldn't be safe.

"This was my idea," she reminded herself over and over again.

"It was a tragic Tuesday in downtown Atlanta," Maxine Daly began. The Channel 2 News logo on her pocket stood out against the black of her blazer. "Yesterday afternoon, a pedestrian was killed in a hit and run accident in front of his office." Even though traffic accidents happened every day, her voice rang with excitement.

"We're at the scene now. I have with me Miss Victoria Jaecar, eyewitness and a coworker of the victim. Can you tell us what happened?"

"Yeah. Sure." Tori had replayed the events of James' death in her mind countless times, but actually talking about it felt like trying to finger paint a photograph. "He was headed to lunch, I think. Over there." She gestured at the crosswalk. Only a faint smudge of red on the white paint hinted that someone had died there. "An SUV came around the corner going way too fast. I thought it would hit us both. I got lucky, but James, he... h-he..."

"Horrible. How horrible!" Maxine rescued her. "Our streets are no longer safe. When will the mayor do something about reckless drivers plaguing our city?" she asked no one, clenching he fist. "What did the culprit look like?"

"He was..." Tori's voice caught in her throat. She swallowed. "...tall. Dark hair, maybe?" What if Mrs. MacGillivray was watching? Or her children? What would they think of her using James' story to help three strangers with a grudge? Would they want justice, or peace? "I didn't get a good look at him. I..."

All this thinking was getting in her way. She had to push through it.

Roy had prepared Tori for this interview, stressing that she should only lie by telling the truth. "The driver just sped off." A lie. "Like he didn't even care." The truth. Both left a bitter taste on her tongue.

"Local police are working day and night to identify the culprit. A reward is being offered for any information leading to his arrest." Maxine held her microphone out for Tori. "Thank you for telling us your story. Is there anything else you have to say to the good people of Atlanta?"

Tori leaned forward over the microphone, making sure to give the camera a clear view of the golden powder baggie tucked in her breast pocket. She counted one... two... three... If he was watching,

Orion had to have noticed it by now. She said the first thing that came to mind. "Use your turn signals."

Maxine promptly withdrew. "You heard it here first, folks." She stepped in front of Tori, taking up the entire shot. "I'm Maxine Daly with Channel 2 News. Stories that count, from people who care. Next up, the weather."

It was over. Maxine shook Tori's hand. She and her crew climbed into the back of their van. As soon as they disappeared around a bend, Tori exhaled all the tension pressing against her ribcage. Relax. Breathe. She had to calm down. She had to focus. There would be no more cameras, microphones, or questions. But her performance had only begun.

The trap for Orion Treyvon was set. Tori had given him her face, her location, and her name. There was no telling whether he'd take the bait, or if he did, when. But she knew in her gut he wouldn't keep her waiting for long. He wanted the mystery drug. He wanted it so badly that he'd murdered James in broad daylight for a single, tiny baggie.

Alone, Tori marched down the street. Her hands trembled. She hid them in the much-too-small pockets of her jeans. Every person she passed watched her, tracking her movements. Every shadow stirred with monsters eager to jump out and bite. Every step could be her last. The two blocks to the Winecoff Hotel felt like ten miles.

The Winecoff Hotel was a boutique establishment, reclaimed from the brick bones of one of the oldest buildings in the Atlanta skyline. Its lobby had just enough space for a front desk, a pair of modern couches, a coffee stand, and a stairway that curved up into a spendy restaurant. For the next few days, it would be her sanctuary. She couldn't risk leading Orion to her apartment.

It was strange for Tori to be staying in a hotel on a weekday, especially so close to her office. After what happened yesterday, no one had questioned her when she called in sick. She'd never called in sick before. James would've rather given up beer and football for Lent than give her vacation. In the end, he didn't get to choose.

She was allowed to be here. Still, she slipped through the lobby with the excitement-edged secrecy of a high schooler playing hooky. She reached the elevator bay. She smashed the "UP" button.

The elevator arrived with a cheerful ding.

"Tori? Tori Jaecar?"

Tori must've jumped two feet at the sound of her own name.

A woman in a button-down dress stood inside the elevator. Maena the project manager.

"What in the world are you doing here?" Maena gasped.

Great, just great. Tori hadn't expected to meet anyone she knew here. There was no way she could act like a normal person right now.

"Oh. Hello, Maena. I uh... I needed to get away from..." Her mind scrambled for an explanation. It only managed to scramble itself. "...the pollen. All this pollen is murder for my skin. There's a nice spa here." She didn't go to spas. Maena knew that. She was so bad at lying.

"It's okay, Tori. I get it. Yesterday was a shock for us all." Maena patted her shoulder. "Come on, let me buy you a drink."

Was that a good idea? No, it was not. Orion could strike at any moment. The last thing Tori wanted was to get an innocent bystander involved. Yet she couldn't find it in her to object as Maena led her upstairs.

The spendy restaurant didn't offer much for its high price tags. Sleek, colorful furniture contrasted with outdated white tile floors. Paper menus decorated empty tables. A single bored-looking waiter loitered by the door.

Maena ushered Tori to the bar with the confidence of a regular. Aside from a couple out on the terrace, they were the only customers. That made sense. It was what, nine fifteen? Frankly,

Tori was surprised there was a bartender working at this hour. Classic downtown.

The bartender poured them both a double of scotch then disappeared into the back.

Throughout the years that they'd worked together, Tori had always been wary of Maena. The project manager dressed like a flower but behaved like a fox. Wielding gossip, seniority, and a mature charisma that could soften even the stiffest of managers, she made office life hell for her enemies. But today, something was missing.

Today, Maena was neither flower nor fox. She wore no cherry-red lipstick. Her outfit could only be described as "simple" and her hair hung in a dark mess at her shoulders. Her eyes seemed duller; her cheeks seemed gaunt. And it wasn't just the missing makeup.

"To nine o'clock scotch," Maena offered a toast.

Tori clinked her glass. "To nine o'clock scotch." She didn't care for scotch, no matter what time it was. But Maena clearly needed it.

Bracing herself, Tori took a sip. She held back a cough as the gasoline burned down her throat. Hopefully it would also burn away some of her nerves.

She didn't trust herself to speak. Thankfully Maena spoke enough for both of them.

"I still can't believe he's gone," Maena mused. "Believe it or not, I hated James too."

She certainly didn't act like she hated James. She ate lunch with him. She laughed at all his jokes.

Tori believed her.

"I hated his terrible ideas... His creepy compliments..." Maena traced her finger around the rim of her glass, one lap for each complaint. "...and those god-awful hugs. But I never thought I'd wake up one morning and he'd be gone."

"I know what you mean," Tori replied in a whisper.

Maena lifted her glass with purpose. "Today is the anniversary of my great grandma's death. Here, in the Winecoff Hotel. About a hundred years ago, this whole place went up in flames. Was one of the deadliest hotel fires ever." She smiled dryly. "Never met her. But I think about her every time I walk by this building." In one, long draw, she finished her drink. "Rest in peace, Mee Maw. And James, too, I guess."

She smiled, yet she looked like she was about to cry.

Solemnly, Tori stared into her scotch. She didn't know what to say. She hadn't felt so useless and awkward since her college room-mate's boyfriend burst into tears when their hibachi chef made a volcano out of onion rings. Apparently, he'd almost died when Mount Rainier erupted ten years earlier. All it took was a single spark to bring all that trauma flooding back.

Tori didn't know what trauma flooded Maena, and she didn't have the heart to ask.

"You know, Tori, I've always worried about you. Since the morning you first started, quiet as a church mouse."

Tori glanced up. Weren't they talking about Maena's great grandma?

"My point is, you never know when you'll wake up one morning and someone will be gone." Maena placed a hand on Tori's arm. "Life is crazy. Don't waste it doing something you hate."

Hate. Was that really what Tori felt for her job? Besides James and Dick, she got along fine with her coworkers. Software engineering was an exhilarating challenge; she loved the sweet satisfaction of pulling abstract logic together into something new. Her salary gave financial security—something rare and precious after the energy crisis. She had her bad days, weeks, and months. She wanted more, sure, but so did everyone else.

She'd sacrificed so much to make it this far.

This was what she wanted. This was who she was.

If it wasn't, those sacrifices—the long hours of studying, the lonely years of her youth, and most of all, the missed time with *him* —would've been for nothing.

Nothing wasn't good enough for Tori. Nothing gnawed at her mind in a swarm of gnats until she couldn't stand it anymore and excused herself from the bar. It followed her out of the restaurant, up the elevator, and all the way to her room.

Roy texted that all was clear on the street behind the Winecoff Hotel. Brooks confirmed no one had entered since Tori. And Vince was probably already on his way up from the parking deck to meet her.

All Tori had to do was sit tight in her room and wait for trouble.

She reached for the brass handle of Room 535. She hesitated.

Heat radiated from the door. The unmistakable scent of ash, soot, and char overpowered her. Smoke leaked from beneath the threshold, swirling around her, swallowing her whole. She sputtered and coughed.

"RUN!" a raspy voice rang out.

A pale woman stood behind Tori. Dirt marred her hollow face. Charred clothing hung off her bony body. A glassy film clouded her large, violet eyes. But her most striking feature was the gold-auburn hair that spilled over her shoulders, molten metal from a forge. She was terrible. She was beautiful.

The hairs on the back of Tori's neck stood up. She couldn't believe what she was seeing. She rubbed her eyes. When she opened them again the woman was gone. So was the smoke. But her warning lingered in the air.

Adrenaline sharpened Tori's senses. She surveyed her surroundings.

The thin line of light underneath Room 535's door was interrupted by two shadows. Feet.

Someone was already inside.

CHAPTER FIVE

Fear sent Tori running for the elevators. She smashed both call buttons. Brooks perched in his sniper's nest. Roy watched from the street. Vince was so loud his footsteps sounded like the baseline of a metal song—she would've heard him come in. The someone in Room 535 was not her ally. She had to get out of here.

Precious seconds ticked away. Why was the elevator suddenly so slow?

The call buttons weren't lighting up. The arrows above the elevators had gone dark.

The elevator wasn't coming.

Room 535 clicked open. Without looking back, Tori bolted for the emergency stairs. As she turned the corner, plaster and dust exploded around her.

A black arrow buried itself in the wall where her head had been.

"Like I told you before, Victoria..." Orion, her attacker, taunted. "...I'm not usually the one being chased."

His mastiff snarled at his heel.

How? How had Orion arrived at first!? Tori's detour with Maena had lasted only twenty minutes. Brooks and Roy had guarded both entrances to the building the entire time.

Orion would've had to sprint to the Winecoff Hotel from wherever he was hiding. He would've had to sneak past Roy and Brooks. Then he would've had to figure out which room was hers. After that, he would've had to break inside.

Surely that would've taken longer than it had taken Tori to half-finish one drink. Unless... Horror pricked down her spine.

Orion had been waiting here before the news report. He'd already known her face, location, and name.

The trap was for her.

A traffic jam of thoughts clogged her mind. Where was Vince? Were her parents safe? Why in the world had she involved herself in something so crazy? But one thought shot past all the others. *Run.*

Tori rushed into the stairwell, jumping two steps at a time. She'd only made it half a flight when her senses caught up with her. Thick smoke choked the air, burning her throat, strangling her breath, and bringing tears to her eyes.

Flames blocked the stairwell from below. There was no way down. She was screwed.

No, she was double screwed.

Behind the veil of fire, a dark shape paced back and forth.

Orion had another mastiff. Orion had another mastiff, but this one was larger than a bear—so much so that it barely fit in the stairwell.

Tori prayed that this was all just another hallucination.

At the sight of her, the mastiff barked, loud, baritone, and very real. Its voice echoed like cannon fire.

An alarm screeched. Emergency sprinklers burst into action, bathing everything in stale water and scalding steam.

Tori sprinted up the stairs. It was her only option. Orion trailed only seconds behind, and soon the fire would calm enough for his giant bear dog to pass.

An arrow pierced her calf. She gasped in shock. Her leg buckled. She caught herself on a railing. Choking back the pain, she glanced down. Big mistake.

Orion was only one floor below her.

Seeing him fed the sheer terror biting at her ribcage.

With a wink, he notched another arrow.

Her eyes pinned on that arrow, she stumbled away. She should've watched where she was going instead. Her sneaker slipped on wet concrete, sending her tumbling forward. She might've broken her chin right then and there, but someone caught her by the shoulders.

"You're almost there."

The pale woman had risen again.

Her body was frail, but her grip was iron. It melted through Tori's shirt.

Tori smelled burning flesh. White hot pain seared through her arms. But she couldn't scream. The woman's eyes, so empty and vast, pulled her in.

"You have to live!" the woman whispered. "You have to live so you can stop him!"

A nearby door flew open with so much force its hinges broke. The seventh floor stretched beyond it.

Tori opened her mouth to reply, but the woman had already vanished. She couldn't afford to worry whether she should trust a ghost. She scrambled through the door. It slammed shut, locking with a satisfying metallic thunk. It wouldn't stop Orion for long, but it would buy her time to think.

Tori slumped against the stairwell door. Sweat dripped off her, yet she shivered.

The seventh floor was a dead end. The elevator bays were

vacant. The stairs were occupied. Should she fight? No—Orion was armed and she wasn't. Should she hide? Those hounds would surely track her down. She buried her face in her knees.

This was bigger than her. It was bigger than her company, the outdated software that defined her life, and all the office buildings in Atlanta. And she was useless. Helpless. Hopeless. How could someone like her matter?

A clock ticked in the hallway. Tori was back in a conference room. James towered over its gray walls. Maena lounged at his side, her dress draped over her like the tail of a fox. On giant brown wings, Dick circled them.

Smoke flooded from beneath the door behind her. The air was too heavy. Tori grasped at her throat. She coughed and choked. Her vision went black around the edges.

"Hey. Tori." It was Zach, her coworker. He sat next to her, oblivious to her struggle. "Thanks again for your help."

Tori blinked. She was back on the seventh floor. She could breathe. She could think clearly now.

Maena had been right, in a way. Tori had never enjoyed working as a software engineer. She hated the meetings, the nonstop work, and the monochrome monotony that dragged on and on for years.

But she loved solving problems. Being challenged. Helping her peers. It was those moments—whenever she made someone's life just a little easier—that got her out of bed in the morning.

She wanted to fight Orion. She wanted to fight the monsters of the world.

And to do that, she had to survive.

Tori limped towards the window at the end of the hall. If the stairs and the elevator were off limits, she would have to make her own exit. She was what, seventy feet up? Eighty? There were indoor rock-climbing walls taller than that. She could use the gaps between the bricks as handholds and climb down. It would be fine if she moved carefully and tried not to look down.

As though it could read her thoughts, the window swung inward. A head appeared in the opening.

Tori saw an angel.

Wreathed in afternoon sunlight, crowned in amber and gold, Roy Angelus reached out to her. He smiled, saffron and honey. His lips mouthed her name. Atlanta, sprawling from the patchwork towers of downtown, past the glimmering lake in Piedmont Park, all the way to Stone Mountain, was a backdrop worthy of a cathedral.

It wasn't until Tori climbed out onto a rusty ladder that she realized Roy wasn't flying.

A rickety fire escape groaned beneath their weight. Tori clung to the window frame so hard her knuckles went white. "How did you find me?"

"I had a few hints." Roy jerked his chin upwards. Black smoke curled into the sky, raining ash on the streets below. "I'm glad I found you in time."

The fire had grown wildly. The whole building might collapse soon. That was the least of their problems.

"Orion's inside!" Tori blurted. "And he's got a bow! We'll be easy targets on this thing."

"Then we'd better move." Roy knelt to her level. He offered her his hand.

Something about that out-stretched hand gave Tori pause. It was salvation. It was also an invitation. And even though she'd only known him for twenty-four hours, she already knew that being near this man was dangerous, like being too close to the sun.

Twenty-four hours ago, maybe even twenty-four minutes ago, Tori would've backed away. Tori of Now grabbed that hand like a rope. With his help, she could climb to heights she never dreamed of. She could draw power from the sun.

Ignoring his offers to carry her, she half-dragged half-stumbled Roy down the fire escape. Together, they spiraled all the way to the bottom.

Blue police lights bounced between the neighboring buildings. Fire trucks wailed in the distance. There was chaos everywhere, but no more sign of Orion.

CHAPTER SIX

Black smoke swallowed red brick. Flames licked at charred windows. Ash smothered Peachtree Street in gray. Onlookers gaped in horror as firefighters rescued hotel guests, one by one, from the jaws of hell. It felt so strange to watch the final moments of the Winecoff Hotel on a television screen when not an hour earlier, Tori Jaecar had been in the heart of it all.

After escaping Orion and his hounds, Tori and Roy had reunited with Vince and Brooks. They'd retreated to the suburbs, into an abandoned corner of the Roswell Mill Club.

Tori had eaten at this restaurant maybe a dozen times. Built into the shell of one of Roswell King's Civil War era mills, the Roswell Mill Club was a favorite stop for business out-of-towners who wanted to confirm that plantation houses, fried food, and fifteen-dollar mint juleps were all there was to the South. Its exposed rafters, worn wooden floors, and white shiplap walls gave it a soft, subtle atmosphere. Most importantly, it was only a five-minute walk from their base-condo.

Outside, man-made waterfalls roared through the derelict dams of the mill. The muffled sound of white water usually soothed Tori. Today it made her restless.

Maxine Daly stepped into the center of the screen. "Tonight, Atlanta mourns the loss of one of the oldest buildings in the downtown skyline. A fire broke out in the historic Winecoff Hotel. Behind me, brave first responders struggle against the blaze." Her demeanor was completely different from this morning. Ever so slightly, she trembled.

Tori didn't blame her.

One by one, soot-covered guests stepped out into the light. Parents comforted their children between fire trucks. Stretchers rolled into ambulances. The scene was enough to bring tears to Tori's eyes.

"Several key campaign advisors for incumbent President Arvis were staying at the Winecoff Hotel," Maxine stated. "After the bombing of his campaign bus just last week, one must wonder... Is this yet another attack on our democracy?"

Leave it to the local news to make a tragedy political.

Tori twisted a lock of hair between her fingers. The President Arvis thing had to be a coincidence, right? Orion had killed James because of the drug, not because of secret ties to domestic terrorists.

"Channel 2 will be standing by for more updates. Until then, our hearts go out to the victims and their families." Maxine clutched a hand to her chest. "I'm Maxine Daly with Channel 2 News. Stories that count, from people who care."

Shaking his head, the bartender switched off the television.

Tori picked at her leftover fries. She wasn't hungry. A lump formed in her gut.

Fire safety codes had come a long way in a hundred years. Maena had texted that she'd made it out okay. So far, no one had died. But they couldn't have possibly accounted for everyone already.

The handprints on Tori's shoulders stung like millions of hot needles digging into her skin. Burning to death would be a terrible way to go. And Orion had burned the Winecoff Hotel to get at her.

Eventually Vince couldn't stand the silence. "I still can't believe that New Girl saw a ghost!" His words oozed with envy, not disbelief. "I've been doing this for years and I've still never seen one. Not a real one."

He leaned over Tori. "You sure you didn't get any proof? Maybe a video? A photo with orbs in the background?"

Before lunch, Tori had gambled on Roy, Brooks, and Vince. Even though she was half convinced she'd been hallucinating, she told them everything that happened at Winecoff Hotel. About her drink with Maena. Orion's huge hounds. The ethereal woman who'd saved her not once, but twice.

Her story was so insane, but they took her at her word. They didn't even ask questions.

That didn't surprise Tori as much as it should have.

Roy swirled red wine in his glass, his brows furrowed. "She wasn't a ghost," he said with absolute certainty.

"What are you, a psychopomp? You didn't guide her to the afterlife. You didn't even see her." Vince scoffed. "How would you know?"

"I'm shocked that you know that word, Vince," Brooks commented dryly. He'd been in a glum mood ever since he'd seen Tori's hand-shaped blisters and the arrow sticking from her calf. Whenever he thought she couldn't hear him, he grumbled about innocent bystanders under his breath.

"Uhm." Tori cleared her throat. This time, she wouldn't let the conversation run away without her. "If she wasn't a ghost, then what was she?"

"I don't know," Roy admitted. "But trust me, I know ghosts."

Trust him? Hah. "How about dogs?"

Roy met her eyes. She averted them.

"I'm sorry, Miss Jaecar. Perhaps we should have warned you."

Brooks grunted in agreement.

"Warned me? Does that mean you knew? That Orion's hunting dogs..." Tori fumbled for words. "...that they aren't normal?"

"You also knew, did you not? Before you volunteered to help us," Roy mused. "That Orion isn't a normal villain. That we aren't normal."

"Then what are you?"

"It's a long story."

"I've got time."

Roy closed his eyes, savoring a sweet memory. "Twenty-one years, six months, and nine days ago, I met Brooks on the edge of a battlefield, laying in a pool of blood," he began as though reading a bedtime fable. "I'll never forget how beautiful he was in that river of red, or how the morning sunlight sparkled on the snow—"

"Maybe start at the middle?" she interrupted. "Or the end?"

"We're monster hunters!" Vince blurted as if it was the coolest thing ever.

"Monster... hunters...?" she repeated slowly.

"To be specific, we're hunting the origin of the monsters," Roy clarified. "Well, we were. Before all of"—he gestured around them —"this."

"What do you mean by the origin?"

"For centuries, monsters only lived in mythology," Roy traced a dragon in his leftover ketchup.

"Mythology. You're telling me I was attacked by a myth?"

"Just think about it. This is the Information Age! There are millions of tablets, laptops, and cellphones in the US alone, and every one of them has a camera. Yet not a single person has ever captured proof of the supernatural. Huge shapes underwater, orbs of dust in bad lighting, pixelated figures in misty forests... But never proof." He wiped away his dragon with a napkin.

If there was a point to this monologue, Roy would have to get to it without her. Why would anyone claim to be a monster hunter and then argue that monsters weren't real in the same breath?

"Until now," Brooks sighed.

So there *was* proof. "Wouldn't that have made the news?" Tori asked.

"It did," Roy swiped through his cell phone. "International news." He flipped it around so she could see. A photograph from Mount Rainier's eruption illuminated the screen.

It took Tori almost a full minute to see it. Just barely, she made out wings and a tail in the chaos of ash, fire, and smoke. "That... That can't be real!" She had to argue. She didn't want to believe that a creature capable of wiping out entire cities could exist.

"Something changed," Roy continued as though he hadn't heard her. "Something brought them to life." He shrugged. "Or back to life. Who can really say which?"

Tori believed him. She had to grab the edge of their table to stop from falling as reality crashed down around her.

These men lived in a different world than she did. She'd understood that from the moment she opened their condo door—no, from the very first moment Vince opened his mouth. But she never could've fathomed just how different their world was.

Monster hunters. Tori's mind raced through the possibilities.

"So Mount Rainier..." A monster had caused a natural disaster. What if all the natural disasters in the past decade had been the wrath of some unseen evil? What about the energy crisis?

"And Orion Treyvon..." A human—at least, he seemed human —hunted alongside hounds from hell. How were they bound together? Did they share a goal?

"That means... Everything else..." The words wouldn't come. All she could see, hear, or speak vanished beneath the relentless gaze of two red, hungering eyes.

She fucking knew it.

"Yo," Vince waved his hand in front of her eyes. "You okay

there, New Girl? If you want, I can get you some water. Or whiskey. Or a Prozac?"

"Miss Jaecar." Roy's voice penetrated the void.

Tori straightened.

"Miss Jaecar. You set a trap for Orion Treyvon. You escaped his hounds and his arrows. You've walked through fire. You can handle the truth."

"Mercy. You can't blame her for being upset!" Brooks protested. "She thought she was signing up to fight a man, not a monster!"

Roy ignored him. "Do you regret it?" He cupped Tori's chin, drawing her face towards his. "Facing off against a monster?"

Yes. And very much no.

"I, uh..." Tori knew her answer, but she couldn't speak. Not while he was so near she could feel his breath on her skin and count the colors in his eyes.

Brooks mistook her hesitation for fear. "You don't have to answer that. You don't have to stay here, either." His voice crept louder and louder until it rippled the wine in Roy's glass. "You don't have to think about any of this ever again. It's not your fight! Go back to your life. We can protect you from afar."

"Can we?" Roy chided. "We did such a great job protecting her today."

Vince laughed. "Man, this is nostalgic. You wouldn't believe how much they bickered when I first joined them!"

Tori stood. Her chair screeched across the ground.

Both Brooks and Roy stopped talking. Even the bartender looked up from polishing bottles.

Oh. Tori winced—half from the pain in her leg, half from embarrassment. She hadn't meant to be so dramatic. She searched for courage in the nails and knots in the floors.

"I don't care if Orion is a monster or a man. I can't back out now."

That made it sound like she was trapped. Well, she was. Orion was clearly hunting her. She couldn't go back to her day-to-day life without putting her friends, family, and coworkers in danger. But that wasn't important.

She didn't want to go back. Somewhere in the Winecoff Hotel, in that springtime snow of ash and embers, she finally found herself. Somehow, she knew that if she dared further into that blizzard, she would also find the monster—not animal—that slaughtered Luke on that night eighteen long, lonely months ago.

Tori clenched her fist. "Teach me how to fight. I'll be ready the next time Orion finds me." Next time, no innocent strangers would get hurt.

She braced herself. This was it. This was the point in the meeting when James would tell her to stick to shopping and romance novels. This was when Dick would tear apart her ideas and send her back to her desk in pieces.

Roy eased back in his chair, a victorious king on his throne. "Brooks?"

Brooks conceded defeat. "As you wish."

Vince cheered. "Finally, a sparring partner I can beat!"

CHAPTER SEVEN

Humidity thickened the air. Sweat dripped from her brow. The pine tree woods around the Roswell Mill felt like a Florida swamp. Tori had never truly understood just how much Atlanta sweltered in summer. Not until the heaviness really worked its way under her skin, into her muscles, draining her like a fever.

It took everything she had to keep her breathing steady as she circled her opponent. She needed an opening. She would have one soon.

Tori had noticed a pattern in Vince's fighting style. He was reckless. He would take an elbow to the face if he knew he could trade blows. And it worked. He was tougher than her and could handle more hits.

But he was also impatient. If she evaded him for long enough, eventually he'd rush her. He'd strike with his right hand. He'd leave his legs open. And when he did, she would take him down.

Brooks watched from the sidelines, his mouth in a permanent frown. Just looking at him made Tori tense. He reminded her of her ma watching her and her brother shoot fireworks over the drainage pond behind their house—somehow anxious and calm at the same time.

Meanwhile Roy lounged in a plastic lawn chair, a cocktail in one hand and a laptop on his knees. He wasn't paying attention. He never did.

"Come on Tori. Show me what you're made of!" Vince swung for her, hard.

"Watch your neck," Roy commented without glancing up from his screen.

Tori wasn't going to miss this opportunity. She went for a shoot; dropping to one knee, she tackled Vince's legs.

Suddenly his legs were gone. The next thing she knew, an arm snaked around her throat. He had her in a choke from above.

"You'd better tap," Vince tightened his grip to make a point.

Tori patted his forearm. He let go.

Vince was intentionally leaving himself open, wasn't he? As a trap.

Frustration boiled in Tori's gut.

Being defeated over and over again by Vince sucked. He was so excited to win at something he couldn't help but gloat.

Every.

Single.

Time.

Dude didn't have a drop of humility in his body. But he sure had skills.

She had so much to learn before she could wipe that smirk off his mouth.

"Good try, Miss Jaecar," Brooks called out. "First thing tomorrow I'll show you how to get out of that hold."

"Thanks," she mumbled at the dirt.

The last few weeks of Tori's life had been fantastic: equal parts awesome, equal parts crazy. Because Tori witnessed James' death firsthand—while on the clock, at that—HR granted her short term leave from work without much question. She traded early morning meetings at the office for long group runs along Vickery Creek with Brooks, Roy, and Vince. She couldn't recall ever having so much freedom before.

Thanks to the Winecoff Hotel fiasco, Brooks insisted that she move in with them for protection. At first, the prospect of living with three strange men made Tori uneasy. But what choice did she have? Orion could attack anytime, anywhere. He'd found her hotel room. He'd find her apartment, too, if she went home. She doubted the police would believe her story as easily as people who made a life out of blending fact with fiction. Thus, Vince was kicked out into the living room so she could have a bedroom to herself.

Bachelor life was a huge adjustment for Tori. She hadn't had roommates since college. Vince and Brooks were constantly locked in a battle over trashing their condo and keeping it clean. She could hardly think in all the chaos and noise. But it was nice, too. Like she had a new, dysfunctional little family.

Brooks mixed the kindness of a children's nurse with the sternness of a drill sergeant. He showed her how to throw a punch, pushed her through brutal cardio, and coached her on lifting weights safely. Each day was full of workouts and fighting lessons. Each night, he cooked her tasty meals, taking great care to mind her tastes and preferences.

Vince smoked like a coal train and drank like a rock star, but he was sincerely excited to have her around. He showed her his knife collection. He taught her how to play dozens of card games and didn't mind losing every hand. He dreamed of being a paranormal investigator but had never caught a real monster on film. So he invented fake ones. Together they watched all his videos.

And Roy, well. He didn't quite fit into Tori's game of house.

For the most part, Roy was gone before Tori woke up and

returned after she went to sleep. But some nights he came back early. He stretched out on the couch and played video games with her deep into the morning until Vince's complaining drove them out. Roy told her crazy stories about his family, such as how he and his brother dated the same girl on the same day without knowing, or how he terrorized his wicked stepmom. He teased Brooks for being too strict daily.

Since the fire, there'd been no sign of Orion.

Spring came like a lion. It went like a lamb—soft, quiet, and comfortable.

"Next time, Vince," Brooks suggested. "Maybe let her get you on the ground. She should get some practice transitioning from—"

"Orion won't pull any punches, why should I?" Vince popped the cap off his flask, taking a swig of hot whiskey. Gross.

Tori didn't want Vince to go easy on her. She was years behind him in experience, athleticism, and discipline. In a real fight she wouldn't stand a chance. But she picked up boxing techniques quickly. She admired the brutal effectiveness of jiu-jitsu submissions. She appreciated how wrestling showed her how to leverage her body, despite being small. Combat sports were much more tactical than she'd ever imagined, and she loved strategy games.

She didn't need shortcuts. She would catch up to him eventually.

Except in shooting. She needed to be good at hand to hand, because no matter how clearly Brooks demonstrated how to shoot a gun, she could barely hit a target. Her hands wouldn't hold steady. She flinched with every bang. She'd almost brought Vince to tears when she jammed his precious revolver four times in one session. She couldn't connect with such a cold, cruel machine.

"I seem to remember *someone* breaking his tooth the first time he fired a gun," Brooks stated. "You improved with practice. So will she."

Vince huffed. "That was different! I was about to get eaten!"

"Why don't you two take a break?" Roy interrupted. "I'll take over for today."

Both Vince and Brooks gaped. Roy had never once volunteered to help.

Tori felt as though she'd been told to stay behind after class by a teacher in school.

"...Very well," Brooks said stiffly, warily.

Vince put his hands behind his head. "Damn. Just when it was starting to get fun!"

Roy offered Tori a hand. "May I buy you lunch, Miss Jaecar?"

Gulping, she accepted.

✳ ✳ ✳

The Roswell Mill Club seemed much larger with just the two of them. Roy selected a table for two on the terrace outside. They'd become regulars here, and the staff gave them space. Throughout their meal, Tori's heart pounded in her ears. She hoped Roy couldn't hear it over the waterfalls.

A waiter set two glasses of wine on the table in front of them. Of course. Wine wasn't exactly an appropriate drink for a hot afternoon, but that had never stopped Roy before.

"You and Vincent seem to be getting along."

"You could say that."

Birds chirped in the distance.

"I hope Brooks isn't giving you a hard time."

"Oh no, he's great."

Cicadas buzzed beneath the terrace.

"You're adjusting really quickly."

"Thanks."

A chorus of crickets sang from the park below.

This. Was. Awkward.

Okay, that was a lie—nothing could make Roy seem awkward. It was all Tori.

She couldn't remember the last time she'd been out alone with an attractive man. High school? No, those weren't men. Maybe never. She didn't know what to do with herself. Or her hands. Or her eyes. Should she cross her legs? Order something less greasy than fries?

She took a deep breath.

Sirens. Succubus. Sexy vampires. If Tori wanted to be a monster hunter, she couldn't keep being intimidated by beautiful people. She channeled the energy of the protagonist from her favorite romance novel. In *Bloodsucker for Punishment*, the heroine saved the world from vicious beasts wielding nothing but a sharp wit and an enchanting charm.

Wit. Charm. Tori could do that. But first she had to remember how to talk.

Say something. Anything.

"So, Roy." She flipped through the menu in front of her. Today's special was steak. "Are you a well-done kind of man? Or do you like it raw?"

A pause.

Wait. Shit.

"What do you think, Miss Jaecar?" he replied with a smile.

He hadn't touched a menu. From his point of view, that question came out of nowhere.

"I uh..." Blood rushed to her face. *Bloodsucker for Punishment* couldn't help her now. "The menu. What I meant was—"

"Hold still."

Roy planted his palm on the wall behind Tori, leaning in close. He reached for her collar. His fingers burned hot trails along her skin.

Did the genre of this lunch date change!?

Tori choked on her leaping heart.

Roy plopped back into his chair. A spider as big as a filet mignon crawled over his hand.

"She was stuck on your shirt," he explained.

"Ah." Tori released the breath she hadn't realized she'd been holding. "That's a yellow garden spider. Kinda pretty, isn't she?"

"Very pretty." Roy agreed. He moved to toss the spider over the railing.

Tori caught him by the wrist. "Don't kill her!"

He raised a brow. "Why not? Is it bad luck?"

"Not bad luck. Bad thinking. After the next big rain, there'll be so many mosquitoes out here that we'll get eaten alive." She gestured at a web on the ceiling. "Spiders eat mosquitoes. They're on our side."

"An ally, huh?" Roy studied the spider as if it was the first one he'd ever seen. "Most cultures view spiders as tricksters and thieves."

"Ma used to say they're wise women, weaving the threads of the world, watching over us from their webs."

"Don't female spiders usually eat their mates?"

"Like I said. Wise women."

He exhaled air from his nose.

"Out in the country, these spiders would set up shop all over our house each summer. Dozens of them. Maybe hundreds." She held out her hand. "My brother and I named every last one. After their patterns. Y'know—Charlotte. Dreamcatcher. Spot."

Gently, he transferred the spider to her. "What's this one's name?"

Tori examined the spider. White, red, and yellow concentric rings painted its back. She's seen that particular pattern a million times. It was the logo of Tianyi, the software giant that bought out her company.

First cloud cat, now this. She once read that nature imitated art, but this was getting ridiculous. Even after almost a month of leave, even all the way out in Roswell, she couldn't get away from work.

Swallowing a sigh, she released the spider onto the side of the building.

"Goodbye, Tianyi." For now.

"Miss Jaecar," Roy observed, those brilliant eyes of his pinned on hers. "How are you doing?"

"Good. Great, even. In a couple more weeks I'll give Vince a run for his money."

"You know that's not what I'm asking. Do you still think about... James, was it?"

James MacGillivray, Tori's least favorite subject. Tori would rather discuss steak again. "I think about that day all the time."

"We can talk about it if you'd like. I know it's hard to depend on people you just met, but we've all been through something... similar."

She shook her head. "There's nothing to talk about. James and I... didn't really see eye to eye. On anything. He was kind of a monster himself, actually."

"Then why did you risk your life to capture his killer?"

A complicated question with a complicated answer. When Tori first chased after Orion, she'd simply been caught up in the moment. When she volunteered for the Winecoff Hotel trap, she'd been thinking of Luke. But both times, James was there. In the back of her mind. A dull headache on the edge of her thoughts.

"My brother always said that there's no such thing as a bad person. Or a good one, for that matter. We're just the sum of inter-actions. A million glances in the eyes of the people we pass by. A little different every day." Tori stared at her reflection in her untouched glass of wine. "I didn't do it for James. I did it for the person he was in front of his wife. His lover. His kids." She gripped the table. "...and for the person I want to be tomorrow."

"Your brother sounds like an interesting person," Roy mused.

She smiled at him. "I'm okay. Really."

Roy decided not to press any further. "Good." He retrieved his laptop from his bag. "I hope you'll still feel that way when I'm done with you." He winked. "Ready for your lesson?"

Tori wondered what subject Roy planned to teach. She didn't think she could concentrate enough to spar against him.

"Let's talk about monsters."

CHAPTER EIGHT

Orion's hounds glared at Tori from Roy's laptop screen. Short bios sprawled beneath their photos. Procyon: Canis Minor, three hundred fifty pounds, 90cm. Sirius: Canis Major, twelve hundred pounds, 175cm. Can understand English, Russian, and Greek. Capable of tracking a scent from a hundred miles away. Below their profile, the word "immortal" sent a shiver down her spine. Injuries might slow them down, but they'd regenerate good as new. Even severed limbs.

"No matter how strong you become, you'll always be weaker than the average monster," Roy explained, wielding a paper straw as a teacher's pointer stick. He enjoyed playing professor.

"A werewolf must be killed with silver or lightning. You must burn the wound when you cut off a hydra's head or it'll grow back as two. A minotaur is ten times stronger than a man, but also twice as slow. Knowledge, not strength, is our deadliest weapon against them."

Tori curled her hair between her fingers, absorbing the information. It was a lot to take in.

As a kid, she'd believed every fable, folktale, and superstition her ma told her. As an adult, she saw patterns in those stories come to life in the behavior of others. Boogeymen grew up into criminals and scam artists. Fairy godparents saved the day in the form of supportive family and friends. There were entire industries devoted to helping people find their Prince Charming.

She'd always believed that there were things beyond human understanding—the inner workings of time, the human soul, entropy of the universe. Who was she to say that those things couldn't materialize as monsters?

But somehow, she'd always thought that monsters would be more mysterious.

Roy spoke of them as if he was reading from a textbook. There would be a quiz later.

"A werewolf? Hydra? Minotaur? Orion's pet dog almost killed me," Tori mumbled.

"Don't worry, I haven't seen a minotaur in ages. And you'll probably never go anywhere near a hydra's den."

"That's... reassuring," she lied. She'd hoped that monsters would be rarer given that they'd been extinct for so long. The thought of facing such a menagerie was terrifying.

In a way, it was exciting, too. A new world of possibilities awaited her. If werewolves, hydras, and dragons existed, surely good counterparts existed as well. She would love to meet a unicorn. Or maybe an angel!

"There are a few things all monsters have in common. Monsters don't have blood; they have ichor. Ichor is colorless, but it reflects light with a gold or silver sheen." Roy demonstrated by swirling his glass of honey-hued wine. "Many monsters hide behind pretty faces, masquerading as humans. But the truth always flows in their veins."

"I'll start carrying around a pincushion."

He shook his head. "You, Miss Jaecar, should never risk touching ichor. Most monsters have silver ichor, which will make you very sick." He crushed his paper-straw-pointer in his fist. "Contact with gold ichor will kill a human instantly."

Talk about a complication. Tori couldn't imagine slowing down Orion's hounds without drawing a little blood. "What's different about the gold ones?"

Roy's gaze drifted to the cloudless heavens. "Most monsters aren't born. Not from nature, at least. They're made. Through curses. Black magic. Unfortunate crossbreeding between things that shouldn't breed." He was choosing his words carefully. "The gold ones are the makers."

"Like an alpha werewolf." Tori never dreamed she would reference *Bloodsucker for Punishment* for anything other than romance, yet here she was. "Or the original vampire."

"Like an alpha werewolf or the original vampire," Roy confirmed. After a pause, he added, "Except there's no original vampire. They're created when the wrong person is buried improperly."

Bummer. "How do you know all this?"

"My family has been involved with monsters for centuries—of course, more so in the past few decades. Most of what I know came from them. And good old trial and error."

"Trial and error?" Tori frowned. She'd chosen a field where almost any question could be answered in minutes by searching the internet. On purpose. Experimental science was best left to the actual scientists. Or, in this case, soldiers.

"Yes. We learn the hard way. We almost lost Vince a couple of years back when he forgot how to fight a werewolf. Kept trying to run it over. Then he crashed into a power line." It sounded like a fond memory. "I'll bet he remembers what to do now."

Tori swallowed hard. She'd always been good at quizzes. She thrived under pressure, and quizzes had always felt like life-or-death situations—how could she win merit scholarships with a "C" on her record? But now the life or death threat was real.

Sensing her doubt, Roy scooted his chair to her side of the table. "Let's switch to something more familiar. Help me figure out what your ghost *actually* is."

"Alright." Her ghost was less intimidating than werewolves, hydras, and minotaurs. Her ghost was one of the good ones.

"Hmmm, where to begin..." He opened a file to take notes. "Did you see a brass leg?"

* * *

The afternoon slipped away. Night fell in to take its place. Tori's head danced with dreams of boogeymen, nature spirits, blood sucking succubi, and Roy, after a little too much wine.

Learning about the many monsters that could appear as a haunting woman had been surprisingly fun. Roy was an amazing storyteller. He got into character, gesturing alongside the heroes and villains. His voice rang with emotion in every scene, as if he'd been there. But by the time lunch-turned-dinner ended, they were no closer to understanding Tori's ghost than they'd been when they'd started.

None of the explanations fit. None of them were even close.

Despite Tori's objections, Roy insisted on handling the bill. He stepped away to pay.

With a parting wave to the restaurant staff, Tori headed outside. She leaned against the wooden railing of the patio, gazing at the waterfall below. Running water whispered in her ears. A breeze wandered through the trees. It was so peaceful here. It was hard to believe she was so close to urban Atlanta. It was even harder to believe that somewhere out there, this gentle night teemed with monsters.

Movement caught her eye. Tori leaned over the railing for a better look.

Armed with bayoneted rifles, men in gray coats escorted

women alongside Vickery Creek. Ropes bound the women's dirty, bruised hands. Tears dampened their tired eyes. Misery carved into the lines of their faces, black, white, and everything in between. In the distance, children cried for their mothers.

Above the sad scene, a young boy climbed the old Roswell Mill. He raised an American flag over the roof. Only, it didn't have enough stars or stripes.

History wasn't Tori's best subject, but she would always recognize the Union flag. This time, she knew she wasn't hallucinating. Some strange magic had transported her back to the Roswell Mill of the Civil War era.

Soon Roswell King's empire of brutality would fall forever. Those men were Confederate soldiers fleeing General Sherman's advance. Those women, the workers of the mill, could not be left behind to potentially aid the enemy. And so they, too, would suffer the worst of war.

Abruptly, violently, Tori doubled over. She coughed and sputtered as she inhaled thick smoke. The stench of burning flesh invaded her lungs. Screams overpowered the roar of the waterfalls.

Shielding her eyes, she struggled to access the situation. Flames devoured the mill. Black clouds strangled the sky. The men and their guns had been lost to the chaos.

A glint of gold glittered among the holocaust of red. Undetected, on the opposite bank of Vickery Creek, a woman ushered the mill workers away from danger. A woman with radiant hair. The ghost!

She was different from the Winecoff Hotel. At the Winecoff Hotel, she'd flickered like a candle at the end of its wick. Here, she exploded with the color of a firework show finale.

Violet and blue feathers threaded through her blazing locks. Elegant scarlet cloth wreathed her athletic body. Her skin almost glowed in the darkness.

A boogeyman, spirit, or succubus? No, Tori had met a goddess.

"You're wrong," a voice in the back of her mind protested.

At once, the fire was gone. And so was the goddess. Instead, a frail figure quivered before her.

"Then what are you?" Tori asked in a hushed tone, afraid she might disappear again.

"Death," the ghost replied. Weakness clung to every word, every movement. "Fire." Her melodic voice echoed like chimes in the wind. *"Resurrection."* A spark burned in those hollow, faded, amethyst eyes.

"Were you here during the Civil War?" It couldn't be possible, and yet Tori already knew the answer.

"I was. I am. I always will be."

"Then what about the hotel?"

For a long, weary moment, the ghost remained silent. She peered at the full moon. "I caused that tragedy, too. Like this city, I die and am reborn in flame. The cycle is timeless." She raised her hand, covering the moon with her thumb. "And this phase is ending soon."

"What do you mean? How can I help you?"

"The one you call Orion is the beginning of the end." She faced Tori. "His masters will use my end to bring great ruin. So great that this mill and that hotel will seem like embers in ashes." She clenched her feeble fists. "I can't stop him. I can't stop them." She reached out to Tori, tangling her fingers in her sleeve. "Great Hunter, promise you will stop *me!*"

Tori could not stand against such intensity. "I... I promise!"

Heat seared through Tori's body. Involuntarily she closed her eyes. And then she saw it.

A thick, orange fog hung in the air. Charred apartment complexes lined barren streets. Windowless skyscrapers marred the horizon. Copper-stained flames licked their bones. There were so, so many bodies.

It was another disaster. But where? And *when?*

"Tori."

Her name summoned her back to reality. Tori jumped. Her shirt was charred to ruin.

Roy leaned in the doorframe, his arms crossed over his chest. "Where have you been?"

CHAPTER NINE

Tori peeked into the hallway. She was too afraid to move. Just around the corner, with nothing between them but light and air, lurked a monster. It tossed and turned in their living room, making the strangest noises.

The monster's name was Vincent Lenoir. He sprawled across the couch, dead asleep. Tori figured he needed the rest—almost every night, she heard him fetching a beer, or playing solitaire, or groaning through his nightmares until morning. She usually tried not to listen. But tonight, she had to disturb him. They were going to be late.

Brooks was out buying groceries. Roy, per usual, vanished with the setting sun. She had to wake Vince herself. But she knew for a fact, through many warnings from Brooks and a whole week of being avoided after she walked in on him once, that Vince slept in nothing but boxers. What if he forgot the boxers this time?

Tori compromised by covering her eyes as she marched into the living room. "Wake up, Sleeping Beauty!" she cried out. "The tour starts in ten minutes!"

No response.

She cracked her fingers. Relief lowered her hand. Vince had passed out in his jeans; he was only half-naked. His shirt draped across a pile of clothes on the floor. He was practically a baby and she wasn't thirteen anymore—she could handle shirtless.

Or so she thought. Vince's exposed back captured her attention in a different way. A roadmap of scars mapped the journey of his life. Deep claw marks carved between his shoulders. Something had clearly stabbed him once. He was practically a baby, yet he carried more cuts and scratches and tears than she could count.

A stallion, midnight blue inked with black, reared across his shoulder blade. Its hooves struck above his heart. Behind it, twelve stars crowned a mountain top. Tori wasn't surprised at all that Vince had a tattoo, but knowing him, she would have expected something more... metal? Like a dragon lighting a cigar with a smoking gun, on a motorcycle. This picture was so specific that it had to have some hidden meaning.

It occurred to Tori that aside from the brief boxer incident, she'd never seen Vince stripped down before. No matter how much he complained about Atlanta's weather. No matter how mercilessly the sun beat down upon their spars. Maybe this shameless loud-mouth wasn't so shameless after all.

"Nancy," he mumbled under his breath. "I swear, I didn't know..."

Tori's heart stuck in her throat. She recognized that tone. It was the tone she heard for the first time when she found Luke's body. It was the tone that tugged at the edges of her memory every evening, without fail, ever since.

Vince didn't deserve to be trapped with that tone. Not alone.

"Hey. Vince." She nudged him, gentle and slow. "I'm going to borrow your car—"

He jerked upright. "No you're not!"

A pause.

He blinked. He rubbed his eyes.

"I am if you don't get ready in about two seconds. If we're late, they'll start without us."

Finally, Vince seemed to register that she was there. Hastily he pulled on his shirt. He shotgunned an energy drink. "Cool your jets! We still have plenty of time."

Typical Vince. He always had something in his mouth—a beer, a cigarette, his lower lip—in a way that reminded Tori of a teething Rottweiler puppy. Tough yet disarming.

But that mouth of his wasn't cute.

Crossing her arms, she counted down. "Two... One..."

* * *

"On nights with a full moon, if you listen very closely..." The woman inched so close to Tori that she could smell the tobacco on her breath. "...you can still hear the drowned girl crying for help!"

A teenage girl whimpered. Her mother hugged her close. Others swarmed the "haunted" old well of Bulloch Hall, snapping selfies and posting them online. Tori wasn't impressed.

Maybe these ghost tours were pointless. She and Vince had attended half a dozen of them in the past two weeks, all over Atlanta, and there was still no sign of her burning ghost. There hadn't been any sign of her at the mill, either.

"This shit blows," Vince whined. At first, he had been stoked to tag along and play bodyguard for Tori. When nothing happened once, then twice, then a third time, his excitement devolved into impatience. He complained constantly. On the last tour he'd been so loud that they'd almost gotten kicked out.

Tori gave him a hard look. "Then why are you filming?"

"It's not like I'm having fun or anything." He panned his phone's camera over the well. "I need some new material. I haven't uploaded anything to my video channel in what, a month? Even if there's like, a shadow that looks kinda weird, I bet I could make an episode about it."

"Glad you're taking this seriously," Tori sighed as she trailed their energetic tour guide down the street.

"What's there to take seriously? Old houses and spooky noises?"

His phone dinged. He lowered it to answer a text.

"Folks, gather up. This is our next stop!" The guide gestured to a large white gate. "Please don't block the street. They're holding a reopening celebration and we don't want to get in the way."

An imposing plantation house with white columns and yellow walls posed behind a wooden fence. Live oak trees hung with fairy lights and blushing azaleas framed its manicured lawn. Expensive cars parked all the way up its long driveway, a line of glittering ants on a cobblestone picnic blanket.

Another old house. Tori didn't care to find out what Vince thought about that, so she focused on their speaker.

"Welcome to Mimosa Hall. Built by one of Roswell's founders, John Dunwoody, this historic home is named for the flowering trees that flourish in its many gardens."

Thunder rumbled softly in the distance. Ugh, the weather in Georgia was so weird. There wasn't a cloud in the starry sky.

"Holy shit," Vince gasped.

Tori tuned out the guide. Had he finally spotted something!?

"That right there is an honest to goodness Porsche 918 Spyder." He pointed at one of the cars decorating the lawn. The sleek red convertible put the word "super" in supercar; it was so flashy it probably caused three accidents on the way here.

"Oh. It's a car." Of course it was a car.

"Not just any car. It's THE car. It's a hybrid, but it pumps plenty of octane through its naturally aspirated eight-cylinder 887 horsepower engine. It was the first street legal car to break the 7-

minute barrier on the Nürburgring track!" he said, all without breathing.

Tori couldn't keep up. And he called *her* Usain Bolt.

"There were only 918 ever made! And now I've seen two of them," he bragged, as if it was his proudest achievement.

Didn't this guy hunt monsters? Save lives?

"Though, the first one did hit me. On the same day I met Roy and Brooks, out in Pennsylvania—"

Another guest shushed him into silence.

"But Mimosa Hall has another name," the guide rambled on. "You see, tonight isn't its first reopening. Or its second. In 1841 and again in 1958, this estate was steeped in tragedy. On the eve it opened, during an event just like this one—"

The girl from before screamed, startling the whole group. Including Tori.

The guide recovered first. "What in Sam Hill's name do you think you're doing!?"

The same thought crossed Tori's mind. Vince had hopped the fence and was sprinting top speed towards Mimosa Hall. She opened her mouth to curse him, but at the sight of glowing eyes, she forgot what she was going to say. She bolted after Vince.

A mastiff! No, *the* mastiff. If that really was Procyon, Orion might be nearby!

The mastiff disappeared behind Mimosa Hall. In front of it, Orion emerged from his SUV. Sunglasses concealed his eyes, but Tori would never forget how tall he stood, how he oozed bravado, or how he moved without making a sound.

A fitted suit showed off his wide shoulders. He'd left his ax and bow behind. He was here on business. Without noticing the commotion at the gate, he headed inside.

"Wait Vince, calm down!" Tori had to tackle Vince to prevent him from barging inside. "Wait a second! Look!"

Reluctantly, he relented. *"What?"*

Tori dragged him to the nearest window. The curtains were only half drawn. Inside, beautiful people wearing even more beautiful finery gathered around antique furniture. Champagne waited on silver trays. Candlelight sparkled on a crystal chandelier. Most importantly, a man in black with a headset in his ear guarded the door. This party had security.

"There's no way they'll let us in. We'd stand out too much."

Vince wore a dirty t-shirt and distressed jeans. Tori sported a zip-up tech hoodie, a tank top, and shorts. They were far too underdressed to pass for guests. They wouldn't even pass for maintenance staff.

"So what? They let Orion in." Vince grumbled. "He stands out too. He's fucking giant and he's wearing sunglasses indoors. At night!"

"He must have been invited."

"Doesn't matter. We can't let him get away!" He drew his gun.

She stopped his hand. "I know that! But if you wave that thing around, we're going to end up in prison."

"Then what are we supposed to do?"

"Let's sneak inside."

"How?"

Grasping for ideas, she sized up Mimosa Hall. The main floor hummed with activity, but the upper floor was quiet. Starting there was probably their best option. But how could they get up so high? The building's second story windows had to be at least fifteen feet off the ground and its brick walls were too smooth to climb.

Together, Tori and Vince circled the lot.

A single-story porch protruded from the back of the house—perfect stepping-stone. From its roof, Tori could simply walk up to a window.

"There!" she rushed over. She stood on her toes. The roof was barely out of reach. "Give me a leg up, will you?"

Before she could object, he wrapped his arms around her and hoisted her into the air.

Tori scrambled onto the roof to escape his grip. "W-warn... Warn me next time!"

She'd scold him properly later. Before that, she had to help him climb up, too. If only she could find something to tie a rope onto... and some rope.

Laughter echoed from the nearby gardens. Someone was coming.

"Forget it," Vince whispered. "There's no way you could pull up someone as yoked as me. Go on without me."

"But..." Tori bit back her protest. He was right. The roof of the porch was bare. There was nowhere for her to hide except inside Mimosa Hall. And if they wasted any more time, she'd be discovered. She had to complete this adventure alone.

Alone. The word spread through her mind like blood in water, attracting a whole swamp full of alligators. Everything had happened so fast that it'd never occurred to her that she might have to face Orion without Vince. She wasn't ready.

"Hey," Vince interrupted gently. "You got this."

She slapped her cheeks. Again, he was right. It was too late to back out, anyways. She nodded and crawled towards the nearest window.

He flashed her a thumbs up. "Don't do anything stupid!"

With that, he slipped off into the night.

Tori took a deep breath. The window opened without resistance. She crept inside.

A king bed, dated upholstery, and clashing prints greeted her— but no party guests. The bedroom sat dark and empty. She exhaled in relief. So far so good. Now to find out what Orion was up to!

She lowered her ear to the floor. The confused murmur of voices mixed with classical music made it impossible to make out anything. She had to get closer.

She snuck through the bedroom door into the hallway. The hallway ended at emerald-carpeted stairs. At last, she heard words.

"What about Russia?" a woman argued. "We simply can't ignore the latest threats!"

"Pah," an old man dismissed. "It's just posturing."

Tori inched down the stairs for a better look.

Two couples sipped cocktails in the foyer. Surprisingly, Tori recognized one of them. Standing near the stairs was the owner of Bronze Age, one of the many fossil fuel giants that'd struck it rich during the energy crisis. She'd seen him on television a lot lately. His trophy wife hung on his arm.

A red, white, and gold banner reading "Arvis Always" arched above the hallway entrance. This was a campaign fundraiser.

Tori's thoughts returned to Maxine Daly's theory that the Winecoff Hotel incident had been an attack against the president. Was that why Orion was here? To cause another disaster? No, that didn't make sense. He seemed welcome. He had waltzed through the front door.

The couple opposite Mr. Bronze Age was strikingly attractive. The woman, who somehow pulled off classy and bold at the same time in her low-cut silk gown, traced her fingers up the arm of a sharply dressed man.

"What do you think, my Far East friend?" she asked.

Her man stood out in two ways: he was Asian—probably Chinese—whereas everyone else was white as the flowers on a Georgia magnolia, and he was young. Compared to his date. Maybe even compared to Tori.

He brushed her off. "This is why I hate campaign events..."

Mr. Bronze Age's wife clutched her pearls. "But can you imagine it? A war in this day and age?"

"There there, my dear." Mr. Bronze Age patted her shoulder. "We have enough nuclear arms to drive Russia back to the Classical era. They wouldn't dare attack us."

Tori wrinkled her brow. This wasn't new or helpful information. Every day, the news spun horror stories about Russia's dictator. It was a major presidential campaign issue.

"But if Senator Pallas gets into office..." Mr. Bronze Age scowled so hard his mustache stretched into a goatee. "...we will have so much more to worry about—oh, hello there, Orion. You're late."

Orion? Curiosity conquered fear. Tori ventured to the bottom of the stairs.

"I'm just in time for the main event," Orion replied.

Mr. Bronze Age smiled. "Introduce me to the guest of honor?"

Orion held out his arm. A woman took it delicately. She stepped into the center of the foyer, swirled in a satin dress, a bourbon rose. "This is—"

Unable to help herself, Tori gasped. Hollow, amethyst eyes. A frail demeanor. Hair like the sun. His date was the Winecoff ghost, but she wasn't ghostly at all. She was here in the flesh. With Orion. Willingly. Saying hello.

Orion halted mid-sentence. His gaze met Tori's. He smirked.

Shit. He'd heard her gasp!

CHAPTER TEN

Tori backtracked to the upstairs bedroom of Mimosa Hall. She had a head start—perhaps enough of one to escape before Orion alerted his hounds. But escape was far from her mind.

Orion had killed James. He'd burned the Winecoff Hotel. He'd driven her from her job and her home. And then he'd vanished for weeks. Not even Roy had been able to track him down. She might not get another chance—she had to stop him tonight.

Scrambling onto the roof, she texted Brooks and Roy their location. Next she dialed Vince.

"Yo, I'm uh..." He sounded like he was running. "I'm a little busy right now."

"Orion saw me." She shimmied down a porch column and surveyed Mimosa Hall's back yard. No Vince. "Where are you?"

"Hell if I know. These mutts have been on my ass since you went inside." She could hear the squeak of a fence gate in the background. "Whoa. Did you know this place has a pool?"

He was still on the grounds. She could work with that. "Meet me by the hydrangea garden?"

Silence.

"...You see a bunch of huge bushes with blue flowers?"

"I'll be there in five."

"But will *you* be there, Victoria?" With his hands buried in his pockets, Orion emerged from Mimosa Hall's rear entrance.

Hearing her name in his mouth filled Tori with both dread and anticipation.

Backing away, she taunted, "What happened to your date?" He didn't have his ax or his bow. If she could stall him for long enough, reinforcements would arrive.

"Date?" Orion laughed. "Oh no, she has other plans." He removed his sunglasses and tucked them into his suit pocket. "Tonight, it's just you and me."

She didn't like that hungry look in his eyes.

Nevermind. No more stalling.

"Thanks, but I think we should see other people!" She bolted towards the gardens.

Mimosa Hall's many gardens proved worthy to be its namesake.

As Tori raced through the darkness, she passed a pond teeming with tadpoles, enough statues to decorate a haunted house, and a wonderland of exotic plants still blooming late into summer. Mimosa trees with pink, delicate blossoms lined the cobblestone path.

"An evening stroll through flower gardens? I didn't know you were such a romantic," Orion licked his lips, following along. "Procyon! Sirius! Forget that stupid brat. Bring me the girl."

Padded footsteps thundered towards Tori. Having hounds on her heels hastened her step. She'd spent an entire month training for this. Yet the real thing pushed her oh so much further than those group runs at Vickery Creek. She poured everything she had onto the road before her, and then a little more.

When Vince appeared in front of her, she almost collapsed with relief.

"Glad to see you're still in one piece." He managed a smile.

Judging his looks, he was the one who was lucky to still be in one piece. Mud and leaves covered him head to toe. His clothes were much more distressed than before. "What's the plan?"

Plan? She'd hoped that *he* would have a plan. Wasn't he supposed to be the veteran here? "That's... still a work in progress."

"Of course it is."

The hydrangea garden surrounded a stone fountain. At the center, a handsome sculpture with a winged helm spilled water over lily pads and moss. The gentle trickle whispered secrets in Tori's ear.

Back at the waterfalls of the old Roswell Mill, she and Roy had discussed Canis Minor and Major at length. The canines had no convenient weak spots. But there was one trait that floated to the top of Tori's thoughts: their scent. If they could track a target from hundreds of miles away, their sense of smell had to be incredible.

Tori and Vince couldn't lose these dogs. They couldn't get the jump on them, either.

Right on cue, Procyon lunged from the hydrangeas. His teeth sank into Tori's arm.

Tori's cries of pain were immediately drowned out by a skull splitting bang.

The hammer of Vince's revolver fell twice. One gunshot cracked into Procyon's chest and the other his foreleg.

Vince followed up with a swift kick to the mastiff's throat.

Yelping, Procyon toppled backwards.

Before Tori had a chance to recover, Sirius erupted from the darkness.

The bear-sized beast crouched over his fallen brother, protecting him with a paw as big as Vince's head. He snarled.

At least, Tori assumed he snarled. She couldn't hear anything besides a high-pitched ringing in her ears. But she could see.

Orion cut a harsh figure against the moonlight. He mouthed something about "a loser drinking alone in the bushes" at Vince, who flipped him off. The once pristine path was painted in shredded flowers, Tori's blood, and sweet-smelling silver ichor.

Alcohol. Moonlight. Blood. "Vince." The combination sparked a flicker of an idea. It wasn't a good idea, but it was better than nothing. "Do you have some whiskey?"

Vince tossed her his flask. He never went anywhere without it. The worn pewter vial was still half full. Soon to be completely empty.

"Please. Keep the big one busy!" she instructed.

He saluted with two fingers.

This Vince was a different person from the Vince who gloated whenever he beat her. His attitude was gone. He trusted her. He cooperated without question or hesitation. He didn't even swear.

He fired at Sirius. Very faintly, she heard him shout "Come here Big Boy! Wanna play fetch?" as he hurried into the next garden.

Sirius roared after him.

Tori still had to deal with Procyon. She fled in the opposite direction of Vince.

The smaller-but-still-huge hound bounded after her.

She lured Procyon into a hedge maze. She darted around strangely shaped bushes and fingerlike branches with the grace of an owl hunting in a forest. Any dead end might literally be the end. But she had to lead him deeper into the labyrinth. She couldn't let Orion witness what came next.

As she turned a corner, Tori uncapped Vince's flask. She was ready. But she still needed an opening. If she screwed up, Procyon would cripple her within seconds. She couldn't leave this to timing and luck.

Procyon tore through a hedge, cutting her off, blocking her path. He gathered his terrible strength beneath him. He opened his jaws wide.

A white rabbit burst from the underbrush.

The interruption startled both predator and prey.

What perfect timing—and insane luck.

Tori dumped the flask all over Procyon's face, into his eyes and nose.

Procyon's howls of rage exploded through the night. They made Vince's gunshots seem quiet.

But hey, apparently Tori's hearing was better.

Without a backward glance, she sprinted towards the hydrangeas, towards Orion. It didn't take her long to find him casually sitting on the stone wall of the fountain. She dove, throwing all her weight at him.

He caught her by the wrists. "*This* was your plan? To split us up? To fight me head on? You're underestimating me, Victoria. Don't you know?" He leaned closer. "I'm the greatest hunter who ever lived."

Tori wished that she was deaf again. She headbutted him.

He cursed in that same strange language—Greek or Russian, according to Roy's notes—and let her go.

This time, when Tori tackled him, he went down with her.

They hit the cobblestones.

Orion hadn't been lying earlier. He knew his way around a fist fight. Maybe even more so than Vince.

Despite everything Brooks had taught her, despite putting up a solid struggle, Tori couldn't win. She couldn't even hold him off.

He pinned her beneath him.

Both of them panted, covered in blood.

"You're stubborn, you know that?" he growled between breaths. He squeezed her wrists so hard they bruised. "I'm going to teach you some manners." He raised his fist.

Something knocked him off her. It smashed him into the stone wall of the fountain with a sickening snap.

Procyon towered over him, stinking of liquor.

A business card floated through the air like a flag of surrender.

"Procyon!" Orion raged. "GET OFF OF ME!"

Tori jumped to her feet. She felt as if she'd just placed first in a marathon. Her plan had worked! Vince's whiskey not only blinded Procyon, but also threw off his nose. He'd mistaken his owner, who was covered in her blood, for her.

The massive mastiff's mistake dealt more damage than Tori or Vince ever could.

Even after Procyon backed away, Orion struggled to stand.

"Sirius, where in Tartarus are you!?" he barked.

Sirius stumbled into the clearing, streaked in silver.

Vince rode on the hound's back with an arm wrapped around its neck. He pressed the muzzle of his revolver into its skull.

Sirius froze. Even if he'd heal, a point-blank shot to the brain had to suck. And it would take a long time for him to grow a whole new head.

"Poor Orion. Attacked by your best friend."

That smooth voice washed the fear and tension from Tori's shoulders.

"That's gotta hurt"—Roy emerged from the darkness, clutching at his heart—"right here."

Brooks trailed him, shotgun at the ready.

Vince eased off Sirius' back, carefully keeping his gun in place.

"Damnit!" Orion seethed. "I should've known you'd get in my way again!"

"Me?" Roy pointed at himself. "I didn't lift a finger."

"Then how do you explain the rat?" the giant hissed.

A white rabbit with eyes like starlight—the same one that'd distracted Procyon in the hedge maze—watched from a safe distance. It flicked its ears back as though it knew it was being insulted.

Tori hadn't noticed it until now. Had it followed her from the maze?

Roy shrugged. "Lepus has always hated you, Orion."

Lepus? The hare had a name? Tori's expression twisted with confusion.

"You might know him as the Easter Bunny," Brooks whispered to her.

That didn't clarify anything. Was she really supposed to believe that the Easter Bunny himself had helped her out? If they were telling fairy tales, this struck her as more of a Brer Rabbit situation; the ravenous fox had been outwitted by his dinner.

"Fuck you. Fuck him too," Orion braced against the stone wall behind him. "You think you've won?" He fumbled around inside of his jacket. "I'm not done yet!"

He held a small baggie over his head. "You want this, right? COME AND GET IT!"

Golden powder inside glimmered in the moonlight. The drug!

In a swirl of amber and scarlet, the Winecoff ghost came to Orion.

Fairy dust filled in her faded eyes. She saw the bag and nothing else. She needed it to survive. She reached for her salvation.

Tori had a bad feeling about this. "No, don't!" She grabbed the ghost's arm. Her fingers found only air.

The ghost vanished. She reappeared moments later in the branches of a magnolia tree. She inhaled the gold powder slowly, lovingly. She bloomed, the brightest flower in the garden. Warmth colored her complexion. Her hair curled around her, rich and vibrant. Copper, violet, and blue feathers furled around her, forming into wings.

As Tori gazed upon her, framed by the night sky, with the party glowing in the background, a realization crossed her mind like a memory. "...Phoenix Hall."

"What?" Vince looked at her like she was speaking Greek or Russian.

Fire, death, and resurrection. "Phoenix Hall. That's this

mansion's true name." They were in danger. "This estate has burned down and been rebuilt, twice."

"You know that they say," Orion laughed. "The third time's the charm."

The magnolia tree burst into flames around the ghost... no, from her.

In mindless ecstasy, the ghost basked in the flames. With each breath, with each pulse pumping the mystery drug through her veins, the holocaust grew stronger and wilder. It devoured the magnolias, the hydrangeas, and all the mimosa trees. It melted away the sanguine dress and the women beneath, leaving behind a monstrous, beautiful bird. And then that, too, burned.

"So she's a phoenix!" Roy seemed more intrigued than concerned.

Brooks slung his weapon over his shoulder. Fire reflected in his eyes. "We can't fight this. We have to get out of here!"

"What about Orion?" Vince objected. "We're so close to finally catching that bastard!"

"Are you volunteering to carry him?" Roy asked.

Tori had to admit, the mental image of Vince fireman carrying a squirming Orion out of a burning building was pretty entertaining.

Sirius took advantage of the chaos. He slammed his paw into Vince's chest, launching him through the veil of fire.

Vince hit something solid with a sickening crack.

"You should be more worried about yourselves!" Orion jeered as he climbed onto Sirius' back. "When my 'date' is through with you, there won't be anything left of you to bury..."

In one magnificent leap, Sirius cleared the flames.

Procyon limped after him, over burning coals, regenerating as quickly the heat gnawed at his skin.

The monsters disappeared into the smoke.

"Vince!" Brooks yelled. He didn't care about Orion.

"God damnit..." Vince groaned, hidden behind the blaze.

Thank God, Gandhi, and Buddha—he was fine. For now.

The flames swiftly conquered Phoenix Hall, climbing all three stories. Yellow brick faded to black. The roof collapsed, destroying the priceless antiques beneath. The classical music gave way to honking horns as those expensive cars poured into Roswell's sleepy streets. The elegant estate transformed into hell on earth.

As though it had a will of its own, the inferno encircled the hydrangea garden. They were trapped.

Tori dropped to her knees. The air thinned. Cinders stung her dry eyes. She watched helplessly as smog eclipsed the moon with all the fury of a nuclear mushroom cloud.

"This is... I don't believe it..." Brooks gasped.

"No need to hurry. Take your time," Vince coughed. "I'm definitely not running out of oxygen or anything..."

Roy steadied Tori with his left hand. With his right hand, he drew that serpent-entwined sword from its sheath on his belt.

Tori didn't understand how a sword could help them.

"Mercy." With how Brooks said the nickname, he might as well have been saying "Master" instead. "There isn't another way out of this. You're going to have to—"

A CRACK, followed by an "ouch!" from Vince, finished his sentence.

Water overwhelmed the hydrangea garden, parting the ocean of fire. Through the ash and soot and steam, Tori saw Vince clutching his temple. He stood at the center of what used to be a fountain. The former-fountain's wing-helmeted statue had toppled over, striking him on the way down. Its weight crushed the stone wall and unleashed the flood. Behind him, a path opened through hell.

What perfect timing—and insane luck.

Roy seemed to think so, too. His eyes never left that statue, even as Tori dragged him along the path. Together, they left Phoenix Hall in their dust.

CHAPTER ELEVEN

For once, Tori agreed with Vince—Atlanta was far too hot.

The monster hunters had spent the past ten minutes in silence. From the empty parking lot of Bulloch Hall, they watched as Phoenix Hall, its neighbor, died screaming. Even blocks away from the blaze, smoke scarred the night. Summer in Georgia was usually humid, but Tori's hands, eyes, and throat were so dry that all she could think about was plunging into cold water and losing herself in the current.

Drifting away would also free her from the frustration that seared in her chest. Tonight, she and Vince had outmaneuvered Orion. Sirius had been neutralized. Procyon had been badly injured. Orion, despite having no obvious weaknesses, learned the hard way that everyone was weak to being slammed into solid rock. Without the phoenix's presence, this would've been over.

But the phoenix had been there. So here they were, no closer to capturing Orion than they'd been at the Winecoff Hotel. Another building burned. Another piece of history disappeared from the world—history they needed to understand the future.

Phoenix Hall was not part of the terrible future the phoenix had shown Tori. It wasn't the end of the destruction. It wasn't the promise she needed to keep.

Her head hurt—more so than it had after she headbutted Orion. Needing support, she leaned against a wooden fence. "President Arvis' donors... They knew Orion. They treated him like a friend. He even introduced them to the phoenix!"

Vince finished her thought. "They crashed their own party."

"But what would President Arvis gain from that?"

"Ah, Miss Jaecar..." Roy sat on the fence next to her, swinging his legs like a kid on a swing set. "This is why I never liked politics. Too much scheming and misdirection."

"Mercy, you love politics," Brooks corrected.

Vince kicked a trash can. It rolled until Brooks stopped it with a glare.

"Apparently Vincent hates politics too," Roy teased.

A growl rumbled deep in Vince's throat. He shoved a cigarette between his lips. "I'm going for a smoke break. By myself." He disappeared into Bulloch Hall's estate.

Roy, Brooks, and Tori exchanged glances.

Vince looked like an adult, but he acted like a teenager. His outburst should've annoyed Tori. Instead, it reminded her of this morning. Of his nightmares. Of his broken voice. Sighing, she clenched her fists. Some things never changed—she would always be a big sister, through and through.

"Don't worry. I got this one." She trotted after him.

Tori found Vince behind Bulloch Hall itself. The grand white plantation house with Grecian columns overlooked a grassy yard. Wooden rocking chairs creaked on its front porch. Live oak trees formed a thick canopy above, hiding them away from the world.

Vince stared at the old well "haunted" by a drowned girl from their ghost tour. He seemed to have forgotten about his unlit cigarette.

"Hey," Tori whispered, not wanting to startle him. "You hear that drowned girl?"

"Not yet." He clutched his temple. "I must've hit my head when I hit that statue, 'cos all I can hear is Orion laughing at us. I can't believe he got away again!"

"Sorry. Guess I'm zero for two on this whole monster hunting thing..."

"Sorry?" The word jerked Vince right out of whatever muck he was wallowing in. He clasped her shoulders. "Tori. Never apologize for things that aren't your fault." He squeezed for emphasis. "You were super cool out there!"

Tori winced, half from the pain of her latest bite wound, half from embarrassment. In her world, compliments often had sharp edges hidden beneath them. She was strong, *for a girl*. She was civilized, *for a scholarship kid*. She was smart, *for a southerner*. When she couldn't find one, she didn't know what to do with herself.

Vince mistook her wince for doubt. "You're a natural, Tori. I've been hunting monsters full time since I was fourteen and I never would've thought to trick one of Orion's hounds. You've been at this for what? A month and change? A month in, I couldn't even hold a gun without shaking." He laughed weakly. "Fuck, the first time I shot at a monster, I shook so badly that the recoil broke my front tooth! Would've died if the tunnel hadn't collapsed on it."

She latched on to the words that weren't about her. "That's... probably because you were only fourteen." Fourteen surprised her. A fourteen-year-old was only a freshman in high school. An actual baby.

She tried to imagine herself learning to fire a gun instead of studying for exams, playing in the fields with her brother, or reading romance novels in the library. No, not just firing a gun— firing a gun at something. She wasn't even certain she could bring herself to shoot at something as an adult.

"No more sorries," Vince insisted. "I should be the one apologizing. You're hurt. You should be back there with Roy and Brooks getting patched up, not slumming it with me. Though you do owe me some more whiskey..."

This was one of Tori's brother's secret techniques. When he was upset, he joked around. When she tried to press him about it, he changed the subject to her. He hid behind a wall of humor and self-deprecation, or, in Vince's case, swearing, booze, and long excited speeches about cars.

She wasn't fooled. She grasped at the heart of the matter. "Vince... We'll beat Orion next time. We were so close tonight. We'll only get closer."

Vince couldn't look at her. "For all these years... all those monsters... all those innocent people Brooks, Roy, and I failed to save..." He chewed on the end of his cigarette. "I used to think that monster attacks were natural. Random. Cruel. But natural. Bad things happen to good people all the time, and that's just the way it is."

His voice caught in his throat. At last, he lit his cigarette.

"Orion was the first person to prove me wrong. And also the first monster I can't seem to kill."

Kill. That term struck Tori twice as hard as "fourteen" had. She'd never stopped to consider just what kind of life a person who collected knives, didn't mind losing at cards, and dreamed of being a paranormal investigator while fighting real, dangerous monsters every day, might've led.

"Forget Orion," Vince spat. "I came to see a ghost."

He traced his fingers along the chipped paint on the haunted old well's wooden frame.

"If ghosts are real, then this girl didn't stop existing when she died. She's still here. She still got to see the world grow up around her."

Tori got the sense that Vince wasn't talking about the drowned girl.

She approached the well, peering between the cracks of the weathered boards that sealed off its mouth.

"The girl who died in this well was a slave," she mused. Unlike Vince, she'd been paying attention to their ghost tour guide. "Most likely only one of many who died on this estate, desperate and scared, her name forgotten. But this place attracts hundreds of tour groups a year. People have picnics on the lawn. Get married in the gardens. As if the passage of time erases all the suffering that happened..."

She gripped the edge of the well. "I hope ghosts aren't real. I hope that time does soothe suffering—that instead of being stuck here, that girl is sunning herself in a field of flowers, free in whatever afterlife she believed in." That Luke's soul wasn't trapped in that snowy wood, alone, forever.

Vince met her eyes. For a moment, he looked as if he wanted to tell her something. Something personal. He thought better of it. "I hope that the next time we see Orion, we send him straight to Hell."

He blew a smoke ring into the air. It floated higher and higher, merging with the last, black breath of Phoenix Hall.

Together, they returned to the parking lot.

Roy and Brooks hadn't waited idly. Boxes of pizza, a pack of sodas, and an entire tub of cheese puffs sat on the bed of Roy's truck. Roy shuffled a deck of playing cards. Brooks offered Vince a shining bottle of Kentucky bourbon.

Vince sized them up. "What the hell is this? Bribery?"

"Yes," Roy replied.

"...Thanks."

Vince snatched that bottle of bourbon and hopped into the truck bed.

Finally, they could all move on from Phoenix Hall.

"So..." Tori began. "What now? I'm pretty sure Vince and I are over ghost tours."

Roy's gaze rose to the mushroom cloud choking the treetops. "After tonight we can all agree—that drug is more dangerous than we thought."

"So what?" Vince grumbled between bites of meat lover's.

Roy gave Brooks an apologetic look. "We're overdue for that visit to my sister's."

Begrudgingly, Brooks nodded.

Tori's heart sank into her stomach. She'd known this day would come eventually. Roy's mysterious, well-connected, drug-expert sister lived far away. He and Brooks had delayed their trip to train Tori.

The end of their delay had two major implications: Tori and Vince might not see them for over a week, and Tori had officially graduated from monster hunter academy. Whether she was ready or not.

Roy offered Tori a soda. "I'll miss you too, Miss Jaecar."

She accepted it glumly.

Wait, what? *Miss her?*

Vince sulked into the tub of cheese puffs. "Why can't I ever visit your sister?"

"As for you two..." Roy ignored the question. "You can follow up on our newest clue."

"...Newest clue?" Tori repeated. They'd learned much from today's adventure, but none of it could help them unravel Orion's schemes. Had she forgotten something important?

The white rabbit from Phoenix Hall landed on the overturned trash can with a satisfying thump. He clutched a business card between his teeth. The same business card that had fallen from Orion when he crashed into that fountain.

"L-Lepus?" She wasn't sure about the Easter part, but this was no ordinary bunny.

"Lepus here was kind enough to retrieve it for us." Roy explained. "The enemy of our enemy."

Brooks sensed her confusion. "Orion has been hunting Lepus for ages. Ever since they both were placed in the, er... It's a long story. Ancient history, really."

"You can understand him?" Tori squinted at their fluffy friend. He was cute, but he was definitely not saying anything about Orion.

"Someday you'll understand him, too," Roy assured her.

That wasn't the answer she'd expected. Could she really learn to talk to animals?

Vince grabbed the business card. He read it aloud, "Whether rain or shine, trust Channel 4 for the weather." He squinted at the small print. "Ugh, Missouri?"

Missouri? Why did that sound familiar? Tori moved closer to see the business card for herself. A meteorologist's name, number, and address had been circled in pen underneath a clipart of the sun. Grace Batya. She was based in St. Louis, Missouri.

Suddenly it clicked. Tori had seen this business card before— on James' desk. It was one of the sentimental trinkets he packed into that sad cardboard box, mere hours before he died. Why did Orion have it? More importantly, why did he bother to steal it before securing the infamous, incriminating drug baggie?

"That business card belonged to James. Before he died, he said he was moving to St. Louis."

Vince shrugged. "Maybe James just thought this 'Grace' lady was hot."

"Maybe. But she's worth investigating, isn't she?"

"...St. Louis is a nine-hour drive from Atlanta."

"I can drive," Tori countered.

"Perfect," Roy clapped his hands together. "You can take Vince's car."

Preemptively, Tori flinched. She expected Vince to shout "over my dead body!", or something about infidelity. His car was the love of his life.

"We can take turns," Vince suggested.

Again, Roy, Brooks, and Tori exchanged glances.

"What?" Vince huffed so loudly that it scared Lepus away. "If Grace is really that hot, I sure as hell want to meet her."

CHAPTER TWELVE

Rain tapped away at the roof, the tick of an invisible clock, scratching against his skull. Groaning, fifteen-year-old Vincent Lenoir pulled a pillow over his ears. It didn't help. The moon shone through his hotel window, a bright beacon in a clear sky. The noise was inside his head.

Guilt and regret leered at him from the corners of his room. Children's faces haunted him in the knots of the wooden ceiling above. A monster with a long braid lurked under his bed. He was awake now. He knew better than to try to go back to sleep. He hadn't made it through a night without nightmares in weeks.

Yawning, he sat up. Time to self-medicate. He tiptoed into the main room of their suite. It was empty. Good. If Brooks caught him sneaking about, he'd never hear the end of it. As quietly as he could, he dug out a can of beer hidden in their ice bucket. A voice stopped him dead.

"Mercy, you're a monster." It was Brooks.

Vince peered over his shoulder. Light glowed from under the door of Roy's room. Were they having an argument? That was nothing new, but they were usually less secretive about it.

"Am I?" Roy mused. "I don't recall eating anyone."

Brooks always picked these fights. He had strong opinions on everything. Vince wasn't old enough for cigarettes and alcohol. They ate too much junk food. They had to stop hunting monsters; he was a child, not a soldier. Roy constantly undermined the old man. He was so blatant about it that Vince sometimes wondered if they were even friends.

Roy and Brooks had dragged Vince to hell and back. He'd known them longer than he'd known anybody else. But he still knew nothing about them. He couldn't resist this opportunity to eavesdrop.

"We can't be his parents," Brooks insisted. "We aren't qualified."

"Why not? We've both been parents before." After a pause, Roy added, "The thing with the bull hide doesn't count. We're not even sure if it was me that—"

"You're kidding, right? None of that counts! And I... I can't." Brooks choked on his words. He changed the subject. "What about Maylee and Nancy?"

Those names drew Vince in. He pressed his ear against the door. Nancy Kingfisher was Vince's best friend ever—the only other teen he'd known for more than a few months. A brilliant artist. Whenever he thought of her, he thought of a painted blue stallion, an orange horizon, copper flames, and a dead city.

Maylee was her kid half-sister.

"Maylee has her father."

"And Nancy?"

Roy dismissed this one less quickly. "... She has Maylee."

"Damn you, Mercy!" Brooks seldom swore. He had to be furious. "He needs a home. He needs stability. And God, he needs therapy. We can't give him any of that." He sounded desperate. He sounded sad. "Please! Take this seriously. Just this once."

For a long while, Roy didn't respond. "I am taking this seriously, Brooks," he finally breathed. "I'll guide them both to the crossroads. From there, it's up to them." A sharpness cut the edge of his voice. "Or would you prefer I did nothing and let the world burn?"

"And what if, after all you've done, nothing changes?"

Another long while passed.

"I trust you, Mercy," Brooks sighed. "But sometimes you make it very, very hard."

A door opened and closed. One of them must've left for the adjoining bedroom.

Well. Vince really needed his beer after all of that. He didn't know how to feel about their plans for his future, and he didn't understand half of what they said. He could figure it out between now and morning.

"Can't sleep?"

When did Roy come into the main room? "I..." Vince hid his contraband behind his back. He blurted out the first thing he could think of. "I don't want therapy!"

Roy exhaled a laugh. "There will be no therapy tonight." He sank into an armchair. "Let's play a game instead, shall we?" He patted the seat across from him. "I, too, need a drink."

An hour, a card game lesson, and six losses later, Vince still didn't know how to feel. This was his first time playing rummy, but Roy had stayed up with him through countless sleepless nights, always with a different excuse. It was familiar. Comfortable, even. It chased away the demons waiting in the dark.

It wasn't a coincidence. Roy knew about Vince's nightmares, didn't he?

It pissed Vince off that a lunatic like Roy pitied him. And it pissed him off even more that deep down he appreciated the company.

Frustrated and ashamed, he wanted to curse Roy out for looking down on him. He settled for breaking the silence. "Roy.

Why does Brooks call you Mercy?" He'd asked the same thing a million times before. He didn't expect a real answer.

Roy surprised him. "It's an old nickname of mine. Brooks... I think it's important to him to remember where we came from." He seemed distant while he spoke. "We've been through a lot together."

"Against monsters?"

Roy shifted back in his chair. His gaze drifted to the window. The bitter winds of winter tore at helpless trees. "Much worse."

Vince glanced up from his cards. When he did, he didn't see Roy. He saw a mouth full of fangs, then a second, then a third. He saw a serpent-tailed woman with hollow, hungering eyes. He saw lava billowing over houses in the shadow of mountain-sized wings. "What could possibly be worse?" he snapped despite himself.

His outburst drew Roy's attention back inside. He frowned.

Ugh. Why did Vince feel like he was being pitied again?

"Vincent," Roy drew a card. "Do you believe in God?"

Of fucking course. Roy dodged his question.

"If God does exist..." Vince clenched his fists. Nancy had dreamed so big and loved so much. Now she was alone in the world. And Vince... Vince had always been alone. "...then he's a monster himself. What kind of God lets such horrible things happen to innocent people? To teenagers? To children?"

"Well then..." Roy didn't finish his sentence. He simply set down a trio of jacks. He had so many points and Vince hadn't even played yet. Roy would win on his next turn. Maybe that was his way of shutting down the conversation.

Ugh, not again. Vince was too worked up to focus on the game. After this round, he'd retreat to his room. He drew his last card.

It took Vince a few seconds to register—no, believe—what he was seeing. Because his hand was out of order, he hadn't noticed that he'd only needed one more number to complete a ten card straight. The number in his hand.

The lucky seven of spades. Finally, he had won! Finally, he'd defeated Roy!

Roy smiled. "How about fate?"

* * *

Cars hummed in the distance. The gentle lullaby almost lured Vince back to sleep. Groaning, he rolled onto his side. At least, he tried. The passenger seat of his old Ford Mustang wasn't big enough for a grown man to really stretch his wings.

Wait. Passenger seat?

Vince jerked awake. There was no seven of spades, no motel, no Roy asking cryptic questions to distract him from his memories. Instead, a woman with crazy hair and even crazier guts gripped his woodgrain steering wheel. Outside, they sailed through an ocean of gray and brown. Nothing but highway, more highway, and empty fields.

First, Vince remembered his shock and awe that a random office worker who didn't even own a car could drive a manual. Second, he remembered the hot Atlanta sun, and all the fires burning beneath. Lastly, he remembered the deal he'd struck with Tori.

"I fell asleep?" He rubbed his pounding head.

"You fell asleep," Tori confirmed.

"How long was I out for?"

"Since maybe five minutes after we passed Chattanooga."

"Where are we now?"

"Shawnee National Forest. Y'know, I never knew there were swamps this far north!"

Shawnee National Forest was just outside Missouri. Most of their road trip was already behind them. Vince had missed most of the drive—a drive he and Tori were supposed to split right down the middle. He'd always been terrible at keeping promises, but he couldn't blow off the only friend he'd made since he was a teenager!

"Shit, my bad."

"I don't mind. I can finish if you want more sleep—"

No fucking way. The pity in her voice twisted like a knife.

"Pull over at that truck stop, will you?" he insisted. He'd crossed more than two thousand miles chasing Orion all by himself. He didn't need her help. Her march was over, here, at this nameless exit.

Nothing helped Vince start his day better than fresh air and an armload of snacks. He returned from the truck stop with beef jerky, a six pack of energy drinks, and sour apple candy.

Tori greeted him with an are-you-serious look.

He knew that look well. She was judging him. He didn't care. After a few more Phoenix Halls and Winecoff Hotels, she'd be lucky to get by with just a junk food habit.

Her attention shifted to the hollowed-out shell of a missile in front of her.

The missile towered over fifty feet, Vince wagered. Taller than the truck stop's sign listing gas prices. What a lame tourist attraction—almost every major exit had one of these bad boys propped up along the interstate.

"Did you know that during the Cold War, there were almost a thousand missiles hidden throughout Missouri? And most of them were nuclear!"

First Shawnee National Forest's swamps. Now a rusted old dud. This Tori chick was interested in everything. What a nerd.

"It's Missouri. What else were they gonna do with all the empty space?"

Soon, they were on their way. Vince put the pedal to the medal, as if going faster might somehow make up for the time he'd wasted sleeping. Going faster also helped distract him from the uncomfortable silence in his passenger seat. He'd crossed more than two thousand miles chasing Orion all by himself, and he had no idea how to navigate small talk.

"Um." Tori opened her mouth, clearly searching for a subject. "So... Are Brooks and Roy a thing?"

"Hell no!" Vince blurted. "Why would you even suggest that!?" After a pause, he clarified, "I uh... I don't give a shit if two dudes wanna, y'know..." He could see it now—Brooks blushing despite himself as Roy finally backed him into a corner. Trauma bonding at its worst. He shook his head, banishing the thought. "Just not THOSE two dudes. They've never even hugged in front of me."

Brooks deserved someone less flighty than Roy, anyway. Old dude seemed like he'd already been put through the ringer in the romance department.

The three monster hunting men had saved their fair share of attractive people, in many different shapes and colors. Brooks treated them all like patients in a pediatric ward. And he flinched whenever he was touched.

Judging from the way Tori stared, she hadn't expected such a strong reaction.

Vince cleared his throat. "But they sure bicker like a married couple, don't they?"

Tori nodded. She didn't have a response for that.

Fuck, this was awkward. Vince lit a cigarette.

Tori tried again. "That's a cool lighter. Where'd you get it?"

He studied the silver lighter between his fingers. It was silver with a raven etched into its side. He hadn't really looked at it in years. "My friend Nancy gave it to me. Around when I first met Roy and Brooks."

"Nancy. Is that who you keep texting when you think no one's looking?"

"No, that's one of my video channel subscribers," he huffed. "And I know you're looking!"

"How long ago was that? When you first met Roy and Brooks?"

"I don't know. Right before the last presidential election, I think. Maybe four or five years? Does it matter?"

Vince could see Tori doing the mental math. He hated math, and he especially hated when people thought there was some kind of magic formula to determine whether or not his life story was sad.

He couldn't tell how Tori's calculations worked out.

"How did y'all meet?" she asked in a perfectly neutral tone.

"During a school field trip, I got lost in a cave. A hydra tried to eat me. Definitely would've died down there if I hadn't run—literally—into Roy and Brooks." It was a miracle Vince didn't have nightmares about that day, too.

"Lost miners used to use fire to follow air currents back to the surface," he quoted a teacher whose name he'd long forgotten. "As it turns out, you don't need fire when you have Roy-fucking-Angelus leading the way."

"That sounds like an unpleasant memory. Sorry for bringing it up."

"Uh uh uh, didn't we agree to no more sorries?" Vince scolded with a wag of a finger. "I swear, Tori. You gotta work on that confidence. Otherwise, I'll always be a better monster hunter than you."

"That's fine, 'cos I'm a software engineer, not a monster hunter."

"A software engineer who doesn't engineer software anymore. How long can you keep dicking around with us before they fire you?"

"I have... a month or so left before they start asking questions."

"And after that?"

"...I don't know. Come to think of it, how do you monster hunters even make money?"

"We don't," he laughed. "Well, I sometimes do odd jobs here and there. Whenever Brooks refuses to buy me more cigarettes. But usually, I don't pay for shit."

"Then who's paying for all of this?"

"Roy's family is loaded. Cheap bastard ought to put us up somewhere nice for once..." Proudly he patted the dashboard, a man and his most prized possession. "This baby's all mine though. Saved up and bought her when I turned eighteen."

Eventually their chatter tapered off. Vince blasted metal music to fill the void. After about an hour, Tori squirmed as though her eardrums would burst if she listened to another song.

"Can I charge my phone?" she begged.

His Mustang only had one power port, one of those plastic things that plugged into the lighter.

"Sure." Vince yanked his phone out of its dock. "But if you play any of that screeching they call pop music I'm turning this car around."

She nodded and plugged in. Before she had the chance to play any pop music, her phone vibrated so violently she almost dropped it. When she caught it, her thumb brushed the "answer" button.

A voice echoed over the car speakers. "Vee? Is that you?"

Tori froze.

Vince did, too. Phone conversations in general made him anxious.

"H-hello Pa," she mumbled, her eyes downcast.

Apparently, those crazy guts of hers turned to mush before her parents.

"Oh thank the lord!" Tori's Dad gasped. "Ma and I have been SO worried about you."

Vince pretended he couldn't hear. Turning away, he cracked his window.

"I hear something happened at work," Tori's Dad continued. "I hope you're taking care of yourself."

Tori didn't—no, couldn't—reply. Whatever guilt she felt, she couldn't put it into words. Especially not in front of Vince.

"I know we haven't always been the closest, but I want you to know... You can always come to me, okay? I mean, if you need anything. If you don't want to talk to Ma. I... I get it. After what happened with your brother, we just don't wanna lose you, too."

Just barely, Vince stopped himself from arching a brow. Tori mentioned her brother all the time. As in, every day. She'd never once hinted that something had happened to him.

"Okay," she breathed "Thank you."

They crested a hill, revealing a police car with a radar gun. The van in front of them abruptly braked. Vince slammed to a stop within inches of its bumper. "Learn to drive!" he shouted. "You weren't even speeding!"

Slowly, everyone processed what he'd done.

Tori's Dad recovered first. "Is that... Is that a *boy* with you?"

Tori hung up on him. She mouthed "sorry" at Vince. She couldn't manage anything else.

"Same." Vince muttered.

Once again, silence reigned. Tori probably needed another nine hours of it.

Vince only gave her five minutes. "Yo. You do know that you can, like..." He shifted in his seat. "None of us care if you tell your friends and family what you're up to. Hell, you can tell them everything. We're not the Illuminati."

"I know that."

"Cool." That was that.

CHAPTER THIRTEEN

Somehow, they made it to Missouri without any more awkward conversations.

The engine of Vince's car whined as it climbed a steel bridge. Tori pressed against her window. Outside, the sunset reflected off the Mississippi River. A silver arch spanned the rosy horizon. "The Gateway to the West," she breathed in awe.

Vince eyed her. "When you're up close, it's just a hunk of steel."

"You've been to St. Louis before?"

"Yeah. Passed through right before we came to Atlanta, actually."

He chewed his lower lip. "Not that I want to hang out with you or anything, but... if you're into tourist stuff, we should check out the raceway across the river." He patted his dashboard affectionately. "I've always wanted to see what my pony and all 375 of her horses can really do on the open road. And Roy and Brooks aren't usually into stopping to smell the roses. Unless those roses are, like, full of blood and tears or something."

Weren't all roses full of blood and tears? Luke had loved them, once upon a time, and his relationships had always ended in a bloody mess. That was why Tori never dated seriously. She had enough thorns in her life from work.

"Maybe later." Stretching, she popped her back. Her body didn't appreciate all this sitting. "We need to get to the TV station. The evening broadcast just ended. Grace probably gets off work right about now."

Vince nodded. "Can you pull up the directions?"

Twenty minutes later, they arrived in front of a balcony-wrapped office building surrounded by, as Vince so aptly put it, tourist stuff.

The Channel 4 station cast its shadow across a sprawling park, staking manifest destiny over the riverside. Behind it, an old court-house lorded over a bustling downtown. A stone church with golden lettering glittered on the next block.

Tori could walk to her Gateway Arch from here. Like Vince's raceway, it would have to wait. They'd reached their destination. And they already had an obvious problem.

Channel 4 had many exits, but their automatic gates quickly closed behind passing cars and people. A security checkpoint blocked the only entrance. A yellow sign marked its booth. Employees only. No trespassing!

Tori and Vince circled the block twice. This was no Phoenix Hall. There was no back porch they could climb.

"Well, this sucks," Vince complained.

"We could pretend to be relatives of an employee?"

He pointed up the street. "We might not have to!"

Another woman climbed into a compact sedan parked along the curb. Tori could sum her up with a single word: delicate. Her platinum blonde hair tied into a neat bun. Her lavender skirt suit with shoulder pads only emphasized her dainty frame. She defi-nitely shopped in the petite section. Without her high heels, she would've barely come up to Tori's chin, and Tori wasn't tall.

Whipping out her phone, Tori compared her to the image search results for "Grace Batya". She was a match. There was no doubt about it. "You're right!"

Tori pumped a fist. "Follow that car!"

Vince revved his engine.

They tailed Grace from a few cars behind. She led them away from the city center, past a stadium, skyscrapers, and enough bars to drown a college town. The excitement of their high-speed car chase wore off after they hit their fourth red light. Then they turned onto an interstate packed bumper to bumper with traffic. Rush hour. Tori felt as though she was in Atlanta.

Eventually Grace turned into a parking lot of a pink stucco building. The letters "Mississippi River Specialists" hung above the entrance. Could that name be any more vague? It could be pest control services, plumbers, or a real estate company.

Vince parked at a nearby restaurant. Tori started after Grace, but he stopped her.

"Hey. I've been thinking..." He popped his trunk. With a level of care and precision she'd never seen him show towards anything except maybe his car, he picked through his knife collection.

He held out a dagger with a wine-bronze sheen, just like Roy's sword.

"Here. The next time you get Orion on the ground, put him in the ground." He belatedly remembered she'd never killed before. "Or, uh, stick him where it hurts or something."

Tori didn't know how to feel about putting anyone in the ground, but Vince had a point. Orion was stronger than her. Probably Vince, too, for that matter. A weapon would close the gap between them.

She accepted the dagger, turning over in her hands.

"According to Roy, this dagger was forged by a legendary blacksmith in some distant volcano. So was my gun. I don't know if that makes it work better or anything, but that's pretty metal, isn't it?"

"Extremely metal." She strapped the dagger's leather sheath to her waist, hidden beneath her hoodie.

After making sure the coast was clear, they followed Grace inside the mystery Mississippi River Specialists building.

An empty reception desk greeted them. A row of uncomfortable-looking chairs lined the wall. White walls framed speckled vinyl floors. Two hallways stretched beyond the entrance, helpfully marked "A" and "B".

Tori frowned. While she was glad that they didn't have to come up with an excuse for being here, they were now officially trespassing... and they still didn't know where they were!

Grace was nowhere to be seen. But the clicking of her high heels led the way.

Holding her breath, Tori followed the sound into the hall. Vince trailed behind her.

Besides that persistent tapping, the building was eerily silent. Strange equipment—a weird computer on a cart, a rack of oxygen masks, and metal gas cylinders—guarded the corridor. As they crept deeper into the unknown, they passed photographs of employees in scrubs.

Tori ran her hand along the wall as she walked. Her fingers found the edge of a bulletin board. Finally, a clue!

A dry-erase calendar and a hand-written schedule took up most of the bulletin board. By piecing together the various dates, procedures, and names, she puzzled out that the Mississippi River Specialists building was some kind of medical facility.

That realization made the fliers posted all over the bulletin board seem all the more ominous. A news article mourned missing children all over St. Louis. A memo warned nurses not to take patients outside after dark. A sticky note reminded staff to double check the locks on the doors and windows before heading home from their shifts.

The fliers told a blood-chilling story—summed up by a hand-drawn sketch of a hulking humanoid with dark hair covering its body and glowing red eyes. It was labeled MoMo.

"Some kind of monster..." Vince whispered, voicing Tori's thoughts.

In their horror, they failed to notice Grace's footsteps growing louder.

Her slim silhouette appeared at the end of the hall.

"Hello?" she called out. "Is someone there?"

They had to hide. Now.

Seizing Vince by the elbow, Tori dragged him into the nearest unlocked room.

Only a fraction of the size of Tori's studio apartment, the dark suite reeked of dried flowers. A plastic dresser dominated the space. Praying to God, Gandhi, and Buddha, she ducked behind it.

Vince slipped around what appeared to be a twin bed.

The doorknob turned. A switch flipped.

Fluorescent lights burst to life, revealing a small bedroom suite. A woman, who despite her white hair seemed surprisingly young for a place like this, slept in a medical bed near a window. Wires connected her to glowing monitors. Carnations in various stages of bloom covered every flat surface. Some of them were so withered they must've been here for years.

"Finally!" Grace cried out. "I've been searching for a nurse for —" Confusion twisted her expression. They were not nurses.

Vince yelped.

Tori raised a brow.

Grace discovering them wasn't great, but it wasn't exactly scary.

"Er..." He held out his arm, unsure what to do. "Can I help you?"

The woman in the bed had him in a death grip. Her monitors screeched.

"Please!" With her free hand, she clung to his t-shirt. "*Please.*

Please save my daughter! I couldn't stop her, but maybe you... Maybe she'll listen to her—" Her strength failed. She collapsed.

The alarms calmed to a slow, regular beep.

"MOM!!" Grace burst into tears. "Oh Mom...You're still with me!"

Vince clutched his wrist like it was broken.

A nurse exploded into the room. "I knew it! Those alarms couldn't go off on their own. Grace, you know visiting hours are over!"

"But—"

"Grace. Your mom's in a coma. I know that's hard for you, but you can't keep messing with her monitors. Come back in the morning!"

The nurse herded them back to the front desk.

Grace whimpered, "Why don't they ever believe me?"

Vince shifted uncomfortably. "Can we talk somewhere else? This place gives me the creeps."

After seeing that memo on MoMo, Tori wasn't keen on sticking around, either.

"Grace, why don't we buy you some dinner?"

CHAPTER FOURTEEN

Vincent Lenoir had never had a more awkward meal before. Shrinking against the back of his chair, he sipped hot chocolate from his mug. He avoided any sudden movements. He didn't want to draw attention to himself.

He, Tori, and Grace were the only guests at Lemp Mansion, the restaurant across the street from Mississippi River Specialists. Tori totally had this without his help.

Lemp Mansion put the word "old" in "old-fashioned". Blushing pink curtains and mahogany molding complimented green patterned wallpaper. Formal tablecloths spread across antique tables. Paintings of average-looking rich people in funny clothing decorated the walls. Behind the wooden bar, the same average-looking rich people leered from stained glass windows. Crimson, purple, and gray light shrouded the whole place in a dark, heavy atmosphere.

Since the moment they'd met, Grace Batya had not stopped crying. Makeup streaked down her cheeks into her food. She didn't notice. The Lavender Lady clung to Tori's arm like a life preserver in a stormy sea.

Tori, who'd turned as pale as the ghosts who allegedly haunted Lemp Mansion—there were cheesy posters advertising them all over the damned walls—patted Grace and made soothing noises. She was doing great. A real natural.

"I'm so sorry!" Grace sputtered for the fiftieth time. "I don't know what's come over me."

Vince was very glad to have backup. Grace didn't seem to care who she clung to. Normally, he wouldn't mind rubbing up against a pretty girl, but this situation called for talking, too. None of his combat training had prepared him for this.

"It's okay," Tori lied gently.

Finally, Grace managed a complete sentence. "You must both think I've lost my mind." She wiped her eyes and then released Tori. "I'm sorry... I was just surprised. And relieved. Mom has been in a coma since... Since my father... S-since that monster..." She sniffled. She tried again. "It's been years since I've heard her voice."

Vince couldn't imagine what that was like. He'd known Roy and Brooks longer than he'd known anyone else, but that didn't compare to being raised by someone. If he could no longer see Roy or Brooks, would he cry, too?

He banished the thought. Hell no. No way!

"The doctors say that she's..." Grace swallowed. "...that she's b-braindead. But they're wrong. You heard her! She spoke to you!" She slammed her hands on the table.

Silverware crashed onto the floor. She winced.

Softly, she concluded, "She's still with me. I hope."

"Hope" stirred something deep and painful in Vince's chest. He stared down into his hot chocolate. He doubted Grace's mother reaching out to him meant anything. And if it did... Stories that featured him usually had less than happy endings.

"There's always hope," Tori quoted a souvenir t-shirt hanging on the wall.

Grace took a deep breath. She straightened.

"Anyways. Who are you two?"

Geez, TV types were something else. Vince had never seen anyone recover their composure so quickly and absolutely. She seemed like a different person.

"I'm Jay—" Tori began.

"Vincent Lenoir," Vince interrupted. Sorry Tori, not today. Lying to women was not his style. "Perhaps you've seen my video channel? I'm a paranormal investigator."

"Jaecar." Tori corrected smoothly. "Tori Jaecar."

"You're a... paranormal investigator?" Grace peered around as if noticing that she was inside a restaurant for the first time. The color drained from her face. "This isn't... this isn't Lemp Mansion, is it!?"

"I think so?" Tori confirmed.

"Oh no!" Grace leapt from her chair. "I can't be here."

"What? Why not?"

"This place is evil! Are you here for Billy?" When Grace saw their blank looks, she elaborated. "William J. 'Billy' Lemp, Jr owned the Lemp Brewing Company, one of the biggest breweries in pre-prohibition America. He was one of the three Lemps who committed suicide in this manor. Though, if you ask me, Elsa was a murder, not a suicide."

"That Billy?" Vince shoved his thumb towards one of the advertisements at the entrance. He wasn't impressed. Someone had died in most historic buildings. And in his experience, the more profitable a ghost story was, the less likely it was to be true.

"Ever since the I-55 expansion wiped out the tunnels beneath this mansion, Billy's ghost has been seeking revenge on St. Louis. He appears as a handsome man in a designer suit, who wears gloves to protect himself from germs—and the blood of his victims."

Tori frowned. "This ghost kills people?"

"They say he's still out there cheating on his poor wife. He

lures unsuspecting men and women into the bedroom and BAM!'"
She crushed a packet of coffee creamer.

It wasn't clear to Vince whether Grace was afraid or enjoying herself. Maybe both.

"Oh no!" she gasped. "He killed himself in this very room!" She tossed a pinch of salt over her left shoulder. She turned the pockets of her skirt suit inside out.

Either way, Vince wasn't afraid. And he was starting to enjoy himself. "Don't worry, Grace. I'm a professional. Nothing can hurt you as long as I'm here."

Tori rolled her eyes, but Grace didn't see.

After a long hesitation, Grace sat down. "O-okay. Thank you, Vincent."

"Please. Call me Vince."

"Thank you, *Vince*." She managed a shy smile.

Now that tears no longer muddied her face, Vince couldn't help but notice that this new Grace was enchanting. Like a nymph, she carried herself with a subtle airiness that complimented her snowy, almost-unnatural hair. Hidden strength thundered in her stormy blue eyes. Even in poor lighting, her fair skin glowed. She reminded him of a swan on a frozen lake. Tori was more like a stubby hawk on a power line.

"...Wait a second." Grace tilted her head to one side. "If you're a paranormal investigator, why were you with my mother?"

"Actually, we were looking for you," Vince replied.

"Wh-what?"

Tori passed Grace the business card.

"Oh." Grace deflated, disappointed. "Is this about work? You followed me all the way to a long-term care facility for work!?"

"Not... exactly," Vince admitted. So much for not lying. He and Tori should've used their time in the car together to come up with a game plan.

"We didn't mean to intrude," Tori apologized. "We're searching for someone. He had your card. Have you ever met a man named Orion Treyvon?"

"Really tall. Lumberjack shirt. Wears sunglasses inside," Vince added.

After a moment's deliberation, Grace shook her head. "I'm sorry. If I have, I don't remember him."

Tori sighed. "Maybe James really did just think she was hot."

Grace grimaced.

"Oh?" Tori leaned closer to her. "Do you know a James? How about a James MacGillivray?"

Immediately Grace shouted, "NO!"

She blushed. More quietly, she explained, "I m-mean. I met him once. He asked for my phone number. A lot."

"Where did you meet him?" Tori pressed.

"At Channel 4. It was, uh... Back before the last election... Oh!" Grace hit her palm with her fist. "He was there for a campaign event! James was a local businessman who endorsed President Arvis." She lowered her tone. "Personally, I'm voting for Senator Pallas. Wouldn't it be great to have a woman in charge for a change?"

"The last election? Why would anyone keep a random business card for that long?" Tori wondered. "Even James would give up eventually. He had other skirts to chase."

"Keep it? I didn't give James a business card," Grace shuddered at the thought. "'Whether rain or shine, trust Channel 4 for the weather.' I came up with that slogan just this spring. Isn't it clever?"

"So... Someone gave this business card to James right before he quit?" Tori twisted her curls between her fingers. "Do you think it was Orion? No, that doesn't make any sense. If Orion gave it to James, he wouldn't need to steal it back."

Vince mulled it over. "Oh," he blurted out. "Orion's planning to kill Grace."

"Wh-what?" Grace's voice jumped an octave.

Tori glared at him, "Don't just say things like that out of nowhere!"

"Sorry. It's just..." Vince held up a finger. "James worked with Orion somehow. Otherwise, he wouldn't have the, uh. Stuff." He raised a second finger. "Orion burned down the Winecoff Hotel with President Arvis' people inside. Then he burned his campaign event at Mimosa Hall. If you ask me, he's either sabotaging the campaign or helping it. Doesn't matter which." He raised a third finger. "Grace here works for Channel 4, a major news network that endorses President Arvis."

He curled his fingers into a fist. "If you were Orion, wouldn't you be interested in James' connection to Grace? At least enough to investigate further."

"That doesn't mean he's planning to kill her!" Tori argued.

"Ah, yeah. Perhaps not. That's just what Orion does—tie off loose ends."

Grace cleared her throat. "Could you two please fill me in?"

Vince and Tori exchanged glances.

"Okay. So." Vince never learned how to sugar coat things. "Orion Treyvon is an assassin. He murdered James. We don't know why."

"That's..." Grace closed her eyes and reopened them. Nope, not a dream. "How am I supposed to believe all that?" A realization struck her. "You said this assassin had my card!?"

"You might want to lay low for a while. Just in case," Tori suggested. "Do you have any family you can stay with?"

"You two are definitely not paranormal investigators!" Grace exclaimed. "What are you? Scammers? The FBI? I can assure you, I'm totally broke!"

"Closer to Illuminati," Vince mumbled.

Tori kicked at him under the table. He dodged.

"Look. I'll be honest." He took Grace's hand. "This stuff sounds crazy and we don't have any proof. You can go home.

Forget about us. Call the police if you want. You've helped enough."

Silence answered.

The three diners listened to the distant clatter of dishes being washed.

Grace inhaled for three seconds and exhaled for six. "This Orion guy... You say your assassin might be involved with Channel 4." She twiddled her thumbs. "Would it help you to check out the Channel 4 headquarters? I could show you where we hold our campaign events."

Vince didn't understand women. After witnessing a murder and being attacked by an assassin, instead of, say, being traumatized or something, Tori had forced her way into his car. She'd almost died inside the Winecoff Hotel, yet that only made her sign up for more danger.

Here Grace was, volunteering to help two strangers who were clearly lying to her—or at least withholding information—break into her workplace. She was risking her livelihood. Maybe even her life.

Was Vince the weird one? When he'd first met Roy and Brooks, he'd told them to get bent. He never would've signed up for this monster hunting madness if it weren't for Nancy.

No, that wasn't it. Grace had to know more than she let on.

That, too, was worth investigating.

Vince couldn't wait. "Please, show us everything."

Grace nodded. "We have an early show in the morning. We'll do it tonight."

"Are you sure about this?" Tori worried. "We could get you in huge trouble."

"I'm sure. Mom is really a good judge of character."

"Well then," Vince stood. He was tired of sitting. He was even more tired of talking.

"Let's go make some news!"

CHAPTER FIFTEEN

Grace signed Vince and Tori through the Channel 4 security checkpoint. They were her cousins visiting from afar. She was giving them a backstage tour after hours so they wouldn't bother anyone. The guards didn't spare them a second glance.

The main entrance of Channel 4 consisted of concrete floors, an exposed ceiling, and black walls wallpapered in colorful branding. Powerful lights formed a canopy above. Beyond the front desk, a hallway wandered through a glass jungle of computers, conference rooms, and cubicles.

Grace gestured towards a pair of double doors at the back of the lobby. "Our campaign events are held in the main studio."

"What are we waiting for?" Vince couldn't wait to see a professional film set.

They proceeded down a long hallway. Well-lit posters from Channel 4's history dominated the space. Twin archers battled a serpentine dragon. A handsome thief guided teenagers through an ancient tomb. A thundering man and a dove-like woman embraced on a grassy riverside, surrounded by carnations, swans, and tranquility.

"Our network owns several other channels," Grace explained. "Movies and TV shows make for better conversation starters than pictures of newscasters." Her smile couldn't conceal her envy.

The hallway led to a second pair of double doors outlined by rope LEDs. A large red "ON AIR" sign crowned them. It was switched off.

Vince shifted impatiently from one foot to another. As soon as Grace swiped her ID card, he dashed inside.

The main studio was nothing like Tori had imagined. There was no fancy architecture, no imposing stage, and no seating for an audience. It was just an enormous room with rigging for lights and cameras. A crescent-shaped desk framed by a cardboard city skyline waited at its center. A green screen hung a short distance away.

Vince bee-lined for the news set. He plopped into the anchor's chair.

Tori thumbed through a stack of papers on a folding table. Broadcast schedules, lunch bills, a memo about the office fridge. Useless. "Is there anywhere in particular we should look?"

"Um... During President Arvis' campaign events, we decorate the entire studio with red, white and gold. I don't know what you're looking for, but it could be anywhere." Grace stepped in front of the green screen. "The year I met James, we shot testimonials from St. Louis locals here."

"Thanks, I'll check around there." Tori explored the area around the green screen. One by one, she popped open plastic storage bins. Wires. Camera equipment. Metal clamps. More wires.

Meanwhile, Grace distracted Vince. "You said you have a video channel?"

He perked up. "Yeah! Remember those late-night shows about paranormal investigators? I grew up on them. Always loved how they bring abandoned, forgotten places back into the spotlight." He leaned back, propping his sneakers on the glass top of the desk. "Since I travel so much, I figured I'd give it a shot, too. My channel's called *Haunt Hunt*. It's gonna be real big someday."

Of course it was. Tori rolled her eyes. Vince had what, two subscribers?

"That's so amazing! I wish I could be as creative as you." Grace brushed a loose lock of hair behind her ear. "You know, I'm not really a meteorologist."

"Oh?" Vince straightened, leaning towards her. "Do you also hunt haunts?"

"You got me." A smile flashed across her face. Like lightning, it was gone as soon as it appeared. "No, I meant that I don't do any actual weather forecasting." She nudged an old television on a rolling cart. "I read this prompt every morning." Holding an imaginary microphone, she pantomimed, "Stay inside tonight, St. Louis. We're going to have some hail!"

She sighed. "I've always wanted to actually act. Like in a story."

"Maybe we can do a collab together after this."

"Really? I'd love that!"

"You can play my lovely sidekick!"

Tori circled the room twice. Mirror panels covered the far wall. Stacks of folding chairs and waited in carts. Even the trash cans had been emptied for the night. Everything was perfectly ordinary. But she would find something out of the ordinary eventually. She had to. If she didn't, they'd officially be out of leads, and she might never stop Orion or find out just what killed Luke.

"Aren't you already Roy's and Brooks' sidekick, Vince?" she mused.

"Roy?" Grace tilted her head. "Brooks?"

"They're my..." Vince chewed his lower lip. "My umm..."

"Mentors?" It had seemed that way to Tori.

"No!" Vince barked. "They're my... coworkers?"

"Older coworkers," Tori corrected. "Who mentor you."

Vince grumbled.

Grace giggled.

"Whatever," he huffed. He fumbled with a pack of cigarettes.

"You can't smoke in here!" Gracie cried.

"Can't or shouldn't?" Smirking, he retreated.

She chased after him.

Vince held the pack of cigarettes over her head, out of her reach.

More giggling.

Frustrated, Tori gave herself a break. She approached the mirror wall. She rolled up the sleeve of her hoodie. Drawing in close, she examined the ugly, bruising swelling around her stitches from Procyon's bite. Brooks had taught her how to hide it with concealer. Mostly.

She twisted to get a better angle. Something impossible caught her eye.

She inspected the last panel on the mirror wall. It was identical to the others except for one flaw—she had no reflection. It showed the set, the floor, and the lightning, but not her.

Her heart fluttered. "Y'all?" she called out.

By her next heartbeat, Vince was at her side.

Grace followed as fast as she could in her purple pumps.

"Damn." He ducked in and out of the broken mirror's view over and over again. "This is so cool!"

Tori pressed her hand against the glass. It gave. With a screech, it swung to reveal a stairway. She couldn't see the bottom. "Any idea where it leads?"

Standing on her toes, Grace peered into the darkness. "I've never seen this stairway before. I didn't even know the station had a basement!"

Vince flicked on his phone's flashlight. "I know how to find out!"

Together, he and Tori plunged into the unknown.

"W-wait for me!" Grace hurried after them. "My coworkers are going to be amazed when I show them this tomorrow."

Showing her coworkers would be easier said than done. The stairwell ended in a tunnel full of doors—as in, hundreds of them. Two by two, they stretched down the tunnel for miles.

As soon as Vince, Tori, and Grace set foot on the concrete floor, fluorescent lights buzzed to life. Chinese characters clearly labeled each door. Unfortunately, no one in their party could read Chinese. They had no choice but to select a door at random.

Tori turned the nearest handle.

They emerged into a second tunnel full of new doors. And then a third. And then a fourth.

The tunnels all looked the same, and their geometry was impossible. It was as if each open door carved a new hall into infinite space. This place was a maze.

Tori checked her cell phone. It had zero bars of signal. Great. "I'll draw out a map. Otherwise, we're going to get lost."

"We're already lost." Vince complained.

Somewhere deep within the labyrinth, a door slammed.

A warm breeze rushed through the corridor. It carried the stench of rotting flesh. The ground trembled beneath heavy footsteps.

The hair on the back of Tori's neck pricked up. Instinctively, she backed against a wall.

"Wh-what's that?" Grace whimpered.

Vince shushed her. He opened the nearest door and slipped behind it. "Come on, get down. And put that phone away!"

Tori crouched next to Vince. Her pulse pounded so loudly in her ears that she could no longer hear the monster. She heard the distinct metallic click of a hammer being drawn.

Vince had left the door cracked. He held his revolver ready.

Tori prayed to God, Gandhi, and Buddha that he wouldn't need to use it.

Thump. Thump. Thump. The monster reached them. It halted before their door.

Long, hairy arms. Biceps as big as her head. A hulking shadow over seven feet tall. Tori couldn't make out much more through the gap. She didn't want to.

The monster sniffed at the air.

Once.

Twice.

A strange gurgle rumbled from its throat. It lumbered on.

Many more minutes passed before Vince, Tori, or Grace dared to speak.

"I can't believe it. That was MoMo!" Grace gasped with dismay "No wonder there have been so many sightings lately. He's hiding in the heart of the city!"

"MoMo?" Tori repeated. That was an awfully cute name for a monster. And it was the same name as the drawing on the bulletin board in Mississippi River Specialists.

"MoMo. The Missouri Monster," Grace breathed. "They say he's an ape man who feasts upon livestock, dogs, and children who stay out too late."

"Good thing you're not a child," Tori stated. "Or livestock. Or a dog." She wracked her brain for a monster from Roy's notes that matched this one's description. "What do you think he is, Vince? A werewolf? Some kind of giant?"

Grace buried her face in her hands. "My horoscope said that my life would take a fateful turn today. I didn't realize that meant I'd turn into a bigfoot's dinner!"

"It doesn't matter what he is," Vince observed. "As long as Grace is with us, we should avoid a fight."

Once again, Tori was surprised by how reasonable Vince could be when things got dangerous. "Should we leave?"

"Please!" Grace begged. "Let's get out of here!"

Vince agreed. "If we still can."

They couldn't.

Once the coast was clear, they returned to the corridor they'd been in before MoMo appeared. But it had transformed. The doors were blue, not gray. Single Greek letters replaced the Chinese characters.

Tori referenced her notes. One by one, she held them up to the labels of the blue doors around them. None of them matched.

Grace sank to her knees. "It's changing!"

"It is, isn't it?" Vince's voice quivered—not with fear, but fascination.

Right now, he reminded Tori of Roy. Somehow that calmed her down.

"We're trapped." Grace sniffled. "If we don't get eaten, we're going to starve to death!"

"Maybe not?" Tori pointed out the only door that differed from the others. Faint light peeked from underneath it.

Vince made a cheers gesture.

"It's not a dead end until you can't go any further."

CHAPTER SIXTEEN

Tori opened the door. A massive warehouse sprawled before her. Dim fluorescent lights cast it in an otherworldly glow. Crates, barrels, and mysterious shapes wrapped in plastic tarps filled it to its stone roof. Rusted iron scaffolding groaned under their weight.

Stepping inside, she brushed her fingers along the bumps and ridges of the wall. "Where are we?"

Eager to be out of the exposed hallway, Grace brushed past her. She pointed at a red, peeling number 7 painted over a yellow background.

Below it, Tori could just barely make out words. "World... Fair?"

"The Louisiana Purchase Exposition of 1904," Grace recited from memory. "It was a huge showcase of art, technology, and architecture from many countries. Some of the buildings from it are still standing." Her brow wrinkled. "But most of them are nowhere near my office."

"This was a vault," Vince observed. "Still is, I guess." He pried open the closest box. It contained rectangles wrapped in paper.

Ripping one released a cloud of white powder into the air. "...Cocaine?"

Pinching her nose, Tori nudged the discarded lid. A fire symbol marked it, dead center. "Is cocaine flammable?"

"Yes," he answered too quickly. He stuck his finger into the mess, then stuck it in his mouth. Gagging, he spit it out. "Ugh, that's definitely not cocaine!"

"Stop sticking random chemicals in your mouth!!" Tori scolded, clutching her chest. It'd been so long since Vince had done something so stupid that she'd forgotten to worry about it. "For all we know that's deadly poison!"

He shrugged, "I don't *feel* like I'm dying."

Grace wandered further into the warehouse. "Lack..." She squinted at one of the larger containers. "Lackawanna Coal Mine!"

Vince looked as if he'd been kicked in the gut. "What did you say!?"

"Never heard of it." Tori climbed onto the Lackawanna container. Leaning down, she peered through the gaps in the sheet metal. A distinct earthy scent. Irregular dark lumps. It contained coal. *So much* coal. She rubbed her temple.

A few decades back, the oil fields of the Middle East and Canada had abruptly dried up. The world never fully recovered from the resulting energy crisis. The price of fossil fuels permanently skyrocketed into orbit.

Tori was standing on a million dollars. If most of these containers also had coal inside, this warehouse could be worth more than Channel 4 itself. "What's this doing under a news studio?"

Grace hugged her arms. "I-I don't know."

Both women jumped when a container suddenly toppled over. Vince tore through its contents like Christmas wrapping. Coal snowed upon the floor. He was making a mess. He was also making a TON of noise.

"Vince!" Tori tried to stop him. "Turn it down a notch! Or seven."

If he could hear her, he gave no indication.

Gold shimmered within the black. Sweet perfume, honey and saffron, overpowered all other smells. Tori reached into the coal and retrieved a golden apple. It was beautiful. It was the most perfect thing she'd ever seen. She stood on the beach of an island, under an amethyst sunset, in the loving embrace of dusk. Luke wrapped his arm around her shoulders, alive and whole.

Before them, Roy splashed into the surf. He pulled off his shirt. Sunlight beat wings against his magnificent, unscarred back. Winking, he offered her his hand—an invitation oh-so-different from the one at the Winecoff Hotel.

If only this could last forever. Every inch of her soul screamed, "It can. Try it. *Take a bite!*"

"Tori, look over here!"

Grace's outburst shattered the spell.

Reluctantly reality returned. Tori slapped her cheeks. She shoved the apple into her hoodie's pocket before it could captivate her again.

Hundreds of golden apples taunted her from the coal.

"Are you alright?" Grace whispered.

"I think I know how James' drug is made..." Tori breathed. Merely holding an apple had almost driven her mad. She couldn't imagine inhaling one.

"Drug?"

"It's a long story. What did you find?"

Grace gestured at a heavy-duty laptop at her feet. Vince's rampage had knocked it to the ground. Luckily it survived the impact. White, red, and yellow concentric rings painted its case.

Tori would recognize that logo anywhere. "Tianyi!"

"Who?" Grace leaned over her shoulder.

"Tianyi is a Chinese software giant. Well. They were. Lately they've been buying up all kinds of companies. They also bought my company, just after I joined. It caused so. Much. Drama."

At last, Tori was in her element. She flipped the laptop open.

A black and white terminal prompt lit up its screen. It was unlocked!

Happily, she invited herself in. The command to run a program suspiciously named "IOU-list" appeared. She smashed the enter key. Angry errors flooded the screen.

Grace peered over her shoulder. "What's wrong?"

"I think... A bunch of database connections failed." Tori squinted at the errors. "We have to be on a Tianyi network for this to work. One sec." She dug through several menus. The only other interesting file on the system was a document that outlined how to lock and unlock a computer. Too little too late. "Do you have a flash drive?"

Grace produced a pink, cloud-shaped flash drive from her key ring.

"Thanks." Tori copied the IOU-list over and stuffed it in her pocket. "I'll play with this once we're somewhere safer."

"Maybe you should take the laptop, too—"

A crash echoed through the chamber. Vince destroyed another crate.

"Vince. Please!" Tori begged.

At last, he relented. Covered in soot, he stumbled back to the women.

Like Tori's golden apple, the words "Lackawanna Coal Mine" had transported him into his memories. Whatever he was searching for there, he didn't find it.

"Sorry about that," he mumbled. "I'll explain later. I—"

The distinct clicking of high heels, drawing closer and closer, interrupted any further discussion.

The trio exchanged glances.

Grace wasn't moving.

"Damnit, Vince!" Tori cursed. "We have to hide."

"Not in here!" Grace cried. "After the mess we made, they'll search this room top to bottom."

"Come on." Vince grabbed them each by an arm. "I see an exit!"

His exit led to what appeared to be a second vault. This one was not a warehouse.

Water dripped from the ceiling, streaking into a moldy drain in the stone floor. Steel cells lined the walls. An angel statue, taller than the church outside the Channel 4 building, held a banner spelling "CREATION" above her wings. Broken at the waist and missing her face, she looked like she belonged at the entrance of a haunted house. Or perhaps a graveyard.

Grace whimpered. "Is this a dungeon?"

The same thought crossed Tori's mind. She pressed further inside the new vault, surveying her surroundings. That angel wouldn't be too difficult to scale. Maybe they could hide behind Creation.

Movement caught her eye. Her stomach cartwheeled. "Someone's in here!" She rushed to a cell and tugged at its locked door.

Behind the bars, a girl and boy huddled on a bench. They didn't react. They weren't moving.

"They're just teenagers," Tori could hardly breathe through the fear and concern bubbling up her throat.

After a long, horrifying moment, the girl rolled over.

"Thank goodness. They're still alive! Quick. Vince, Grace. Help me find a key. Or a crowbar—"

With a loud metallic clack, a spotlight switched on.

A man basked in its glow, not five feet away from Tori. "Welcome, ladies and gentlemen, to the world's stage," he announced.

How had she not seen him? How had she not heard him coming?

The man dressed with drama in a designer suit, chandelier

earrings, and satin gloves, but it was his self-satisfied smirk that left the biggest impression. It dripped with charisma, red wine and lipstick, hot oil on bare skin. His honeyed hair complimented a face that could only be described as a work of art.

If Roy was a marble sculpture, this man was a Renaissance painting framed by jewels and gold. He was breathtaking. No, *stunning*.

Vince and Grace stared, speechless.

Slowly, sensuously, the man removed a glove. "Humanity has come so very far in the centuries past." He flashed Tori a radiant smile. His free hand gripped... was that an ice cream cone?

"We've invented airplanes, x-rays, television, wireless communication..." While he spoke, he dipped his index finger into the cream. He sucked it clean. He never broke eye contact with Tori. "...even ice cream."

A chill shivered down her spine.

"But no matter how much time passes, some things never change. Did you know?" He stepped towards her. "This vault where you and I stand today once housed slaves destined for the World Fair's 'Anthropology' exhibit. A human zoo. For 'savages.' The public *ate them up*, dignity and all, for the bargain price of a nickel."

This guy was dangerous. He was also magnetic. She needed to run, but she couldn't look away.

"We prey on each other. We devour the weak. We lock them in cages and cubicles. Why?" He leaned closer. Ugh, he smelled good too. "So that we can feel better than them. To show off our 'progress'."

"It's him!" Grace gasped. "Those gloves... That suit.... That arrogance... He's Billy Lemp! I bet these tunnels go straight to Lemp Mansion. He's here to punish us for trespassing on his family's legacy!"

Disdain rumbled in the man's throat. "How dare you compare

me to that lascivious loser!" He tossed his frozen treat over his shoulder. It crunched when it hit the floor.

Much to Tori's relief, he backed off. "My dear Lavender Lady..." He stalked towards Grace instead. "While it's true I've all the glitter and class of a billionaire, I'm here in the name of human progress. Not business. Not love."

Vince blocked his path. "You call this"—he motioned at the cells—"progress!?"

The man laughed. "Of course." He patted the cell with prisoners. "These days, we only feed Asterius two kids at a time."

"I don't see what's so funny about that," Vince growled, clenching his fists.

The man sized up Vince.

"Leon," he purred. "Leon Narcissus."

"Wh-what?"

He drew an engraved pistol from beneath his lapel. He pointed it at Vince.

"When you're burning in Tartarus, that's the name I want you to scream."

CHAPTER SEVENTEEN

Tori shoved Vince. She was too slow.

A crack thundered through the vault.

Vince hit the ground. "Fuuuck!" he cursed, hugging his calf. Blood seeped through his jeans.

"Like I'd miss at this distance." Narcissus blew his gun's smoking barrel. Calmly, casually, he seized Vince by the collar. "Dear. I'm going to get scolded because of you." He licked his lips. "How are you going to make it up to me?"

"Let him go!" Tori shouted.

"But that's not what he wants," Narcissus traced a finger along Vince's chin. "Is it?"

Vince faltered. A heartbeat later he tangled his fingers in Narcissus' golden hair, dragging him into a kiss.

Tori blushed. Grace covered her eyes with her purse.

Breaking the kiss, Narcissus purred into Vince's ear, "Kill them. Kill them so we can be *alone*."

Without hesitation, Vince dove at Tori.

The sudden attack caught Tori off guard. The next thing she

knew, they were a mess of limbs on the floor, struggling against each other, covered in dust and mud.

He was bigger. He had more experience. But he was no longer thinking. No matter how she kicked or punched him, he went straight for her neck. Her cocky sparring partner had been replaced by a wild animal.

She could outsmart a wild animal. When he grabbed at her throat, she snatched his wrist. She locked his arm against her chest. Bridging her hips, tripping his injured leg, she threw herself into a roll. He tumbled off. She scrambled away.

Big mistake. Vince tackled her exposed back. He trapped her legs with his own. He hooked his elbow around her neck and squeezed. She thrashed with all her might. She scratched at his skin. He didn't budge.

She couldn't reach the knife he'd given her. She couldn't breathe.

In their practice matches, once she tapped, he always released her immediately. It'd never occurred to her just how much stronger than her he was. Panic clawed through her system. He meant to kill her. He meant to kill her, and there was nothing she could do to stop him.

Her vision blurred. Darkness swallowed her surroundings. She closed her eyes.

The aroma of baked peaches and brown sugar overcame her. Her ma washed dishes in front of the kitchen window. Her brother skipped inside through a screen door. Standing on his toes, he offered her a poppy. She accepted it and stroked his hair.

Tori ached. It was a dull, throbbing ache, deep within her soul. Oh, how she missed those simple times. The countryside had been so much kinder to her than the city. How many summers had she hunted critters in those woods? How many fish had she caught in the drainage pond behind her house? Perhaps she never needed to join Brooks, Vince, and Roy to escape her office life. She was home. She could rest.

Screeching tires. Burning flesh. A golden apple.

She couldn't die. She couldn't let go of it all. If she let go, who would stop Orion, free the phoenix, and save Atlanta?

The baying of distant hounds echoed in her ears. A woman with three faces stood over her, smiling.

Gasping, Tori opened her eyes.

The spotlight behind Narcissus exploded violently, scattering glass everywhere.

A large wedge buried into Vince's shoulder.

"Get off of her!" Grace emptied a can of pepper spray into his eyes.

Shouting in pain, he released Tori.

Coughing and choking, Tori got her hands and knees. Her head spun.

Abandoning her high heels, Grace wrapped an arm around Tori's waist. She dragged her to her feet. Together, they hobbled for the nearest door. They'd just barely reached it when a brick exploded inches from her nose.

Vince would not be defeated so easily. Tears streamed down his red face. Below the glass wedge, his left arm hung limp. Red gushed freely from his leg. Somehow, he'd managed to stand. He tracked them with his revolver.

Life was so unfair. Tori couldn't hit a stationary target with a handgun. Meanwhile, Vince, despite being possessed, blinded, and mad with pain, could hit them from across the chamber.

He fired again. She braced herself.

At the last second, as though it'd been struck by an invisible force, the bullet curved sharply to the left. It smashed an impressive hole into the wall.

Tori clutched Grace's arm. Gritting her teeth, she summoned whatever strength she had remaining and ran.

Vince limped after them with surprising speed.

Narcissus applauded his champion, in a lazy, unhurried tempo. He made no attempt to chase—chasing was beneath him.

Tori pushed mystery door number three. It opened into a bare, claustrophobic tunnel. They rushed onward, paying no mind to the disorienting twists and turns of the corridor. It didn't matter if they got lost. If Vince caught up to them in such tight quarters, they'd be easy targets. They had to keep moving.

"I never should have gotten involved," Grace softly sobbed.

Their road forked. One path led to stone stairs that curved upwards. It smelled sickly-sweet. The other led further and further underground. They had a life-or-death choice to make. Without any information.

Tori hated gambling. Even though her family bought dollar scratchers every single holiday, the most she'd ever won was another play. She'd lost every mandatory office raffle. The one time she'd played poker in college, they'd bet with candy for fun, and she still ended up losing boatloads of money after a piece of peppermint stuck in her windpipe and she had to go to the ER.

She swallowed hard. Unconsciously she stroked her throat. She could still feel Vince's hold on her. Her body remembered that primal terror, losing consciousness, that hopeless darkness.

Grace went straight for the stairs. To her, the surface meant safety.

A starving fox wandered through the woods. It stumbled across a rabbit laying across a deer path. Its mouth watering, it leaned in to take a bite. A sickly-sweet scent filled its nose.

A thousand generations of the fox's ancestors screeched in warning. To them, that sickly sweetness reeked of death.

The fox bounded off.

Tori tugged Grace away from those stairs. They continued along the downward path.

Before Tori had the chance to regret her decision, they found a door. As soon as they burst through it, the ground shuddered beneath them.

The door behind them vanished.

So it was true. This place really did change at random intervals. Good. That meant that Vince couldn't follow them here.

Grace collapsed to her knees. "What... What's happening?" Sniffling, she pulled a handkerchief from her purse. She dabbed her eyes. "Why is MoMo in this maze? What did that man do to Vince?"

It was Tori's turn to quote Roy. "I'm sorry, Grace." She dropped down next to her, placing a hand on her shoulder. "Perhaps we should have warned you."

"Warned me of what!?"

What indeed? Where could Tori start? She'd known that their enemies were monsters, but this was on an entirely different level from the ghosts, hellhounds, or even the burning phoenix she'd encountered so far.

This labyrinth itself was magical—it had a will of its own. MoMo could be anything. As for Narcissus... Narcissus reminded her of Orion. He'd implied that he was human, but there had to be more to him.

She was in over her head, too.

She started at the beginning. "So uh. You remember Orion, right? He's not just an assassin—"

Someone laughed.

Or maybe that was just the sound of heavy machinery groaning to life.

Fluorescent light flooded the room.

They were inside an office, kind of. Rows and rows of computers—server racks, probably—buzzed in the corner. Across from them, filing cabinets with heavy padlocks guarded unknown secrets. Wires spiderwebbed into dials and control panels. A single

desk dominated the floor. Behind it, a frosted glass marker board covered the wall.

This looked like a scene out of a high-tech research center, not some forgotten basement from a hundred years ago.

"Did the Louisiana Purchase Exposition of 1904 have anything like this?" Tori asked. Uneasiness bubbled in her gut. She prayed to God, Gandhi, and Buddha that there was an innocent explanation for all of this.

"No way! I doubt the Lemp Brewing Company needed computers. And Channel 4 keeps pretty much all its equipment in the studio or our news vans." Grace traced her fingers along the glass marker board. "Where in the world are we?"

The frost melted away beneath her touch. It wasn't a marker board. It was a window.

The window revealed another vault.

Tori's uneasiness boiled over into nausea. She couldn't swallow what she was seeing.

Beyond the window, the largest vault of the three they'd discovered stretched into the shadows. Inside, an arsenal worthy of the Fort Knox awaited duty. But this was no government stockpile.

Among the guns and explosives, Tori spotted a familiar wine-bronze sheen on a helmet and a spear. Sirius and Procyon napped beneath a map of all the missile silos in Missouri. In the distance, something sparked in with the intensity of a fallen power line.

Magical weapons. A menagerie of monsters. Hundreds of golden apples.

Someone was preparing for battle.

CHAPTER EIGHTEEN

A slender thread twisted around a rusted coal cart in the tunnel of a mine, splitting in every direction, a tiny hydra with a dozen heads. Vincent Lenoir clutched his aching temple. Where was he?

He grasped a string at random. He followed it until it stopped at the base of a news anchor's chair. Right, he'd survived the Lackawanna Coal Mine. He was inside of the Channel 4 studio instead. That made sense. Now, where was everyone else?

Tori and Grace were gone. Brooks and Roy were worlds away, yet somehow Vince could see them.

Another thread tugged at Brooks' heart. It fastened around Roy's finger.

Hundreds more burst from Roy. One of his thickest threads reached Vince's heart, too.

Vince forgot about it once he noticed the one wrapped around his neck. He tugged at it desperately.

At its other end, a bull stared him down. It lowered its horns. It charged.

The thread snapped.

Stinking, stagnant water dripped onto his forehead. Vince

jerked awake. Pain lurched through him, churning his stomach. He heaved all over the concrete. Dazed, he gazed at an unfamiliar ceiling. Wait, this was familiar. He was in the vault of Creation. He was laying at its very center, on top of that nasty drain.

Slowly, much more carefully, he tested his limbs. His left arm no longer worked. His leg felt as though it was made of sand. A dust storm raged inside his head. He couldn't think. More importantly, he couldn't remember anything.

Blood mixed with the mud. He was wounded. Badly. "Brooks...? Roy?" he cried. No one could save him. Brooks was across an ocean with Roy. Tori and Grace had fled without him. He was alone, like he'd always deserved.

Movement caught his attention. He wasn't alone, after all.

He eased onto his elbows for a better look. In the corner of the room, huddled in a cage, a teenaged boy and girl watched him. Their faces twisted with fear.

He could figure out what the fuck had happened to him later. Right here, right now, these kids needed his help.

"Hey!" He struggled to stand. "Hold on a little longer. I'll get you out of there!"

The girl raised a finger to her lips to shush him.

Groaning on its hinges, a door swung open.

Vince dropped to the ground. He was so battered and bruised he'd lose a fight with wind. Playing dead was his best option, even if it wasn't his style.

A growl rumbled through the vault. Heavy footsteps thudded towards him.

A hoof nudged his side. It had to be MoMo.

Vince cracked an eye.

The hoof disappeared.

He rolled over, a mere half-second before it stomped where he'd just been laying.

Under that huge hoof, cracks spiderwebbed in the stone floor.

So much for playing dead.

Adrenaline surged life through Vince's broken body. He scrambled to his feet. Limping as fast as he could, he put some distance between himself and MoMo. His progress was so slow that the monster didn't bother to chase him. He couldn't escape and they both knew it.

Playing dead had failed. Flight wasn't possible. Vince had to fight.

He drew his revolver. It was much lighter than usual. When had he used so much ammo? Only three rounds remained in its cylinder. Damn. He'd have to budget his shots. This was gonna suck.

Frustration rumbling in his throat, he faced the beast of the labyrinth.

Grace had been wrong. MoMo wasn't an ape. Long, sharp horns curled from his head. Brown fur covered his skin. Thick muscles rippled within his hulking chest. His cloven hooves pawed at the pavement. He was half man, half bull—a minotaur!

A hazy memory drifted through Vince's mind. A man draped in red and gold. A speech on humanity. A joke about feeding. Leon Narcissus. "You must be Asterius."

"I see Narcissus still talks too much," the minotaur grunted.

He charged. The earth quaked beneath him.

Holding steady, Vince fired. His shot went wide. It was impossible to control his gun's recoil while he was so weak from blood loss!

He had no time to dodge. Gritting his teeth, he braced for impact.

When Asterius reached him, he grabbed the bull by the horns. Somehow, he avoided being gored. But he lacked the strength to pull himself out of danger completely.

Rearing, the monster threw him into a brick wall.

Vince's ribs snapped like toothpicks. Fuck. A direct hit would've killed him. Another hit like that would kill him anyways.

And Asterius wasn't done with him yet. He circled to charge again.

Vince couldn't get up. He aimed his revolver between Asterius' eyes and squeezed the trigger.

The minotaur was smarter than a bull. He veered out of the way.

There wouldn't be another opportunity. Vince held his breath. He emptied his last chamber.

The bullet grazed the beast's shoulder.

Asterius snorted. "Your aim is terrible."

With a weak laugh, Vince dropped his gun. "I wasn't aiming for you."

The minotaur's great head turned just as the boy and the girl fled into the hallway. The door to their cage hung open. A hole smoked where its lock had been.

"You shouldn't have bothered." His tone trembled. "They... they can't be saved."

If Vince didn't know better, he'd think the minotaur was sad. "They have a chance."

It was over. He had no fight left. But he'd won where it mattered. If God and Fate were real, that had to count for something. Could Nancy's mother see him now? Would Brooks be proud of him? Would Roy, who once guided him out of the darkness, hold his hand as he returned to it for good?

"MoMo!" Grace shouted.

Grace? Grace wasn't who Vince expected to welcome him into the afterlife. Maybe he was hallucinating. Maybe it was wishful thinking.

Asterius hissed, "What's this?"

Grace stood in the doorway. She waved a red handkerchief over her head like a matador's cape. "I b-bet..." Her eyes were puffy. Her cheeks flushed a rosy pink. She'd been crying recently, yet she tried her best to be brave. "I bet you can't catch me!"

Frustrated, and maybe a little offended, the minotaur lumbered towards her. "What a waste. More young calves to the slaughter."

Above them, the lights shut off. The vault disappeared behind a veil of pitch black.

Soft footfalls. Grace was running.

Asterius hesitated. He couldn't track her.

A cell phone flashlight shone beneath Tori's face. "Yo, hamburger meat! Over here!" she jeered from the opposite side of the room. "At this rate you won't catch either of us."

"Enough," the minotaur snarled. "Don't underestimate me!" With surprising speed, he charged at her.

Her phone's glow vanished.

An echoing crash shook the entire vault.

The lights snapped back into action, illuminating the battlefield.

Asterius had underestimated Tori and Grace.

The software engineer perched precariously on top of a steel cell.

Inside the cell, Asterius was trapped.

The weather woman slid a padlock onto its door. She added a second, then a third.

No matter how viciously the minotaur bashed against the bars, they didn't budge. He roared. "You can't cage me!"

"Apparently they can," Vince taunted. "Why didn't I think of that?" Talking. Hurt. So. Much. He coughed, leaving specks of blood on his palm.

Tori rushed over. "Come on." She wrapped an arm around him.

"I can't believe we just did that!" Grace cheered, half terrified, half thrilled. She tucked Vince's revolver into her purse. After a pause, she also snagged her heels. "I was so sure we were going to get eaten."

"We still can," Tori warned. "That cage won't hold him for long!"

With an ominous bang, Asterius thrashed inside his cell.

Completely terrified, not thrilled, Grace helped Tori lift Vince. Together they carried him into the labyrinth of doors. The excitement following Asterius's defeat faded quickly.

Tori attempted to map their path, but whenever her notes started to make sense, the tunnels changed. They were lost. This was hopeless. Minotaur or no minotaur, they were no closer to safety than they'd been before Narcissus showed up. And Narcissus was still out there.

All the while, Vince slipped in and out of consciousness. A warm breeze embraced him, coaxing him into dreams. A high school teacher stood over him, lecturing in a monotone drone, "...Lost miners used fire to follow air currents back to the surface..." He struggled to move. "Air... Air and fire!"

Grace almost dropped him. "Wh-what?"

He dug his lighter from his pocket. He switched it on.

When the breeze picked up again, the flame flickered towards a single door.

Tori caught on immediately. "Let's follow that current!"

Five gusts and six doors lately, they emerged into the parking lot of Lemp Mansion.

Fresh air and silver moonlight revitalized Tori and Grace. But Vince still wandered in darkness. The dreams had stopped. The nightmares had ended. He couldn't see, but he could feel a river around him. A ferryman's pole disturbed its flow.

Through the rush of water, he heard Grace sob. "He's not going to die, is he!?"

A voice pierced the depths, so crystal clear it could've been in Vince's ear.

"Not if we can help it!"

CHAPTER NINETEEN

Tori had never seen anyone look at another person the way Roy looked at Vince.

Once her ma came terribly close, on the night of Luke's funeral, as she stared down at his empty casket knowing that she'd never again smile as he laughed at his own jokes or argue with him about his boyfriends and girlfriends. She'd never see him graduate from the medical school he'd worked so hard to get into. She'd never walk him down the aisle.

On that night, everything good and bright inside her died. It had killed her that there wasn't enough of her son left to bury. She withered, so bitter and full of guilt that after only a year and some change, Tori barely recognized her anymore.

Perhaps Tori herself had worn that awful mask when she found Luke's body in the snow. Or whenever she saw his photograph on her desk, collecting dust. Or whenever she came home to an empty apartment, accidentally cooked an extra portion for dinner, or dialed his number just to hear his voice on his answering machine.

Losing her brother had carved a river into her soul, into which she poured all the anger, desperation, and despair that raged beneath her skin every day, even now. Each night, she drowned in that river. Each morning, she fought her way back to the surface. The part of her strong enough to break free from that current was gone, underground, forever.

So when she saw Roy, so uncertain and afraid, his perfect composure finally shattered to pieces, she wondered just how much Vince meant to him. When she saw Grace sobbing into her handkerchief, Brooks so scared he couldn't speak, and Vince sprawled over the picnic table, bleeding through his gauze, struggling to breathe, she saw herself.

She'd only known Vince for what, maybe two months? Whether eighteen months, eighteen hours, or eighteen years passed, it was too soon for another visit from Death. The pain was enough to tear her in two. *Again.*

Yet with that river flooding up over its banks, she couldn't cry.

After reuniting with Roy and Brooks, their group had retreated to a park just up the street from Lemp Mansion, safe from the prying eyes of security cameras, late-night diners, and neighbors.

The park was sleepy, with dried out grass, a faded playground set, and a green metal eating area beneath a stand of pine trees. Above them, the moon held her breath. It was well past midnight. Even in the heart of the city, a peaceful stillness reigned.

But there was nothing peaceful about the scene silently unfolding before Tori.

Deftly, desperately, Brooks treated Vince. He extracted the hunk of glass. He tested that lifeless arm. He cleaned and applied pressure to that ugly, oozing gunshot wound. Somehow, he managed to keep his hands steady while the rest of him trembled.

Roy watched, uncharacteristically quiet.

Grace wept enough for everyone else.

Vince just... laid there. Mangled. Broken. He hadn't moved in ten minutes, save for the shallow, ragged rise and fall of his chest.

Bruises swelled on Tori's neck where Vince's hands had been.

Her throat ached when she breathed. That ache became agony whenever she tried to talk. She didn't dare wonder just how close Vince had been to killing her. She didn't dare wonder how close to dying he was right now.

"He's... he's going to make it," Grace whimpered. "Right? We were supposed to film an episode of *Haunt Hunt* together!"

Brooks glanced at her. He glanced back at Vince. "He's... lost a lot of blood." He could barely choke out the words.

"We have to get him to a hospital!"

With an unreadable expression, Roy slipped onto the bench next to Tori. "Miss Jaecar. Tell me. What did you find inside Channel 4?"

A labyrinth. A minotaur. An incubus. A mystery program. And among all of that, a secret base with a secret arsenal. She stared at the ground. If only one of those magical weapons could heal Vince. But they couldn't. None of the new information was useful.

"Tori..." Grace tugged her sleeve. "The apple."

Tori had almost forgotten her forbidden fruit. She dug it out of her hoodie and placed it on the table between them. This time, its sweet aroma sickened her. They'd gone through so much to steal it. It couldn't be worth it.

Brooks' face wrenched as if his heart had stopped. "Your sister guessed correctly."

"An Apple of Discord," Roy whispered.

"Discord?" Grace inched away from the apple. "What's an Apple of Discord?"

"The treasure of the Hesperides, the seed of strife, the harbinger of war..." Roy mused. "Those apples grow only from a single tree, in a garden where the sunset meets the west, watered by the tears of the world." He drew in a long breath. "To taste one is to taste pure power. *Immortality*. They're the envy of gods and men alike."

"Whenever history mentions an Apple of Discord, many people die," Brooks explained.

"These apples... They're used to make James' drug, aren't they?" Tori asked.

Roy nodded.

"I bet they can make hundreds of doses from one apple," Brooks thought out loud. "A mere sliver of such power.... It'd be enough to drive a phoenix mad. To turn a hearth fire into a holocaust."

"And it'd be insanely addictive," Roy concluded.

Tori was beginning to see the picture in Orion's puzzle. Like the arsenal hidden beneath the Channel 4 building, like the drug, the phoenix and the minotaur were weapons. Orion, Narcissus, and whoever they worked for were preparing for war. Why? And why in Missouri?

She couldn't process that. Not yet. "How does any of this help Vince?"

"What are a few flesh wounds to an immortal?" Roy sounded so certain, but he didn't smile, his body language was stiff, and he drummed his fingers on the bench in an erratic beat.

Roy was conflicted. Nervous.

To Tori, that was as ominous as smoke from a wildfire.

It took her a moment to put together what he meant. When she did, her own wildfire of doubt razed all but one thought to the ground. "You can't be serious!"

Grace's gaze bounced between them. "What is he talking about, Tori?"

"You just finished telling us how dangerous these apples are!" Tori gripped the edge of the picnic table. "Now you want us to feed one to Vince?"

Unflinching, Roy endured her wrath. "Only a bite. Enough to get him through this."

"Only a bite? Of *immortality?*"

"Wouldn't want him to outlive me," he laughed wryly.

Brooks pursed his lips. "Mercy... I don't..."

Roy searched Vince's sleeping face for an answer. "If it's him, it'll be fine," he insisted with all the confidence he could muster. More softly he added, "Besides, what other options do we have?"

That was a good question.

For the first time since he'd rescued her at the Winecoff Hotel, Tori truly looked at Roy.

He knew more than he let on. He *always* knew more than he let on. To have enough time to count all his omissions and half-truths, she'd need to be immortal herself. She'd be a fool to trust him. She'd also be a fool to attack an assassin, climb into a stranger's car, and follow an angel down a fire escape, through fire and brimstone, nine long hours north of home.

She was still here. And here, as she had done on those first days, she let her shepherd guide the way.

She drew her dagger. She cut into the golden apple.

Brooks tensed.

Grace hid behind a nearby hedge.

Resting his chin on his palms, Roy watched with anticipation.

The lure of power was stronger than the lure of death. As soon as Tori held out a slice to Vince, he stirred. He snatched it from her fingers and gulped it down.

They waited. Nothing.

She shifted restlessly. She turned to Roy. "Should I feed him another piece?"

A knuckle nudged her shoulder.

"You... Tori, you..." Vince groaned like the engine of his beater on a steep hill.

His breathing had stabilized. Color had returned to his cheeks. Even the defiance had returned to his eyes. Yet there was something different about him that Tori couldn't quite place.

"You promised we'd go to that raceway!"

CHAPTER TWENTY

Everyone was acting so fucking weird. Vincent Lenoir furiously sliced up his chocolate chip pancake, trying to ignore how Brooks hovered around him as if he might disappear in a puff of smoke, or how Grace jumped whenever a car passed by, or how Tori avoided him all morning. Only Roy seemed normal—if drinking red wine with his breakfast could be considered normal.

Vince sighed. He shoved his plate aside. He'd lost his appetite.

If any person in their group had the right to act weird, it was him. He was the one who'd almost died last week. Or so he'd been told. Aside from a terrible pounding in his head, dreams about tangled thread, and a dull ache in his chest if he inhaled too deeply, he was fine. He'd slept for almost seven days straight; he'd never been more rested. In his line of work, occasional injuries were to be expected.

He wanted to get back to work already. He wanted revenge against that stupid cow named Asterius. He wanted to check if those teenagers had escaped the labyrinth. If so, surely they'd have made the news by now?

Instead, he was at a diner, across the street from the World

Chess Hall of Fame of all places, gutting out another painfully awkward meal.

Grace's apartment's tower was up the road.

In a surprising role reversal, instead of Grace moving in with Roy, Brooks, Vince, and now Tori, they crashed with her. Since their adventure at Channel 4, they'd barely gone outside. For Vince, laying low was as excruciating as reality TV with pop music in the background.

Grace was his silver lining. She was sitting pretty for a woman her age—her west end apartment had a fancy lobby, three bedrooms, two full baths, and a view, albeit distant, of the sprawling Forest Park. She gushed about finding a crazy good deal on rent every time they rode the elevator.

She watched every episode of *Haunt Hunt* with him, made him snacks, and lit lavender-scented candles everywhere to, as she put it, "speed up his healing". She wanted to help in any way she could. Nothing helped him more than having his own personal nurse.

Well, a nurse besides Brooks. Brooks was the doctor. And old.

Why Grace gave them the time of day after they'd dragged her through hell and back was beyond Vince. She'd known them for, what, two hours before they'd entered Channel 4? By his count, within another two hours, they'd almost gotten her killed a dozen times. But he wasn't complaining. He didn't even complain about sleeping on a pink couch under a blanket with cute animals hand-stitched into it.

He was ready to complain now.

The diner's atmosphere was pleasant enough. Bright lights and high ceilings gave it an airy vibe. Chalkboard menus and neon letters colored the walls. Televisions hung behind the bar. The problem was with the people at Vince's table. They'd been here for thirty minutes without exchanging thirty words.

Vince had enough. "What're you two doing here? I thought your sister lived in Europe."

"I'm a fast swimmer." Roy winked.

Brooks shot Roy a disapproving look. "Roy's sister is staying in the United States for the foreseeable future. Not too far from St. Louis."

"So I can finally meet her?" Vince pressed.

"There's no need," Roy brushed him off. "We already know what James' drug is for, thanks to you, Miss Jaecar."

Thanks indeed. If Brooks or Roy reminded Vince to thank Tori one more time, his head was gonna explode. He owed his life to her sticky fingers and that legendary Apple of Discord. Supposedly. He wasn't sure he believed that had actually happened. If he'd really taken a bite out of immortality, wouldn't he feel... different? The only thing unusual in his stomach was a guilty knot so big he couldn't enjoy his food.

Tori gazed out the window like she was waiting for someone. Her meal sat untouched on her plate. She looked overwarm for someone who was currently indoors in the heart of summer. A scarf draped around her neck, hiding the bruises he'd given her.

He didn't remember their fight or Leon Narcissus. Whenever he tried, vague sensations flooded his system—a smooth voice, hot skin, and an overwhelming desire to prove himself. He couldn't thank Tori because he needed to apologize first, and because he couldn't remember what he'd done, he didn't know where to start.

"I'm glad we've solved one mystery," Tori replied. "But what about the rest of them? Why is there a magical military stockpile beneath Channel 4? How did those hallways keep moving? Who are Orion, Narcissus, and Asterius really, and, more importantly, who are they working for?"

"Orion. Narcissus. Asterius," Grace listed off. "Those are all names from Greek mythology."

"Are they?"

"You're from Atlanta, aren't you? Haven't you seen Orion's Belt? In the south, it's visible all year long!"

"Is that the constellation with three dots in a line?"

"Yes! It's part of Orion the Hunter," Grace confirmed excitedly. "Legend has it that Orion was the greatest hunter to ever live. The gods placed him in the stars when he was killed by Apollo out of jealousy... or by Artemis for assaulting her handmaiden... or by Gaia for vowing to hunt all the creatures on Earth to extinction..."

"That sounds like something he would do."

Vince frowned. "Sounds more like a bedtime story to me."

"It *is* a bedtime story. My mother would tell me tales about the stars every night. Before she... well." Grace patted her cheeks to re-center herself.

"Near Orion the Hunter and his two hounds, there's Asterius. Better known as the Taurus, the bull of the labyrinth. Slain by the great Greek hero Theseus." Tugging at the sleeve of her lavender sweater, she showed off a charm bracelet with an emerald stone. "I'm a Taurus myself, actually. That's why I'm reliable and so, uh, terrified of change."

Vince wasn't surprised in the least that Grace was into astrology. He was extremely surprised that astronomy connected two of their enemies. What if all their enemies were connected by stars? Had the secret behind his nightmares been hanging over his head all along?

"We're being attacked by bedtime stories!?"

"Dead ones, apparently," Tori observed.

"I wish they'd stayed dead."

"Hmm..." Grace tapped her chin with a finger. "Narcissus sounds familiar, but he isn't a constellation. Is he dead, too?"

"Narcy fell in love with his own reflection in a pool of water," Roy recited cheerfully. "It was a fatal attraction—he dove in and drowned."

Her blue eyes met his, searching. She decided he was serious. "So... you guys regularly meet characters from Greek mythology?"

"I've been waiting a long time for someone to put that together." Roy stared at Vince while he spoke.

Vince narrowed his eyes. How was he supposed to know any of this stuff? It was Roy's fault he didn't finish high school, not his.

"Isn't the phoenix myth, uh..." Tori wrinkled her brow. "Egyptian? Chinese? There are so many options."

"What if all myths from all cultures are true?" Roy seemed thrilled by the possibility. "Monsters from Greek mythology masquerading as memories passed down from generation to generation."

"So, if Orion, his hounds, Asterius, and Narcissus are all from Greek mythology..." The secret behind Vince's nightmares wasn't over his head after all—it was behind him. One by one, he recalled the monsters he'd hunted over the years. "What about the werewolves? And the vampires? And the hydra that almost ate me in the Lackawanna Coal Mine?"

Roy tapped his index finger. "Lycaon's fifty sons, transformed into wolves as punishment for treachery." He tapped his middle finger. "Vrykolakas, corpses condemned to wander the world of man forever." He hesitated, studying the lines in his hands. "...The Lernaean Hydra, guardian of the Underworld."

Each response begged for a million more questions, but Vince could only think of one. He started to ask it, but the words wouldn't come out. His mouth had gone dry. A lump clogged his throat. Rain tapped away at the roof, the tick of an invisible clock, turning back time. He was a scared fourteen-year-old again, standing at the crossroads of his life.

What about Spearfinger, the Cherokee witch wielding obsidian claws, who thundered down from the Appalachian Mountains, who devoured children's livers? *Which Greek asshole murdered Nancy's mother?*

Tori was nothing if not a good listener. "Wait, Lackawanna Coal Mine?" she mouthed, so softly only Vince heard her.

Grace accepted the truth with more grace than Tori and Vince combined. Especially considering she'd only met them a week ago. "Orion, Narcissus, Asterius. In their myths, they don't meet. Why are they working together?"

"After months of trailing behind Senator Pallas, President Arvis is leading the polls."

The diner's owner had switched on the televisions.

"Last night, authorities apprehended a suspect in the arson of President Arvis' fundraiser at Mimosa Hall. He is believed to be a member of the Russian SVR."

Of course. Vince rolled his eyes. The news always blamed supernatural stuff on Russia.

"Patriotism and love for our great leader is at an all-time high. We'll show those cheating Russkies that they can't interfere with our democratic process—"

In tandem, the screens changed to a football game, then a cooking show, then a car commercial. The diner owner didn't like politics, either.

What now? Vince wasn't keen on continuing their Greek mythology discussion. He couldn't interrogate Brooks and Roy about his past in front of Tori and Grace. Everyone else seemed to know more on the subject than he did, anyways.

"Sun Tzu, the Art of War..." Tori whispered under her breath. "All warfare is based on deception."

"Bless you," Vince grunted.

"It's President Arvis. He's involved, somehow."

Roy rested his chin on his palms. "And what makes you think that, Miss Jaecar?"

"It's just a hunch, but... President Arvis runs on a platform of security, authority, and nationalism. He thrives on fear. The Winecoff Hotel, Mimosa Hall, and I'd bet the bombing of his campaign bus were false flag operations to garner public sympathy."

Vince leaned back against the leather of his chair. "What the hell is a false flag operation?"

"Err... At my office, there's this project manager, Maena," Tori began, wetting her lips. This was going to be a long story. "Once James asked her to do a quarterly report. To get out of it, she wiped her hard drive. Oh no. A virus! The IT department was sabotaging her to make engineering look bad! By the time James finished screaming at everyone with 'tech' in their title, he forgot about the original work. It was worth it to Maena, even if she lost her files."

Vince's career in monster hunting didn't involve quarterly reports, hard drives, or IT departments. "In English, please?"

"In false flag operations, you attack yourself and blame someone else. When you need an excuse to pick a fight."

Grace tilted her head. "If President Arvis really is involved... Who does he want to pick a fight with?"

Roy clapped his hands together. "Let's find out!"

CHAPTER TWENTY-ONE

Midnight drifted lazily down the Mississippi River. Cars hummed along the highway. Bugs only Tori could name sang along. The distant Gateway Arch glowed in the moonlight, a silver streak of hope above the black labyrinth below. It was a quiet, easy evening. But the only thing that brought Vincent Lenoir peace was the overpowering stench of burning rubber.

Finally, two long weeks after dying and coming back to life, he'd made it to his raceway.

Bleachers—huge enough to make a high school football stadium seem modest—framed a classic NASCAR loop. Within that loop, Vince's new best friend, the road course, twisted around harrowing turns. Black skid marks scarred the pavement. Dents bruised the guard rails.

Even though the track was now still, it radiated energy. Character had been carved into every inch of every mile, upon which countless men risked everything to feel alive.

Vince had insisted on coming here to celebrate his full recovery. He'd wanted to have a go around a track since he was nine, when he caught a glimpse of Barber's first turn on his way to Birmingham. He couldn't risk getting killed again before he got the chance. By the end of the year, he planned to empty his entire bucket list. Even if it meant hanging out alone with Roy.

"Was it everything you dreamed it would be?" Roy asked with a smile.

He lounged on the tailgate of his lifted Dodge Ram truck.

This raceway's parking lot could hold hundreds of cars, but tonight there were only two. It was closed. They were trespassing, naturally.

Tori hadn't been in the mood for tourist attractions, especially when it required committing a misdemeanor. Grace had refused to leave her apartment for fear of offending the new moon, whatever the hell that meant. Brooks stayed behind to play bodyguard. They'd learned their lesson about splitting their group from the Winecoff Hotel fiasco.

Vince soaked in the heat and gasoline fumes oozing from his Mustang. "Everything and more."

His car was an old gray mare. In her youth, she was meant for drag racing, not caressing wild curves in the dark. He'd worn her tires until they were as smooth as the profile of a vintage Corvette, trashed her suspension, and melted her brakes. Yet whenever he looked at her, he fell in love all over again.

Not that he understood anything about love. But cars? Cars he understood. Ever since his foster mother taught him how to do donuts in front of an abandoned Walmart, he'd worshiped them. Behind the wheel was the only time in his life he felt like he was in control.

"How was it for you?" Just this once, he'd lent Roy his Mustang.

"A little slow," Roy said with a smirk.

Vince kicked an empty can at him. But he wasn't actually mad.

It'd been ages since he'd hung out with Roy like this. While Vince was a teenager, Roy was a constant fixture in his life. They'd play cards almost every night. Test out the latest and greatest videogame. Vince had even hugged him once. Willingly.

Over the past six months or so, something had changed between them without Vince noticing.

He popped a cigarette in his mouth and fumbled for his lighter.

"I would've liked to see the look on your face, y'know. When you thought I might die. I don't think I've ever seen you flustered before."

"It's not too late. We can do a redo. Bring you back to the brink of death."

"Wouldn't be the same."

"The understatement of the century."

A question burned in the back of Vince's mind, black, angry smoke that not even a dozen laps around the track could smother. "Roy. Why didn't you tell me? That the monsters we hunted for all those years might be connected to each other?"

"Are you an expert in Greek mythology, Vincent?"

"That's not what I'm asking."

"...Would you believe me if I said I didn't know?"

Vince laughed weakly. "Not a chance."

Roy leaned back on his palms, searching the stars for the right words.

Vince wondered if he was looking at specific constellations, and, if he was, whether those wanted to kill them, too.

Whenever Roy was silent like this, a monologue would surely follow. "In Greek epics the lines between good and evil—between monster and man—are clear. Arachne's pride weaves her into a spider. Narcissus' fatal flaw, his pride, kills him in the end. Theseus slays the man-eating minotaur and saves the day. Reality isn't so straightforward."

Roy held out his hand.

Vince handed him his cigarette.

The strawberry blonde took a long drag. "I always suspected

there was a method to the madness that binds you and me. But even I don't know how, why, who, or what." He allowed smoke to escape his lips. It drifted into the heavens.

"I don't know how Greek monsters disappeared in the classical era. I don't know why they're back now. I don't know if President Arvis is really our main villain, or what he might want. I don't know what's going to happen. But I do know..." he trailed off.

"What?" Vince prompted.

Roy always had all the answers. It wasn't fair for him to come up short when the answer Vince needed was so important.

"Do you remember Nancy's mural? Back in Monongahela?"

Of course, Vince remembered Nancy's murals in her hometown just outside Monongahela National Park. She'd painted a blue stallion behind the town's only bar, a volcano of deadly animals along the diner, and, on the back of the church, a six-winged angel baptized in copper-tinted fire.

Although striking, the images had seemed random to Vince. He'd always half-suspected they were drug induced. Nancy had been a pretty straight-laced teenager, but anyone who'd lost her father so young had a right to have a few bad habits.

"I mean, yeah. One of them is tattooed on my fucking back."

Roy shook his head. "Not that one." He returned Vince's cigarette. "Back in Atlanta, the phoenix showed Tori a vision of the future. In that vision, she saw orange fog, copper-colored fire, and a dead city."

Orange fog. Copper-colored fire. A dead city.

Vince could see Tori's vision as if he'd been there himself—charred buildings, ruined skyscrapers, and a smog-choked horizon. Roy's description was identical to Nancy's mural on the church. "That has to be a coincidence, right?"

"Vincent," Roy sighed. "Don't you understand by now?"

He leaned in, lowering his voice to a whisper.

"There's no such thing as a coincidence."

* * *

With bated breath, the hero crept into the boiler room. Water rushed through leaking pipes above him. He gripped his flashlight so hard his knuckles turned white. But not as white as the infamous White Lady who haunted these depths, searching for her lost children.

"Legend says that the White Lady kidnaps any unfortunate soul who crosses her path... never to be seen again!" the hero narrated.

Laughter echoed through the boiler room. Someone was behind him.

The hero broke into a run.

When he turned the corner, he stood face to face with tired, hungry eyes.

Grace screamed.

She grabbed Vince's arm. She couldn't watch anymore.

Haunt Hunt episode "Not that Kind of White Lady" played on the television in the center of Grace's living room. Vince never did find a monster in that Manhattan skyscraper's basement. Instead, he'd stumbled upon a bunch of maintenance workers smoking pot and playing cards in the middle of their shift. It was a fond memory. He'd won a hundred bucks off those guys by betting on rummy.

Tori sighed. "How does that scene still scare you, Grace? We've watched this episode like seven times."

It was a good thing Grace's apartment was so ridiculously big—Vince and Tori spent so much time in her living room that they were practically roommates. Gradually their stuff blended in with Grace's feminine decor.

Energy drink cans glittered beneath colorful crystals hanging over the windows. Candy wrappers littered whatever surface space wasn't already occupied by potted plants. Romance paperbacks piled high on a hand-painted coffee table.

Vince currently shared an L-shaped pink velvet couch with Grace. Tori sat in a fluffy white armchair, hugging her knees. In the quaint open-concept kitchen, Brooks brewed strawberry herbal tea. Roy dug through the fridge, searching for God knows what.

"Thinking about the White Lady just makes me so emotional." Grace sniffled into Vince's sleeve. "A mother who can't see her kids. I can't imagine being so lonely!"

"It's okay, Grace," Vince patted her shoulders, doing his best to ignore the warmth melting through her sweatshirt, her hair that smelled of lavender, or how her touch sparked electricity up his skin. "I'm sure those maintenance workers are still down there dodging work to this day. She's got plenty of company."

"So do you, Vincent," Roy teased.

Vince detangled himself from Grace.

One by one, Brooks handed out mugs of tea. "Maybe you three should watch something more to Miss Batya's tastes?"

Grace shook her head. "It's okay! I really like Vince's—"

Tori switched the television over to basic cable. Siren Song, the latest and greatest singer to dominate the nation's pop charts, took center stage.

"—I love Siren Song! She's my absolute favorite—"

Plugging his ears, Vince snatched the remote from Tori. He changed the channel to the news.

"—Oh, that's my coworker, Mrs. Homer! This is good, too."

Like Tori, Grace was now a slacker. She'd called in sick every morning since the labyrinth. Monster hunting seemed to have that effect on people. A real career killer.

"Thanks," Vince accepted his drink from Brooks without looking up from his phone. Half-heartedly, he answered a text from one of his channel's two subscribers. Dude asked a lot of questions for someone with the username "Sun Tzu". Wasn't that some kind of brainiac philosopher?

Vince was wiped out from last night. He and Roy had chilled until track workers started showing up for their morning shifts, and then a little longer. Not that he would've slept much either way.

"Got anything with some actual kick? Like espresso? Or a double shot?"

"You're free to go to the diner and buy whatever you'd like," Brooks replied stiffly.

"That reminds me. Now that Vince is officially better..." Grace tapped her index fingers together. "...are you planning on moving on soon?"

Now that was a question worth answering. Over the past two weeks, the monster hunters hadn't made much progress on the whole Greek-mythology-meets-President-Arvis thing. But they weren't really trying.

Vince's kiss with Death had drained them all, even Roy and Brooks. They'd needed some peace and quiet to recharge. It was the longest vacation any of them had ever given themselves.

Brooks nodded. "Most likely."

"Where are you going?" Grace continued.

"That still remains to be seen."

As far as Vince could tell, they had three solid options. They could return to Atlanta to resume their hunt for Orion the Hunter. They could head to Manhattan, President Arvis' hometown, and try to dig up some dirt. Or, as a wildcard, they could move their vacation to a ski resort near Monongahela. Have Tori judge for herself whether Nancy's paintings were coincidences or not.

Vince wasn't keen on the prospect of seeing Nancy again after so many years. They hadn't parted on the best terms.

Grace's shoulders slumped. "So you're done with St. Louis?"

Vince opened his mouth to comfort her, but his voice caught in his throat. Something on the television brought all his thoughts to a screeching halt.

Tori saw it, too.

The headline "St. Louis in Mourning" came and went. Beneath it were two photographs of kids. THE kids. This story was about the teenagers Vince had freed from the cages in the vault of Creation.

Horror spread through Vince's gut. With each word the anchor spoke, it grew sharper.

The girl had been visiting town for a dance competition. The boy was a local businessman's child. They hadn't even been declared missing when a jogger stumbled upon their remains floating in the Mississippi River. DNA testing confirmed their identities. Over a month ago.

"They... They were already dead?" Tori whispered.

Brooks gazed into the tea leaves at the bottom of his teapot. "... Yes, Miss Jaecar. They were already dead."

The resignation in his tone dragged Vince to his feet. "You knew!?"

"Roy and I... We crossed paths with them on our way to you. We knew immediately."

Sometimes Brooks looked younger than he was—when Vince listened to him for once, Tori mastered some new skill, or he found an excellent sale at the grocery store. Right now, he looked like he'd been locked in that cage under Channel 4. Only instead of a month, he'd been there since 1904.

Vince never understood why Brooks blamed himself every single time someone got hurt.

"For what it's worth," Brooks added. "Because you freed them, Vince, they were finally able to cross over."

"What the hell is that supposed to mean!?"

"Congratulations, Vincent." Roy patted him on the back. "You've finally seen a ghost!"

Reeling, Vince stumbled away from them. How could Brooks think that would make him feel better? How could Roy be so nonchalant!?

Ever since he was small, long before his plunge into the supernatural at Lackawanna Coal Mine, Vince had wanted to meet a ghost. Ghosts were proof that the other side existed—that there was more to being human than struggle and suffering. That he might have a soul.

He'd missed his childhood. He had already wasted so much of his life. If he had a soul, maybe, just maybe, he'd get another chance at happiness.

He'd always wanted to see a ghost, but not like this. These ghosts were almost as young as he'd been when he met Roy and Brooks. They hadn't had lives to waste.

Vince buried his face in his hands. Why was he always unable to save the ones who deserved it most? He was so focused on his own pain that he didn't notice Tori retreating across the room.

"I... I need some air," she muttered.

Before anyone could respond, she disappeared out the door.

CHAPTER TWENTY-TWO

Tori drowned in an ocean of blue, gold, and crimson. Angels swam around her, drenched in light. With its sprawling mosaics, the Cathedral Basilica was opulent and grand. Even on a Thursday morning, it bustled with tourists. It was nothing like her old one-room church back in her hometown. It was close enough.

She settled in a pew far from the entrance, where it was quiet. Incense soothed her labored breaths. Before her, a priest stood at a table full of tiny candles in crimson cups. He lit one with a small brass lighter. He mouthed a prayer.

Tori had been raised as a Baptist. She'd never seen a votive candle in church before. She hadn't attended Sunday service since college, much to her ma's dismay. She wasn't sure what she believed in. Yet she found herself following in the priest's footsteps. She stopped in front of the flickering flames. They whispered of wishes and promises, of triumph of good over evil.

Should she light a candle for those teenagers' souls? For James? For the people who'd died in Atlanta's fires? How many candles would she need before this was all said and done, with Orion safely behind bars?

Perhaps he would need one, too.

She'd never thought about what Roy, Brooks, and Vince would do when they hunted Orion down. Maybe they killed people as well as monsters. They had so many guns. Would they turn them on him as readily as Vince had turned his on her under Narcissus' mind control? If so, would he deserve it?

"I am the light of the world. No follower of mine shall ever walk in darkness; no, he shall possess the light of life."

She knew without looking that Roy had joined her. Of course. With Orion still at large, it wasn't safe for her to be alone. That wasn't what she really wanted, anyways.

There was nothing to say. She wasn't upset with him. She was the one who'd asked to fight alongside him, Brooks, and Vince. She'd watched James get murdered before she'd met them; she'd known what she was getting into. But she hadn't understood the toll death would take on her. How much it would make her think of Luke.

No wonder Vince drank all the time. She would do anything to numb this stinging, doubt-edged guilt.

"I would have liked to meet him," Roy mused.

Tori followed his gaze to a sculpture of Jesus hanging on the wall. "You would?" Roy didn't strike her as the religious type. Why would he be? He didn't seem phased by anything. He already had all his answers.

"No one has seen him for thousands of years, yet his words carry the same power as the day he spoke them." The glow from the candles reflected in his eyes. "Blind faith. There's something beautiful about that, don't you think?" His gaze drifted upwards. He wasn't admiring the vast domed ceiling, but something beyond it. "If myths are real, and we know they are, who's to say he isn't real, too?"

That was a comforting thought. That would be so much better than angels or unicorns.

Tori hugged her arms.

"Roy. Why didn't you tell me? That the monsters were from Greek mythology?"

"Would you have believed me?"

Maybe. "No, probably not," she admitted.

It was one thing to feel as small as a rabbit beneath Sirius' mighty paws. To stare the Devil in the eyes, with the proof of his power painted crimson on the snow. Folklore and fairy tales tucked her into bed each night. They were real. She could see them. Feel them.

But to accept that some unseen, unknown power had changed the rules of reality? That was something else entirely.

"I don't deal in faith, Miss Jaecar. I want you to draw your own conclusions from what you see with your own eyes. I want you to *know*." Roy searched the faces of the twelve apostles painted above them. "Orion, Narcissus, and Asterius are just lackeys. We're up against something greater than all of them."

That, she already knew. She'd known it from the moment she first dragged Orion to the ground. Someone was giving him orders. Something had brought ancient legends back to life. She dared not guess at what could be capable of that, or, even worse, what it would mean about the afterlife. There was so much more to Greek mythology than its heroes and villains.

Roy's fingers brushed the petals of a crocus someone had arranged in front of a votive candle. "Did you know? The tradition of leaving flowers for the dead originated in ancient Greece. They believed that if flowers blossomed on a loved one's grave, it was a message from the next world. That they'd found happiness in the ever-blooming meadows of asphodel, in the embrace of eternity."

Closing her eyes, Tori tried to imagine Luke standing in Roy's endless field of flowers. It was too pretty a picture for such an ugly murder. There'd been no body left behind for her to offer a bouquet. An empty coffin rotted beneath his headstone.

"It's been almost two years since I lost my brother, Luke. Lucien Anestis Jaecar," she confessed like a sinner. His name felt forbidden on her lips. It'd been trapped in her memories for far too long. "My twin."

The word "twin" sparked the faintest flicker of surprise in Roy's expression.

"My younger twin. My other half," she whispered. "He was killed, Roy. By a monster like Orion's hounds, only worse."

The river in her soul rushed over its banks, flooding her with emotions she couldn't hold back. Tears welled in her eyes. The last thing she ever wanted to do was cry in front of Roy, but the relentless current crashed through her, dragging her under.

"The day I met you... The only reason I got into Vince's car... It wasn't because I'm brave, or strong, or capable of saving anyone. I did it because after twenty months, two days, and nine hours, there hasn't been a single second—not now, not ever—that I haven't missed my baby brother."

Roy spoke of flowers and messages. Of something greater than them all.

She couldn't swallow the truth about such things, or those poor teenaged ghosts, when her lungs were already so full of pain that she couldn't breathe.

"I couldn't stand it anymore. All that silence where there should've been laughter. All that solitude. All that never-ending gray. If I didn't do *something*, I'd spend the rest of my life waiting to see him again."

Now the tears flowed freely.

"And if I put myself in danger, maybe, just maybe that wait would end a little sooner."

She choked. She was drowning.

A touch on her hand calmed the waters. Fingers closed around hers and pulled her to shore. Roy guided her across the boundary of the living and the dead. Together, they returned to the here and now.

Compared to that raging river, the cathedral was deafeningly silent.

Tori dried her eyes with her sleeve. "S-sorry, I don't know what came over me..."

Now that she'd poured her heart out, she was empty.

Shame dripped in, drop by drop, filling the void.

She'd never broken down like that in front of anyone before. Not even Luke.

Roy's grip on her tightened. "Never apologize for who you are, Miss Jaecar."

"I'm apologizing because I just started crying out of nowhere. Because I miss some guy you've never met, who has nothing to do with anything."

"You started crying because you have a reason to cry."

A pause.

"I won't pretend to know what it feels like to lose a sibling, but I do know a thing or two about people's ability to change. You'll always miss Luke. But you're also brave and strong, and fully capable of saving others."

Another pause. He met her eyes.

"Miss Jaecar. Many people will die before this is over. For them, we can only offer flowers and hope that Hades is a kinder ruler than Death. But as long as I am here, you need not fear Hades or Death. You and I... Vince, Brooks, and perhaps Grace, too... We will save more than we lose."

He squeezed her hands in his.

"You can have faith in that."

Tori believed him.

Roy had underestimated her, in a way. She'd already changed since meeting him. While she didn't care about her own safety, she cared about the orange horizon, windowless skyscrapers, and charred bodies that waited in her future.

Together, they would change that future. They would ensure that good triumphed over evil with their own two hands. And when she finally reunited with Luke, he would be proud to call her his sister.

She exhaled, long and slow, letting all her built-up anxiety and agony escape her chest. She would be okay. "We can do this," she agreed.

He smiled. He released her.

She hadn't realized just how much she'd been leaning on him. She almost had to grab him again to catch herself.

"Let's... Let's go back!" Heat burned in her cheeks. As if crying in front of him wasn't bad enough.

He nodded.

Roy led her out into the morning sun, wreathed in red, yellow, and white.

Tori winced from the sudden change in lighting. When her eyes adjusted, she saw a path forward. "Roy." She retrieved Grace's flash drive from her pocket. She'd almost forgotten about it. "Remember this flash drive I told you about earlier? From the vault underneath Channel 4."

He sized up the flash drive. It was pink. It sparkled. "Narcy sure has interesting taste..."

He did, but this was Grace's flash drive, and that was beside the point. "There's a program on here. It seemed important, but I couldn't get it to run."

"Right, you'd mentioned that. Does it need a password? An RSA key?"

Why did it not surprise Tori that Roy knew what an RSA key was for?

"No. I suspect it won't work unless I'm on a Tianyi network."

She opened her work email on her phone. "But I have a plan." This was it. All those boring years at her fintech firm would finally pay off. She'd be the hero of host-not-found errors.

"Oh?" He was usually the one with the plan. Twice now, she'd usurped him.

"I can't wait to hear it."

CHAPTER TWENTY-THREE

"What!?" Grace clasped her cheeks. "You've never been to a zoo before?"

"Nope. Never really got the chance." Zoos were part of the normal childhood that Vincent Lenoir had missed out on. Government housing programs didn't have the budget for outings, and he couldn't imagine Roy and Brooks taking him. Besides, lions, tigers, and bears weren't exotic compared to mythical beasts.

She turned to Brooks. "Can we go now? Please?"

Vince, Grace, and Brooks had come to Forest Park searching for Tori. No matter how peaceful the past two weeks had been, the danger was still out there. It wasn't safe for her to be alone.

Vince, too, had been spooked by those teenaged ghosts. But he had experience, cigarettes, a full flask, and a junk food habit to help him pay down the costs of failure. He couldn't accept that bad things that happened to innocent people weren't his fault, but he could board up those feelings with the other skeletons in his closet. He could cope.

Today's odyssey ended quickly. Just as they arrived at Forest

Park, Roy texted that Tori was safe. That he had the situation handled.

Vince, Grace, and Brooks could've gone home. No one wanted to.

Flowers bloomed along the sidewalks. Sun-baked grass and sprawling oak trees flourished as far as the eye could see. The enormous park was full of life. And after such an emotional morning, they all needed some sunlight.

Brooks sat with a leg crossed on a stone retaining wall. Deftly, meticulously, he re-organized his medical kit. "Isn't the zoo on the opposite end of Forest Park?" He'd insisted on waiting for Roy and Tori somewhere public, where it would be harder for them to be attacked without witnesses.

They loitered at the edge of an ice rink that'd been converted into a shuffleboard area for the summer. It wasn't a popular location on a weekday morning, but joggers and dog walkers passed by frequently enough.

"Miss Jaecar and Mercy should be back soon. I don't think it's a good idea."

Vince exhaled his relief. Grace looked so excited that he would have gone along for her sake, but after his recent visit to Narcissus' human zoo, he wasn't keen on more iron bars and cages. "It's kinda hot out, anyways."

Grace was a different person in the daylight. She didn't belong underground, surrounded by death, or cooped up in some fancy apartment tower. Despite the horrors of the labyrinth, she practically glowed with optimism and cheer.

Vince had never met someone so bright before.

"That's okay. We can stop and smell these flowers instead!" Grace selected a blossom. She offered it to him. "Pink. For gratitude. We never would've made it out of the labyrinth without that lighter of yours!"

Yep, way too bright. He averted his eyes. Accepting her gift, he twisted its stem between his fingers. It was familiar. "Are these the same flowers you had in your mother's room?"

"They are!" She was pleased that he remembered. "These are carnations. My mother loved them." She cupped one between her hands. "Aren't they pretty?"

"Y-yeah," he mumbled.

Pretty indeed. Somehow, as she smiled into those pristine petals, she seemed sad and happy at the same time. He wondered what it felt like to remember a parent so fondly.

He gestured at an impressive plant with dozens of cream-colored flowers. It towered almost as tall as Brooks. "What's this one called?"

"That's a hydrangea."

"Really?" That brought him back to Mimosa Hall and its moonlit gardens. "Tori showed me some hydrangeas once, but they were blue."

"There are many different kinds of hydrangea. It's a versatile, hardy plant," Grace explained, plopping down next to him on a bench. She held up a forked leaf like a kid doing show and tell. "This one's an oakleaf hydrangea. We had a huge bush of these in the back of our garden, near the... near the..."

The leaf fell to the ground.

"Near what?"

"*Narcissus*. Our hydrangea was near our daffodils, also known as narcissuses." She hit her palm with her fist. "I thought that name sounded familiar!"

"Well," Brooks breathed. "It sure doesn't seem like he was turned into a flower..."

"Is that how his legend ends?"

"According to mythology, yes."

Vince blew air through his nose. "Not if I have anything to say about it." That ending would be far too pleasant for a man who'd threatened his friends.

"Maybe revenge isn't a good idea, Vince. What Narcissus did... that was some kind of mind control, wasn't it? Who knows what other powers he has up his sleeve?" Grace's voice trembled in the breeze. "Wouldn't it be better to avoid seeing him again?"

Grace was a total mystery. The woman was afraid of her own shadow... and cracks in the sidewalk... and ladders... and black cats. And their visit to Channel 4 had been one fresh terror after another.

As far as she was concerned, Vince, Tori, Roy, and Brooks were strangers. And suspicious as hell. They'd given her no reason to trust them. He would've expected her to run as far away from them as possible by now.

Yet she'd invited them into her home. She slept soundly at night surrounded by guns, with nothing to protect her except a thin door.

He chewed his lower lip. "Grace... Don't take this the wrong way, but why are you still here?"

"Wh-what do you mean?"

"I mean, why'd you stick around after we almost got you killed? You don't know us, and this isn't your fight."

She recovered the hydrangea leaf from the ground. She traced a finger along its veins. "I'm coming with you. If that's okay," she whispered in a tone even smaller than she was.

The look on her face made Vince's heart drop. He hadn't meant to reject her. "Of course it's okay! It's just... We'll catch the bad guys soon. You don't have to be involved." There was still hope for her. She could lead a normal life. "You're not... like us."

"No, I'm not." She clenched her fists. "That's why I have to come with you."

"What do you mean?" Brooks asked gently.

She faltered.

Without thinking, Vince placed a hand on her arm.

Grace's stormy eyes met his. She dug a handful of colorful

paperclips out of her purse. She held up a blue one. Slowly, purposefully, it bent itself into the shape of a horse.

Brooks nearly dropped the bandage he'd been wrapping.

Her performance reminded Vince of twisted spoons. He'd never seen anything like it, except in one of those Vegas magic shows that aired on late night television. "You're... psychic?" He reached for the tiny horse.

She lost her concentration.

Static shocked his fingers. He yelped.

"Magnetism, then?" Brooks guessed. "Using electricity."

She nodded.

"Ever since my mom's accident, I've been able to, uh. Do things that others can't. Impossible things. Like attracting cans from across the room." She placed the horse in Vince's palm, giving him an apologetic look.

"And it's been getting stronger. So much stronger. Back in the labyrinth, I deflected a bullet! Isn't that supposed to be nearly impossible to do with a magnetic field?" She crunched her remaining paperclips in her grasp. "What if I'm a monster, just like Orion, Narcissus, and Asterius?"

"Grace, you're not a monster—"

"How would you know!?" she blurted out. "My mom is young and healthy. The doctors never figured out what caused her coma. A real medical mystery. My father did something to her. He's one of the monsters you hunt. I've never been more sure of anything in my life!"

She faced Vince, desperate, pleading. She grabbed his wrists. "I need to find out who he is—no, who I am. It hurts to leave Mom behind, but... if I don't come with you, I'll never know!"

Vince recognized her expression. It was the expression of a person who carried a crushing weight on their shoulders. Who'd been betrayed by their parents. Who didn't care what happened to them anymore. He also recognized that determination in her tone—that pain of being abandoned, rejected, and left behind.

For the first time since he met Brooks and Roy, he found himself standing on the shores of an unknown sea. He braced against the bitter cold. The warmth of this month's temporary home was nothing but a faint glow in the distance, drowned out by the lights of the city. Above him spanned millions of stars, one for every adult in the world. There were so many, yet not a single one wanted him. He was alone.

Grace was alone, too, wasn't she? Without her mother.

He closed his fist over the figurine, careful not to damage it. It was a treasure.

"Don't worry, Grace." He didn't have a clue who her dad was. He wasn't sure that her powers were related to their mission. But he wouldn't abandon her to navigate that vast, endless sky on her own. "We'll help you find those answers," he promised.

Neither of them would ever be alone again. Not if he could help it.

Brooks looked as though he wanted to say something but changed his mind.

Come on Old Man, read the room!

"Right, Brooks?" Vince prompted.

"...Right," he agreed stiffly.

"Oh thank you!" Grace threw her arms around Vince, dragging him into a hug. "I was so worried you wouldn't want me slowing you down."

"D-don't thank me yet." God, she smelled good. Blood rushed to Vince's cheeks. He covered his face with his arm, but he was too late. Brooks was already staring him down, daring him to do something stupid.

As if. He couldn't think about that stuff right now. All he could think about is how he hoped Grace wouldn't regret her decision. The path before them was long, winding, and paved with heartache. He didn't deserve thanks. Even if he managed to keep this promise, he wasn't going to make her happier.

"Do you need some water, Vincent? You're looking a little red."

Vince almost fell out of his seat. He separated from Grace.

Roy leaned on the railing of the shuffleboard courts with the biggest grin Vince had ever seen. Tori hovered at his side. Fucking hypocrite.

Vince smoothed down his t-shirt. "You're back."

"We've been back." Tori dashed towards their bench. In an uncharacteristic burst of affection, she threw her arms around Grace.

"Grace, your power is incredible! It was you who saved us in the labyrinth, wasn't it? You stopped that bullet. And you exploded that spotlight! Thank you!"

"Welcome to the party, Miss Batya," Roy hummed, offering her his hand.

Grace blushed from all the attention.

"Th-thanks." She shook Roy's hand. "I'll do my best not to get in your way."

He winked. "I'm *positive* you'll be a huge help."

"If chicks keep joining at this rate, we'll be outnumbered soon," Vince observed. He, Brooks, and Roy had lived the bachelor life for what felt like forever. He was looking forward to the end of that era.

"*Women.*" Brooks corrected. "I'll be glad for that, since Mercy and I have clearly failed to teach you manners."

Chicks, women, people. It didn't matter. Vince's world was growing, little by little.

"Vincent will have plenty of time to practice his manners tomorrow," Roy announced. "We have a long drive ahead of us."

"That's right!" Tori pumped her fist. "Next stop: New York City!"

CHAPTER TWENTY-FOUR

Vincent Lenoir watched with bated breath. In the ombre glow of the failing sun, filtered through a wreath of trees, Grace was a divine princess descending from heaven. She didn't notice a mere mortal like him.

She pinched a steel-jacketed bullet between her fingers. Slowly, carefully, she aimed.

With a satisfying crack, she shot another bottle off a post.

Vince and Tori cheered.

Vince, Grace, and Tori lounged around a quiet park along the bank of a ruined canal. Leafy trees, crumbling stone, and a tangle of gravel paths hid them from the road. They were alone, save for the ducks that picked through the water lilies.

Per usual, Roy had run off on some unknown errand as soon as they'd parked. Meanwhile, Brooks had volunteered to find a place to crash for the night. And so, their charges enjoyed what would likely be their last opportunity to relax for a long while. By blowing stuff up.

"Do it again!" Vince raised a beer over his head, a toast to her success.

"That was almost eighty yards!" Tori cried. "You're getting so good at this."

"Th-thanks," Grace blushed.

"If you get much better, we won't need Vince anymore," Tori teased.

"Hah hah," he grumbled. Her joke wasn't funny.

Grace tilted her head. "Why's that?"

Weeks had passed since they'd escaped Channel 4. In all that time, Tori hadn't mentioned her fight with Vince once. Although he was happy to follow her lead and pretend it had never happened, they were both bad pretenders.

A heavy tension lingered between them. It was crushing. It was awkward.

Vince would let it suffocate him before he dared open his mouth. He wouldn't make her remember her defeat, even for an apology.

"Never mind that." He patted Grace on the shoulder. "She's right. You're amazing, Grace." Touching her felt sacrilegious. But she didn't pull away. "I knew you were someone special from the moment we met!"

Tori gagged on her drink.

"Tori! Are you okay?" Grace gasped.

Defeated, Tori flopped backwards. "No. My back is killing me." She stretched out in the grass. "Since when did saving the world involve so much driving?"

"Since you decided we had to go visit some office fifteen hours away," Vince replied.

All three of them were stiff and restless after spending the entire day crammed into Vince's car. Their road trip had ended maybe an hour west of their final destination: New York City. More specifically, Tianyi's North American headquarters. The Beijing software giant occupied fifteen floors of the historic Wool-worth Building.

St. Louis and New York City weren't exactly close, and the highways between them were far from scenic. Whenever Vince closed his eyes, he saw Pennsylvania license plates.

To make matters worse, the back seat of his Mustang was... intimate. They'd taken turns sitting with their knees shoved against the center console. Vince didn't understand why Brooks had refused to let Tori ride with him and Roy. Wasn't she his new favorite?

At least Vince and Tori had Grace with them this time. Whenever things got weird between Vince and Tori, Grace saved the day with small talk. Her bag had an infinite supply of snacks. Somehow, she'd even convinced them to play road trip games.

At first, both Vince and Tori had been too self-conscious to get excited over billboards with the letter "Z" on them or solving extra-hard clues in I Spy. But they were both so competitive they warmed up to each other.

Vince talked about his dream of owning a classic car with modern upgrades. Grace explained the traits of the 12 different zodiac signs—both astrological and Chinese—in extreme detail. Tori complained about her brother's crazy exes. And then the conversation turned boring.

Once Tori and Grace brought up work, it was all over for Vince. The two women commiserated about pointless meetings, sexist coworkers, and crappy bosses for so long that he'd resorted to playing road trip games by himself. They might as well have been speaking a foreign language.

He'd never sat at a desk, written a resume, or had anything resembling a career. When he was a teenager, he'd worked odd jobs here and there, but his money almost always got stolen or confiscated. It wasn't a good memory. For that matter, neither was New York.

Gasping, Grace pointed at the horizon. "Look! I can see the city from here!"

New York City glowed as bright as the sunset, a heavenly

paradise at the end of the hero's journey. And to Grace and Tori, it was one. Neither woman had ever been there. There, somewhere in that concrete labyrinth, they would find what they were looking for.

But for Vince, it was a step backwards in time—to the humble beginning of his journey. Once upon a time, he'd lived near New York City. He hadn't been back since meeting Roy and Brooks. And although he would never admit it, deep down, he was afraid. The monsters that lurked in his memories were more terrifying than Orion, Narcissus, and Asterius combined.

Tori frowned. "Why don't we fly between cities?"

"You can't fly with weapons." Or at least that was the bull-shit excuse Roy always gave Vince. Roy and Brooks took airplanes regularly. They'd clearly figured that one out. He wasn't stupid.

Dutifully Grace cleaned up the glass from her target practice. "I'm glad we got to ride together. It feels like I've gotten to know you both a little better."

"Nothing says friendship like listening to the entire eight disk catalog of Siren Song." Tori lied. "I can see why she's topped the pop music charts for so many years."

Grace lit up. "Oh, I'm so glad you like her too! Her music gets into my soul. When I hear it, I think of my mother, healing sunlight, and drowning in wine." She clutched at her chest, her hand over heart. "Sometimes, I feel like she's the only one who really understands me."

Siren Song's voice reminded Vince of nails on a chalkboard, but he wouldn't dare say that now.

"I know what you mean," Tori lied again. "We should listen to her again on our way to Tianyi. For extra inspiration! Don't you agree, Vince?"

He didn't like the look she was giving him.

"Maybe I'll listen with you!" a fourth voice announced.

Vince almost fell off the fence he was sitting on. "Jesus Roy! Do you always have to sneak up to people like that?"

"I don't know about my mother..." Roy emerged from the parking lot. His truck was nowhere in sight. "...but I sure could use a fountain of wine." He smiled at Vince. "Seems like you could, too."

"How about an IPA instead?" Tori tossed him one from their twelve pack.

In one fluid motion, Roy caught the bottle and popped the lid off on his belt buckle. "Is Brooks not back yet?" He took a sip.

"Nope," Vince grunted. "Maybe the old man broke his hip. Or maybe his dementia finally kicked in."

"Well... In that case..." Roy tapped his lip thoughtfully. "Miss Jaecar. Do you mind helping me for a moment? I'd like to review our plans for Tianyi."

Tori scrambled to her feet. "O-of course."

"Perfect!" He slipped his arm around her shoulders. "This shouldn't take long..." He guided her in the direction he'd come from. It was a good thing he had a grip on her, because she almost tripped twice as she followed. She was too busy paying attention to him to watch where she stepped.

Roy didn't need help reviewing any fucking plans.

Now Vince understood why Brooks hadn't let Tori ride in Roy's truck. Watching Roy flirt so shamelessly made him want to give him a piece of his mind—fucking hypocrite. But Tori looked so damned happy that he kept his mouth shut.

"Be safe!" Grace waved goodbye.

Once they disappeared into the distance, she plopped down next to Vince. Her toes dangled inches above the ground.

Until now, he hadn't realized just how short she was. Her high heels were impractical, maybe, but they certainly added presence. Without them, with her right at his side, she seemed so delicate. Like she would break if he squeezed her too hard. No one would guess from a glance that she could fire a bullet with the force of a gun.

Someone special indeed.

Finally, Vince was alone with Grace. He'd wanted this chance all day, but now that he had it, he had no idea what to say. He couldn't sit still. He couldn't even think. He needed a cigarette. Would she judge him if he smoked in front of her?

"So, uh. How long have you been a weather girl?" He cleared his throat. "I mean, weather woman." Damnit Brooks.

"A few years." She peered into the still, dark waters of the canal. "Time flies, doesn't it?"

"Do you like it?"

"I suppose so."

"That almost sounds like a no."

She shook her head. "I wanted to be a meteorologist since I was a little girl."

"Then why..." Why had she suddenly slumped? Why wouldn't she face him?

"We're so small, aren't we, Vince?" Wistfully, she turned her gaze upwards. "I've always been in awe of this world we live in, and even more so, the fact that people can look up at that great wide sky and read the future." She made a square with her thumb and index fingers and held it so the moon was in the center frame. "Where will tornadoes form? When will spring flowers bloom? Will it snow for Christmas?" She dropped her hands. "It wasn't until after college that I realized that meteorology these days is all computers and math. I've, er. Never been the best in academics. So I became a weatherwoman instead."

"Being a weatherwoman is cool. I never could've done it," Vince countered. He didn't understand the difference between a meteorologist and a weatherwoman. What he did understand was how it felt to be ashamed of school performance. He understood that perhaps better than anyone. "I'm probably worse at academics than you are. Whenever I try to read a textbook, all of the letters get jumbled in my head. Numbers, too."

She smiled, sympathetic. "Even if I had been good at academics, it wouldn't be the same. Weather loses a bit of its magic when it's reduced to numbers." Her smile faded. "And forecasting loses its mystery when you're just a pretty face reading a script. I always thought I'd be able to move people if I worked hard. But I'm just too..."

"...Is that why you want to try acting?" he asked softly.

Her face lit up. "A-ah, you remembered that?"

For once, he knew exactly what to do. "Hell yeah I remembered that! You're going to be my leading lady..." He hopped off the fence. "...starting right now!"

"R-right now?"

"You heard me. Who knows how long Roy will monopolize Tori? And we'll be as old as Brooks before he's done picking a motel." He brandished his phone like a sword. "This is the perfect opportunity to film the next thrilling chapter of *Haunt Hunt!*"

"I don't know if I..." She wouldn't meet his eyes, but he could tell she was interested.

Sunset. A still, black river. Crumbling buildings. This park was a prime for a ghost story. "In today's episode, the new heroine Grace Batya rescues the hero Vincent Lenoir from the vengeful Lady of the Lake!"

"L-Lady of the Lake?"

"The Lady of the Lake was one of the most successful women of her era..." He gained momentum. "...but after her husband and son died under mysterious circumstances, she rowed off into the mist, never to be seen again." He leaned closer, lowering his voice. "Alive, that is. Now her spirit haunts waterways, dragging unsuspecting men to their deaths to keep her company!"

Too much. Grace shrank away. "Th-that's... is that a real thing? Is there one here!?"

"What? No. I just made that last part up." Vince withdrew, rubbing the back of his head. "There are a zillion legends like that. Remember the White Lady? And Lamia, La Llorona, etcetera. We're in the wrong part of New York to see the Lady of the Lake, anyways."

That was the appeal of *Haunt Hunt's* ghost stories, after all. They were fascinating, mysterious, and most importantly, fake. Tonight, Vince and Grace would save the day without risking their lives.

"O-oh. Okay! What do you need me to do?"

"Hmm... Let's start with the opening." Vince surveyed their surroundings. A large, heavy, rotten gate spanned the canal. It hung ajar. Murky water pooled between its doors. An opening.

"Here, stand on this." He patted one of the stone walls the gate was attached to. "There I can get a nice wide shot of you, the canal, and the woods."

She nodded.

He offered her a hand as she climbed the wall.

"Alright. Just hang out there for a sec." Holding up his phone, he backed away until she was visible head to toe on his screen. "I'll say a few words. Then we can move onto the first scene."

But the words never came.

When Vince looked at Grace through his lens, he was speechless.

The atmosphere wasn't spooky—it was ethereal. As moonlight kissed her pale skin, her divinity was undeniable. She completely outshone the drowned canal and shattered the forest around her. She wasn't like him. She was powerful. She was radiant.

His camera refocused.

A shadow loomed behind her. It held a sickle to her neck.

Vince's blood ran cold. His body went numb. Despite the heat of summer, he could see his breath in the air.

A monster? No, this was a person on a horse. A person without a head.

Even without expressions, the headless horseman's intentions were clear. It reeked of death and oozed with rage. It wasn't friendly.

When Grace noticed its reflection in the water below, her face twisted with terror. She screamed.

Vince dropped his phone and drew his revolver. By the time he found his trigger, before his phone even hit the ground, the headless horseman was gone.

He rushed to Grace. He scooped her off the wall.

She trembled, but she was fine.

Relief knocked him to his knees.

She threw her arms around him, tears clouding her eyes. "What was that!?"

He hugged her close. "I don't know."

The feeling returned to his fingers. With her body against his, he warmed up quickly.

"What's going on here!?" Brooks scolded as he approached from the parking lot. "I leave you alone for five minutes..."

"Brooks! There was a..." A what? Vince couldn't identify anything from what he saw. "Something attacked Grace."

Instantly the parent transformed into a soldier. "Is she okay? What about Tori?"

"She's with Roy."

Brooks' frown confirmed Vince's theory about their car situation.

"Protect Grace, okay Brooks?" Vince begged. "I'm gonna take a look around. Make sure it's not still hiding somewhere."

His weapon drawn, he scaled the wall Grace had been standing on.

A shock of yellow caught his eye. A sticky note?

He lifted it into the light.

Nine numbers scrawled in black ink across the crumpled paper —a curse that brought his whole world crashing down.

"Vince..." Brooks picked up on his shock. "What is it?"

"A phone number." Vince would never forget who it belonged to.

How the hell did a headless, horse-riding, sickle-wielding shadow know Nancy Kingfisher?

CHAPTER TWENTY-FIVE

Vincent Lenoir had never visited a place more appropriately named than Sleepy Hollow. The journey here guided him and Grace through magical woodlands, brick buildings, and lush fields, all with the scenic Hudson Valley as a backdrop. On a weekend, the small town would've been crowded with tourists. Early on a workday, it was quiet, still, and slow.

Vince and Grace had spent the last hour exploring the Sleepy Hollow Cemetery. Inside, a church watched over scattered headstones, a teacher and his students. Giant old trees worshiped a flawless sky. They passed monuments to the rich and famous. Grace stopped to read the plaques on every single one. They were alone the entire time, except for the occasional walker, a groundskeeper, and an elderly couple, all of whom smiled and waved as they passed.

The graveyard wasn't mysterious or sinister like their Headless Horseman had been. It was peaceful.

But Vince wasn't at peace. He couldn't rest until he had some answers.

After their encounter with the Headless Horseman, he'd pulled an all-nighter researching monster folklore, a task so boring he normally couldn't stick to it for longer than ten minutes. He found no leads in Greek mythology. There were two promising prospects closer to home.

One was the dullahan, a demonic fairy that wielded human spines and killed with a single look. Metal, but probably not their culprit. Vince and Grace were both still alive.

The other was the Headless Horseman of Sleepy Hollow, the spirit of a British soldier doomed to an eternal search for his missing head. At midnight, under the full moon, he rode through the streets of the small town just north of New York City. Supposedly.

Stubborn and sleep deprived, Vince had insisted on hunting his haunt the next morning. Grace, who felt responsible, begged to tag along. Meanwhile Tori, Brooks, and Roy stayed behind at their motel to prepare for their upcoming appointment at Tianyi.

Nancy Kingfisher wasn't responding to Vince's calls or texts. That was nothing new, of course. It'd been years since the fight that had gotten her kicked out of Maylee's father's house—a fight that'd been Vince's fault.

Vince only ever made Nancy's problems worse. She had too many bad memories associated with him. She never wanted to see him again.

He didn't give a fuck what she wanted right now. The monster from last night might not be some undead redcoat, but it was definitely dangerous. He needed to know that she was okay. Besides, she didn't need to see him to pick up her damned phone.

He kicked an innocent pinecone off the gravel path.

Grace examined a blue and gold sign with rapt interest. It claimed that the Headless Horseman legend had climaxed in this very spot, which was probably bullshit. She ran her fingers over the raised letters one by one.

"What are you doing?"

"Shhh..." Her focus was so intense that he was surprised she heard him. "I'm trying to listen."

Listen? Suddenly he was interested. As far as Vince understood, Grace's powers revolved around metal. So far, she'd only used them to smash things. It would be wonderfully convenient if she could do more. "Has metal ever spoken to you before?"

For a long, uncomfortable moment, she ignored him.

Finally, she leaned back. She nodded in satisfaction.

"Nope!" she replied. "Never."

He opened his mouth to ask for clarification, but he thought better of it. Instead, he drowned his confusion with a sip from his flask. So what if her behavior was a little weird? It was a little cute, too.

Moving on from the sign, she spun in place. "I just feel... connected to this place. Like I've been here before." Broken sunlight brushed her skin, giving her an ethereal glow. Her Elysian eyes fell on a bridge. "Oh. I have."

Vince stepped onto the bridge. "You've been here before? When?" Nothing about it seemed special. The plain wooden structure spanned a shallow stream. The water below was as sleepy as the hollow. Could there be a hidden torrent hidden beneath that calm, clear current?

Averting her eyes, Grace twirled a lock of hair between her fingers. "In a dream."

"A dream?"

"Lately, I've been having the same dream over and over." She followed him onto the bridge. "A man holds a woman in his arms. He tucks a carnation behind her ear." Swooning, she hugged her shoulders. "He's handsome, put-together, and strangely electric. Ah, and he has a beard!" That was an important detail. "Though I'm not usually into men with facial hair."

Good to know. "What about the woman?"

"She's... How should I describe her?" She stared at her reflection in the creek below. "Her hair is light, even more so than mine. She's slender. Pretty. Fragile. Like a songbird in a cage. Only the cage is wide open. She's too busy looking at him to think about escaping. But then someone approaches. The man disappears, leaving the woman alone at the crossroads."

"What happens next?"

"I wake up. I'm not sure who they are, but I'm one hundred and fifty percent sure they were on this very bridge." She tugged at his sleeves. "It sounds crazy, I know. But I believe it was real."

Was she really worried he would think she was crazy? Vince took her hands and squeezed them lightly. "I believe you." Compared to her communion with a signpost, her dream was crazy normal.

Besides, this wasn't his first rodeo with dreams grounded in reality. If only he, too, had seen star crossed lovers instead of Spearfinger's eyeless scowl.

"Mom always told me that dreams are messages from heaven."

"Do you think your dream has something to do with the Headless Horseman?"

"Maybe." Grace was back to her bright and bubbly self. She bounded across the bridge. She climbed onto a mossy boulder for a better view of the area. "Maybe we can find some clues nearby!"

The Headless Horseman didn't strike Vince as a romance fan. Perhaps this graveyard had other supernatural stories. "I'll see if I can find anything online." He squinted at his phone. No service. "Or not."

So close to New York City, dead zones were more mysterious than ghosts. His phone must've broken somehow.

He started towards Grace. He stepped off the bridge. "Hey, can I borrow your—"

Death metal drowned out his question. Someone was calling him.

"What the fuck?" Vince checked his phone again. "Tori Jaecar" flashed across the screen under four full bars of signal.

He headed back where he came from.

The music abruptly stopped.

Once was an accident, twice was a coincidence. If it happened a third time, they might've found their clue.

Right on cue, Siren Song shattered the silence.

Vince winced. He would never get used to that dramatic, ringing voice. It wasn't just grating; it was familiar. Hearing it made him feel like he was forgetting something important. But how could screeching about painting the town with color or boring boy-meets-girl stories be important?

"That must be Tori," Grace guessed. She dug her phone out of her purse.

"Don't answer that!" he shouted.

Starting, she dropped it to the ground.

"My bad." He hadn't meant to scare her. "I mean... Can you bring that over here? I want to test a theory."

Obediently she delivered the device.

Her ringtone fell silent against the gentle hush of running water. Just like before.

She caught on. "Ooooh. What could be causing this? The bridge?"

Not likely. There were patterns to phenomena like these. "Like you said earlier, we're at a crossroads." Vince hopped over the railing. He landed in the stream with a splash. There was more lurking in this stream than water. He'd bet his car on it.

He kicked around the riverbed. Nothing but rocks, sand, and bottle caps.

A cloud drifted overhead, blinding the sun.

Drenched in shadow and wet up to his waist, Vince shivered.

"Vince!" Grace cried. "Behind you!"

He wheeled, fists raised. The sight of a woman below him drained away all his fight.

She was breathtaking. A tangle of wild hair swirled around her flawless face. Large dark eyes full of curiosity peered up at him. She floated in the swell, motionless and harmless.

The shade shifted.

A sliver of light kissed her skin.

The serene spirit vanished. A horrible monster with sharp scales, bony limbs, and a lipless smirk full of teeth replaced her. A ridge arched from her back like a sail. She rose from the depths, clawing at him, trying to drag him under.

Suffocating fog swirled in his head. Lamia. La Llorona. *The Lady of the Lake.* How long had it been since he last breathed? Why couldn't he now?

Desperate, he drew his revolver.

"Wait!" Grace hugged his arm against her chest. Her warmth reached him.

He faltered.

Delicately, as though handling glass, she released him. She turned to his attacker.

Leaning closer, she brushed a hand along the monster's cheek. She maintained eye contact, unphased by that horrible appearance, never letting go.

"You're beautiful," she said in a trancelike whisper. She meant it.

The word "beautiful" cut through the Lady of the Lake as cleanly as any knife. A mournful cry escaped her lips.

Wounded on the inside, she fled downstream.

Oxygen flooded Vince's lungs. He collapsed into the shallows, gasping for more. Each breath dispersed the fog, little by little. It left behind a dull pain that gnawed at his thoughts. It was difficult to speak. "How... How did you know to do that?"

The spell broke. Grace clutched her chest with the same hand that had touched the beast. "I don't know." She remembered something. "Wasn't the Lady of the Lake supposed to live somewhere else?"

"Guess she moved."

"What should we do?"

His gaze drifted in the direction the Lady of the Lake had gone.

The stream glittered before them. It called to him; a siren's song; a road to their destiny.

He recalled the map posted at the entrance of Sleepy Hollow Cemetery. That was... the Pocantico River? It emptied into the great Hudson, which spanned half of New York.

Groaning, he stood. Water dripped from his jeans, t-shirt, and jacket. He was gonna need some new clothes.

"Our little adventure just got a lot bigger."

And more annoying.

CHAPTER TWENTY-SIX

"You can't be serious, Vince," Brooks stated flatly.

"Serious as a heart attack," Vincent Lenoir stood his ground. "This is important to me."

The word "important" strained Brooks so much that an actual heart attack wasn't out of the question. Sighing, he switched off the burner of the old electric stove in front of him. Tonight's spaghetti sauce would have to wait.

For once, their run-down motel suite had a kitchenette. It even had a white-speckled pot and a spatula. He didn't have to jerry rig a coffee pot or boil water in the microwave. Making dinner should've been easy.

"You want to waste your time searching the entire Hudson Valley for some unknown monster? Instead of coming to Tianyi with us? And you're going to drag Miss Batya along with you?"

Vince wouldn't let making dinner be easy. "Glad you understand."

Even before meeting Tori, Vince, Brooks, and Roy had encountered unknown monsters on a regular basis. Compared to the threat of a presidential plot, or some prophecy that doomed Atlanta, neither the Headless Horseman nor the Lady of the Lake could be considered important. But for Vince, grand stakes didn't compare to ones with a face and a name.

Not one, but two ghosts haunted Nancy Kingfisher's phone number.

There was no such thing as a coincidence.

Something, somewhere had gone terribly wrong.

"It's fine, isn't it?" Tori suggested. "We're less likely to get caught if we sneak two people into Tianyi instead of four. Besides, do you honestly think Vince could pass for an office worker?"

Normally Vince might've asked her what the hell that was supposed to mean, but even he knew to keep his mouth shut while she was helping him.

Brooks looked to Roy for backup.

Roy, who couldn't care less, shrugged.

Grace did her best to disappear against the beige walls. She didn't like arguing.

"It's not about that," Brooks insisted. "It's just so... selfish."

"You're calling me selfish for worrying about my best friend!?"

Brooks untied his leather apron. He hung it on the back of the chair next to him. He wore it so often—cooking, gunsmithing, or even at the laundromat—that it'd become part of his mask. While had it on, he was a caretaker, not a calloused killer. When the apron came off, the gloves came off. He planned to fight this battle.

"Every time we go on one of these missions, we're risking our lives. Our best chance of survival is to face them together. Especially since Nancy's already—"

He bit off the end of his sentence. It'd been a mistake.

"Already *what?*" Vince pressed.

Stiffly, reluctantly, Brooks whispered, "Nancy's been missing since her stepfather kicked her out."

In a flash, tension flooded the room. It would explode at any moment.

"Miss Jaecar. Miss Batya," Roy coughed. "I'm suddenly in the mood for sushi. Care to join me?"

The innocent bystanders couldn't evacuate fast enough.

Grace had barely closed the front door behind her when Vince swept Brooks' spaghetti sauce right off the laminate counter.

A crash. Crimson stained the carpet. Hot, sticky liquid clung to shards of glass. Vince never really got modern art, but as he stared down at the disaster at his feet, he saw himself in those scattered droplets.

In one long, runny streak, he mingled with Roy and Brooks. Their truck trailed blood along the road, across the country.

In the broken jar, he noticed the circles under his eyes. Ragged nights reflected in the broken pieces. He tossed and turned in a cramped back seat, on a pullout couch in a cockroach infested motel, alone, under a cold, starless sky.

There was a smudge of red for each bullet he'd fired. There was a smear for every Spearfinger stalking through the darkness, for every mother lost in between, and for every life smashed into dirt by cruel, unfeeling evil.

Roy, Brooks, and Vince had failed to save someone so many times that Vince had stopped counting. Now he'd failed to save Nancy Kingfisher, the only someone who'd ever understood him.

"Vince." Brooks seldom swore. Instead, he breathed that name in an infuriatingly even, unemotional tone. He disapproved.

Vince would've preferred to be cursed.

"Calm down. I know you're upset, but there's no reason to break things—"

"Calm down? After you and Roy fucking lied to me for years!?"

"You don't know how long Roy and I searched for her. She's alive, but she doesn't want to be found," Brooks explained. "We didn't tell you because we knew you'd react like this."

"Oh. You wanted to spare my feelings. How kind of you. Too

bad you didn't think to spare my feelings when you strong-armed a lost fourteen year old into fighting monsters with you."

For his entire adult life, Vince had chased at Brooks and Roy's heels. He'd abandoned high school without looking back. He'd sacrificed his sanity for the better good. And sometimes he actually helped. He murdered a man-eating werewolf. He rescued a doctor from his vampire girlfriend. He snatched a damsel in distress from the claws of banshees. It was never enough.

The people he couldn't help haunted him, day and night, in the bottom of every bottle of whiskey. Nancy was the last person—no, the last thing—on earth who connected him to the living.

Spearfinger, the Cherokee boogeyman, had murdered Nancy's mother.

But Nancy was stronger than Vince. She moved on. She got her therapy. Throughout his teenage years, she'd phoned him every week to complain about school, chatter about comics, and give progress updates on her dream of being a famous singer. He ached for those fleeting glimpses into the life he was missing. He didn't even mind when she gushed about boys.

That window was shut. Forever.

All because he'd opened his big mouth.

And that bastard, Nancy's stepfather.

Nancy's stepfather was so self-centered he made Roy disappear-for-days Angelus seem responsible by comparison. The professional musician lived in his own fantasies. He hid away in his studio, or on some scenic horizon, or at the top of a high rise halfway across the world, in some endless search for inspiration. He couldn't function in modern society. He didn't try.

Whenever that piece of work did remember he had a daughter, he doted on Maylee. Meanwhile he barely remembered to feed Nancy.

Literally. Vince watched from afar as Nancy grew weaker and thinner, a bay tree wilting and withering in winter. Her dream faded. One night she blacked out while driving back from class. She woke up in a hospital, wired to a half dozen machines, speaking nonsense in a panic. Roy had called it dactylic hexameter, a kind of poetry. To Vince, it was a cry for help. She could've died. Yet her stepdad didn't even bother to check on her.

She deserved better. After all she'd been through, she deserved to be happy.

Vince had told her as much. Every single day. And finally, one night, he'd convinced her to tell her stepdad, too. Loudly. With lots of screaming.

Her stepdad could not be reached with words, no matter their volume, no matter their meaning. He kicked her out of his house. Someday, once she grew up, she would thank him. It was all in the name of tough love.

Love? What a sick joke.

Vince didn't know a thing about love. He might have felt it once for Nancy, but their past had become too muddied with guilt and regret for him to be certain.

The monsters he faced bared their fangs and claws from the darkest corners of his nightmares. What hope was there for humanity if they also lurked among family, in broad daylight?

Brooks could be one of them. Easily. The tired old man had witnessed the same tragedies, defeated the same villains, and suffered the same losses as Vince. He'd even served in the military. He'd survived the raw, senseless devastation of war. He knew just how fucked up it was to raise a child as a soldier. He bickered with Roy about it regularly. But what else did he do about it?

Nothing. Absolutely nothing. He molded Vince into an Olympic athlete. He cooked him tasty, healthy meals, pushed him through brutal cardio, and coached him on lifting weights. He showed him how to fire a gun, how to cripple a moving target, and where to stab to deal the most damage. He dutifully, thoroughly went right along with the madness. He was obeying a commandment from heaven: thou shalt not win arguments with Roy.

Because of Vince's stupidity, Nancy was gone forever.

Because of Brooks' indifference, Vince had to suffer that loss all over again.

"But that's not important, is it, Brooks? What do I have to live for, anyways?" Vince uncapped his flask with his teeth. He emptied it down his throat.

"You're acting like a child," Brooks stated with practiced patience.

"No, Mom, you're treating me like a child."

"I still don't understand how 'Mom' is supposed to be an insult." Brooks shook his head, perplexed but perfectly calm.

It wasn't fair. He shouldn't be allowed to stay calm. Not while Vince and Nancy struggled against a crushing current of isolation and violence that threatened to drag them under whenever they closed their eyes.

"Then why don't I help you understand?" Vince had to destroy that composure. He had to confirm for himself that Brooks was human. "You're not my mom. You're not my dad." The words flowed faster and faster as painful memories surged through him. He couldn't breathe. Not until they were all out of him. "You're not my parent. You're not anyone's parent." Brooks had said so himself, once upon a time. "Not anymore! You're a lost cause, just like me."

His statement sank and expanded, filling the space between them, blood in water.

"You can't protect me," Vince gasped for air. He'd been shouting. "The only thing you can do for me..." His throat burned. He was at his limit. "... is fuck off!"

The swell subsided, spent.

In its reckless fury, it washed away everything but silence.

Brooks looked fine, but he wasn't. He couldn't make eye contact. His inhales were slow; his exhales were jagged. He gripped his spatula a little too tightly. The flimsy plastic handle cracked and bent. "Very well," he replied. Through sheer willpower, he kept his tone steady.

He swept out of the apartment. The door closed behind him with a final click.

Vince realized too late that he had gone too far.

Now that he'd driven away his mentor, he was alone, without Nancy, surrounded by monsters. The walls crowded around him. The room felt tiny, claustrophobic. The white speckles of Brooks' pot glared at him, a million tiny eyes, calculating, judging.

Brooks hadn't forced him to do anything. Brooks never harmed Nancy.

It was him. It was all his fault.

He had to escape. He rushed outside, into the parking lot.

CHAPTER TWENTY-SEVEN

A cool, crisp evening embraced Vincent Lenoir like an old friend. A breeze tousled his hair. And then an autumn chill clawed at his skin, sobering him in an instant. He did not want to be sober. He reached for his empty flask.

A gentle hand grasped his shoulder.

"Vincent," Roy whispered.

The timing of his arrival was suspicious. Somehow, some way, Brooks had summoned him.

Vince lowered his flask. The idea of Brooks, the stern, stoic captain needing reinforcements humbled him. "It's Vince," he corrected. His heart wasn't in it.

It didn't matter why Roy was here. His presence was a mercy. A second chance. A truck stop in the middle of the desert.

"Okay Vince," Roy relented. "Why don't you and I go for a walk?"

Vince lacked the energy to object. Obediently, he followed Roy into the parking lot, then up the road. In Roy's company he was a little less on edge; the cold felt a little less biting. He buried his hands in his pockets. He braced himself for the scolding that would surely come.

Roy never spoke. He led them away from their rental, up the street.

Sprawling evergreens and old A–framed buildings lined their path. They wandered through the middle of nowhere. The locals had long since settled for the evening. It was quiet. Still. Serene. Compared to cities that never slept and the roaring highways they normally explored, it was another planet.

Step by step, the tempest swirling inside of Vince subsided. Frustration replaced fear. Shame replaced anger. Together they drained away his bitterness, leaving behind only regret, pooling in his chest.

Their journey ended on a bridge over a railway. A stone rail guarded tracks below. Above everything, a billboard advertised a charity fund for victims of Mount Rainier's eruption. The volcano loomed in its background, king of all monsters.

Swinging his feet over, Vincent sat upon the stone wall. He breathed in, slow and deep, taking in the billboard. "You think whatever caused that is still out there?"

Roy settled next to him. "Maybe."

"Can we kill it?"

A dry laugh. "Maybe. I bet you can."

Vince hugged his knees. "About Brooks..." He swallowed. "I don't... I didn't mean..." His words stuck, thick and lumpy as glue.

"I know," Roy assured him. "He does, too."

"What happened to his kids?"

"You should ask him."

"I'm asking you."

"Their mother, she..." Roy leaned back on his palms, searching the night sky for inspiration. "Let's just say she wasn't meant to be a mother."

"They're not... did she...?"

"She did."

Vince had been afraid of that answer. Brooks' children weren't gone, they were dead. And he had used them against him as an insult. He couldn't imagine what that would feel like. He'd only just met Nancy's mother before she died, and he could never forget her.

He buried his face in his hands. He was the absolute worst.

"I met Brooks shortly afterwards," Roy continued, his expression unreadable. "That's probably the only reason he ever spoke to someone like me."

Vince peered up at him from between his fingers. "You have kids?"

"I do."

"Where are they?"

"They're all grown up now."

"Why not make them into monster hunters instead of me?"

Roy hesitated. "...They have their own monsters to hunt." He turned to Vince. "Besides, as Brook once put it, I'm not qualified to be a parent."

"Well that's great to hear from one of my..." Vince trailed off.

Brooks brought him chicken soup when he was sick with the flu. He patched the bullet holes in his favorite jacket. He taught him how to change the oil of his car and tie a tie.

Roy snuck out with him in the early hours of the morning to bars, clubs, and midnight movie showings. He coached him on talking to girls. He showed him how to shrug off the small things. To live unapologetically. To accept who he was.

Both of them had lives of their own with complicated pasts, difficult families, and uncertain futures. Yet they were always there for Vince. They kept him healthy. They kept him sane. They forgave him when he wasn't at his best.

Vince didn't understand why they'd invested so much into him. No matter how many monsters he helped them kill, there would always be more. No matter how many people they rescued, others would be eaten. Nancy would still be alone. Brooks' kids would still be dead. Roy would keep fighting with or without him.

"Roy," he choked through that oppressive burden. "What's the point? To all of this?"

"Not even I know the answer to that."

Of course. Roy had given Vince so much already. That was too much to ask.

Roy nudged him, leaning closer. "...Do you want to know *my* answer?"

Vince raised his head. "What?"

"You." Roy poked him in the chest. "You were the last thing I expected to see in that coal mine. After ages of trying to solve the mysteries of the universe—of fumbling around in the dark with no clues—you surprised me." He smiled. It was a fond memory. "After that I realized that this world also surprises me. Constantly."

He toyed with his cellphone. "The collective knowledge of civilization can be carried around in a tiny glass box. Your average corner store contains food from six of the seven continents. People invent new technologies and stories by typing words into a computer, without setting foot outside. Who could have imagined such wonders a thousand years ago? In a thousand years, what will come next?"

He gained momentum. "What's the point of it all? I won't preach philosophy or religion to you. You wouldn't like Aristotle. And what is God to an ICBM?" His eyes drifted up to the heavens. "For me... There is no point. And that is the point. I don't know what will happen next. I can't predict how it will end, or even if it will end. So I want to see as much of it as I possibly can."

Vince didn't know what to make of Roy's speech. It was the most his mentor had shared about himself in one sitting, and, even worse, it started with him. "Even if most of what you see is ugly?"

Roy patted him on the back. "Especially if most of what I see is ugly."

Could Vince live like that? No. Definitely not. Unlike Roy, he didn't care about modern marvels or knowing unknowns. The horror in his heart was too heavy. No amount of wonder could keep him afloat. But he had a different reason to keep on going. Two of them, to be exact.

"Roy," he whispered.

"Vince?"

"Where did Brooks go? I need to..." Heat rose to his cheeks as Vince said something he had never said before. "I need to apologize."

This time, Roy was not surprised. "Let's go get him." He offered a hand.

Ignoring it, Vince hopped off the stone wall. "Ladies first." He wasn't a child. They could walk together, but he would walk by himself, if only to prove to himself that he could.

Smirking, Roy led him into the darkness.

Vince paused. "Oh. One last question."

"Yes?"

"...What's an ICBM?"

CHAPTER TWENTY-EIGHT

The long hours of the afternoon came and went. Vincent Lenoir sighed. In the end, Brooks was right—this had been a waste of time.

Vince and Grace had combed the entire Hudson Valley with nothing to show for it except fast food wrappers and a pile of drenched clothes in the back seat. Finding a single monster in an entire region was as impossible as finding a good show on cable TV at two in the morning.

Vince had no regrets as he sat atop Tarrytown Lighthouse, his feet dangling over the edge. He couldn't shake the feeling that he was supposed to be here, enthroned in his tower, high above the Hudson River. Something important lurked nearby, out of sight. He just had to breach the surface to find it.

That feeling kept him awake well past midnight.

In an odd way, he shared kinship with this old, out-of-service light house. Cobwebs clung to the walls where pictures and curtains once hung. Only scrapes on the floors remained in the once cozy living quarters. Its beacon slumbered, forsaken and forgotten. The world didn't want its light.

Soft footsteps tapped along wood, then steel.

Grace approached. If she wanted to survive as a monster hunter, she really had to stop wearing high heels. Vince ought to tell her as much, but he couldn't imagine her without them anymore.

"There you are!" She settled next to him. A breeze teased a lock of unruly hair that'd escaped her bun. The crescent moon shone behind her, a halo of silver. She breathed in, tasting the traces of salt in the air.

Aside from a jumbled text message about an old coworker from Tori, Team Tianyi hadn't contacted them. Their mission had to be going well. Right now, they were probably busy running Narcissus' secret program.

Tonight, Vince and Grace were alone.

Vince had stretched his pocket money to book them two rooms at a motel down the road. After dropping Grace off for the evening, he'd escaped on his own. Apparently, she couldn't sleep, either.

He'd underestimated her. They were trespassing. To climb this lighthouse, he'd had to hop a fence and enter a locked building. He'd dealt with the lock for her, but Grace still had to cross a narrow bridge, creep inside, and ascend three stories in the dark.

He never dreamed she'd go so far to find him. She didn't seem like a rule breaker.

Then again, she did sneak two suspicious strangers into Channel 4.

"You should be in bed," he teased with a smirk.

She huffed. "So should you!"

Shrugging, he lit a cigarette.

Her gaze sank. She watched water lap against the rocky rip rap below.

"I... I had that dream again." Her voice trembled like a buoy in the river.

Vince glanced up at her. It might've been the moonlight, but her eyes shone as though they were damp from tears.

The Songbird Lady from Grace's dream totally sucked.

So what if the love of her life had abandoned her on some bridge in a graveyard? Vince had been abandoned before, too. It hurt. The wound never closed. But a little pain was good for the soul. It wasn't so bad that he'd haunt innocent girls, even if he knew how.

Grace switched to a safer subject. "See that constellation up there? The one that looks like a dipper?" She traced a shape, connecting the dots. "That's Ursa Major, the Great Bear. She's protecting her cub, the Little Bear. Seeing them together reminds me that Mom is watching over me." She dabbed her eyes with her sleeve and smiled. Thinking about her mother comforted her.

Vince's thoughts drifted through the past five years, through Brooks' home cooked meals and Roy's countless games of cards. His chest ached. He took a drag from his smoke and exhaled, banishing it all into the night.

"Not a fan of bears?" She leaned down to his level. "How about nymphs?" She pointed out another spot in the sky. "That little cluster off to the side is called the Seven Sisters."

"The Seven Sisters, huh? Can't wait to get attacked by them."

"Not everything wants to attack you!"

He grunted noncommittally.

She gave up and plopped down next to him.

He offered her his flask.

After a moment's hesitation, she took a sip. "You grew up with Roy and Brooks, didn't you?"

"You could say that." Roy and Brooks kidnapped him when he was already a teenager. They didn't get credit for all the suffering before that. He raised himself.

"Do you have any other family?"

He narrowed his eyes at the word "other." "No."

"Parents? Siblings?"

Ugh. She wasn't going to let this go.

"They died. Eaten by sharks."

A pause.

Her hand gripped his arm, offering strength. "I'm... I'm so sorry! That must've been terrible. No wonder you didn't want to talk about it." She wilted, a flower in a windowless room.

Guilt tugged at his heartstrings. His lie had been so obvious that he hadn't expected her to believe him. "It's okay, Grace. It happened a long time ago."

She met his eyes.

He wondered what she saw.

"You've been through a lot, haven't you, Vincent Lenoir?"

It was his first time hearing his full name from her lips. What a waste.

He recognized her gentle tone and knowing expression. Pity was the last thing he wanted from her.

Digging his fingernails into his palms, he turned away.

But she wasn't done with him yet. "I didn't mean it like that."

He flinched. Had she somehow traded her electrokinesis for mind reading?

"It's just... You've been everywhere. You've defeated so many bad guys. You filmed every single one of those episodes of *Haunt Hunt*—you're making your dream into reality, by yourself, whatever it takes. Meanwhile, I was born with superpowers, yet I've always been afraid to leave Missouri."

She cupped his chin, drawing his face towards her.

"I admire you, Vince. And I want you to know... From now on, you don't have to be alone, because you'll always have—"

Was that a promise? A confession? Or did she mean to add Roy, Brooks, and Tori's names to her own? He would never know the end of that sentence.

A brilliant flash of lightning lashed the heavens. Thunder rocked the earth.

The long delay between them meant that the danger was far away.

Even so, Vince's ears rang. Electricity pricked down his spine.

"We should head back," he warned. "It's going to..." Storm?

A sudden realization struck him. It was a clear night. Literally seconds ago, he and Grace had been stargazing. There hadn't been a cloud in the sky.

Now angry black thunderheads devoured the stars one by one.

He leapt up. He grabbed Grace. They had to get inside.

She tugged against him. "Vince, look!"

He followed her rainbow-painted fingernail out to the Hudson River.

A massive, old-fashioned boat stalked through the river. Two barren masts rose above its empty deck. Mist swirled around unmanned oars that propelled it forward in silence. It glided on the surface without creating a wake. A ghost ship. It was a fucking ghost ship!

Vince had once done a *Haunt Hunt* episode about the lost flagship of Henry Hudson. As punishment for choosing fame and glory over the safety of his sailors, the legendary explorer had been cursed to wander these waters forever.

Under different circumstances, seeing one of his stories come true would've made Vince's year.

Right now, it confused him.

What did Henry Hudson have to do with a mourning mother?

The Lady of the Lake loomed over the helm. Her long locks unfurled behind her, a sail in a hurricane, capturing the fury of the tempest for their own. Her eyes bounced back and forth, shore to shore. She was on a mission. She was searching for something.

Or should he call her Captain of the Lake?

Now that she was upright, her chest seemed awfully flat.

Grace noticed where he was staring. Her mouth pressed into a thin line.

He averted his eyes downward to the stones below.

The once calm waves now thrashed against the rip rap, hungry for a victim. They lurched higher and higher, climbing closer and closer.

A violent gust tore at Vince's back.

His footing slipped. Headfirst, he plummeted over the railing.

Stupid. Why did he stand so close to the edge!?

Instinctively he shut his eyes. He waited to be crushed against solid ground.

Death would not be so swift.

He missed the rip rap, plunging into the Hudson River.

The current swallowed him whole. He couldn't pull his arms away from his sides. In the absolute darkness, he couldn't tell which way was up. It didn't matter.

For the second time in forty-eight hours, his lungs screamed for air. Panic flooded his system. He was drowning. He couldn't think.

Something hooked around his waist. It jerked him like a fish on a line.

He opened his eyes.

The muddy water stung, but not as much as the horrible sight before him.

The Lady of the Lake floated not an inch from his face. She opened her great jaws. Razor sharp teeth lined them, gum to gum.

Vince didn't—no, couldn't—care. His oxygen-starved brain wandered from his body, suspended in space, frozen in time.

The monster's bony limbs entangled his.

Huh. She was a he after all.

His last drop of consciousness drained away.

CHAPTER TWENTY-NINE

Rain tapped away at the roof, the tick of an invisible clock, counting the seconds until Vincent Lenoir came to. Agony, not air, filled his lungs. His head felt like an engine that hadn't had an oil change in a hundred thousand miles. Was this the afterlife? No, he wasn't dead. Not yet.

Vince was fourteen again, in the woods of Monongahela.

Nancy whimpered next to him in the mud.

Her mother, Yona, drew back the creaking string of a bow.

Above them, the black sky wept.

Vince opened his eyes.

Spearfinger stared down at him. Well, her empty eye sockets did.

She'd once appeared before him as the woman of his dreams—a black-haired bombshell with a smile that cut right through him.

Now she'd ripped out her own eyes. Scales speckled her gaunt skin. Jagged stone tipped her fingernails. Her long, lovely legs had disappeared into a diamond-patterned tail. She was definitely not hot anymore.

"Fate has terrible power. You cannot escape it by wealth or war.

No fort will keep it out, no ships outrun it," Spearfinger hissed at Vince.

Yona fired an arrow at the monster, her long braid blowing the wind like a banner.

The attack bounced harmlessly off Spearfinger.

"When the sun sets upon the burned horizon, you'll see!" Spearfinger swung her tail at Yona.

Yona fired another arrow. It was pointless. The tail swept her off her feet.

"It will fall, a prelude to the black music of mourning. A song of suffering that turns time back to dust for man!" Spearfinger howled, seizing Yona by the throat. "He will kill our children—destroy our ancestors' future!"

Spearfinger tightened her grip. "It's your fault." Shaking with rage, she squeezed with all her might. "AND IT'S ALL YOUR FAULT!"

A spine popped. Then it crunched.

Vince hugged Nancy to his chest, muffling desperate sounds that no human should ever make. He didn't want her to see. He didn't want to see. But he could hear. And oh god, did he hear. Death did not whisper—it screamed, it tore, it shouted! He saw nothing, but Yona's head ripped off with such an awful snap that he'd hear it for the rest of his days.

Lightning flashed. The downpour clawed at his skin. Darkness threatened the edges of his vision. Somehow, Vince stood. Nancy wept in a ball at his feet. He'd failed to protect her in the way that mattered most. He could not fail her again.

Spearfinger's shrieking sounded distant, like a radio with a bad signal. Vince was no longer afraid. Only rage remained. He was unarmed. He was hurt. But deep down, he knew he was still stronger than the monster. She would share this grave with Nancy's mother.

The storm clouds snarled, echoing his will.

Spearfinger lunged.

Another flash of lightning. A smaller flash matched it.

Spearfinger's jaw shattered in a torrent of tissue and silver blood. Before she could scream a second bullet shredded her windpipe. A third split her skull.

Vince turned away.

Her body hit the mud. She died in a rumble of thunder.

Roy stood behind her. He lowered his smoking revolver.

Vince was dead. Well, not really, but he wished he was. His lungs, his stomach, and his head screamed as if he'd been the one that'd been shot. He could hardly even feel them. Instead, he replayed Nancy's mother's death over and over again in his mind. Thwack. Pop. Crunch. *Rip.* Always followed by Nancy's cries. Nothing could be more excruciating.

Roy placed a hand on his shoulder.

It was a lifeline. Vince grabbed the older man's wrist.

"Don't move, Vince." Roy wrapped his arm around Vince's waist. "It's okay." He pulled him into an embrace. He shielded him from the rain.

Warmth chased the nightmares back into the darkness. Human contact. When was the last time Vincent Lenoir had been hugged? Why here? Why *him?*

"You're safe," Roy promised.

Anguish bubbled up and over. Tears welled in Vince's eyes as he threw himself at Roy. He sobbed into the stupid monster hunter's stupid t-shirt. He sobbed for Nancy's mother. He sobbed for Nancy and Maylee. Most of all, he sobbed for himself.

Life as he knew it was over. He could never forget Nancy's mother. He would never forgive this snake, even after she rotted, even after she crumbled to dust. He would never return to New Jersey or his boring-ass high school. Evil was real. People were suffering. There was no going back now.

Safe. "That's a lie. Damnit Roy, that's a lie!" He would never be safe again.

Grace glowed on the horizon, a lighthouse in the fog.

Roy smirked at him. "Do you need some water, Vincent? You're looking a little red."

Wait, water?

Water was the last thing Vince needed. He was drowning.

* * *

Vince startled awake. He rolled over, grasping at the ground. The bottom of the Hudson River was oddly soft.

"It's about these twins who are both amazing archers."

He cracked open an eye. He sprawled on a shag rug, safe and dry.

"In the latest chapter, the heroine faces a pair of giants. She transforms into a doe and dashes between them. They try to strike her and hit each other instead!" An unfamiliar voice narrated so enthusiastically Vince could practically hear a dorky grin in the words.

Vince was in a dark room. It was filled with the kind of cheap, battered furniture he'd expect to find in a college dorm. Colorful magazines littered every surface, spilling onto the carpet. Beyond the lone window, the storm that'd almost killed him raged on.

Grace sat on an overstuffed futon, very out of place, listening politely. On the coffee table in front of her, a comic book opened to a two-page spread of a man that for some reason reminded Vince of Maylee Kingfisher.

He tried to speak but all that came out was coughing.

"Vince!" Grace rushed to his side. "You're okay!"

"Okay" wasn't the word he'd choose to describe himself. His head churned with the fury of a thousand hangovers.

He flashed her a thumbs up. "I'm alive."

"Thank goodness! I was so worried. You really scared me."

Behind him, cinders smoldered in a fireplace. That explained why his clothes were dry. What was left of them, at least. Someone had stripped off his shirt and tucked him under a knitted blanket.

He smirked at Grace. "You didn't give me CPR, did you?"

"No, that was me." The Lady of the Lake meekly raised his hand. He hugged his knees in an armchair next to Grace's futon. "Did you know you have a chipped front tooth?"

Jerking upright, Vince grabbed for his revolver. Shit. Someone had stripped him of his weapons, too.

The comic book loving, (male?) Lady of the Lake watched him. His wild hair had been tamed into a messy ponytail. A baggy hoodie concealed his bony limbs and ethereal skin. He looked kind of like a supermodel wearing a potato sack.

Lightning cracked. For only a flash, a lipless shark was among them.

The shark seemed worried.

Was his concern for Vince or about what Vince would do to him?

"Hi. I'm, uh. Akheilos." When no one responded, the Lady of the Lake rubbed the back of his head. "It's a mouthful, I know... Louis works too!"

Vince glanced at Grace.

Her clothes were clean. No dark circles lined her eyes—she'd slept since last night. She clutched a half empty teacup. She was already well acquainted with this "Louis."

Vince read the room. They weren't in any danger. Still, he couldn't bring himself to relax. Louis helping them contradicted everything he'd learned about monsters over the past five years. He had to have ulterior motives.

"...Hi. I'm Vince," he replied through clenched teeth.

"Do you need anything? Coffee? Milk? Donuts?" Louis headed into the compact kitchen, only a few steps away. "Sorry, I don't have guests often." He rummaged through the cabinets. Miscellaneous objects dropped to the floor. A box of cereal. A cracked ramen bowl. Packets of takeout chopsticks. "Oh, and I have some leftover taquitos from the twenty-four-hour store down the street!"

This guy's lifestyle would give Brooks nightmares.

"He saved your life, Vince," Grace stated the obvious. "As soon as you fell, he dove right into the river. He pulled you to shore. He even got you breathing again." She clasped her cheek. "Oh Louis, you were so brave!"

Silence.

She cleared her throat expectantly.

"Thanks," Vince muttered. "I guess."

Grace clearly trusted Louis. She hadn't lived the life Vince had. She had yet to witness the ugly truth of being human; she didn't know how little the world cared about the innocent and weak.

Although Louis seemed harmless, muscles packed his frame head to toe. Even though he slouched constantly, he towered over them. Those predator teeth weren't for donuts or taquitos. He could overpower them whenever he wanted.

"Ah, I'm getting ahead of myself. I should explain." Louis abandoned his search for food and returned to the living room. "For starters, this is how I really look." He spun around, showing off his perfectly normal, perfectly mortal body.

Vince crossed his arms over his chest.

"I'm not lying! I was popular before I got cursed."

Vince found that even harder to believe. A comic book nerd would've never been popular at his high school no matter how pretty he allegedly was.

"My curse... It makes my appearance, well. Y'know. And it screws with technology whenever I get nervous, which is why I never passed my driver's test. But hey. Now I'm an expert swimmer. And the whole boat thing is sweet, isn't it?"

"How did you get cursed?" Grace asked.

"I pissed off the wrong person. My fault, really." He didn't seem eager to elaborate.

That was fine because Vince didn't care. "Why are you helping us?"

"Why wouldn't he help us?" Grace retorted. "It was the right thing to do!"

"Ah to be honest... Don't get mad, okay?" Louis tugged at the hem of his hoodie. "I've been following you two since you were at that canal."

Vince leapt to his feet. "So *you* were the one that threatened Grace!"

"What? No! I don't know anything about that, I swear!"

Grace placed a hand on Vince's shoulder.

Scoffing, he backed down.

Shrinking away like a kicked puppy, Louis mumbled, "I just... I overheard something about a ghost story."

"You followed us halfway across New York for a ghost story?"

"Because I need help finding a ghost from a story," Louis explained. "Specifically my mother," he added. "She's the ghost."

"I'm sorry for your loss," Grace stated solemnly.

"Oh, uh. She's not dead as far as I know. But there are a lot of legends about her. La Llorona, Lady of the Lake, etcetera. She's cursed like me. Only worse. She suddenly disappeared several years ago. I've been searching for her every night since then, hoping she'd recognize my ship, but... nothing." His gaze drifted out the window. He sailed somewhere far away, far beyond the tempest's fury. "I'm worried about her. Really worried."

"Don't worry, Louis. We'll definitely help you." Grace assured him.

"Speak for yourself." Vince was tired of this shit show. He fumbled around the room. Where the hell did they put his shirt?

"Please! I don't know what else to do," Louis begged, clasping at Vince's hands. "If I don't find her... If she forgets I'm alive, she'll…" He shook his head, unable to bear the thought. "You're an expert on ghosts. Help me figure out where she went!"

Vince wrenched free. "How're we supposed to do that?"

"Go to her old hideout. I'm sure there'll be clues there."

Roy had sent Vince on enough fetch quests for one lifetime. "This region is full of creeks, canals, and flooded subways. Why don't you expertly swim there yourself?"

"I can't. It's too close to New York City. What if someone sees me in the light? Also, those subways are scary. There are alligators down there, y'know."

Vince didn't immediately argue.

Louis seized the opportunity to press harder. "Please. Help me with this one little thing! If you do, I'll help you with your Headless Horseman." He pledged his hand over his heart. "I'll scour the entire Hudson Valley if I have to!"

"Vince. How long could it possibly take?" Grace pleaded.

Vince studied her expression. If Tori, Roy, and Brooks had contacted her, she would've said so by now. Besides Nancy's phone number, they had no leads on the Headless Horseman. They hadn't caught sight or sound of Orion, Narcissus, or Asterius.

He didn't see a way out of this. Not without disappointing her.

Sighing, Vince admitted defeat. "…Where's this hideout?"

"It's called Sibyl's Cave."

The color drained from his face.

Grace tilted her head to one side. "Where is that?"

Vince answered before Louis. "Hoboken, New Jersey."

CHAPTER THIRTY

Mist and smog strangled the afternoon sun, casting Hoboken in an eerie, somber glow. Rain droplets danced atop the pavement. Moisture clung to every surface, clouding the windows of cars and the letters of street signs. The air felt thick and heavy.

Vincent Lenoir had lit his cigarette three separate times, and three separate times it had smoldered and died. The weather was perfect for caving. Not.

He peered into Sibyl's Cave. The stench of mildew, mold, and rot overwhelmed him. Brown fluid seeped from the ceiling. Trash mingled with the mud. Back before monsters were real, before he ever dreamed that people like Brooks and Roy existed, he often snuck into this very grotto to smoke. It was even more gross than he remembered.

He was glad he'd skipped breakfast. If he hadn't, he'd surely be tasting it again.

Grace ran her fingers along the iron gate that blocked off Sibyl's Cave. "How far does it go?" Someone had bent the bars to form an opening.

He squinted into the mouth of the cavern. "Hell if I know."

The main room wasn't very large. He'd have to crouch to make it ten feet in. But there could be more to it, hiding beneath the surface.

The cave was as artificial as the gothic-style arch that crowned its entrance. Some rich dude had it carved out of the hillside hundreds of years ago. Who could truly know the depths of such vanity?

"They keep filling it in and it keeps opening back up. Guess Shark Boy's mom doesn't like having a concrete front door."

Hugging her arms close to her chest, Grace ventured inside. Her footsteps drove rats from their hideaways. "Why would she live like this?"

Her question surprised Vince. Were there not any homeless people in St. Louis?

Blankets piled upon flat surfaces. Cans, empty bottles, and other useful trinkets sprawled around them. Shark Boy's mom clearly was not the only resident of this tourist attraction. It was filthy, but it was safe from prying eyes. That was the most many in post-crisis America could hope for.

If Vince hadn't met Brooks and Roy, he might've ended up here, too.

St. Louis was no utopia. It was Grace. She was too innocent. Too naive.

"Louis said she was cursed, but so is he. And his apartment is..." She struggled for the best word. It hadn't exactly been clean either. "...better."

Louis. That name soured Vince's mood. Thanks to yesterday's tireless tempest, they'd been forced to spend all afternoon with Louis. The meek merman was so starved for company that he hung around no matter how much Vince swore and scowled. In turn, Grace swore and scowled at Vince.

Okay, so Grace never swore. Her scolding was almost as bad. She claimed he was being rude. She accused him of being embarrassed about the mouth-to-mouth CPR. As if he would care about something so childish!

Someday she would understand. He wasn't being rude. He was being awfully considerate. For her, he shared the same space and breathed the same air as a monstrous would-be perhaps-already murderer. Who cared how Louis acted in front of them? What mattered was what he did in the shadows, behind closed doors, under pressure.

Like right now. Louis waited underwater, out of sight, back by the road.

Ugh. Vince was paranoid enough without knowing danger literally lurked behind him.

"Maybe she's into mineral water?" He lingered in front of a pool of murky water. "They dug this tunnel to get to a spring that has healing powers."

"Does it really have healing powers?"

He pressed his hand against a wet stone and held it up so she could see. A sticky film clung to his fingers. "What do you think?"

She grimaced.

They continued into the cave. Soon the weakened sunlight could no longer fight back the darkness. Dense, pitch-black emptiness surrounded them. Nothing disturbed it except their soft exhales and a constant drip, drip, drip.

Grace took Vince's arm. She was on edge, too. But not because of Louis or the atmosphere.

Vince's cellphone lay dead at the bottom of the Hudson River. Normally that wouldn't stop Brooks from nagging him for not checking in for two days.

Brooks, Roy, and Tori still hadn't contacted them.

Last night and this morning, Grace had tried to call them half a dozen times. By the third time she hit a voicemail inbox, she was worried.

But Vince wasn't. Roy dropped off the face of the planet all the time. And Brooks? He was probably busy keeping Tori in line. There was definitely no way something could've gone wrong at Tianyi. And if something had, it definitely wouldn't be his fault for going to Sleepy Hollow instead.

Ever so slightly, his fingers trembled.

"So, uh." Grace switched on her phone's flashlight, flooding the drowned chamber in an LED glow. "We're hunting a ghost, right? Are there any here?"

"I think that was a figure of speech."

"Oh."

"But there *was* a body discovered here once."

"O-Oh!" Her grip on his arm tightened.

Memories of late-night television flickered in mind. He wished he'd paid more attention. "It happened shortly after Sibyl's Cave opened to the public. She was a woman from Broadway. Her killer attacked her on her way home and dumped her outside. They never found him. Some famous poet wrote about it and everything."

"That's so..." She trailed off, at a loss for words. "Sad" wasn't enough. "Why do you know so much about this cave?"

"I, uh." He cleared his throat. "Lived nearby."

A creature burst from somewhere below.

It screeched as it scrambled over their feet.

Grace screeched louder. "Eek! Another rat!" She squeezed Vince so hard it hurt.

Just barely, he glimpsed white fur fading into the distance. It was no rat. What the fuck was a rabbit doing underground? Did they even live in New Jersey? Aside from Lepus at Mimosa Hall, he'd never seen one outside of a cage in a pet store.

An exotic animal. He narrowed his eyes. "Hey Grace. Lemme borrow your phone."

She obliged.

He surveyed the area the rabbit had come from with her cellphone's flashlight. A rectangular line caught the light. It was an entrance. Hidden behind an outcropping, a stone-faced door hung ajar just wide enough for a fluffball-shaped rodent to fit through.

He nudged the door experimentally. When it closed, it fit so snugly against its frame that the seams vanished. They never would've spotted it if it hadn't already been open.

He'd been curious about the rabbit before. Now he was down-right suspicious.

Grace was not suspicious at all. She reopened the door. "Hello, Miss Louis'—I mean Akheilos'—Mom!" she shouted. "Your son is really worried about you!"

Vince clapped a hand over her mouth. Her voice echoed for what seemed like an eternity.

She pushed him away. "Why are you worried about someone hearing me? We're looking for a missing person. Wouldn't it be nice if she found us?"

"She's been missing for years, Grace. We don't know what else might have moved in since then," he explained in a hushed tone. "What if whatever killed that Broadway woman also killed her? What if it's still here?"

Huffing, Grace proceeded into the secret passage. "What if you're wrong and Louis' mom is the one that's still here?"

Together they explored what appeared to be a makeshift apartment. The rooms were dusty and damp, but they were also cozy and lived in. The first room was a kitchen with steel shelves, a propane-fueled stove burner, and weird hooks on the walls. Beyond it, an alcove with a folding table and chairs served as a dining room. It led into a living room composed of a battered loveseat, a coffee table made from a crate, and a laptop that wouldn't turn on no matter how much Vince mashed at its keys.

The more they uncovered, the more tension drained from his shoulders. Little by little, he started to believe Grace. They weren't being watched. No ambush waited ahead. If there was anything dangerous in this place, it would've attacked them already.

Last but not least, they entered the bedroom. A twin bed sat upon a moth-eaten rug. Old polaroids wallpapered the walls, with barely a spec of space between them. It was hard to make out any details in the dim light. A camping lantern leaned on an uneven chest at the foot of the bed. With a push of a button, it burst to life.

Vince would've rather been attacked by all the monsters he'd ever met than have the images before him scarred into his mind. They were photographs of children. Girls, boys, teens, and toddlers of every race, shape, and size. Some were outside. Some were in their houses, sound asleep. Some laid unconscious in the kitchenette. There were hundreds of pictures, and not a single one featured Louis.

"Vince..." Grace whispered. "Is that...?" She couldn't finish her sentence. It was too horrible to say.

It was Vince. It was Vince standing in front of Hoboken Group Home for the first time. It was him at thirteen, smoking a cigarette inside this very cave. It was him with Nancy, hiking in the woods, mere weeks before his fateful field trip to Lackawanna Coal Mine. Fear and disgust churned in his stomach. He'd never felt so violated.

One by one, he ripped them down. He shredded them into confetti. He would destroy every last picture. Then he would burn them. And then he would burn everyone and everything involved in taking them.

Grace raised her hand, unsure whether she should stop him.

She didn't have to.

A sinister smirk sliced him to the bone.

His fingers framed a nostalgic memory. His foster mother wrapped her arm around him. They smiled behind the wheel of her old Toyota in the parking lot of a Walmart, years before he'd moved to the east coast.

A figure loomed in the rear-view mirror. It was a black-haired bombshell with a smile that cut right through him. She clutched a camera in her claws.

He rubbed his eyes. He pinched himself. No matter how he tried to wake up, the nightmare was still there. He was awake. This was real.

Spearfinger of Monongahela had been stalking him since he was small.

Rage rampaged through him, a wild stallion, trampling all other emotions. Hundreds of ugly possibilities bucked in his chest.

Somewhere outside, something boomed.

Sibyl's Cave lurched violently.

Hot air and ash exploded through the corridor. Pebbles fell around them. Pots and pans clattered to the floor.

"What was that?" Grace screamed. "What's going on!?"

Thrown off balance, Vince landed on his back with a thud. The sharp pain forced him back into the present. His head spun. Snakes and sharks chased the edges of his vision.

Snakes and sharks? A sudden realization sobered him. He jerked upright. "This was a trap! Louis' mom, she's actually—"

A second blast rocked the cavern to its core.

Ominously, the earth groaned. Cracks spiderwebbed across the ceiling. Dirt rained from the sky. The light drizzle rapidly became a downpour. Soon, they'd be buried alive.

Grace grasped his hand. "We have to get out of here!"

They bolted towards the mouth of the cave.

The entire tunnel system buckled and shook. Rocks crashed around them. Vince lost count of the number of times they narrowly avoided being crushed.

Sunlight peeked around a corner. The exit was near!

A boulder trembled above it. If it collapsed, it would block the opening.

Desperately Vince and Grace picked up speed.

The boulder slipped. They weren't going to make it. They were going to die in this grimy hellhole, outsmarted by a fucking fish.

Something shifted inside of Vince. Hope flooded his system, as though he'd drawn the winning card in poker.

His sneaker stuck on a ledge. He tripped, launching face first into the sludge. His revolver toppled out of its holster. It fired.

The bullet bit a hole in the ceiling. Water trickled through it.

"God damnit!" He grabbed his gun.

Drip. Drip. Drip. That relentless leak returned.

With a boom, the roof collapsed.

A huge reservoir of water emptied onto their heads. The torrent swept them off their feet, past the boulder, and out of the cave. It dumped them unceremoniously into the Hudson River.

Coughing and sputtering, Vince climbed onto the street. He dragged Grace out with him. He'd never let go of her.

She let go of him. She hugged the asphalt as if it was a long-lost friend.

They'd survived.

Somehow.

Smoke, singed with the stink of gunpowder, coiled from Sibyl's Cave's broken mouth.

Louis the Shark Boy was gone.

CHAPTER THIRTY-ONE

Cars rushed down the street, splashing mud on the sidewalks. People passed, chatting and smiling. The city was alive. Somehow, so was Vincent Lenoir. He sat on the stairs of a church, soaked to the bone. He could hear and see it all, but it was distorted, as though hidden behind rain-streaked stained glass.

Right now, if Orion, Narcissus, or Asterius found him, he'd be dead meat. He didn't care. How was he supposed to care when his past had been tainted? Why should he survive when Nancy's mother might've been killed because she'd met him?

Hoboken Group Home, the nondescript townhouse next door, cast its shadow over him. A tricycle rusted in the yard. Faint laughter echoed from the second story.

He'd come here without thinking about it. He didn't understand why.

He'd refused to even set foot in New Jersey after his fateful field trip to Lackawanna Coal Mine. Nothing good had happened to him in foster care. He had no use for memories of adults who brushed him off as a lost cause, for bigots and their lashing belts, for the old men who made him call them "father". Back then, he didn't matter.

If only he still didn't matter. Those times had been simpler. He wished he was innocent. He longed for a home that never existed. He craved Nancy's teasing, disapproving teachers, and fist fights under the bleachers.

"Vince." A hand tugged his sleeve.

For a moment, Vince thought that Roy had appeared. He'd explain away the darkness. He'd laugh and then everything would be fine again.

The relief was as fleeting as smoke in the wind. It wasn't Roy. Roy was missing.

Grace gazed down at Vince. Her eyes were full of pity.

That pity should've pissed him off. Instead, it made him feel guilty.

Brooks was right again—Vince was selfish. As soon as he and Grace had escaped Sibyl's Cave, he'd run off on his own. Louis could've been hiding in an ambush. There could've been more explosives. He couldn't help it; he needed to be anywhere but there, with Spearfinger.

Vince shouldn't have left Grace behind. He owed her an explanation.

"Grace, I—" His voice broke. "Sorry" sounded too self-serving.

Kneeling, she pressed a finger to his lips. "I know. It's okay."

Her words struck Vince like one of Sibyl's Cave's explosions. His bad boy act crumbled; his foundation collapsed. He buried his face in his hands. Hot tears coated his fingers.

Okay? He'd never been okay. He couldn't even blame Roy and Brooks for that.

For as long as he could remember, Vincent Lenoir had been a mess. Desperate for attention, he acted out in school. Afraid to be vulnerable, he hurt everyone who ever cared for him. He was too stupid, too stubborn, and too reckless to be responsible for other peoples' lives.

He was a nine-year-old in the passenger seat of an old Toyota. His foster mother showed him when to hit the clutch and shift into first gear. The car picked up speed. When he turned the wheel, its tires skidded, throwing them into a spin.

Vince had never forgotten that thrilling, weightless feeling.

A week afterwards, his foster mother had abruptly disappeared. He'd assumed she quit. Social workers regularly gave up after he put tape on their mouse sensor, lit firecrackers in the bathroom, or replaced their coffee creamer with laxatives.

What if she hadn't quit? What if Spearfinger had gotten her?

Roy often told Vince that there was no such thing as a coincidence. The timeline was a little confusing, but if Spearfinger had been at Walmart, Hoboken, and Monongahela, she'd stalked him for his entire childhood.

Vince couldn't deny it. He was cursed. No wonder his parents had abandoned him. Someday, once Grace got to know who he really was on the inside, she'd abandon him too.

Today, Grace stayed. Turning her back, she scooted in front of him. She blocked the view from the road. No one could see him cry.

Her small act of kindness rippled through him, growing into waves that eroded the last of his resolve. The wounds on his heart festered and bled, flooding out onto the pavement. He cried until every last drop was spent. Then he shuddered in silence.

Grace waited without judgment.

Exhausted, Vince rested his forehead on her shoulder.

"I grew up here. In Hoboken Group Home. And in Birmingham. And in Pittsburgh. And in Chicago. But mostly here, in that building, in the second bed from the window. I only lived in this group home for eighteen months, but those were the last eighteen months I had to be a kid." He didn't understand why he was telling her, but he couldn't stop the words from flowing.

"My parents aren't dead. Well, they might be. I don't know." He lowered his hands, studying the lines of his palms. They were winding. "The woman who gave birth to me dumped me at a church. She's probably still out there, but I'll never have a mother."

He retrieved the yellow sticky note from the Headless Horseman from his pocket. It was so pale and faded from water damage it was no longer legible.

"This phone number is from the first friend I made after Roy and Brooks adopted me." *Adopted.* He'd never admitted that he viewed them as parents before. "Her mother sacrificed herself to save us from a monster. A monster I followed into the woods like an idiot. The same monster in that photo from Sibyl's Cave—Louis' mom. It was all my fault."

"Vince." Grace took him in her arms. "None of this is your fault. Louis' Mom killed her. Not you. You're just another victim."

"I'm nobody's victim," he snapped. His words had no bite. Spearfinger had already taken everything—he was empty, drained, done.

And yet Grace reached him anyway. He leaned into her warmth. His heart quickened as new emotions ebbed through him, filling the gaps in his soul little by little.

Her grip tightened. "You're right. You're fearless. You're a hero." She stroked his hair. "But you suffer, too."

His fingers closed around her sleeve, holding on. She made him feel safe. Wanted. In her embrace, he forgot all about the rain. He could imagine a future where who or what they were didn't matter, where he never saw a monster again. *Home.*

The feeling was magnetic. He couldn't pull away. Not even as it carved against his ribs, aching deep in his hollow chest. Each touch, every heartbeat, made him long for more.

He hated it. Het let go.

Grace was a divine descending from heaven. She was afraid of everything, which only made her strong. She fought for her mother —for love—even after all these hopeless years. She liked him, even as dangerous and broken as he was. She'd forgiven him where Nancy never could.

Vince didn't deserve it. He was an asshole. Over the past few days, he'd dragged her around chasing ghosts he didn't even bother to warn her about.

She had her own hardships. Unlike him, she actually had a mother—a mother who was both near and out of reach. No wonder she'd wanted to help Louis so badly.

"You lost your mom like Louis, didn't you? I don't know what you're going through. But if it feels anything at all like..." He clutched his chest. "...like this..." His fingers curled into fists. "I'll do whatever it takes to help you cure her."

She pulled his chin towards her.

Helpless to her touch, he met her gaze.

Somehow, they'd gotten so close to each other.

"Thank you," she whispered.

He could taste her lavender breath on his lips. His pulse pounded louder with each sweet exhale, a duet.

Heavy raindrops fell upon them, washing away the trials of the day.

They didn't notice.

Here, tangled with Grace under an overcast sky, with all the city laid out before them, Vince felt something he'd never felt before. Not when facing certain death. Not when he moved for the umpteenth time. Not when he liked her, but he didn't *like* her. He was nervous.

"Vince. No matter what happens..." She leaned in as she spoke. "...you and I will always be—"

Vince, who was intimidated by nothing, realized with a painful shock that the stakes were too high for him. He couldn't do this.

Grace wasn't some girl he could use up and toss aside. What if she changed her mind? What if her feelings were spent after one kiss? What if he screwed up and made her hate him? He couldn't imagine himself in a relationship, committed to another.

It was a fear he'd never experienced before. He couldn't feel anything else.

He jerked away and just like that it was over. Before he knew it, he'd fled down the block.

"Wait!" she called after him. "Vince, you can talk to me!"

He couldn't hear her. Even if had, he wouldn't have listened.

She rushed after him.

Escape was the only thing on Vince's mind. He bumped into a stranger.

"Ouch!"

He knew that voice. A million memories assaulted him. They forced him to his knees.

An amber-skinned woman sprawled in front of him. Headphones covered her ears. Piercings glittered on her brow. Her black hair pulled into a long braid like her mother's. She'd changed so much, but Vince would always recognize her. *Nancy Kingfisher.*

Grace caught up to him. Her mouth dropped open. "Siren Song?"

What? Wasn't that some pop singer? Why did Grace call Nancy that?

Vince didn't get the chance to ask. As soon as he reached for Nancy, a nearly invisible string pressed into his neck. It tightened into a noose, cutting off his air supply.

Instinct took over. He forgot both women and clawed it with all his strength.

When it didn't break, Grace helped him.

Together, they snapped the line.

He was free. Kind of.

While saving his neck, they'd both brushed against, stuck to, and tripped over countless more threads.

Vince struggled against them. They didn't budge. He could barely move.

They were trapped in a giant spider web.

Nancy—and Siren Song—had disappeared during the confusion.

Half-suffocated, he wasn't sure he hadn't hallucinated her in the first place. Either way, she made perfect bait.

"You must be Vincent Lenoir and Grace Batya." A business-woman with a figure eight body and an ominous smirk emerged from the shadows. Her strappy stilettos made Graces' heels look like baby shoes.

Under different circumstances, Vince would've been interested in getting to know her. Right now, he was only interested in getting out of there. "In the flesh. Why don't you let us down so we can greet you properly?"

She scoffed.

"Not a chance. You and I have some business to settle."

CHAPTER THIRTY-TWO

Time had not been kind to New York City. The once glittering skyscrapers slowly decayed behind rotting plywood. The once crowded roads were too cracked and uneven for cars. Rats had conquered the streets. They boldly darted between towers of trash, underneath the feet of pedestrians. Tori wished that they hadn't walked.

She'd read about Hurricane Triton in school. Reading about the disaster didn't compare to seeing it in person. Over a decade had passed since the storm had devastated Manhattan Island, but its mark was carved into the battered sidewalks, mildewed store-fronts, and tired faces of passersby. It had rained for six days and seven nights. It would be thousands more before the city would heal.

New York City was President Arvis' hometown. He'd served as governor for a decade before being elected. But instead of cleaning up the damage, rebuilding anything, or providing support for those who'd lost everything, he'd simply closed the flooded subway, boarded up buildings, and moved upwards.

Magnetic rail trains hung from arches high above their heads.

Covered sky bridges connected hotels, apartments, offices, and shopping malls. Massive LED screens blocked out the sun. The heavens above were artificial, colorful, and exciting—the pinnacle of human progress, the pulse of the world.

Tori's gaze lingered on a homeless man on a corner, huddled with a starving dog. Mud caked his clothes up to his chest. Even in the heat of summer, he looked cold.

Roy noticed. "You can't help them all." He twirled his serpent-handled umbrella, which concealed his antique sword, in his fingers.

"That's just an excuse to do nothing." She rifled through her wallet. No cash.

Wordlessly, Brooks opened his bag. He pressed something into the man's palm.

All over the United States, year after year, the middle class had shrunk until only a tiny sliver remained between the rich and the poor. Here, that sliver was gone. It made Tori sad. Or perhaps she was just sad to be returning to work.

Taking a deep breath, Tori approached the Woolworth Building. Roy and Brooks trailed closely behind.

The Woolworth Building, nicknamed the Cathedral of Commerce, dominated its surroundings. Once the tallest building in the world, its sixty stories of ornate Gothic architecture and thousands of windows cast a long shadow over the squalor below. Gargoyles leered from their perches. Oxidized copper, gold, and blue trimmed its many roofs and turrets.

On the way here, Tori had researched its history. Unlike the Winecoff Hotel and Mimosa Hall, so far, there'd been no major tragedies inside. The architect had been so paranoid about the risk of fires that he'd carved salamanders on every floor, believing that animals who could walk through flames and live would share their magic with his masterpiece.

The Woolworth Building had been commissioned by a business tycoon who'd owned the Victorian era equivalent of Walmart. It was a beautiful, staggering monument to greed.

It was fitting, then, that it housed the North American headquarters of Tianyi.

A three-story Tudor arch crowned the main entrance. Mercury, the many-winged god of commerce, and Ceres, the grain-wreathed goddess of agriculture, protected either side.

At the sight of the deities, Brooks tightened his grip on his briefcase. He'd hidden his shotgun inside.

Together, the monster hunters continued through the sliding glass doors.

The Woolworth's Building's main lobby was as grand as the Cathedral Basilica. Dark coffered ceilings gave way to vaulted mosaics of green, blue, and amber. Grecian marble glittered on the walls and floors. Elevators with gold-etched doors waited around a security desk. Beyond them, a grand staircase curved up to a mezzanine with storefronts.

Under different circumstances, Tori would've explored and taken pictures. Instead, she stood, stiff and uncomfortable.

"Ah," Roy pranced up the stairs. He thumbed an order into a screen in front of one of the shops. "I was hoping for a chance to grab some coffee."

"It's going to be a long day," his tone implied. As per usual, he was the only one among them who wasn't anxious.

"Mercy," Brooks observed. "You sound like Vince."

"Good." Roy winked. "What would happen to our team morale if we didn't have someone around to complain?"

A waitress handed him his drink.

Tori didn't know how to feel about Vince running off to chase ghosts from his past, but she didn't mind spending time with just Roy and Brooks. Both men were reliable, reasonable, and considerate. No one cared who touched the car radio. Today, they'd even dressed up.

Brook in professional clothes reminded her of a military officer —thick glasses, starched collar, and all. Being around Roy, with his slicked back hair, navy sport coat, and strawberry-printed dress shirt that pulled ever so slightly at the buttons to compliment his muscles beneath, made her feel like she was the heroine of a romance novel.

But it would've been nice to have Vince the newly immortal fighter and Grace the human railgun with them in case something went wrong. Instead, they were off gallivanting around Hudson Valley.

"I'll complain enough for all of us if we run into anyone I know," Tori shifted uneasily in her kitten heels. The prospect was unlikely, but possible.

"That's the spirit!" Roy toasted her.

Brooks frowned. "You don't like your coworkers, Miss Jaecar?"

"It's not that, it's just..."

To gain access to Tianyi, she'd told her HR department that she was considering moving to New York City. She didn't want to have to lie to anyone else. She already felt claustrophobic; the weight of her deception squeezed her shoulders. Or maybe that was the stiff button-down shirt she was wearing.

"Don't worry, Miss Jaecar," Roy assured. "If we do run into someone you know, I'll take care of it."

Why did that sound so ominous?

They proceeded to the elevators and ascended the great tower.

The Tianyi North American Headquarters occupied fifteen stories of the Woolworth Building. Its entire first floor had been turned into a lobby. Only an abstract, imposing front desk, a few chairs, and access card protected elevator bays filled the enormous space.

They were up so high that Tori's ears had popped. The air was thinner. Black marble covered every surface. Stone sculptures decorated the walls. The atmosphere was heavy, cold, and uninviting.

She'd read somewhere that corporations chose this aesthetic to make negotiators uncomfortable. It worked.

Steeling herself, she approached the front desk. "Uh, hello?"

"Do you have an appointment?" The receptionist didn't look up from his computer.

"Yeah. I'm Victoria Jaecar. I also have Zach Godfrey and Richard Mercer with me."

Roy made a peace sign. Brooks nodded by raising his chin.

"Oh, it's *you!*" Suddenly he seemed interested. "You're from that subsidiary in Atlanta. The one with the dead director!"

His excitement slapped Tori in the face. The Tianyi employees she'd met before had always been dismissive towards her company but wow. They were talking about a person who'd died in front of her.

"You saw what happened, didn't you?" So he knew. And he was asking questions like it was the latest episode in a cheesy soap opera. "Was he really...?"

Tori opened her mouth and closed it. What could she say?

Brooks frowned. "Was he what?"

"It was all over the news." Immune to his disapproval, the receptionist showed off a tabloid article on his phone. "His wife put a hit on him for cheating! Was he really sleeping with coworkers?"

Coworkers? Just thinking about that word being plural made Tori's stomach lurch.

Her expression was the only response needed.

"The nerve of some people! If you ask me, he got off too lightly."

Roy cleared his throat. "Excuse me."

As if noticing his presence for the first time, the receptionist sized him up. "Well hello there." He liked what he saw.

Roy placed a palm on the desk, leaning closer. "I'm Zach Godfrey, one of Victoria's teammates."

"How can I help you, Mr. Godfrey?"

"Please, call me Zach."

"Zach."

"I'd love to tell you *all about* Director MacGillivray, but we're in a rush. We can't be late meeting his replacement. You know how it is. Perhaps you and I could continue this conversation later? Over drinks...?" He flashed a smile.

The receptionist was blinded. He completely forgot about James.

"R-right. Later, then..." Peeling his eyes away, he keyed something into his computer. "Don't worry, Zach. Your new director will be way better—I hear they were hand-picked by the CEO's son himself, and the CEO's son is very selective."

"So am I."

For some reason, this conversation bothered Tori more than the one about James.

A metallic ding announced the arrival of an elevator behind them.

"Twenty-seventh floor. In the conference room on the left," the receptionist stated, shamelessly sliding a business card underneath Roy's fingertips.

Smoothly, Roy slipped it into his coat pocket. "Thank you."

Brooks and Tori herded him into the elevator.

Once the doors closed, Tori exhaled a sigh of relief.

"Don't you dare, Mercy," Brooks warned. He spoke in a whisper, but in such a small space, she heard him anyway. "We don't have time for—"

"That remains to be seen." Roy's voice was full volume. He had nothing to hide.

Well, he didn't. What Roy did after they finished here was no one's business. But when Tori closed her eyes, she saw him in a smoky room, the lights dark and intimate, curled around someone else. That image shook her more than all the might Tianyi could muster.

A hand gripped her shoulder. She opened her eyes.

"Miss Jaecar," he promised. "I'm only messing around."

Oh god, he'd noticed.

God heard her prayer. The elevator opened. As soon as the gap between the doors was large enough for her to fit through, Tori rushed out. She wanted to die from embarrassment. The fastest way to do so would be in the heart of enemy territory.

The twenty-seventh floor was a maze of concrete and metal. Glass cubicles sprawled in every direction. A large conference room with a heavy wooden table and an incredible view waited at the end of the main hall.

"Come on, Richard," Roy hooked his arm through Brooks' and escorted him inside.

Their plan involved splitting their group. Tori would search for a way to run Narcissus' mystery program. Meanwhile, Roy and Brooks would stay behind and stall the new director. One person poking at random computers was a lot less suspicious than three. With so many people around, even if she got caught, she shouldn't be in any danger.

Act like you belong, she recited in her head as she wandered into the main office space. She passed a dozen people going about their workdays before she reached the first desk. She passed a dozen more before finding a desk without an owner.

This was her chance. Tori plopped into the desk's chair. She attempted to join the WIFI network on her own laptop. It rejected her immediately. She lacked some identity software. She would have to do this the hard way.

Her hands trembled. She switched on the old school computer underneath the desk. A Tianyi login screen appeared on the monitor. On a whim, she entered her username and password. Nope, of course not. She tried several more sets of credentials—Zach's, her office's IT manager's, standard admin passwords—without better results.

This was her specialty. But she was a programmer, not a hacker. Given enough time, with enough messing around with the operating system, she would definitely find a way to run Narcissus' IOU-list on this computer without logging in. She didn't have time.

The meeting with the new director would start at any moment.

She trusted Roy and Brooks, but how much time could they possibly buy her? Ten minutes? Thirty? Every second was precious.

She would use brute force if she had to. But it'd be better to get lucky.

To get lucky, she needed a clue. She rifled around the cubicle. Crochet needles, a flier from a Senator Pallas rally, a photo of a pet tarantula...

A glossy shine underneath a stack of papers caught Tori's eye. She nudged them out of the way.

A mustache, greasy hair, and heavy-lidded eyes stared up at her. James! He was much younger in this picture, but that leer of his was unmistakable. What was he doing here? And who was the platinum blonde songbird of a woman standing next to him?

"Excuse me. This is my desk."

Tori jumped out of the chair.

A woman loomed behind her. Clean, confident, and condescending, she practically oozed with power. A pencil skirt and a skin-tight blouse hugged her figure eight body. A black jacket slung over her shoulders. Her red lips pressed into a thin line. She tapped her stilettoed heel impatiently. "Can I help you?"

How long had she been there!?

Backing against the desk, Tori mumbled, "S-sorry! I'm from out of town. I got lost on my way back from the bathroom and was looking for a map of the office." Her excuse didn't sound convincing, even to her.

"Come with me," the woman ordered, seizing her wrist.

Her grip was gentle.

Tori easily broke it. "Sorry, but I'm super late for an important meeting. I came all the way from Atlanta to meet my office's new director of engineering. I can't keep him waiting." If this new director was anything like James had been, fear of irritating the boss would scare off even the strictest of rule-followers.

"...Adeline Webb."

Why was Adeline introducing herself? Was she not listening?

"Sorry! I, uh, really need to get moving..." Tori inched towards the hall.

"You must be one of the three Atlanta employees who requested a transfer."

Her words paralyzed Tori in her tracks.

"Nice to meet you, Victoria Jaecar." Adeline offered her a manicured hand. "Starting from today, I'm your new boss."

CHAPTER THIRTY-THREE

Breathe in, breathe out. Blind to her surroundings, Tori followed Director Webb back towards the elevators. She had to calm down. So what if there was a crack in their plan? It'd been fragile from the start.

Her enemy was leading her to her allies. Roy and Brooks were experts at improvising. Together, they'd figure something out.

Webb marched straight into the main conference room. Its doors closed behind them with an ominous click.

The faintest of frowns flickered across Brooks' face when he saw them. He hid it with a stiff smile. He pulled out chairs for the women. "You must be Adeline Webb." He offered her a hand. "It's a pleasure."

Roy, who lounged with his hands behind his head and his feet propped up on the desk, greeted them with a curt wave.

Webb ignored Brooks' hand. "That's Director Webb, thank you." She claimed the head of the table. She crossed her legs, a queen on her throne. "Let's get started."

Meekly, Tori settled next to her.

"Our first topic for discussion will be your complete disregard for company policy."

Not a great start. Tori buried her sweaty hands in the pockets of her jacket. "I'm sorry about earlier, I..." She would never be good at lying. "...I really was lost. I didn't know what else to do."

"Oh Tori," Roy teased. "You'd get lost in a circle." He was backing up her story.

Brooks joined in. "Stop it, Zach. Can't you see she's already embarrassed?"

At least that part wasn't a lie.

Director Webb's glare hardened. "You must be Zach Godfrey."

Roy winked. "At your service."

"And Richard Mercer?"

Brooks nodded.

"Mr. Mercer, do you smoke, by any chance?"

"Never."

"You look *awfully* mature for forty," she observed.

He was unphased. "I get that a lot, unfortunately."

"That explains why you haven't progressed very far in your career." She smiled as though she hadn't just insulted him. "Sales is such a *superficial* field."

Her attention shifted to Roy. Her smile faded.

"Speaking of superficial... I've never seen a mid-level software engineer who dressed in SMS from head to toe."

Honestly, Tori hadn't believed Vince when he told her that Roy was rich. He looked like a million bucks, but they only rented run-down rooms and drove everywhere in aging cars. Vince avoided toll roads and Brooks coupon shopped at grocery stores. He prepared as many meals as possible at their base, even if it meant cooking on coffee makers or clothing irons. Surely he wouldn't have learned such niche skills if he didn't have to.

But SMS? If everything Roy currently wore was from SMS, it

had to be true. SMS, short for Spin, Measure, and Shear, was famous for being over-the-top expensive. Software engineers earned a healthy living, but a single shirt from SMS cost more than a month of Tori's salary.

Why hide his wealth? And why didn't he bother to hide it now?

"Thank you," Roy replied.

"That wasn't a compliment."

"You recognized quality right away. Is there any greater compliment?"

Tori wasn't sure they were talking about fashion anymore.

He straightened. "And since you have such an eye for quality..." Placing both elbows on the table, he rested his chin in his hands. Mischief glinted in his eyes. "...I'm looking forward to working together."

No response. Director Webb didn't seem to like where the conversation was going. She switched to an easier target. "Victoria. As for you..."

"Y-yes?"

"Do you know the first thing I did when I was appointed as your superior?"

"N-no?"

"I looked up my new reports on social media." She smirked, a spider with a fly trapped in her web. "People post so many pictures online these days."

Shit.

James never would've bothered to do something so tedious in a million years. Why did Tianyi have to replace him with someone who actually cared?

They were screwed. They were SO screwed. They'd been screwed before they even set foot inside the building. This meeting was a trap like the Winecoff Hotel had been. Would everything here also burn to the ground?

"Why don't you tell me who you and your friends really are?"

"Director Webb!" A man burst into the room. He was out of breath. "Director Webb! You're the only manager I could find. You gotta call maintenance—"

Red lights flashed. A siren split the air. Tori's ears rang. She regretted thinking about the Winecoff Hotel. This fire alarm couldn't be a coincidence—the timing was too perfect. Maybe she'd somehow summoned the phoenix.

"Oh. Oh no. I'm too late." The intruder slumped. "We're all going to have to go down all those stairs—"

"Enough! What's going on?" Director Webb hissed.

"Someone spilled coffee in the copy machine. It caught fire!"

Dazed office workers haunted the halls like vampires seeing sunlight for the first time in centuries. The solemn and serious floor quickly devolved into chaos.

"I..." Director Webb rubbed her temple. "You..." Her gaze swept over Roy, Brooks, Tori, and the intruder.

"Stay put. I'll be back!" With that, she trailed the man out of the conference room. She locked the door behind her and disappeared around a corner.

Roy clapped his hands together. "Time for Plan B!"

His coffee cup from earlier was gone.

"Plan B?" Tori repeated.

Neither Brooks nor Roy seemed the slightest bit flustered by the current situation. This Plan B was their Plan A.

Waltzing over to the entrance, Roy retrieved the receptionist's business card from his pocket. He folded it neatly in half. Then he forced it in between the lock and the door frame. In one smooth gesture, he unlocked the door. He opened it, a gentleman. "After you, Miss Jaecar."

They escaped into the corridor.

No one so much as looked in their direction.

Tori exhaled her relief. "Okay, what's this Plan B?"

"We're stealing a laptop," Brooks explained.

Stealing a laptop? That would be one step in the right direction and two steps in the wrong one. It was much harder to break into a corporate computer than out of a glass room. "If you do that, I'll be a criminal!"

"Accomplice, actually," Roy corrected.

Brooks elbowed him. "Don't worry, Miss Jaecar. We'll return the laptop as soon as we're done with it. With any luck, no one will even realize it's gone."

Their luck hadn't exactly been great lately. She clenched the hem of her jacket.

Roy picked up on her skepticism. "It's not a crime to run out on your boss! Tianyi will be suspicious of you, but that's not enough to do anything about it."

"...What will we do with someone's locked laptop, anyways?"

"I know a guy who can get us in."

She wondered why they didn't bring someone so convenient with them in the first place. "And what about connecting to Tianyi's network?"

"Tori... I know it's not a perfect plan." Brooks gave her an apologetic look. "But I don't think we can afford to have any more meetings with Director Webb."

Finally, a statement she agreed with.

Gently, Roy nudged her further out of the room. "We're wasting precious time. Go on ahead. We'll meet you downstairs."

His words were straightforward, but his tone implied something extra. *Trust me.* Tori nodded, unable to meet their eyes. Trust wasn't the issue. She believed that they would steal that laptop. That they would solve this problem. That they wouldn't sully her name. The issue was that all those things involved "they" instead of "us."

Roy and Brooks kept her at a distance. They didn't need her.

This wasn't new. Roy and Brooks often hid secrets from Tori.

And Vince and Grace, for that matter. Roy never explained where he went at night. Brooks balked at danger for anyone but himself. They always had some sort of Plan B, C, or D between only them. They were the adults. The other monster hunters were stuck at the kid's table.

Somehow, Tori had assumed that things would be different without Vince and Grace around. But why would they? She was a newbie and an outsider. She had no one to blame but herself for this disappointment.

She just wished they would trust her, too.

She patted her cheeks. She quarantined those feelings in the back of her mind. *Later.*

"Got it. I'll meet you downstairs." Saluting with two fingers, she melted into the flood of people streaming under exit signs. She didn't love the idea of descending twenty-seven flights of stairs. At least the exercise would clear her head.

The swarm surged down the hall. Tori's role in the heroics was over. She didn't need to think. She barely registered the many twists and turns that took her to the back of the building.

Eventually the wailing fire alarm stopped. It did not stop the exodus of bored office employees, eager for fresh air and a paid break.

She reached the last corridor. It ended in emergency stairs, sunglasses, and satin.

"What in the name of the Twice Born are you doing here?" a familiar voice barked.

Orion. Orion was up ahead!

"Whatever I want."

That purr could only belong to Narcissus.

"You seemed like you could use some company."

Suddenly every nerve in Tori's body was firing on high alert. Orion and Narcissus barred the path between her and the exit. *Together.* She prayed to God, Gandhi, and Buddha that dogs weren't allowed inside the Woolworth Building. Procyon and Sirius would smell her in seconds. Why had she agreed to split up from Roy and Brooks?

"Company?" Orion spat. "You're just one of that whore's pawns."

"That may be true at the moment, but someday this little pawn is going to cross the board and become a queen," Narcissus dismissed. "When that day comes, I hope you'll still be in play."

They were coming closer. She needed to hide!

She jiggled a random door handle. Locked.

A man next to her noticed. "Did you forget something? Don't worry, maintenance will unlock all the conference rooms after they finish the headcount downstairs."

"I don't need your help!" Orion snapped.

"Don't you?" Narcissus pretended to examine his fingernails. "They almost captured you last time, didn't they?"

There was nowhere to hide. Blending into the crowd wasn't an option, either. This hallway was far too narrow. Tori would have to brush shoulders with her enemies to pass them. And if she turned back, against the flow of traffic, she'd stand out too much.

"So what? You didn't do any better, even with the minotaur!"

"That's precisely my point, dear. Fate favors those brats."

Breathe in, breathe out. She had to calm down. The answer was clear: her only way out was through. When they were almost upon her, she'd make a run for it. She just had to reach the stairwell. Then she could lose them in the maze of floors and people.

"Orion, it doesn't matter if you're a giant, a demigod, or the King of France..."

They were almost upon her. She could already smell Narcissus' cologne. Daffodils with a subtle hint of star anise and had never been quite so intimidating.

"...You're also a pawn like me. And pawns are fated to be sacrificed."

She steeled herself, ready to bolt.

"Victoria! Get back here this instant!"

Director Webb's outburst turned many heads, Tori's included. Her new boss paced back and forth at the mouth of the hallway. Her pointed glare darted from face to face.

Director Webb hadn't spotted Tori yet, but she would soon. More importantly, she'd attracted Narcissus' attention. His curiosity piqued, he surveyed the area. It would take a miracle to slip past him now.

Tori was cornered. She had to do something, fast.

Too slow. Narcissus' eyes met hers.

Her heart stopped. Did he recognize her?

A strong grip yanked her into a dark office. A hand muffled her cry of surprise. The door shut behind her.

Before Tori registered what had happened, someone's back crashed against the door.

"We're nothing alike!" Orion growled. "I'm no pawn. I'm Orion Treyvon, the greatest hunter who ever lived, and I'm going to live forever!"

She could just barely make out his outline through the blinds on the door. He'd shoved Narcissus, unknowingly saving her.

Orion grasped the lapels of the other man's jacket. "If you get in my way, I'll kill you too."

Unimpressed, Narcissus placed a palm on his chest. "At least buy me dinner before you put your hands all over me."

Scowling in disgust, Orion retreated.

An uncomfortable tension stretched between them.

As though he'd spilled a glass of fine wine on the floor, Narcissus sighed. "Suit yourself, Orion Treyvon. I'll stay out of your way." *What a waste,* his tone implied. He brushed invisible dirt off his lapels. "I prefer my own company anyways."

They had nothing left to say to each other. At last, they continued on their way, vanishing into the depths of Tianyi.

The hand covering Tori's mouth fell away.

She'd almost forgotten her kidnapper! She wheeled to face them.

A familiar woman stood before her, prim as a fox.

Maena, the project manager, smiled.

"Sorry, I didn't mean to scare you!"

CHAPTER THIRTY-FOUR

One ring. No answer. A second, then a third. Still nothing. Eventually, the pattern was broken by a loud beep. "Oh, uh! How do I record? ...I think I got it. Hello, sorry I missed your call. This is Grace Batya, twenty-three, waning crescent moon in the 7th House of Taurus with Jupiter—" Another beep cut her off.

Defeated, Tori dropped her phone into her pocket. It wasn't unusual for Vince to get caught up in something and become unreachable, but she'd hoped that their new party member would be more responsible. Grudgingly she accepted reality—she wasn't getting any backup tonight. With a heavy sigh, she returned inside.

Smoke, leather, and cinnamon overwhelmed her senses. She winced. Out on the balcony, high near the summit of the Woolworth Building, the unforgiving sun banished all shadows. In stark contrast, the interior of the Black Sheep restaurant was dim, lit only by red-shaded lamps, candles on tables, and a trio of black-tinted windows high above her head. Even in the middle of the afternoon, it felt like a Saturday night. That was probably the point.

Gradually her eyes adjusted. She didn't love what she saw.

Well-dressed men and women lined the bar. In a corner of the room, Roy lounged in a tufted armchair. He clasped a glass of fine wine in his hand. Maena posed at his side, leaning her stool on two legs to get just a little bit closer. The vulnerable, real woman Tori had bonded with at the Winecoff Hotel was gone, buried beneath smoky eyes and painted lips. Roy and Maena looked like a pair of tropical birds in their natural habitat—colorful, eye-catching, and exotic.

Meanwhile, Tori looked like a middle schooler who'd stumbled into a liquor store. She regretted wearing such a plain outfit; her black jacket, basic pants, and white shirt were the classic software-engineer-at-an-interview uniform. Software engineers couldn't afford to eat here.

At least she wasn't alone. If she was too young for Black Sheep, Brooks was too old. He stood behind Roy, stiff and silent, avoiding eye contact with anyone. Especially Maena.

If Tori didn't know better, she would've thought he hated her. But how could he? This was their first time meeting.

Roy greeted her with a smile. "No luck?"

Tori gave him a thumbs down.

"Can't say I'm surprised," Brooks muttered.

Their luck had been terrible from the moment they'd set foot in New York. On their very first night, Vince and Grace had been threatened by a headless horseman. Out of all the desks in Tianyi, Tori had chosen Director Webb's. In a swarm of hundreds of people, she'd run into their two deadliest enemies at the same time. And they had nothing to show for it.

After Maena had snatched her out of harm's way, Tori had called Roy and Brooks to warn them about Orion and Narcissus. Avoiding a fight was more important than grasping for clues. They regrouped at Black Sheep to brainstorm a Plan C.

It was difficult to brainstorm in front of Maena. Tori hadn't been able to shake her.

"That's enough for now, Miss Jaecar." Roy patted a seat next to him. "Shouldn't you catch up with your friend?"

Gripping Tori by the wrist, Maena dragged her into the chair. "Yes, let's catch up! It's been what, a few months? So much has changed, so fast. You look good!"

Good? Despite herself, Tori glanced at her reflection in Roy's glass. She had the same freckled face, dry skin, and frizzy curls as always. Dark circles smeared under her eyes. If anything, she looked worse than before. She didn't understand.

Maena's hands inched upwards. She squeezed Tori's bicep. "It would take me years to get results like these! You *must* tell me your workout routine."

Blood rushed to Tori's cheeks. "O-oh yeah, sure!" She'd never stopped to notice how her body had changed since she'd started training. Her once slender frame had hardened and grown. She could see the outlines of muscle under her skin. Good indeed.

Somehow, this realization humbled her. Without Roy, Vince, and Brooks, she never would've dreamed of getting so much stronger, inside or out. "It's all thanks to Brooks. He's helped me so much you'd think he was my personal trainer."

Upon being named, Brooks flinched.

Guilt eclipsed her gratitude. She shouldn't have said anything.

Mercifully, Maena moved on without him. "To be honest, Tori... I never expected to see you again."

"Me neither," Tori admitted.

Maena's glass of scotch, long since drained of spirits, sweated on a coffee table in front of them. She reached for it.

"Life is crazy, huh?"

No kidding. So many consecutive coincidences had happened for them to meet. Tori started with the biggest one. "What were you doing in Tianyi?"

"Remember our last meeting?"

Of course she remembered. Orion's arrows had left permanent

scars. She'd never forget the stench of burning flesh. She could still feel that visceral terror or the desperation that'd kept her alive.

"I almost died that night." Maena swirled ice around her cup. "The Winecoff Hotel burned down on the anniversary of my grandmother's death. Fate was telling me to leave Atlanta. I quit the next morning. Had an apartment in NYC by the weekend."

Tori bowed her head. "I'm sorry."

"Hah." Maena dropped her glass back onto its coaster with a jarring clink. "I'm not. I needed a good kick in the ass! My life back in Georgia was going nowhere."

"Why'd you move to New York City? Do you know anyone here?"

"Not a soul. I wanted to start over." A dry laugh. "Who would've guessed my only job offer would be from Tianyi? I should've saved myself the effort and transferred."

Maena put on a brave face, but Tori could tell that her pride was wounded. She could fix that. "Your effort wasn't wasted. Isn't Tianyi very selective? And they pay way more than our company!"

"You're sweet." Maena smiled at her. "But I wasn't looking for money."

Roy slid a fresh glass of scotch over to her. "I'm sure you'll find what you're looking for."

Her smile widened. Her eyes never leaving Roy, she accepted the drink. "Speaking of selective... Tori. Introduce me to your new friends." She punctuated the thought with a long sip.

Tori followed her gaze to Roy and Brooks. Selective? How was she selective?

Without a doubt, Roy was attractive.

Now that she looked a little harder, Brooks had his own appeal. His strong jawline, wide shoulders, and salt and pepper hair gave him a masculine, rugged edge.

For some reason Director Webb's accusation came to mind.

Roy was superficial. Absolutely.

255

He himself was hot. Brooks was handsome. Vince's attitude was terrible and he reeked of smoke and beer, but he had potential. Lots of girls were suckers for bad boys. And Grace's whole career revolved around her appealing to a wide audience.

Roy was collecting beautiful people.

Only Tori was a normal human being. And she'd invited herself to the party.

"My bad, I should've started with introductions. This is Maena Dixon, a project manager from my former, er, current job. Maena? Meet Brooks Wyman and Roy Angelus." She pointed out each person accordingly.

Brooks nodded.

Roy smirked. "Hello Maena."

"Hello boys."

A pause.

"Tori. Aren't you going to tell me how you know them?"

"Um..." Tori wracked her brain for a believable answer. "I um..."

"Your boyfriend?" Maena guessed jokingly. "And his dad?"

Roy clutched at his chest. "I should be so lucky."

Tori had to say something before she got any more flustered. "Relatives!" she blurted. "They're my relatives."

Maena raised a brow. "Relatives?"

They looked nothing alike. Skin tone, eye color, hair color —nothing!

"Distant."

She should've said she was adopted.

Maena laughed. "You're a terrible liar." She waved a hand dismissively. "If you don't want to tell me, just say so."

"O-oh, okay then." Tori felt like a wad of gum on the sidewalk.

"But." Inching closer, Sherri raised a finger. "I'm not going to completely let you off the hook. What were you three doing inside Tianyi?"

Tori shrank away.

"Since I saved you from the fire drill, you owe me that much!"

Maena had a point. She'd saved Tori from oh so much more than a fire drill. She deserved to know it.

Tori had barely mouthed the name "Director Webb" before Roy cut her off.

"We were trying to run a script on Tianyi's network."

Roy was the last person Tori expected to open with the truth. She was stunned.

Maena tilted her head. "A script?"

In a roundabout way, Roy had given Tori permission to stop lying. "Honestly, I don't know what it does," she explained. "But I do know that it's important."

"Know" was a strong word. For all she actually knew, Narcissus' IOU-list could be a lunch order. But Narcissus didn't seem like the type to pay for his own lunch. He definitely didn't care for computers. If he bothered to carry around a laptop just for that one script, it had to be dangerous.

Maena's smile faded. Her eyes fell.

For a moment, Tori feared that she'd offended her somehow.

"...It has something to do with James, doesn't it?"

"You catch on so quickly, Miss Dixon," Roy hummed. "Tell me, how do you feel about road trips, jiu-jitsu, and ghost stories?"

Where was this recruiting pitch when Tori had showed up at their condo!?

Brooks' glares could've melted iron.

Maena didn't reply. She stared at the coffee table as though counting the rings in its wood.

Tori would have agreed to a date with Orion in exchange for knowing what Maena was thinking. Did she suspect that they were involved with the murder? Or worse, that Tori had been involved with James?

Abruptly, Maena placed her work bag on the coffee table. She unzipped it. Her computer and employee ID card were tucked neatly inside.

"Oh no, I'm late for an appointment!" She jumped to her feet. "I'm in such a hurry. I hope I don't forget something on my way out."

Tori's jaw fell open. "You don't have to—"

"No, I do," Maena insisted. "I have to go. This is an appointment with destiny."

Luck. Fate. Destiny. Those things had nothing to do with this. Tori and Maena were, at the most, acquaintances. This script business was, at the least, suspicious. They could sabotage Tianyi. They could steal corporate secrets. And with her ID, they could blame it all on her. She had to have more information before making such a risky decision.

Grabbing at her sleeve, Tori protested, "Just let me explain—"

Maena silenced her by pressing a finger against her lips. "All of these years, I worried about you. I was wrong. You're not the church mouse. I am." She shook her head. "I should have been more worried about myself."

There was no argument for that. Tori relented, slumping back into her chair.

In one long gulp, Maena finished her remaining scotch. "To nine o'clock scotch." She toasted with the empty glass. She frowned. "But it's like four something, isn't it?" She shrugged. "I need a better password."

With one last smile, she exited the restaurant.

CHAPTER THIRTY-FIVE

Nine o'clock came and went, then ten, then eleven, then twelve. People trickled in and out of Black Sheep in a constant stream of color and change. The bottles of the bar glinted like a thousand watchful eyes. Every time the front door opened, Tori flinched. She saw Orion's leer, Narcissus' grin, red eyes, and knife-sized fangs. Soon she might see them for real. In a couple more hours, she, Brooks, and Roy would infiltrate Tianyi again.

Tori would have preferred waiting in the stinking, flooded subways to waiting inside the Woolworth Building. Roy insisted they were safe here. So many floors stretched between Tianyi and Black Sheep that even Orion's hounds could get lost searching for them, and they couldn't openly search in all these crowds.

Still, she couldn't quite forget that she was being hunted. The sixty-story skyscraper was too small, too exposed, too claustrophobic.

Desperate to escape, Tori fled onto the balcony.

All day, the balcony had been her sanctuary. She soaked in the warm evening air. Slowly, the tension left her shoulders. Her breathing steadied. The world flowed around her, indifferent, with better places to be, drowning out the monsters.

The danger was somewhere out there, not here.

She relaxed. She felt younger.

Feeling young was the problem, wasn't it?

If she felt more confident—if she had more strength and experience to offer—she wouldn't be so anxious. She wouldn't make so many mistakes. Roy and Brooks might actually trust her.

"Mind if I join you?"

Tori had escaped reality so successfully that she didn't hear the glass door behind her opening.

Roy lingered at the door, a vampire waiting for an invitation.

Did she mind? No and yes. Over the past several weeks, she'd spent more time alone with Roy than she had with anyone else. And she spent that time with surprising ease. He was smooth and intoxicating, all ambrosia and wine.

But she was fruit salad and grape juice. He made his designer clothes look even better. She dressed in clearance t-shirts and hoodies. His features were flawless, whereas she had wild hair and a swarm of freckles that made it look like she constantly had chocolate stuck on her lips.

Whenever she was around him, Tori couldn't focus on anyone or anything else. And as she contemplated the line between a crush and desire, she couldn't help but draw a different conclusion: she didn't compare to him.

She sighed. She nodded.

Roy sat on the railing next to her, his back to the world.

He was here to cheer her up, wasn't he? Back inside, she'd fidgeted so much for so long that even Vince would've noticed she was nervous.

She braced herself. Roy's pity often stung.

"I'm sorry for what happened back there," Roy began.

Tori glanced at him. Coming from his mouth, "sorry" sounded

like Greek. She didn't dare guess what he meant. He probably didn't even remember flirting with the receptionist, Maena, and Director Webb.

"Brooks and I should've gone over everything with you before we set foot in Tianyi. In our line of work, something always goes wrong. There's always some sort of Plan B, C, or D. We got too used to Vince, who never cares about the details."

"You don't need to apologize for that. I get it. I'm a newbie and an outsider," she said to her knees. "Besides, everything worked out in the end."

"Newbie? Outsider?"

"We met three months ago."

Tori didn't get why he was so confused. Her schoolteachers had always assumed she couldn't afford field trips. Her college roommates had never invited her to clubs or shows. Whenever he could, James left her out of decision-making meetings. She was used to being excluded.

"Tori," Roy whispered. Her name lingered between them, a wish, dandelion seeds in the wind. "You're not a newbie. Vince, Brooks, and I hunted Orion for months, but you're the one who lured him to the Winecoff Hotel. You're the reason Vincent is alive. You're even the reason we're in New York City!"

There was power in a name. The velvet sound of "Tori"—not "Miss Jaecar"— pulled Tori's gaze to his. That change, as subtle as a poet, moved her as much as his speech. It was a symbol. A change in point of view. She was no longer Miss Jaecar, an awkward girl afraid of standing out. She was Tori, an equal—and a woman.

"You are no outsider. You're clever, creative, and brave." Roy continued. "You press on when you're scared; you problem solve when you get stuck." His tone softened. "Whenever you're thinking really hard, you play with your hair. Your cheeks have the most charming dimples, only when you smile. You're a voice of reason in a theater of madness—sweet soothing music that melts like chocolate on your lips."

He paused for breath, a welcome mercy. Tori had forgotten to breathe.

Each phrase, each stanza, drew her closer and closer.

She touched a freckle on her lip.

"Someday, Tori, you'll be a great leader."

Tori realized, right then and there, that there was no line between a crush and desire. They were born of the same longing. Both were greedy and selfish.

She wanted more of this, whatever it was, whatever it cost.

"You can say all that about me, but I don't know anything about you."

"Yes you do," Roy swung to the far side of the railing, standing on a thin ledge. He didn't so much as glance at the staggering drop behind him. He was too busy looking at her. "You know that I'm not afraid of heights."

Tori recalled how her first mission had ended. High up, on the fire escape of the Winecoff Hotel, he'd invited her into heaven. She'd mistaken him for an angel.

"You know that I'm a genius at video games. That I stay up all night, most nights. That I love travel, stories, and challenges. That I like you as you are, and..." He hesitated.

He exhaled, releasing a great weight from his chest.

"...and that Brooks will kill me if I ever look at you the way you look at me."

It was no mistake. Roy *was* an angel.

Tori's crush and desire were her sins to confess. Her greed and selfishness. Her shame to carry. She'd suffered for months and would've suffered for many more if he hadn't said something. He was being kind.

This kindness sounded like a rejection.

Tori knew a lot about Roy after all—he'd never let Brooks stop him from doing anything.

She turned away from him. "I'm that obvious, huh?"

"Not obvious. Honest."

With a gentle grasp, he cupped her chin and guided her face back towards him.

"Tori. I'm not afraid of Brooks. I'm... not even sure I'm afraid to lose him. That's the real reason I've pretended not to notice you all this time."

She didn't understand.

"I'm... so much older than you. And I'm not talking about age. I've been through so much I could never explain it all. I'm surrounded by death. I'm addicted to conflict and danger. I don't know where I'll end up, from day to day. I lie so often I sometimes forget what the truth is. And I'm a terrible father, too."

Gripping the railing between them with both hands, he backed away.

"There's a distance between me and everyone else—a distance not even someone as clever, creative, and brave as you can cross."

Tori had done the math on their ages so many times she'd lost count. It worked out fine, even by her ma's standards. In the Cathedral Basilica, with its votive candles and flowers, she'd made her peace with death. His unpredictability prevented her from sinking into her old, gray routines. And she'd known that Roy was a parent from the very first moment she saw him and Vince together.

None of that mattered.

He was flawed, just like her.

Hearing him say so only made her want him more. To get her hands on him. To find all his scars and imperfections.

Tori lacked experience in the romance department. But Roy had just accused her of being brave. *Twice.*

She placed her hands on top of his. She leaned in, so near their noses almost touched.

She breathed him in, saffron and honey.

"You once told me to draw my own conclusions."

Tori had held Roy's hand once before, at the Winecoff Hotel. This couldn't possibly be the same thing. This touch—so small and innocent—set her system on fire. Her heart pulsed to a sweet, soothing, burning rhythm. A magnetic heat pulled her in.

And she wasn't alone.

He laughed. "You shouldn't take me so seriously."

"Then I won't." Tori had stumbled upon a boundary Roy could not cross. She would cross it for him, again and again, until all that distance he dreamed of disappeared. "After all this is over... Once there's no threat of monsters and war... When I no longer get scared or stuck..."

It was her turn to give him an invitation.

"Let's go back to Roswell Mill Club and find out just how far I can go."

Amusement sparked in Roy's eyes. He loved a challenge.

"After all this is over."

CHAPTER THIRTY-SIX

Tori was at home in an empty office. Back in Atlanta, under James' "leadership", she'd pulled all-nighters almost every month to meet his crazy deadlines. Now that it was well past midnight, she was in her element.

The monsters hiding within Tianyi had all gone to sleep. There was no flirty receptionist to distract her. The army of workers had retreated with the evening rush hour, warm in their beds, far from here. Hopefully Director Webb, Orion, and Narcissus had moved on, too.

The twenty-seventh floor of the Woolworth Building was no longer a maze of concrete and metal. Without any lights, the glass cubicles and conference rooms disappeared. Without people, the atmosphere was eerily still. The cavernous space was an abandoned ruin, forgotten and forbidden to all.

Tomb-raider Roy led them into the unknown. He made a game of pointing out security cameras to avoid. He was so accurate and confident that if Tori didn't know better, she would've assumed that he was the one who'd installed them.

They stopped in a corner, hidden from view.

Roy borrowed a rolling chair from the nearest desk and offered it to her. "You're up."

Nodding, she opened Maena's laptop. She typed in the password and plugged in Grace's flash drive. Unconsciously holding her breath, she navigated to the IOU-list program. She felt like she'd been waiting for this moment all her life. She hit enter.

Building. Loading. *Success!* The databases connected. Thousands of lines of text scrolled past her. She squinted, attempting to make sense of them. Shipper. Consignee. Bill of lading. Package identifiers and names. It might as well have been printing Chinese.

Gripping the back of her chair, Roy leaned over her shoulder. "So? What does Narcissus owe?"

She didn't have an answer. She'd never seen logistics logs before.

"Here," Brooks pointed at one column. "Most of it's coming from St. Louis." He gestured at another. "Oil, coal, weapons, and explosives too... The labyrinth must be some kind of distribution center."

His explanation dispelled a lot of the mystery, but not all of it.

For starters, some of the items made no sense. "Wedding gifts" were being shipped from a garden in St. Louis. "Helen of Troy" had been sent to Atlanta. And the last line in the list stood out so much from everything else that it had to be dangerous.

"Minuteman?" Tori read out loud. "Destination: anywhere?"

Roy leaned in more. "Cryptic."

It was odd, hearing that from him.

Brooks frowned, "What do you think, Mercy?"

"Hmmm, what *do* I think?"

God. Roy was so close to Tori that she could feel his breath on her skin. All the blood surged away from her head, fogging—no, *steaming*—up her thoughts, luring her back to Black Sheep's balcony. She squeezed her eyes shut.

When she opened them, he was even closer. He was looking right at her.

His fingers brushed her cheek.

She flinched.

He broke an almost-invisible string with a snap.

It'd been attached to her temple. How had she not noticed?

"We have a problem." He seemed excited. That was a bad sign.

Abruptly he yanked Tori's chair backwards.

Less than a second later, in an explosion of keys and plastic, an arrow smashed into Maena's computer. The archer had good aim—the single shot obliterated both the onboard hard drive and Grace's flash drive. The IOU-list was gone.

Well, this copy. Both Tori and Roy had it on their machines, too.

Orion appeared from the hallway, twirling an arrow between his fingers. He smirked. "Hello Victoria. Didja miss me?"

Such a dramatic entrance. Tori half wondered if he'd been hanging out with Narcissus after all. Why else would he leave cover to shit talk?

"Like a dog misses his bone," Roy replied with a grin. "I hear you're going to live forever, oh Greatest Hunter of All Time." He twisted his umbrella and drew the snake-entwined sword hidden inside. He pointed it at Orion, a challenge. "That's quite the claim. Let's find out if you can back it up."

Orion's smirk faltered ever so slightly.

No way—was he intimidated?

"And the legends call *me* arrogant." Lowering his bow, he unstrapped his ax from his back.

He'd barely wrapped his fingers around his weapon when Roy was on him.

Roy was fast—faster than Vince and Orion combined—so much so that Tori could hardly keep up. He slashed at Orion's chest.

Orion parried with his ax's handle.

Roy planted his foot between Orion's legs. He shifted his weight into his blade. It bit into the hickory of the ax's handle. It cut through. Easily.

Scowling, Orion shoved Roy away.

Hooking his foot around the back of Orion's ankle, Roy tripped him.

The giant landed flat on his back.

Roy drove his swords downwards, towards his heart.

Again, Orion parried.

"Procyon! Sirius!" he cried, frustration ringing through his voice.

Procyon lunged at Roy from beneath a desk.

Roy also had backup.

With the smooth, deadly accuracy of a leopard catching an impala mid-air, Tori drew her dagger and slashed Procyon across the chest.

Yelping, the hound tumbled to the floor.

Behind Tori, the bark of Brooks' shotgun drowned out a low-bellied, rumbling snarl.

Sirius stumbled, blinded by a face full of buckshot. He crashed into a table. Papers scattered, covering the floor in ichor-splattered snow.

Taking advantage of the chaos, Orion kicked the ground with both feet, sliding out from under Roy. On his hands and knees, he crawled under a desk. He retreated with his tail between his legs.

Together, Roy, Brooks, and Tori chased Orion down the hallway.

In turn, Sirius and Procyon nipped at their heels.

The mad dash ended in a dim, two-story auditorium used for company announcements. Folding seats arched around a raised stage. Above them, a catwalk crisscrossed over complicated light rigging. A large camera hung from the ceiling. Faint LEDs lined the walkways.

Orion scrambled up a hanging ladder to the catwalk.

Immediately, Roy was after him.

Brooks barred the steel double doors behind them. Then he slung his shotgun over his shoulder. He drew a handgun and trained its barrel on Orion.

Tori climbed onto the stage for a better vantage point. For the second time in twenty-four hours, she felt like the protagonist of a romance novel. She couldn't do anything to help. But Brooks and Roy didn't need her help. The handsome heroes would protect her.

Being attacked with Roy and Brooks was a different experience from being attacked with Vince and Grace. Their actions were smooth, prompt, and decisive. Their calm attitude was infectious.

Roy cornered Orion at the edge of the catwalk.

Orion dropped his ax. Backing away, he raised his hands in surrender.

But Mercy did not accept.

Roy brandished his sword. In the low light, its wine-bronze sheen flashed crimson. "Sorry Orion. You're supposed to be dead. It's my responsibility to send you back where you belong."

Orion laughed.

"Even if you kill me, I'll live forever. I'll go down in history"—his smirk returned, more self-satisfied than ever—"as the man who outplayed you in your own house!"

A pair of horns crashed through the wall mere feet away from Tori.

Asterius the minotaur charged her from behind the stage.

He meant to gore her to death. And he was way too close.

No amount of Brooks' training—no owl, no fox, nor leopard—could save Tori now. She had no time to dodge.

Yet time seemed to slow down.

Shock and concern twisted Roy's face.

Brooks didn't speak, but he stared up at Roy with such clear desperation that she could read his thoughts. *Don't let her die.* As If Roy could do something. As if he might not.

Orion grinned, but the smile didn't quite reach his eyes. He was still terrified of Roy.

Roy closed his eyes. He made a choice.

In a burst of light, his sword transformed. A golden rod replaced the blade. The wings of its guard unfurled until they were large enough to carry him through the air. The snakes entwining the handle came to life, stretching to impossible lengths.

One of the great serpents sank its fangs into Asterius' shoulder. The other bit him between the eyes.

In an instant, Asterius' momentum was gone.

The minotaur dropped right where he stood, inches short of Tori. He hit the ground like the fall of a gavel; his judgment was final.

Before Tori could process everything that had happened, Roy was beside her.

He hugged her close.

Honestly, Tori wasn't surprised by Roy's use of magic.

Grace's electricity, Brooks' loyalty, Vince's luck, and her own combat instincts already pushed the boundaries of the mundane world. It was natural that Roy, who led them, wielded something greater.

As Roy's warmth graced her body, as his heartbeat joined hers in hymn, as honey and saffron enshrined her, Tori realized that she'd fallen for an angel. Literally.

Tears welled in the corner of her eyes.

A real angel.

She prayed to God, Gandhi, and Mercy that when Luke had fallen, it'd been into the arms of an angel, too.

"Smile for the camera, will you, 'Roy Angelus'?" Orion laughed, collapsing to his knees. "Wouldn't want that heroism of yours to go unrewarded."

Roy glanced at the camera hanging from the ceiling.

A blinking red light indicated that it'd been on the whole time. But who'd been watching?

Thunder rocked the Woolworth Building—an ominous, bone shaking growl that likened Brooks' shotgun to a whisper. Lightning lashed the night sky. The entire tower shuddered as screeching winds clawed at its frame. The power flickered, helpless against the divine fury of the sudden storm. It was as though the sky itself was enraged by Roy's revelation.

"Mercy!" Brooks gasped. "This can't... That fool..."

The lights died, submerging them in absolute darkness.

All hell broke loose at once.

Sirius crashed through the drywall next to those steel doors, his teeth bared.

Brooks' gun fired.

Roy's sword—no, staff—met something metallic with a ringing clash.

Tori was knocked down by an unseen pair of hands, only to be scooped up by Roy.

Thousands of questions assaulted her from every direction. She wanted to understand the sudden panic, what was happening, and what had been summoned. "Roy, what—"

"I need you to run, Miss Jaecar," he cut her off.

Setting her down, he squeezed her shoulders. "Promise me you won't stop running."

The implication was clear. He was leaving her behind.

No, worse. She was leaving him behind, alongside Brooks, to face the tempest without her. She opened her mouth to object, but no words came out. How could she argue with that trembling touch? With the raw fear in his tone?

Here it was again, that distance between them.

Being attacked with Roy and Brooks truly was a different experience from being attacked with Vince and Grace. Her peers at the kids table needed her. At Mimosa Hall, she'd gathered useful information and outsmarted Orion. At Channel 4, she'd discovered the labyrinth, stolen the IOU-list, and saved Vince from certain death. She made a difference.

But New York hadn't been her city. In five minutes flat, she'd been captured by Director Webb. She'd almost been sandwiched between Narcissus and Orion. Asterius had nearly gored her to death. She'd gotten so much stronger, but she was still so weak.

The best Tori could do for Brooks and Roy would be to get out of their way. She trusted them to survive this, and she trusted her own resolve to get even stronger. Today she would flee, but someday, she'd definitely catch up to them.

She took his hands in hers. "I promise."

With that, she fled into the hallway.

* * *

Tori burst into Tianyi's emergency stairwell. Twenty-seven spirals of steps circled a harrowing drop. She couldn't see the bottom—just looking down made her lightheaded. She grabbed the railing and descended the great tower, a fire drill of one. She wasn't alone for long.

An arrow sliced through her jeans. It rebounded off the wall with a jarring thwang.

Tori stumbled into a run. She'd been cut, but not deep.

Somewhere, Orion had her in his crosshairs.

The whole corridor was pitch black except for the faint glow of exit signs. She couldn't see him. But he couldn't see her perfectly, either. Otherwise, he wouldn't have missed.

"Where are your chaperones?" he jeered.

His voice echoed, chilling her to the bone. It was bad enough hearing it once.

One of Brooks' earliest combat lessons flashed through Tori's mind. Her enemy had the high ground and a ranged weapon. There was no overcoming such a huge disadvantage.

Brooks' guide to fighting on stairs was simple: *get off the stairs!*

So far, she'd gone down four floors. Tianyi's main lobby was three floors further. She still had Maena's ID card. If she escaped there, she could scan into the elevator and ride it to freedom.

Orion had to reload. Tori had a head start—she could make it.

She bolted down the stairs.

Unfortunately, she wasn't dealing with a normal person.

The electricity surged. The lights burst to life just in time for Tori to witness Orion leaping into the center gap.

Orion caught a railing right above her head. Using his momentum from fall, he swung into her.

Pain shocked through Tori's body as it hit concrete.

The lights died again.

Orion pinned her with all his weight. "You didn't answer me earlier. I'm hurt. Because I missed you *terribly.*" He hooked his elbow around her neck, squeezing her throat.

She was trapped. She couldn't breathe. Soon, she'd be unconscious.

But she'd promised Roy she'd escape.

Tori ripped her hidden dagger from its sheath and buried it into Orion's back. The exertion forced the last whisper of air from her lungs.

For a ragged heartbeat, Tori thought she was going to die. In the next heartbeat, Orion recoiled, howling in agony.

She rolled, throwing him off her.

This was her chance. Since he now knew she was armed, it might be her only one.

Wrenching her knife free, she scrambled to her feet. She almost collapsed right back down again. Her head spun, twisting the world upside down. Constellations danced in her vision. She latched onto the railing, holding on for dear life. It slipped underneath her. Her hands were too slicked with blood to maintain a good grip.

If she was going to fall, she'd better fall further down the stairs.

She trundled onwards.

One floor. The spinning slowed.

Two floors. Her senses stabilized.

Above her, Orion stirred. Had she injured him badly enough to end the hunt? What if he bled to death?

A single stairway remained between her and the entrance to Tianyi's main lobby.

She sprinted.

She reached the final step.

Something stopped her ankle. She toppled head over heels.

Tori was falling, but it was fine.

Luke watched from below, a big stupid grin on his big stupid face. His wrinkles were gone. His arms were strong. It would be many years before relentless breakups and even more relentless schoolwork drained that shine from his eyes.

Her brother was the one who had tossed her, and he would catch her, safe and sound.

When was the last time they'd played like this? A decade ago?

They lived those days free from pressure, weightless. In those days, she never could have dreamed what her future would be like. That he wouldn't be in it.

She braced herself for impact with the landing. It never came.

Tori wasn't falling. She wasn't flying either. She was suspended midair by hundreds of transparent threads. She couldn't touch the ground.

Instinctively she struggled.

The threads clung to her clothes, arms, and legs. The more she moved, the more she entangled herself.

The door that led to the Tianyi main lobby taunted her, a mere meter from her grasp.

It swung ajar.

A figure eight body eclipsed the opening.

The spider descended upon the prey trapped in its web.

Director Webb tilted Tori's chin up, forcing her to meet her eyes.

"Victoria, oh Victoria. We didn't finish our meeting."

CHAPTER THIRTY-SEVEN

Li Chenlong was completely in control. The piano pulsed with every beat. The keys bowed beneath his fingertips. Their vibrations rippled through him, calming stormy waters. The satisfaction from each stroke soothed the stinging handprint on his cheek. Complex, exhilarating, yet restrained, the notes wove together into a battle song. It was perfect, just like him.

His father was in New York again, and again they had fought over something stupid.

This time, his father had purchased a shopping mall in Atlanta. At this very moment, the old man was probably off being treated to dinner, smiling and laughing with suits from the West's largest commercial real estate firm. And those suits smiled and laughed along, believing they had swindled him.

No one swindled the CEO of Tianyi. He had a plan.

The problem was, Chenlong could not figure out his plan. Over the last ten years, his father's investments had ranged from impractical to insane. He acquired a failing fintech company. It was so outdated and mismanaged it would have been cheaper to build a competitor from scratch. He bought a St. Louis television network, as if controlling the local gossip in some unimportant midwestern city could accomplish anything.

Then there was the Lackawanna Coal Mine, the literal money pit. Anthracite was valuable. But no matter how many millions of dollars Tianyi carved out of the earth, it would never offset the staggering cost of modernizing a flooded, centuries-old mine. What a disaster. Before they even broke ground, they had to pay off an orphanage to bury the story of a missing kid. *Vincent Lenoir.*

A chord soured, ruining the melody. Chenlong made a mistake. How unlike him.

It did not matter. The CEO's son was many things, but a failure was not one of them. In the end, he always got his way. He would find the music hidden in this cacophony of bad business decisions. When he did, he would use it to destroy his father. He would become untouchable.

Absently, he traced the outline of his chin.

His apartment fell silent. The Woolworth Building penthouse towered high in the clouds, far above the hustle and bustle of Wall Street, a haven from the filth below. Black walls accented exotic walnut floors. Modern furniture filled the empty space. He didn't own a single painting or photograph. He preferred to be alone.

His footsteps echoed as he proceeded into his double-height living room. His servants shuffled back and forth behind the scenes. They dared not disturb him.

His guest was not half as wise.

Senator Pallas waited in an armchair. Slowly, jarringly, she clapped.

She had overheard his playing—including the mistake. Had anyone else intruded on his private time so blatantly, he would have canceled on them.

But Senator Pallas was someone who could not be ignored. Her sharp, silver eyes held him captive. The lines of her face whispered of decades of experience. Her broad shoulders and stately stature commanded attention. She was the judge of the most supreme court, sage of the tallest mountain, keeper of the world's darkest secrets.

She demanded respect, so much so that Chenlong, heir of Tianyi, crown prince of the largest empire on earth, bowed his head as an equal.

"That was amazing," she breathed.

He replied through tight lips. "I was only practicing."

"Imperfections are what make art beautiful, Chenlong."

He scoffed. Imperfections were just imperfections. She could wrap them up with pretty words, but they were still ugly underneath. His Porsche 918 Spyder was a work of art, too, but there was nothing beautiful about the dent in its bumper. He had it repaired long ago, but he remembered every time he saw his car. It was damaged. Weakened. Scarred.

Chenlong had no dents. Her commoner lips soiled his name. "It's Charles," he corrected, drawing a line between them. "At least while I'm in the states." She was lucky he did not insist on "Mr. Li."

He sank into a seat next to her. He snapped his fingers.

A butler approached with a tray. He served a bottle of aged whiskey. After pouring them each a glass, he vanished into the background. The crystal glasses scattered the light, casting the room in an amber glow.

"Thank you for seeing me, Charles," Senator Pallas sipped politely. "I promise I won't be long."

Chenlong did not respond. Such spirits were wasted on someone like her. Politicians only deserved to drink their own poison. He did not understand why a congresswoman had come here, to him. And why in the dead of night?

She had an election to win, of course. Perhaps they were supposed to be conspiring together. Perhaps she hoped to manipulate him into helping her. Did she think he might convince his father to stop funding President Arvis' campaign?

She did not seem that naive. Even if he could convince that heartless sculpture of a man to do anything, he wouldn't. President Arvis' foreign policy was convenient. His United States kept Russia, China's rowdy neighbor, busy. As long as the two superpowers bickered with each other, Tianyi could profit from both of them.

This appointment was going to be pointless. Chenlong should have refused her the moment she requested a midnight meeting. His curiosity had gotten the better of him.

"I came to introduce myself..." Senator Pallas placed a leather box between them. "...and give you this." She opened it delicately.

A watch glittered inside. It was a mysterious masterpiece—not an A. Lange & Sohne, a Patek Philippe, or even a Rolex. No maker's mark blemished its flawless gold. Delicate serpents entwined its intricate clockwork. On its face, a faded woman's diamond eyes fixed him in a paralyzing gaze.

It turned him to stone. The watch suited him so well it was as though it had been made for him. That was the problem.

He had been born on the eve of the lunar new year, a mere hour after the year of the dragon. It was the first time he had disappointed his father. Thousands of disappointments later, he identified with the snake. The wily, alluring zodiac sign suited him much better.

More importantly, his watch collection was a secret. He seldom wore jewelry of any kind in public. It was too overstated for someone of his status. His wealth spoke for itself. He sent acquaintances of acquaintances of acquaintances to auctions to purchase new pieces with the utmost discretion.

He had never met Senator Pallas before. Her present was too personal to be a guess.

The second hand had ticked all the way around the tiny clock before Chenlong found his voice again. "What do you want from me?" he hissed.

"You'll understand soon enough." She sounded like his father. "Think of it as a favor."

"I don't need any favors from you."

"Not yet. But you will."

He snapped the box closed. "I think we're done here."

Without resistance, she stood. "Someday, when you want to thank me..." She set her glass down, punctuating the thought. "Well. You know how to contact me." She winked at him. "It was divine to meet you, little emperor."

Her teasing tone banished all doubt—"little emperor" was an insult.

Chenlong would not be baited. He turned his back to her as she departed.

The door closed. He clutched his temple.

Senator Pallas was a prominent political figure. At some point in her career, she should have learned how to conduct herself. Gifting a stranger in the middle of the night... Digging into his preferences... Poking fun at him like a close friend... He might have expected such childish behavior from a teenage girl with a crush, but not from a world leader. Maybe he had overestimated Americans. His encounters with President Arvis had been similarly unpleasant.

Chenlong peeked at the watch. It was gorgeous, to put it mildly. He should have refused it. There was something forbidden about it, like the railing of a bridge or the exit door of an airplane. Whenever he looked at it, he felt that he was in danger.

Weary, he raised his cup of whiskey to his lips. He hesitated. He reached for the entire bottle instead.

His hand brushed Senator Pallas's glass. Dark red caught his eye.

Wine replaced her whiskey.

His butler would never have wasted fine liquor without asking his permission.

Magic. He was definitely in danger.

In one smooth motion, he swept the glass off the table. It shattered into a thousand stars on the ground. By the time a maid appeared with a broom, he had already retreated into his study.

He dropped into his office chair. Here, surrounded by a fortress of books, nothing could harm him. He switched on his laptop. The hour was late, but it was never too late for work. Work calmed him. Solving problems made him feel like himself. Between nursing his bottle and reading emails, his pulse eventually steadied.

An alert begged for his attention. He clicked on it.

Database connections scrolled past him. Rows upon rows of data filled his screen. Someone was accessing privileged information—privileged information he didn't recognize.

That should not have been possible. He ate, breathed, and lived Tianyi.

Straightening, he dug deeper. He pulled the profile of the employee responsible.

Maena Dixon, a project manager from Atlanta.

Judging from how useless Director MacGillivray had been, Chenlong would be surprised if Maena even knew what a database was, much less what to do with dozens of them. What in the world was she up to? What was an "IOU-list"?

Shipping manifests flashed across his screen. One by one, his father's investments began to make sense. Little by little, adrenaline spiked through his veins. He shut his computer, grabbed his keys, and headed for the elevator.

The snake had his rat.

CHAPTER THIRTY-EIGHT

Cicadas sang to the evening sun, a summer symphony of respite and relaxation. Beads of water hugged her window, glittering like stars. Humidity hung in the air, hot and sticky, smelling of the sweet pops melted on the sidewalk outside. Tori and Luke had been too busy chasing each other through their neighbor's fields to stop, cool off, and eat.

Tori was home. Neither St. Louis nor New York City compared to the wonder of this sleepy cottage nestled deep in the heart of Georgia. Here, she could rest. The roaring roads and whispering monsters of the city faded into the distance. They were nothing more than bad memories. Nothing could harm her.

"'I think I got you this time,' Brer Fox bragged, grinning an evil grin. Wily Brer Rabbit was caught in his trap, so stuck he couldn't move his hands or legs or paws, but he had a plan."

Ma held two fingers up in the moonlight, casting the shadow of a rabbit on the wall. With her other hand, she made a fox. She pantomimed the scene as she spoke.

"'You got me, Brer Fox. But please, for old time's sake, make it quick,' Brer Rabbit begged. 'Roast me, but don't fling me into that briar patch over there. Hang me, but don't fling me into that briar patch over there. Drown me, but don't fling me into that briar patch over there.'"

Ma tucked Tori into her bed. Warmth and affection glowed in her eyes.

"'You're not scared of anything,' said Brer Fox. 'But you are scared of the briar patch over there. So that's how I'll prep you for supper.' He flung him over the fence into the thorns."

Tori knew how the fable ended. She'd heard it a thousand times. It never failed to transport her deep into the past, into a world of magic of mystery, where legends taught lessons instead of pain.

"Brer Rabbit didn't shout or yell. He scuttled through the brambles and brush all the way to safety. 'I was born and bred in the briar patch,' he laughed. 'That's the place I'm at my best!'"

Ma smiled at Tori. "Deception... Ingenuity... Manipulating others... These are a huntress' greatest weapons."

A cat leapt onto her shoulder. A large white spot marked his gray fur. A cloud.

This wasn't Tori's mother. It was Dee, the cat lady from her office park.

After everything that'd happened, Tori knew better than to write this off as a fever dream.

Dee was some kind of monster. She was helping Tori. But why? And how?

"Only prey relies on strength alone. You're better than that."

No, not Dee. *Diana.*

Tori jerked upright. Her childhood bedroom had vanished. Instead, she was in a dimly lit shipping container. Handcuffs bound her wrists. They were chained to a wall. Her leash was so short that she could barely stand in place.

Little by little, memories of Tianyi's stairwell, her battle with Orion, and Director Web's ambush returned.

Her head felt full of molasses. A dull ache in her throat punished her for losing another fight. Her phone and dagger had been confiscated. She was in bad shape, but she was in one piece. For now.

Vince and Grace weren't answering their phones. Roy and Brooks were gone.

Tori was alone with her enemies.

Slowly, she inhaled and exhaled.

The air tasted stale. Moisture slicked every surface. A chill clung to the darkness. She was probably underground. She could worry about that later. The first thing she had to do was get her hands free.

She surveyed the room. A halogen work light illuminated the cramped space. A makeshift guard station—a folding chair with a small table—waited well beyond her reach, empty. Magazines piled next to it. She squinted, struggling for a better look.

They weren't magazines, they were comic books. *The Adventures of the Sun and Moon* titled every cover. On one spread, a female archer fired an arrow from the back of a buck. On another, a man strummed an acoustic guitar. Their features were so similar that they could've been gender swapped clones of each other. They had to be siblings.

Torn pages peppered the ground. Someone had shredded specific chapters. Perhaps they didn't like the ending?

The paper was thick and colorful, like the business card Roy had used to unlock Tianyi's conference room door. It gave Tori an idea.

Before she could act on it, the door swung ajar.

A giant eclipsed the opening.

Orion Treyvon stepped inside.

"Good morning, Beautiful."

The word "beautiful" had never sounded so ugly.

Tori swallowed a swear. It was better to not encourage him.

"What? Not even a hello?" He sauntered over to her. "I think you owe me that much after last night." He spoke so confidently, but his movements betrayed him. They were tense and stiff; he was in pain. Too bad that didn't stop him from invading her personal space.

"Sorry." Tori's childhood values had flown out the window of the Winecoff Hotel. She'd stabbed another person, yet the only thing she was sorry about was not killing him. "I'll work on my aim."

His gaze lowered to the tear his arrow had cut through her jeans. It'd barely broken her skin. "So will I. Not that I'll need to." He traced his gloved fingers along her chain. "If you're like this, I can't miss. Takes the fun out of things."

"You're right. Why don't you let me go so you can not hit me some more?"

"Hah! That's what I like about you, Victoria. You keep acting tough. You keep fighting back. It's so adorable." Leaning in close, he lowered his voice. "How should I make you understand? I'm so much stronger than you'll ever be."

Fear crawled up Tori's spine. Determination chased it back down. If she kept quiet until he lost interest, she might survive this encounter. But survival wasn't enough. She had to escape, save the phoenix, and stop President Arvis. And to do that, she had to keep Orion talking.

"You could start by telling me... Why did you kill James?"

"James? Oh, was *that* his name? You humans are so cute with how you name your animals."

Tori blinked. Unlike James, Procyon and Sirius were actually animals. Didn't Orion name them?

Orion noticed her confusion. "He was our pet for years. He barked when we said bark, fetched when we said fetch, and begged when we said beg. How else do you think he made it to Director?" He shrugged. "He'd still be alive if he hadn't tried to run. I think he

285

was trying to save an old girlfriend's daughter? Something stupid like that."

So the photograph on Director Webb's desk had been relevant after all. The woman standing with James had been his lover, many years ago. Tori wagered that the mysterious mistress was from St. Louis. The fact that James cared about anyone but himself shocked Tori more than the connection.

Orion chuckled. "What kind of loser would risk his life for an ex?"

That was a good question. Tori had better ones. Her handcuffs limited her movement, but they also put Orion at ease. He was volunteering so much extra information. She couldn't waste this opportunity.

"Our pet, you said. *Our.* Do you work for Director Webb?"

"I don't work *for* anyone. Don't you know who I am?"

"Enlighten me."

"I'm Orion Treyvon, son of the sea, the sky, and the crossroads between, giant among kings!" He pounded a fist on his chest. "No one outranks me. There's nothing alive I can't slay."

Tori fought the urge to roll her eyes. The word "narcissist" should've been based off him, not Narcissus.

"Then what are you doing here? Did you die and come back, like Narcissus and Asterius?"

"I didn't die, I was backstabbed." Orion was less eager to brag about his death. "By another hunter. But she's gone, I'm here, and I'm better than ever." He crushed a torn page from a comic book. "I'm slumming around with those degenerates because of a prophecy. If President Arvis' plans succeed, I will become immortal! Like Procyon and Sirius."

A prophecy, huh? Tori recalled the domed ceiling of the Cathedral Basilica. Her childhood church had preached salvation, not predestination. Free will controlled the universe, not divine destiny. *Fate.* Roy mentioned that term a lot.

But Orion spoke with such absolute certainty that she could not deny that he, at least, believed that the future could be predicted. What a terrifying thought. For predictions to be possible, there had to be a script to read from. Otherwise, the prediction itself would change everything.

Tori didn't have time to learn new rules for the universe. Right now, she needed to stay in the moment. "Why go through so much trouble? Why not just steal some Apples of Discord?"

"As if immortality could be stolen," Orion spat. Her suggestion was stupid. "Those apples will drive any normal person to madness. I need all of my senses if I'm going to conquer a new kingdom and rule from the highest throne!"

Oddly, Orion's reaction comforted her. He was so overconfident that he'd believe anything that painted him in a positive light. Her existential crisis could wait until his prophecy came true.

"Once I do..." Orion placed a hand on the wall next to her, cornering her. He cupped her chin. "If you bark, fetch, and beg, I might just let you be Queen Victoria."

He was so close that Tori was afraid he might kiss her. She would have preferred an existential crisis.

Orion was underestimating her. His weight was on the wall, not her. Both of his hands were occupied. Her legs were free.

If she kicked him where it hurt, he would recoil.

If she could get the chain for her handcuffs around his neck, she could knock him out.

If she failed, well. It was best not to worry about what if's.

Adrenaline ticked through her body. She closed her eyes, counting down the seconds.

Three...

Orion grinned. "What's the matter, Queen Victoria?"

Two...

"Don't want to take responsibility for all you've done to me?"

One...

"Well then." He tightened his grip on her jaw. "What should I do to *you?*"

"You should keep your hands to yourself," Narcissus stated flatly.

Tori barely stopped herself from kicking Orion in time.

Her gamble might've paid off against one villain. Against two, she had no chance.

Orion narrowed his eyes. "Can't you see I'm busy?"

"That's not what you said last night."

"What do you want!?"

"You." Narcissus gave him a long, pointed once over. "You following the rules, to be specific. Adeline is the one who captured her, not you. So whatever"—he waved a hand in their general direction—"this is, it'll have to wait until she's done with her."

"Adeline doesn't have to know every little thing."

Narcissus wrinkled his nose as though he had whiffed something rotten. "Are you sure 'little' is the word you want to use?"

"Damnit Narcissus." Orion seized him by the collar. "If you don't shut that pretty mouth of yours, I'll shut it for you!"

"This pretty mouth of mine works on giants too," Narcissus warned, unphased. "Keep on touching me like that"—lovingly he stroked the other man's cheek—"and one of us is going to end up on his knees."

Roaring in frustration, Orion flipped the table. Comics swirled through the air, leaves in an autumn gust. "Know your place, you worthless pawn! As soon as this is over, you're fucking mine."

"Oh Orion, keep talking dirty to me!"

Orion couldn't bear the shame of being teased in front of Tori. He wasn't willing to test Narcissus' abilities, either. He only had one option: retreat. "Fuck this."

Growling, he stormed off.

Narcissus retrieved a hand mirror from the pocket of his blazer. He straightened his collar.

Tori didn't understand what she'd just witnessed. It almost seemed like Narcissus had defended her. But why would he?

"I, um..." She cleared her throat. "Thank you?"

"I didn't do it for you."

Ah. So she was right. He *had* chased Orion off on purpose.

"Thank you either way."

"Be thankful that I didn't have to actually touch that testosterone addled bull-hide of a man," Narcissus complained. "I swear, this power of mine couldn't be any more ironic."

Ironic? Tori frowned.

As far as she knew, Narcissus' power charmed others into doing his bidding. He struck her as the kind of person who would enjoy being worshiped. She struggled to remember his myth. Roy claimed that Narcissus had fallen for his own reflection.

Narcissus had kissed Vince, a stranger. His interactions with Orion had been tense, to put it mildly. Both situations involved romantic acts with a person he did not like.

That was it. It wasn't his power. It was the trigger.

"...Because you only love yourself?" Tori guessed.

Narcissus scoffed. "It's not a sin to love yourself. My only crime was being born too beautiful. Not that someone like you would understand."

Tori ignored the implied insult. "Try me."

"A mountain nymph fell in love with me at first sight." He grimaced as if he were describing a toad rather than a nature spirit. "I don't blame her, of course. But instead of, you know, getting to know me or anything, she followed me around like an echo. When I told her to get lost, I broke her heart. She prayed to the gods for revenge." He drew a line across his neck. "That's all it took. I was cursed. Je suis là, me voilà!"

He shook his head. "To be honest, that's the least traumatizing way my story could have ended." Holding the back of his hand to his forehead, he peered up at the heavens. "Poor Ganymede!"

Under different circumstances, Tori might've pitied the beautiful monster. She couldn't respond. Her grasp on reality slipped between her fingers like water in her palms.

Legendary beasts. Heroes returned from the afterlife. Prophecy, fate, destiny, and now gods. She wished Roy was here to explain it all away. She clung to the last thread of normalcy, the present. "If you didn't get rid of Orion for me, then why did you?"

"Oh honey. Don't tell me you didn't know?" Narcissus looked down his nose at her. "I did it for me. You and I have *a lot* in common." He quickly clarified, "Underneath the surface, that is."

After listening to his backstory, Tori was confident that having a lot in common with him was a bad thing.

Reluctantly, as if she was covered in melted sweet pops, he patted her shoulder. "I felt sorry for you, that's all."

"Sorry enough to unlock these?" She held up her handcuffs.

"Not quite." He smiled. "Anyways. That's enough fraternization for one day. Orion will slither back in here as soon as he realizes I'm gone. Make sure you escape before then!" Without glancing back, he departed.

Tori breathed a sigh of relief. Finally, she was alone.

Orion had punted several comic books in her direction. Grabbing one, she folded a page into a thin rectangle. She wedged it into the catch of her handcuffs. Her bonds popped open.

Cheering, she kissed the comic book that saved her.

Bold print captured her eye. It was the heroine's name. Artemis. *Goddess of the Hunt.*

Tori's hand wandered to her chest. She'd once hallucinated being struck in the heart by a silver arrow. It hadn't been a hallucination, had it? She desperately needed to find the others.

CHAPTER THIRTY-NINE

Vincent Lenoir opened his eyes. He saw nothing. He opened and shut them, again and again, but no matter how hard he tried he could not make sense of the infinite darkness.

His body weighed a ton. Pain pulsed in his temple with such searing intensity he couldn't think about anything else. Water rushed in the distance, yet his mouth was dry as a desert. Was this hell?

No, hell was on earth. It was growing up in a world full of monsters. It was Roy and Brooks gone from his life. It was running away from a girl who sincerely liked him.

He was alive. He wouldn't be for long. His feet were bound together—above him. He hung upside down, suspended in the air, somewhere even more humid than Sibyl's Cave had been. Blood pooled in his head. If he didn't break free, it would overflow and burst. He struggled. A rope snapped.

He landed flat on his back. *Stupid.* He was lucky he didn't break his neck.

"Vince? Is that you?"

Graces' hand found his arm.

For a heartbeat, Vince wished he had broken his neck. In this hell he'd created for himself, he didn't deserve the touch of an angel. He wasn't ready to face her. Fortunately, he didn't have to face anything. In this pitch blackness, neither of them could see shit.

"Yeah. You okay?"

"I think so."

As Vince's headache weakened, his guilt strengthened. He was so afraid of being abandoned that he'd abandoned Grace. Twice. In the span of an hour. Then he literally ran into an almost-girlfriend from his past. So fucking smooth.

His antics got them stuck in a spider web. The last thing he remembered was a sexy librarian type sinking her fangs into his neck. Under different circumstances, it would've been hot.

Her venom hit him like a spinning carnival ride after a night of binge drinking. He had the worst hangover of his life. His lingering nausea was so sickeningly powerful that it might cure him of his thing for older women forever.

"Where are we?" Grace wondered.

A chill gnawed at his skin. "Not hell. Why's it so damned cold?"

"In Greek mythology, it'd be Hades. Not as hot as hell."

"I'm pretty sure I'd know if we were in Hades. That Spider-Lady must've brought us here. Maybe we're in a freezer. She's saving us for dinner."

"Oh no! Spiders hate the taste of lavender! We have to escape before she returns!"

"Let's find an exit."

Silently, wordlessly, they fumbled around on their hands and knees. Vince had never felt so awkward before. He bumped into Grace once or twice, but neither of them wanted to talk, especially not about what had transpired between them.

It was for the best. Their relationship status would not matter for a whole lot longer if Spider-Lady liquified their insides and ate them through a straw.

A thin slime slicked the floor. Sulfur mingled with the musty air. Whenever Grace made a sound, Vince flinched. A thousand serrated teeth snarled at the edges of his vision. This atmosphere reminded him of the Lackawanna Coal Mine. Hopefully, if a hydra appeared, Roy and Brooks would, too.

"Oh? Oh!" Grace exclaimed. "Vince! There's a door!"

Vince crawled in her direction. His fingers traced up a wall. Concrete gave way to cold metal. He grasped a handle. "Of course. It's locked."

"Can you unlock it?"

Unlocking something by feel alone without tools would be a tall order even for Roy. Vince preferred more direct tactics. He stood. Summoning all his might, he slammed his shoulder into the door.

It didn't budge.

His attempt sent someone skittering away from them.

"Who's there?" he shouted.

A flashlight reluctantly winked to life. It revealed a mess of a man.

Vince froze. Photographs of children jammed his thoughts like rush hour traffic.

"Louis?" Grace gasped. "Is that you?"

"Oh. Ah! Thank goodness!" Louis wiped cold sweat from his brow. "I thought you were... you know what? Never mind." He waved from behind a grate in the door. "Hi guys."

Vince and Grace had been locked in a tiny maintenance room, bare except for a rotting electrical panel and crumpled trash.

Grace, at least, was happy to see Louis. "How did you find us?"

Louis flashed a thumbs up. "Turns out the alligators that live down here are actually really nice. They gave me directions."

Down here. Alligators. They were in the flooded subway system.

The mention of more monsters thawed Vince's limbs. He reached for his gun. It was missing in action. "Or maybe he's been stalking us for decades."

"Well, yes. I stalked you here. In a way," Louis admitted, oblivious to the fact that the door was the only thing standing between him and an entire childhood of pent-up anger. "A suspicious-looking woman snuck into Sibyl's Cave right after you. She must have rigged the explosives." His eyes fell. "I'm so sorry! I tried to warn you, but I was so nervous my phone wouldn't turn on. Afterwards, I couldn't find you. So I followed the woman instead." He clutched at his heart. "The experience took years off my life."

"Not enough of them," Vince growled.

Grace pressed her face up against the grate, straining for a better look. "Can you get us out of here?"

"There? No. I never saw any keys."

"Hmm..." She tapped her lip with a finger thoughtfully. "I've got it!"

She lowered her palm in front of the door handle. Her magnetic powers kicked in. Slowly, the bolt of the lock slid backwards, out of the catch. The door popped open.

"Wow, that's so cool!" Louis cheered. "You're just like the Sun and Moon!"

Grace beamed at him. "More like the Stars!" She didn't understand what he was talking about, but she was pleased to be praised.

Enough playing nice. Enough pretending like nothing was wrong.

Vince forced through the door. He seized Louis by the collar, shoving him against a wall.

Louis yelped.

His flashlight rolled across the tile, illuminating a subway station.

Skylights spanned vaulted ceilings. Faint sunlight filtered through the murky water above them. Sludge dripped between their leaded seams. Somehow, despite an era of neglect and decay, the glass held back the fury of the sea.

The words "CITY HALL" sprawled across the far wall. Mosaic patterns, once colorful and bright, now grayed and crumbling, decorated every surface. Muddy rivers flowed over rusted train tracks. Brass chandeliers, darkened with age, hung over the walkways like spiders.

Vince, Grace, and Louis stood in an abandoned subway station. They were its first passengers in a century.

"Vince!" Grace yelled. "Stop it!"

Vince couldn't hear her. "You knew, didn't you?"

"I don't know what you mean—"

"Don't fucking lie to me!" Vince shoved him harder. "You knew what your mother was up to!"

"You're hurting him!" Grace pulled on his bicep. "He clearly has no idea what you're... what you're talking..."

Louis slumped. He couldn't make eye contact. "I knew," he confessed.

"She killed kids, Louis! And you let her!" Vince's voice shook nearly as much as he shook Louis. "Give me one good reason why I shouldn't kill you right now!"

"Lamia," Louis mumbled. "That's her name. I always knew what she was capable of, but as long as she could see me, she didn't hurt anyone. It wasn't until she left Jersey on her own that she... that she actually..."

Vince's hands inched higher to his neck. "Don't worry, you'll be seeing her really soon."

"You mean..." Louis' eyes widened. "She's...?"

"Shot through the head. Remember my revolver?"

Tears streaked down Louis' face. "I'm so relieved!"

Shock stunned Vince into silence. His grip loosened.

"I love my mother. So much," Louis choked between sobs. "She was a queen, you know. A wise, fair ruler. But one day, she had an affair with the wrong man—my father." The story gushed out of him like water flowing from a broken dam. "My father was married. His wife found out about me. So she kidnapped me. My half-siblings too. And my mother, she... She thought she was all alone in the world. Her despair drove her mad. It turned her into a..."

"...A monster," Vince finished for him.

His torrent subsided, its anguish spent.

"Yes, a monster," Louis whispered. "When I found her again, after so many lifetimes had passed, I... I couldn't do it. I couldn't end her suffering."

Peace softened Louis' eyes. He'd fulfilled his purpose. He was satisfied. "Vincent Lenoir, I can never repay you for what you've done for me." He squeezed Vince's fingers at his throat. "Do what you must."

Vince had never seen a monster look quite so human. He faltered. "But why me?" he breathed, desperate, pleading. "Out of all of the kids in the world, why did Lamia want me?"

Louis' face fell. "I don't know." He searched for a better answer. "Maybe it was fate. Maybe she knew that somehow, through meeting you, she would finally be able to rest."

Vince let go. Reeling, he stumbled away. He couldn't listen to another syllable.

Grace grabbed his hand, holding him steady.

"Get out of my sight!" he barked at Louis. "Before I change my mind!"

Louis dropped to his knees, grasping at Vince's hands. "At least let me help you get back to the surface."

"Fine. But after that, I never want to see your pathetic face again."

* * *

Louis led Vince and Grace through the drowned labyrinth.

The City Hall station's entrances had been filled in. Its passengers had no choice but to follow the subway tunnel deeper underground, through twists and turns, for blocks and blocks. Dead silence haunted the passageways like a graveyard. Only rats traveled on these railways—they scampered over the half-submerged tracks.

"Do you think there are any mole people down here?" Grace murmured.

Louis's flashlight flickered. "M-mole people?"

"I read about them in a magazine once. There's an entire civilization of blind, rodent-like creatures living underneath New York City. Someday their armies will rise to conquer the world above."

"Armies?" Louis squeaked. "That's definitely—"

"Bullshit," Vince wasn't in the mood for innocence anymore. "Grace. Mole people are real, but they aren't rodents. They're homeless people. They're doing the best they can to survive." He glared at Louis. "The only monster in this subway is standing next to you."

His accusation ended the conversation.

Their odyssey led them to a dead end. Well, a dead end for anyone who couldn't turn into a Shark-Boy. The path before them dove into water. Louis' flashlight couldn't penetrate the black, bottomless depths.

"What now?" Vince complained. "Did the alligators give you directions to a submarine?"

"Uhm Louis. You didn't happen to bring any other friends along, did you?" Grace asked.

"Friends?" Louis laughed. A pause. "O-oh, you were serious? No."

"Then who's that?" She pointed behind them.

Something big shifted.

The subway quivered in anticipation.

Dust trickled on their heads.

Louis swept the area with his flashlight.

A hulking figure cut a shadow against the unsteady beam. Horns curled from its forehead.

Asterius, MoMo, the minotaur, blocked the entire corridor.

They were trapped between him and the abyss.

Great. Vince's gun had been stolen. Asterius' shoulders were so broad that the monster hunter might not even be able to get his arms around his neck. Without a weapon, fighting was out of the question. That only left flight.

Vince surveyed the room for anything useful. Busted rails curled up from the floors. Corroded pipes leaked on the walls. His eyes stopped on Grace.

Rails. Pipes. Were either of those things magnetic? Ugh. He should've paid attention in science class.

"Vince?" Grace whimpered.

"When I give you the signal, we'll make a run for it," he whispered. "Can you throw some metal to distract him? Once we're close."

She nodded.

Louis fidgeted so much that the hem of his hoodie frayed. "Okay."

"Do you understand now?" Asterius stomped towards them with purpose. "How futile this is. How helpless we are!"

"Speak for yourself, buddy," Vince jeered.

Snorting, Asteris lowered his head. He pawed at the earth.

"Now!" Vince shouted. He seized Grace's arm. Together they rushed the bull.

Vince was so focused on the road ahead that he didn't notice that Louis stayed behind.

Asterius charged. His hooves thundered along the pavement.

Grace's power pulled at the rails and pipes. She needed more time.

The point of Asterius' horn pressed into Vince's chest, above his heart. It tore his shirt. It punctured his skin.

A deafening roar boomed through the subway.

Water crashed into their ankles. The impact knocked everyone to the ground.

Vince and Grace tumbled over each other, past their enemy.

Asterius bellowed with frustration.

"Louis," Grace cried out. "What are you doing!?"

Louis, their Lady of the Lake, towered over the scene. Rapids raged around him. He'd summoned strength from the deep.

"You know, Grace. For some reason I feel like I've known you forever. But you don't really know me, do you?" He faced off against the minotaur. Waves chased along his footsteps. With each ebb and flow, they grew in intensity. He raised his hands over his head. The current surged, rising above them, clawing at the ceiling.

"Vince was right all along."

Vince scooped up Grace. With everything he had, he sprinted towards the station.

Louis smiled as he watched their retreat.

"I *am* a monster."

The tsunami fell, crushing him and Asterius.

The torrent swallowed everything in its path. It lapped at Vince's heels. It gained on him.

He hadn't fully recovered from being poisoned. His muscles shivered and ached. His lungs screamed for oxygen. He reached his limit.

A rope looped around his waist. It dragged him and Grace into the air.

CHAPTER FORTY

The line trembled. She had a bite!

Tori Jaecar pulled the rope with all her might. Rough hemp pressed into her hands. Her muscles burned. She panted for air. She dug her heels in.

Somewhere in Alaska, a mighty grizzly plunged its claws into a river. It dragged a king salmon into the light.

With one final, decisive heave, Tori landed her catch.

Vince and Grace toppled onto the ground next to her.

Wiping the sweat from her brow, Tori breathed a sigh of relief. She hadn't been fishing in years. Luke used to hold onto her rod whenever she hooked something big. Once a mudcat the size of her arm had almost dragged them both under. Now she'd hauled two struggling, full-sized adults out of the water by herself.

Dee—perhaps Artemis—had done something to her. She was sure of it.

Tori shoved a thick, metal ventilation grate back over the opening in the ground. It blended in so seamlessly with the tiles on the floors and ceilings that their enemies below would never notice it.

Well, not unless they knew about this sewer tunnel above the subway.

Unfortunately, that was a strong possibility.

The sewer tunnel had cracked, crumbling walls. A rust-colored patina painted it top to bottom. It was ancient, but new mingled with the old.

Fully functional fluorescent lights hung from the roof, bathing the corridor in sterile light. A pathway had been carved through the rubble. It was clean enough that Narcissus could walk the whole thing without ruining his designer shoes.

The clack of the grate settling into place returned Grace to her senses... kind of?

She scrambled over to the grate. She wrenched at it. It was too heavy for her. Flustered, she held her palm over it. No luck. It wasn't magnetic.

Meanwhile, Vince did nothing. The worry lines wrinkling his forehead made him look older than Brooks. He moaned in pain. He rolled onto his back. He buried his face in his hands.

Although Tori didn't need to be thanked for saving them, she at least expected to be acknowledged. She was happy to see *them*.

"Please, Tori. Help me with this!" Grace gasped between yanks. "Louis is still down there!"

"Louis?"

Tori's gaze bounced between her two companions. She couldn't read this atmosphere. Why was Vince so calm while Grace panicked?

Cautiously Tori reached for the grate.

Vince snatched her wrist. "Forget about him."

"But he helped us so much!"

"Like he helped all those kids?"

Grace had no argument for that.

"Look," Tori was beginning to feel like she was watching an episode of a soap opera out of order. She hated soap operas. "I don't know who this Louis guy is, but that subway flooded right after I grabbed you. So unless one of you has some scuba gear—"

"See Grace? Shark-Boy will be fine," Vince hissed. "But Asterius can't breathe underwater. Are you sure you don't want to help him, too?"

Tori blinked. What in the world was going on between them? They'd been getting along pretty well between St. Louis and New York. Too well, even. Now they bickered like two seagulls that had happened upon a French fry.

Grace threw her arms around Tori. "Oh Tori. I'm so glad you're here!"

Vince sat on his elbows. "How did you find us, anyway?"

"You weren't exactly being quiet down there," Tori laughed dryly. "What were you doing? Holding a cooking competition? There were so many crashes, bangs, and shouts that I wouldn't be surprised if you told me you had a whole television crew running around with you."

"Something like that," Vince grunted.

"But how did you end up underground?" Grace asked.

Tori rubbed the back of her head. "I got stuck in a spider web. It's a long story."

"No way! Us too!"

Tori detached herself from Grace. "We have a lot we need to catch up on."

Golden snakes entwined her thoughts. Had Vince known the true power of Roy's sword? Had Roy and Brooks escaped the fury of the storm? She patted her cheeks. She could worry later. "For now, we need to move. Both Orion and Narcissus are skulking around."

"Asterius, too." Vince stood. "Where to?" He offered Grace a hand up.

After escaping the shipping container, Tori had explored the sewers for so long she'd lost track of which way was up and which way was down. "This place is almost as bad as the labyrinth beneath Channel 4. Let's find an exit before our enemies find us."

The tunnel ended in front of the strangest elevator Tori had ever seen. Scrollwork wove complex patterns around a bronze cage. The cage hung from a cable that appeared far too thin to support its weight. Hydraulic machinery glittered behind it. Above it all, an art deco styled eagle judged them with cold, blank eyes. The intricate yet cold aesthetic reminded Tori of the back of a quarter, tarnished with age, repeated a thousand times.

"If I ever see a time machine, I bet it'll look like this," Grace entered the elevator. She'd forgotten her suspicions about the rabbit with lightning speed. Maybe the exploded cave incident hadn't been as bad as it sounded.

"Ladies first," Vince gestured at Tori.

Tori rolled her eyes as she trailed after Grace.

"Hey. Brooks keeps saying I need to learn manners."

Once they were all inside, Tori pressed the only button. The antique elevator creaked and stretched like a cat after a long nap. It lifted them into the unknown.

* * *

A metallic ding echoed through the ancient elevator shaft as Tori, Vince, and Grace reached the top. Wooden doors rolled out of their way.

Tori stepped into an enormous room. She felt as though she was trespassing in a Renaissance painting. Intricate molding crowned elegant plaster ceilings. Priceless portraits of past United States presidents hung on vibrantly colored walls. Luxurious red carpet lounged upon shining wooden floors. The furniture looked antique, handmade, and older than her great grandma.

Atlanta's museums were small. She could probably buy two or

three of them by selling the decorations collecting dust around her. She was afraid to touch anything.

"This place is familiar," Grace tapped her lower lip with her finger.

Tori and Vince exchanged glances, sharing a rare moment of kinship. Neither of them had ever set foot anywhere half as luxurious as this.

Grace peered through the glass panes of a door. The rotunda on the other side could fit one of Atlanta's museums inside of it. Grand staircases curled up to a circular balcony. Fluted columns supported a domed ceiling. "Ah! We're in New York City Hall!"

Tori saw herself a thousand times, reflected in crystal chandeliers. "This is just a city hall?" The Georgia state capitol building had a gold-plated roof, yet it seemed less extravagant.

"Not just a city hall. It's one of the oldest city halls in the nation. So much happened here." Grace spun, her arms wide. "The center of the center of New York. A stunning backdrop to social affairs, council meetings, bill signings, and even assassinations. Our greatest leaders all passed through these halls. Even President Arvis. This was his home base, back when he was governor."

Dizzy from rotating, she almost tripped. "During the last election, Channel 4 came here for one of President Arvis' speeches. Afterwards, the staff gave me a tour." She beamed. "Can you tell?"

Grace had been here before. That was the best part of New York City Hall's history.

"What do you remember?" Tori asked.

"The whole building is crawling with security. But I think I can lead us to a staff exit."

Vince had ignored Grace's long exposition. Instead, he rifled through cabinets, shelves, and desks. "Before we go.... look!" He gestured at an old cedar chest. Loot glittered inside. Their confiscated possessions waited, ready to be un-confiscated.

"Baby, I missed you so much!" He kissed his gun.

Tori returned her dagger to its sheathe inside her hoodie. She switched on her cellphone.

Disappointment gutted her. Roy and Brooks hadn't contacted her.

She swallowed, pushing the anxiety bubbling up her stomach back down. It'd only been, what? A day or so? Surely they'd call soon.

"My phone!" Grace snatched up her pink case. "I hope my poor adoptable pets are okay. I didn't feed them last night."

Tori opened her mouth to ask what adoptable pets were and why they needed food, but she snapped it shut once she noticed the distinct tap-tap-tap of approaching footsteps.

They ducked into a corner, out of view from the hall.

She closed her eyes, racking her brain for an explanation in case they were caught. Lost tour group, custodians, construction workers... Nothing worked. Tori's clothes were torn. Vince and Grace were drenched and muddy. Not to mention they were visibly armed.

If Tori made it out of here in one piece, she'd practice lying in the mirror until it came to her as naturally as writing a line of code.

When she opened her eyes again, Director Webb stood a few paces down the hall. A man draped his arm around her shoulder. She laughed at some unheard joke.

The high-pitched giggle didn't suit her. It reminded Tori of how Maena giggled whenever James said something gross. It was convincing, but to a trained ear, it was too stiff to be sincere. Director Webb was clever—and fake.

"Arachne," the man promised in an inviting voice—the kind sweet talkers looking for company saved for the twilight hours right before bars closed. "You'll have your revenge as soon as the war is over."

Tori had never seen President Arvis in person before, but she recognized him immediately. A navy suit highlighted his broad shoulders. A manicured beard accented his bold jawline, giving him a mature, put-together look. A strangely electric aura clung to him, pulling her in like gravity, ensuring that the entire room revolved around him and only him. He reminded her of Roy, except where Roy's charisma whispered and teased, his shouted. No, *demanded*.

Director Webb—presumably "Arachne" was an alias, or her real name—ran her fingers along President Arvis' bicep. "Your war will never be over." It was a compliment, not an accusation.

It occurred to Tori, momentarily, that President Arvis was married. Once, on the news, she'd seen his scowling wife in the background. Now she understood why the woman scowled.

"I've brought you almost everything you've asked for," Director Webb pleaded. "That house cat from the South has been defanged. I washed those two insects out of Sibyl's Cave right into my web." She walked her fingers up his arm, one word at a time, a creeping spider.

"So she's the one who... the explosives..." Grace breathed.

Director Webb held her chin up high. "They'll make such tempting bait, don't you agree? Not even Roy Angelus will be able to avoid me for much longer."

"Almost, but not all," President Arvis corrected with a smile. "Why so impatient, my dear? I, for one, enjoy our time together."

She sighed. "Fine. I'll wait. A deal's a deal."

He laughed good-naturedly. "You should enjoy yourself more." His hands inched down her figure eight body to her waist. "Don't you like our plans for Atlanta?"

Tori flinched. What could President Arvis possibly want with Atlanta?

He, the Commander in Chief of the United States, had already teased about a war. That was bad. Insanely bad. She might not have believed her own ears if she hadn't seen the military stockpile underneath Channel 4.

Years ago, the worldwide energy crisis had sparked dozens of wars. To the ruling class, fossil fuels had always been more valuable than human life. The government had simply stopped pretending otherwise.

In a cruel way, Tori's generation had been lucky. The United States somehow avoided fighting another superpower directly. Modern weaponry was so deadly efficient that the smaller proxy conflicts ended before she came of age. She didn't have to witness the brutality firsthand. Her brother didn't have to die defending old men's pockets.

She couldn't imagine a war reaching Atlanta. She didn't want to.

Director Webb smirked. "Like doesn't begin to describe my feelings on the matter."

"Just wait until you see the fireworks," President Arvis winked.

Fireworks. *Fire.* Tori recalled midnight gardens and her phoenix, both engulfed in madness. She clenched her fists. She had a plan to ruin and a promise to keep.

"In the meantime..." President Arvis' playful tone hardened into something more serious. "I still don't believe you about Roy. Even after everything I've seen. His loyalty has never wavered before."

It was Vince's turn to flinch.

Tori didn't blame him. If Roy Angelus' family really was as wealthy as they seemed, it was natural for them to have friends in high places. No one on earth had ever achieved the title of "billionaire" without bribing important politicians. It was practically a prerequisite.

It still felt wrong to hear "Roy" and "loyalty" out of the mouth of a villain.

Perhaps there was a reason Roy never named names when he spoke of his relatives.

"Let me talk to your prisoners," President Arvis insisted.

"Very well. This way."

Uh oh. Tori glanced at Vince and Grace, who'd gone pale. By prisoners, was he referring to them?

For once, the monster hunters had a chance to ambush a monster instead of being ambushed. Too bad the monster was President of the United States.

Tori had worried about stealing a laptop. How was she supposed to attack the president? What if he had secret service guards nearby? She could see her ma's disappointed face streaked with tears—her daughter, at the top of the nation's most wanted list!

President Arvis and Director Webb paused in front of the door.

Vince drew back the hammer of his revolver.

No, no, *no!* Tori panicked. If someone witnessed him using deadly force on the president, they'd never make it out of here alive! She needed to stop him, but how? She couldn't move or speak without being discovered.

President Arvis grasped the handle.

Siren Song chanted the national anthem as his phone burst to life.

He dug it out of his pocket. "Ah." He frowned. "I need to take this somewhere private." He dismissed Director Webb with a wave. "Wait for me outside. I'll only be a moment."

With that, their enemies departed in opposite directions.

Tori gasped for air. Relief and oxygen flooded her system. She clapped her hands over her head, thanking God, Gandhi, and Mercy for their insane luck.

It wasn't luck.

A phone was still ringing behind her.

Reluctantly, she looked over her shoulder.

The phone belonged to a Chinese man who watched them from a doorway by the elevator. He held it out for them to see. Tianyi's red, yellow, and white rings glowed on the screen. It was dialing President Arvis.

How long had he been there? How much had he overheard?

"You must be Victoria Jaecar."

Her name summoned flames in Tori's heart. Yes, she was Victoria Jaecar, the oldest monster hunter here. She had to defend the others. Her fingers crept down towards her knife.

The newcomer could be summed up with a single word: sharp. His dark eyes cut through her, indifferent to her blade. A custom SMS jacket slimmed his athletic, but not too athletic, figure. Not a single lock of hair dared stray out of place. He had a subtle, stylish taste that screamed perfection.

Mere months ago, his absolute confidence would've intimidated Tori into silence. Hanging around Roy had helped her build a resistance to beautiful people. "That's me."

"We don't have much time. They'll be back as soon as they realize I'm not my father. Come on." It was an order.

Tori obeyed. Why not? She had nothing to lose. She'd happily waltz straight into a trap if it meant avoiding a confrontation with the head of state in a government building.

Grace bounded after her, eager to meet their newest friend.

Only Vince stayed put.

"I told you, we don't have time to—"

The two men locked eyes, truly seeing each other for the first time. Shock and recognition paralyzed them both. They looked as though they'd been struck by lightning. Or a sports car.

The newcomer slammed his fist into Vince's jaw.

CHAPTER FORTY-ONE

Luscious desserts. Overflowing spirits. Prime aged steaks, so perfectly tender and rare they could be sliced with a butter knife. And a private room so that no one gave a shit if he ate with his hands. This was the restaurant of Vincent Lenoir's wildest dreams.

The wood-framed walls smelled of oak and hickory. Black leather padded studded chairs. The horns of a bull crowned a crackling brick fireplace. It should've been his heaven on earth. He was too angry to ascend. He could only focus on dark hair, dark eyes, and a glare so pointed he could cut himself on it.

He didn't need to cut himself, because the piece of crap that owned all the above had already punched him. For no fucking reason.

Vince would always remember Charles.

He'd never known his name, but he'd also never forget his Porsche 918 Spyder—the very Porsche 918 Spyder that'd nearly turned him into a skid mark in front of Lackawanna Coal Mine. That masterpiece belonged in a temple to be worshiped.

And Vince had kicked it.

It'd been a crime to scar the beautiful face of that beautiful car.

He should've scarred the beautiful face of the man who drove it instead. But it was too late for that. Just like it was too late for Charles' revenge. As a judge once told Vince when he got caught with an entire rack of RC cars years after shoplifting them, all crimes had their statute of limitations.

They weren't even.

Charles had started a war.

Oh, the things Vince would do to him.

Charles dominated the head of their table, his long legs crossed, gripping the arms of his throne. He was a perfect little leader, with his perfect little grin, without a single crack in his mask. He acted as though nothing had happened.

Meanwhile, Vince nursed his jaw with an ice pack. He would strike back. Later. When Grace and Tori weren't at risk of becoming collateral damage.

The women watched in awe, their food untouched, as "Charles" Chenlong Li, heir of Tianyi and king of royal assholes, dictated their future.

"There isn't much time. President Arvis has a debate with Senator Pallas in Atlanta in two days. We need to stop him there, before this escalates any further."

Two days. Vince hoped that would be long enough for Roy and Brooks to return. Back in city hall, Director Webb had implied that the dynamic duo was on the run.

If Vince had faith in anything, it was that his mentors would be fine on their own. But would their mentees be fine on *their* own?

Charles addressed only Tori. "Tell me. Where did you find that... that 'IOU-list'?"

"Weeks ago, when I was visiting my mother, I heard a strange noise. I went to investigate. In her room, I found trespassers!" Grace recounted, edging in between Charles and Tori. "My mother reached out to one of them, which shocked me to the core. Because, oh, I forgot to mention, she's been in a coma for years. Anyway, I broke down in tears and then Vince told me—"

"In a military base," Tori cut to the chase. "In St. Louis."

"St. Louis," Charles rolled the words over his tongue as though tasting them for poison. "Did anything important ever happen in Missouri?"

"Well," Vince observed. "Grace was born there."

Charles scoffed. He did that a lot whenever Vince talked. "This is why I never involve people like—"

"Like what?" Vince narrowed his eyes. "People like us have been hunting monsters since before you were born with that silver spoon shoved up your—"

"Golden," Charles corrected. He drummed his fingers on the table in a brisk, pulsing rhythm. "Monsters. Is that what you call my talented employee, Director Webb?"

"Director Webb works for you?" Tori gasped.

He leveled her with a look sharp enough to slash a mountain in half. "Obviously."

She shrank away.

Vince's fingers curled into a fist as he fantasized about smacking that smug smirk off Charles' mouth. It was okay to make him feel stupid, but not Tori. Tori had worked hard for her smarts. She had a college degree and everything.

"Why else do you think you survived breaking into Tianyi's office?" Charles asked in the same tone a schoolteacher would use to ask the sum of two and two. "Why else do you think President Arvis never managed to interrogate you?" His eyes fell to the watch on his wrist. A gaudy serpentine hand ticked around a gaudier gold face with some lady etched into it. "Director Webb and I have an arrangement."

Vince rolled his eyes. This was why their group needed Brooks and Roy. Their leadership worked. Brooks maintained order while Roy ran the show. They figured out who knew what, where to go next, and what to do without stepping on anybody. They would've flattened this asshole under the weight of his own ego.

"She sure acted like a monster," Tori argued, squaring her shoulders, bracing for a fight. "And you're interrogating us now. How are we supposed to know this isn't another trap?"

Charles sized her up, slowly, pointedly. "Go ahead then. Ask me anything." He sat back in his seat, yielding the table.

"The 'IOU-list' was Tianyi's data. You should know what it means. What are wedding gifts?"

"A drug. You're already familiar with it." He frowned. "My father has been investing in it for quite some time."

"What about Helen of Troy?"

"The face that launched a thousand ships... In Greek legend, she caused the Trojan War, a conflict so devastating it wiped Troy from the map," he mused. "I believe it's a metaphor. Something that will start President Arvis' war."

"And the Minuteman?"

He shrugged. "You're the American. You tell me."

Wood screeched across the floor as Grace hopped up from her chair. "The minutemen were units of civilian soldiers who fought against the British in the Revolutionary War!" she exclaimed, eager to be useful. "They were known for being ready at a minute's notice."

"Sounds like us," Vince laughed.

"It does sound like us," Tori agreed. She turned on Charles. "But not like you. Why are you helping us?"

"War is bad for business."

"Historically speaking, that hasn't been true at all."

"Listen, Victoria." Charles uncoiled. Although he wasn't quite as tall as Orion, he towered over her, a snake cornering a bird. "You can't afford to be picky with allies."

Tori didn't budge. "I can't afford to trust someone I just met, either."

Vince had to admit—Tori looked pretty badass right now. She stared down the billionaire like some kind of urban amazon, her clothes torn, steak knives brandished, without a trace of fear in those bold, brave eyes.

"How about this?" Charles conceded with a sigh. "I'll fly you three to Atlanta and get you inside the presidential debate. After that, we can go our separate ways. Not allies. No trust required."

Tori searched his expression for the lie. She didn't find one. "Deal."

"I'm cool with that too," Vince mumbled. "Not that anyone asked me."

"Thank you so much!" Grace cheered. "Mr. Char Li, I knew you were a wise soul from the moment I saw you. You have such a white aura!"

Mr. Char Li grimaced as though he'd been elbowed in the gut.

* * *

Dinner turned out to be amazing. Grace unknowingly stumbled upon Charles' weakness: his pride. In her attempts to befriend him, she stepped all over it. She asked him personal question after personal question. She offered him bits of her food to try. By the end of the night, he was Charlie, not Charles.

Whenever she touched him, Charlie flinched away. His composure slipped whenever she said his nickname. It was clear to everyone but her that he would rather be anywhere else, but he endured, all in the name of pretending to be perfect.

Charlie excused himself the moment they stopped eating. He packed them into a cab that took them to a hotel thirty minutes and three bridges from the Woolworth Building. Their enemies were everywhere, he'd said. They'd be safest far, FAR away from him.

Vince folded his arms over the railing of their hotel balcony, high above New York City. He lit a cigarette. Smoke drifted through the air, mixing with the rain. Ashes lazily snowed down on the streets below. People hurried along, tiny as embers, going about their normal lives.

Behind him stretched the grandest hotel suite he had ever seen. It had five bedrooms, three fireplaces, and a kitchen with two separate microwaves. If he slid through that sliding door, he could relax. He could sip complimentary whiskey from a couch bigger than his car. Watch some television. Take a soak in a jetted tub. It all sounded so much better than flying back to that sweltering oven also referred to as Atlanta and getting embroiled in a political scheme.

He couldn't relax. Somewhere on the horizon, in that dreary downpour, Roy and Brooks were fighting without him. He belonged with them, in run down motels in the middle of nowhere. How did he get here?

Someone knocked on the door.

"Yeah?" he grunted without looking.

"Hi Vince." Tori stepped onto the balcony next to him.

Silence.

She opened her mouth, twice, and closed it again.

He wasn't in a hurry. He offered her his cigarette.

Much to his surprise, she accepted.

Pinching it between two fingers, as though afraid it might bite, she raised it to her lips.

She inhaled.

She coughed as soon as smoke reached her throat.

Vince laughed. Leave it to Tori to bring a smile to his face after both nicotine and alcohol had failed.

Grace was the queen of naivety, a songbird in a cage. But in many ways, Tori was just as pure as her.

Pointless meetings. Racist coworkers. Crappy bosses. A loving family she actively avoided. Her life was full of problems and complexities he'd never understand. She survived them all on her own. She kept going through murder, monsters, and madness. Nothing shook her determination to dirty those clean hands of hers.

He fell into this life. She chose it.

Tori was like a heroine from a comic book. Did that make Vince her sidekick? He wouldn't mind if that meant he got to wear a cool cape.

Her breathing steadied. "Sorry, I just... I came to apologize."

Another surprise.

"I keep getting in the way. At the Winecoff Hotel, Roy rescued me. Inside Tianyi, Brooks literally carried me. Back in the labyrinth, you almost killed me. Not because you wanted to, or because of mind control, but because I was weak. I panicked. I forgot." She straightened, mimicking Brooks in the deepest voice she could muster. "The best way to defeat a physically stronger opponent in close combat is to run."

"Tori." Guilt choked Vince as if he'd been the one to burn his throat. He should be the one apologizing. She was older, but he was her senior. He knew better than anyone else how she felt right now. How many times had he cowered while Roy and Brooks stood between him and danger? "You couldn't have possibly—"

"Our enemies won't care about my excuses." She peered down from the balcony, admiring the harrowing drop. "Before I met you, I was afraid to even talk in meetings." She squeezed the railing. "I never want to feel that powerless again. So from now on, I'm going to take responsibility for my actions. Learn from my mistakes. Stop doubting myself. No excuses. Whatever it takes to protect what's important to me..."

She took a second drag from his cigarette. "...including you."

Vince looked at Tori—really *looked*—for the first time since they'd met in that alley.

She wasn't the same lost little girl. With her silhouette against the full moon, smoke drifting from her lips, she was as fierce as a dragon. He believed her promise.

He held out a hand expectantly. "Smoking isn't cool anymore, y'know."

"I know." She returned his cigarette. A pause. "No more running off chasing ghosts for a while, okay?"

"Okay." Unlike her, his promises weren't worth much.

Her knowing grin erased the serious atmosphere.

"Now. Tell me what *really* happened between you and Grace…"

CHAPTER FORTY-TWO

The freight elevator groaned to a stop. Its cage-like doors rolled open. The great beast yawned, inviting Vincent Lenoir, Grace, Tori, and Charlie onto its back.

Atlanta's Ponce City Market had been built into the carcass of a department store headquarters. The chain that'd once possessed this two million square foot monster had died long ago. Its spirit returned in the form of a trendy shopping mall and condos.

Many of the headquarters' original features, such as this rust bucket of an elevator, remained intact. Centuries-old bricks. Steel beams. Air ducts, exposed pipes, and hanging wires. Interior designers called them "character." Vince called them "gentrification." What a waste of a good old creepy building.

"So this is Skyline Park!" With a spin, Grace danced onto the concrete landing.

Ponce City Market's roof had been converted into an adult playground.

The freight elevator exited into an overpriced-looking lounge. Edison bulbs flickered on the tin ceiling. Well-dressed men and women mingled among plush suede chairs. A pyramid of champagne flutes and an ice sculpture of the Atlanta skyline decorated the bar. It was over the top, even for someone like Charlie.

To the right, outside on the terrace, the normal people were quarantined behind floor-to-ceiling windows. Reporters, interns, police officers, and right and left wingers schooled together. They filtered around folding tables, colorful and varied, fish in an aquarium.

To the left, beyond a pair of metal doors, a rooftop amusement park spiraled into the sky. It waited for customers. There would be none tonight. Tonight, Ponce City Market had a different main attraction.

Everyone awaited the show, right, left, and center.

"The presidential debate will be held in an auditorium downstairs," Charlie explained.

"Then what are we doing up here?" Vince grumbled.

The last forty-eight hours had passed like seconds. He, Tori, and Grace had crammed in a month's worth of planning. Their final mission had two main objectives: expose President Arvis and stop Helen of Troy.

To expose President Arvis, they needed evidence that connected him to the IOU-list. To stop Helen of Troy, well. For starters, they needed to figure out who—or what—she was.

Both objectives were a long shot. All the details were vague.

Vince wouldn't have it any other way.

"I told you I'd get you inside the presidential debate, and here we are. Inside the presidential debate," Charlie scoffed. "What were you expecting? Backstage passes? The state box in Ford's Theater?"

Vince flipped him off.

"Oh!" Grace perked up. "That's where President Abraham Lincoln was assassinated—"

Tori shushed her. "Please don't say that kind of thing out loud! I'm sure this place is crawling with secret service agents."

"You're right," Vince surveyed their surroundings. Guards manned every door. "We need to get away from this crowd."

Grace peered over her shoulder at the freight elevator. "I didn't see any other stops on our way up. Does this only go between the roof and the parking lot?"

Tori pulled up a map of Ponce City Market on her phone. "There's another way downstairs." She pointed at Skyline Park. "Out there."

Two men in black blocked the amusement park's entrance. Wires curled behind their ears into their white starched shirts. They were dressed so prim and proper, yet their suit jackets hung unbuttoned and loose. Vince would bet his car they had pistols hidden in the slack.

"We're gonna need a diversion."

Charlie sighed. "Can't you do anything by yourselves?" He smoothed the collar of his flawless SMS suit. Deliberately bumping into Vince as he brushed past, he marched up to the bar. He ordered whiskey.

There was no free food in here, but one wouldn't know it from how quickly vultures descended.

A woman in a low-cut dress eased onto a stool next to him. "Charles Li. What a *delicious* surprise."

Vince gagged.

Even for a room full of millionaires, Tianyi's net worth was a big number. Tianyi's heir was an emperor among kings.

A businessman hovered over his shoulder. "Are you here to support President Arvis?"

"Your father has been quite generous to our cause," a senator added.

A competitor smirked. "Rumor has it he's been meeting with Senator Pallas in secret."

"How illicit."

"How intriguing."

"The last time I saw you, Charles, you told me you hated attending campaign events. Yet here you are." Sulking, the woman glared daggers at Tori and Grace. "And with two other women! I'm jealous."

"I'm sure you are." Charlie straightened, addressing his onlookers. "If you have questions for me, you can direct them to my executive assistant." He'd had enough. Already.

"Wow, your English is so good." The woman gushed.

Ever so slightly, Charlie stiffened.

She traced her fingers up his arm. "I'd love to hear more of it. Maybe at my hotel, after the debate?"

Yep, Vince was gonna vomit. He searched for a trash can, bucket, or bag—anything.

"Excuse me!" Charlie waved down the closest security, the men in black guarding Skyline Park. "This woman here needs a restroom. And a first aid kit."

Confusion reigned.

He dumped his whiskey on her head. Then he dropped his glass.

Chaos overthrew confusion as shards of crystal exploded across the floor.

The woman screamed. Onlookers recoiled. The men in black reacted as though Charlie had thrown a grenade, climbing over chairs and around people to get to him.

Vince would've loved to stick around to see him suffer, but Tori dragged everyone outside.

They had Skyline Park to themselves.

Vince hadn't been to a carnival since he snuck into Kennywood as a kid. He had to admit—this one looked pretty magical. A sketchy steel rollercoaster flew through the air. A three-story slide towered over a kingdom of carnival games. A mini golf course meandered through colorful boardwalks. The view was out of this world. Behind it all, skyscrapers glowed like will o' wisps in the late afternoon sun.

Those skyscrapers were the only thing that glowed.

The power was shut off. The whole fantasyland was dark, empty, and dead.

There were so many shapes and shadows that Vince could hardly tell what he was looking at. He wandered over to the closest carnival game and poked through the prizes. Movement stirred among the stuffed animals. Was that a rabbit?

He blinked. He rubbed his eyes. Nothing but teddy bears.

Ugh. He'd spent too much time in New York City. Now he was seeing rats everywhere.

Grace slipped behind the counter of a water-gun game. A brightly painted fish covered her lower half, giving her a cartoonish mermaid tail. "Look Vince, I'm..." She trailed off. Louis was a sore subject.

A dull ache gnawed at Vince. He cornered it in the back of his mind. He turned to Tori. "Where's that way down you mentioned?"

Tori's phone made an encore appearance. "I think it's over here..." She switched on her flashlight. Its LED beam illuminated double doors. An elevator stood by, open and ready.

"Bullseye!" Vince cheered.

An arrow splintered into a target of the shooting gallery next to him, dead center.

It missed his nose by millimeters.

"There you are, my Queen." Orion perched on the rollercoaster tracks above them. He spun an arrow in his fingers. "I've been looking *everywhere* for you!"

"Queen?" Vince wrinkled his brow.

"Ah, sorry. That's me," Tori raised her hand. "When I told you guys what happened in the subway, I skipped over some sexual harassment."

"Sexual harassment? You thought that was sexual harassment?"

"I was chained to a wall."

The giant's head was so high in the clouds he couldn't hear her. "Here I thought we had something special!" He notched the arrow. "This time, when I chain you to a wall, sexual harassment will be the least of your problems..." His voice stretched with tension as he drew back his bowstring.

Yep, fuck this guy. Vince leveled his revolver at Orion. Excitement and adrenaline held his aim steady. That bastard was what, ten, twenty feet up? He'd be an easy target. And where an arrow made splinters, a bullet would fell the whole damned tree.

Vince shuddered in anticipation. No, wait. The ground was literally shaking.

Someone hit a switch.

Electricity surged through the amusement park. Neon lights flickered in icy blue and fiery crimson. Upbeat, off-key music bounced between the walls. The swing ride awoke from its slumber. Chain-linked chairs danced around it, arms of a many-eyed monster.

A bull paraded through the funfair.

"MoMo," Grace breathed.

Asterius dominated the carnival entrance—the headliner of the freak show: the world's strongest, hairiest man. "This ends here, tonight."

Vince squeezed his gun's grip. "I couldn't agree more."

Orion fired—and so did Vince.

A bullet ricocheted off the rollercoaster tracks as Tori tackled Vince out of the way of Orion's arrow. She hooked her arms through her companion's elbows and dragged them towards escape.

"It's two against three," Vince protested. "We can take them!"

Orion was out in the open, trapped on a rooftop, ready for a showdown. They might never get a better chance to defeat him.

And they needed to defeat him if they wanted to find out what happened to Brooks and Roy.

The past week had hardened Grace. Instead of crying or screaming, she clenched a fist. "Yes. I'll pull down that rollercoaster and give them the ride of their lives!"

"Can doesn't mean should," Tori warned. "Security had to have heard that gunshot."

Vince sighed. She had a point. The Department of Homeland Security was in the house. He was down to clown with a minotaur and a giant, but he didn't want to fight against actual people. Not here, not now.

"Come on!" Tori shoved over a prize display.

A storm of inflatable animals, teddy bears, and mini golf balls raged across the pathway, clouding Orion's view.

They rushed into the elevator.

Vince mashed the door close button.

No response.

"Shit."

The elevator was broken.

Asterius crushed a mini golf ball beneath his hoof with a satisfying snap. Toys wouldn't slow him down. And there was nowhere to run. His enemies had trapped themselves in a tiny metal box, helpless ghosts in a cage.

He charged, trampling everything in his path.

He crossed the threshold of the elevator. Thick fingers grasped at Vince's throat.

Vince shut his eyes. He had always figured he'd die doing something cool. There was nothing more uncool than getting popped like a balloon animal. What would Roy say when he found out? Would Brooks forgive him for making one last mess?

A cable snapped.

In a harrowing freefall, the elevator plunged into darkness.

Something wet splattered across Vince's face.

CHAPTER FORTY-THREE

The world was upside down. Tori's head spun and lurched like a lopsided merry-go-round. She sprawled across Vince and Grace sprawled across her. They piled upon the remains of their elevator in a mess of limbs. They groaned in unison. Somehow, they'd survived the four-story fall to the bottom of Ponce City Market.

The steel cable holding up the elevator had snapped. Grace had used her powers to activate the emergency brakes. Their momentum melted those brakes. Her efforts slowed them down enough that their bones, at least, remained unsnapped when they hit the ground.

Little by little, Tori's senses returned to her. She couldn't see a thing.

"You guys still alive?" she whispered.

Vince moaned. "Ask me in an hour."

"That was awesome!" Grace switched on her phone flashlight.

Tori's heart froze in her chest. Silver blood streaked from Vince's head.

For a moment, she imagined Vince as a monster. A blizzard of confusion, betrayal, and concern swirled through her. He was injured—badly.

A moment later, she noticed a four-foot-long severed horn in the rubble. And a finger.

The ichor wasn't his.

But it would make him sick.

Asterius had been holding onto Vince when the sudden drop transformed the elevator into a guillotine.

"Vince." As Tori's heart thawed, her stomach broiled. She peeled off her hoodie and offered it to him. "You have a little something on your, uh. Just wipe your whole face."

"What now?" Grace asked.

Tori frowned. Modern elevators had many failsafe mechanisms. Steel cables were strong. The freak accident had crippled an enemy. The whole thing was awfully convenient. And there was no such thing as a coincidence.

Grace had clearly been surprised. Tori's powers were limited to herself. That meant their stroke of fortune had something to do with...

Tori's gaze drifted to Vince.

He cleaned up the best he could. When he noticed Asterius' horn, he claimed it as a trophy. He practically bounced with excitement as he stashed it in his bag. He didn't seem sick.

Perhaps she'd underestimated him. After all, he'd eaten that Apple of Discord.

She brushed off the thought along with the layer of dirt that powdered her clothes. She could worry about that later. She settled for being thankful that, for once, fate had twisted in their favor.

Vince peered up the elevator shaft. "The debate hall is above us now. Should we find another elevator?"

Tori never wanted to see another elevator in her life.

"Maybe some stairs."

The ground floor of Ponce City Market was full of stairs. Stores and restaurants lined an enormous room that opened to a second-floor mezzanine. Spiral stairways rose between the levels at regular intervals. Giant fans dangled from the ceiling, sending jagged shadows dancing across wooden floors.

Tori had never been inside a shopping mall after it closed. She now understood why. During the day, Ponce City Market thrived on color, light, and life. At night, that energy slept, trapped behind grates. Lonely chairs and tables circled around the food court. Empty stalls and barren shelves haunted the corners. The mall was a skeleton of its true self, sealed in a tomb, waiting to be reborn.

"The... Great... Fire..." Grace read off a tarnished plaque.

"Sounds like a nickname for Atlanta," Vince grunted. "You'd think they'd turn up the AC a little more for the President of the United States."

Tori traced her fingers along the plaque. It was a memorial for the Great Atlanta Fire of 1917, a horrible holocaust that had razed nearly three hundred acres of factories and homes. A map of the damage etched into the brass, ending with Ponce City Market.

Black and white pictures framed the plaque. Firefighters battled a blaze from horse drawn carriages. A thick, gray fog hung in the air. Charred bodies of apartment complexes lined barren streets. They seemed familiar, as if she was thumbing through her ma's old photo album.

"Uhh, guys?" Vince nudged her.

This tomb had a ghost.

A woman perched on a railing above. She was so thin and frail that Tori almost mistook her for a signpost. White blotches clouded dark, glassy eyes. Her once-beautiful hair had faded from gold to sand. She quivered as she watched them. The mere act of sitting, breathing, existing, took everything she had.

The phoenix had risen from the ashes of Phoenix Hall.

"It's time," she said to Tori.

Vince whistled. "Man, you look like shit."

327

"Vince!" Grace thwacked him. "She doesn't look like shit, she looks... wise."

Tori inched towards her. "No, she looks like she's—"

"Dying," Orion completed her sentence. He appeared behind the phoenix and handed her a sandwich bag filled with golden powder. "That's kind of the point, you know?"

"Why would you want your friend to die?" Grace cried.

After inhaling a tiny baggie of Orion's drug, the phoenix had deleted acres and acres around Phoenix Hall. If she inhaled that entire sandwich bag... Tori stared at the map on the plaque. She remembered where she'd seen those pictures—the phoenix had shown them to her.

The Winecoff Hotel. Roswell Mill. Mimosa Hall. And the Great Atlanta Fire. Atlanta itself was a phoenix, destined to be reborn in flames.

"It's her," she breathed. "She's Helen of Troy."

"What?" Vince complained. "Why didn't you tell us you knew Helen?"

Tori ignored him. The final piece of the puzzle fell into place. At last, she had more answers than questions. "Her name isn't Helen. But her face will launch a thousand ships. Death... Fire... Resurrection... All those disasters..."

She faced the phoenix, clenching her fists so hard her fingers went numb. "You exist outside of time. The last vision you showed me is in the future, isn't it? You're going to destroy downtown."

The phoenix bowed her head in shame.

"Helen of Troy was said to have been the most beautiful woman in history. So much so that kingdoms of men died fighting over her," Orion recited. "Do you want to know how it all started? She was given to a prince as a bribe..."

"...in exchange for an Apple of Discord," Grace finished. The golden sandwich bag reflected in her wide eyes.

"You're the one who came up with the metaphor, aren't you, Orion?" Vince scoffed.

"Oooh, metaphor," Orion sneered. "You're breaking out the big words today."

The more she understood, the paler Grace turned. "But why would President Arvis want to destroy downtown?"

Vince shrugged. "To win a debate?"

The mention of an Apple of Discord transported Tori back into the vault of Creation. Magical weapons, a menagerie of monsters, and hundreds of golden apples surrounded her, ready for battle.

"To pick a fight," she solemnly concluded.

"With who? Isn't he already the bad guy?" Grace whimpered.

In Mimosa Hall, Tori had overheard President Arvis' campaign donors gossip about Russia's dictator. In New York City Hall, Director Webb had whispered of war. Tori had a bad feeling about this.

"My dear Queen." Orion's overconfidence had reached its limit. "You catch on so quickly." He grabbed something under the lapel of his jacket. "Killing you is going to be such a waste."

Snarling accompanied his threat, thunder to his lightning. Sirius and Procyon circled the monster hunters. He'd been waiting for backup.

A click. A pin clattered to the ground.

Orion rolled a round object between Vince, Tori, and Grace. A grenade!

Everything exploded at once.

Grace repelled Orion's grenade. In a rush of powder and shrapnel, it blew open the entrance of a bar. Shards of shattered pint glasses burst through the air.

Sirius lunged.

Vince shot him in the temple.

A hole in the head did nothing to stop the hound's huge body.

Tori yanked Vince out of Sirius's path as he smashed into one of the pillars supporting the second-floor mezzanine.

Cracks spiderwebbed across the column. Ponce City Market trembled. An earthquake would've been more subtle. So much for the secret service not getting involved. Never mind the secret service—at this rate, half of Atlanta would be on the scene before they so much as glimpsed evidence of President Arvis' schemes.

Procyon didn't give Tori time to think of a new plan. He dove at her.

She leapt backwards to avoid his fangs.

A steel cable pressed into her calf. It tightened around her legs, launching her upside down. The next thing she knew she was hanging over the ruined bar.

Of course. She should've known.

This wasn't the Winecoff Hotel, Mimosa Hall, or Tianyi. They hadn't accidentally stumbled upon Orion. They were trespassing in his territory. The Greatest Hunter of All Time had days to prepare for them. What kind of hunter used arrows when he could use traps?

"Remember what I said about the next time I chained you up?" Orion jeered.

As he stood there, his eyes stormed with pride, Tori realized something important. She could see a pattern in the chaos. For all his talk about how she "impressed" him, he still underestimated her. He lowered his guard whenever he felt that things were going well for him. He played with his food.

Confidence surged through her, lighting up every muscle and every nerve. That flaw of his would be fatal. "Grace! The fan!"

Over the next three seconds, the monster hunters' coordination couldn't have been better if it'd been choreographed with months of practice.

One. Grace snapped the iron neck of the ceiling fan. It crashed down on top of Orion and the phoenix, crushing the railing.

The phoenix vanished.

Orion was forced to dodge.

Two. Vince fired upon the steel cable holding Tori.

Three. As Tori fell, she swung her weight into a refrigerator. It toppled over. Beer bottles and soda cans bounced through Ponce City Market like grade schoolers unleashed upon an amusement park. They burst, spraying Sirius and Procyon muzzle to paw.

Orion was distracted, the phoenix was missing, and sticky sweetness clogged the mastiffs' noses.

This was their chance.

"Vince, Grace," Tori shouted. "Go on without me!"

Vince balked. "I'm not leaving you with this degenerate."

Orion had the high ground, but this wasn't the Woolworth Building. Unlike that tower's barren stairwell, Ponce City Market was a briar patch of rooms, walls, and hallways. In this tangle of twists and turns, she could get the jump on him. She was at her best. She could win.

Even if she couldn't, she had to try.

If no one stopped President Arvis, everyone, everywhere would lose.

She met Vince's eyes. "I got this. No excuses."

In those five words, she said all she needed to say.

A pained expression twisted Vince's face.

From the way he looked at her, forlorn and afraid, Tori wondered if he'd ever had to say goodbye to someone he cared about.

"You got this," he conceded.

He held Grace's hand and dragged her into the nearest stairwell.

"I believe in you!" Grace called back with a wave. "You're a Leo, and Leos can do anything they put their mind to."

Orion raised his bow. "I'm not going to let you just waltz out of—"

"Oh no you don't!" Tori wrapped her arms around the pillar Sirius had damaged. She pulled with all her might.

A hunger burned inside her heart where Dee's—no, Artemis'—arrow had struck her.

It'd always been there, in a way.

Since the first time a teacher ignored her raised hand, assuming someone from the country couldn't know the answer. Since the first time her ma cried over the bills that piled up from the mail. Since the first time she crossed the stage of a school graduation.

She was hungry for power over her own life.

Artemis had simply let that hunger out of its cage.

Tori was a predator—a predator who could borrow strength from others like her.

Deep in the tundra, a polar bear hauled a young whale onto the ice.

A satisfying rip. Something gave. She stumbled backwards as the mezzanine above her collapsed. Metal and concrete rained on the floor.

The landslide threw Orion. He tumbled, landing hard in front of her.

She marveled at her own strength. Fishing Vince and Grace out of the subway had been impressive, but this? This was incredible. Unbelievable. Worthy of a Leo.

"Forget them." She drew her dagger. Finally, she would give him what he wanted.

"You and I have a date."

CHAPTER FORTY-FOUR

Vincent Lenoir escaped to the third floor of Ponce City Market. Grace trailed him into a dim hallway with painted concrete walls. It was quiet. Eerie, even.

They were getting closer, but they still had a long journey ahead. This was no presidential debate hall. The main event would have people and fanfare. It also would've been vacuumed.

Vince coughed from the dust. "Ugh. Would it kill them to clean once every few centuries?"

It wasn't just the dust. Anxiety clawed at his throat. No matter how he tried, he couldn't swallow his guilt. He'd never left someone behind with a monster before. Not once. If something happened to Tori back there, he'd never forgive himself. With trembling fingers, he shoved a cigarette between his lips. He fumbled for his lighter.

Grace stopped him.

"Vince. Look!"

It took him a second to spot it.

A single thread ran down the hallway, disappearing into darkness.

He nudged it with his thumb. It was sticky. "A spiderweb."

Director Webb had left a guideline. Or an alarm.

Before Vince could weigh the pros and cons of following the thread to its conclusion, Grace bounded off without him.

Vince sighed. Leave it to the queen of naivety to trust a stranger. He jogged after her.

The spiderweb led them into a large storage room. Boxes piled in cardboard towers. Folding chairs covered in tarps, trash carts, and forgotten stacks of tables surrounded them. There was a light at the end of the tunnel—a gap in the wall barely big enough for two people to peek through.

By the time Vince caught up to her, Grace had already pressed her face up to it, hogging most of the space. He didn't mind squeezing up against her for a look of his own.

"First Theseus and now this. Can't you do anything right?"

Vince didn't need to see a thing to recognize that voice.

Broad shoulders. A handsome face. A full, glorious beard. Striking slate eyes like Grace's, but where hers drizzled, his stormed. President Arvis stood with his hands behind his back, sneering at an injured Asterius.

On the other side, bright stage lights illuminated a spacious brick room. The villains posed center stage on a raised carpeted platform. Podiums guarded them on either side. Above them, a giant eagle clutched a star-spangled banner in talons. Rows of seats encircled them, pews of an expectant church.

Narcissus had a front row seat to the show. In his bold suit, decked out in red, white, and gold, he was a living, breathing campaign poster. He filed his nails. He wasn't interested in the drama.

Next to him, Director Webb sat perfectly upright, careful not to touch her colleague.

Vince and Grace had found the debate hall.

Someone was going to have to scrub that carpet before it could go on TV.

Silver ichor ran in a river between Asterius and President Arvis. The minotaur's right arm was missing. His shoulder wept, sinew and ash. One of his horns had been clipped. Even while kneeling, broken as he was, he towered a head taller than everyone else.

Somehow, President Arvis still made him seem small.

"Get out of my sight," the president spat.

Asterius obeyed. He lumbered off, as passive as a lamb.

"I shouldn't have expected anything from a stupid beast." President Arvis said to someone out of view.

Charlie stepped onto the platform from backstage. "It's so difficult to find reliable help."

Vince bit back a mouthful of swears.

Charlie had promised to go his own way once they got inside Ponce City Market. He neglected to mention anything about going all the way to President Arvis' inner circle. They should've known better than to team up with a guy who stopped driving his one-of-a-kind Porsche just because of a tiny dent.

Charlie's eyes met Vince's.

He knew about the gap. It was a trap.

"This old building has some rats, it seems," Tianyi's heir observed.

That. Fucking. Snake.

If Vince died because of Charlie, he'd haunt him forever.

President Arvis rubbed his temple. "So it seems."

"Don't worry." Narcissus sauntered towards Vince and Grace. "I have a way with animals."

Whimpering, Grace scrambled behind a cardboard tower.

Vince's memories of his first encounter with Narcissus were vague at best. That was a mercy. The sensation of smooth lips, breath that smelled of ice cream, a hot pulse beneath his fingertips, and Tori's desperate cries were already more than enough to cement his fear of the other man.

As Narcissus creeped closer, Vince inched backwards. He didn't understand how Narcissus' powers worked, and he *really* didn't want to understand them better.

He didn't make it far. There was nowhere to run.

Perfectly painted fingernails slipped through the gap in the wall.

The wall wasn't a wall after all. It was a room divider on a sliding rail that cut one huge event space in half.

Narcissus parted with ease, casting Vince into the naked spotlight.

Narcissus, Director Webb, Charlie, and President Arvis stared at him.

Once, in a Vegas casino, Vince had bet away everything he owned down to his boxers. He was a reckless gambler, and even he didn't like his odds of survival.

"Is that a .45 magnum in your pocket, or are you just happy to see me?" Narcissus cupped Vince's chin.

"Fuck off, you ugly weed!"

"Ugly?" Narcissus's face twisted with the confusion of a man that hadn't heard the word in a thousand years. He peered at his palms, dumbstruck. "Am I losing my touch?" He reached out to try again.

"Keep your hands off of him!" Grace threw herself between Narcissus and Vince with the fierceness of a swan protecting her nest.

Narcissus grinned. "Jealous, much?"

Silence filled the now-much-more-spacious debate hall—a calm before the storm.

"Move aside," President Arvis bellowed in a thundering voice.

Narcissus welcomed the excuse to get away from Vince.

One heavy footstep at a time, President Arvis approached. He loomed over Vince and Grace, evaluating them, as though judging their worthiness to enter the afterlife.

Affection softened his hard expression. "Grace! It's really you, isn't it?"

What? Vince didn't know how to react.

From the shock on her face, Grace didn't either.

President Arvis reverted into the commander in chief. "Give us some privacy!"

Director Webb and Narcissus evacuated as quickly as possible.

Charlie lingered long enough to meet Grace's, then Vince's eyes. He retreated without a second glance. For all his pomp and circumstance, the two-faced bastard buckled awfully easily under the weight of true authority.

The warmth of spring returned as President Arvis embraced Grace. "Grace! My long-lost daughter."

Hold up. *Daughter?*

Vince had to admit, now that they were side by side, he could see the resemblance. They both had platinum, thin-as-a-cloud hair. Lightning swirled in their irises. Most importantly, they carried themselves with an otherworldly charisma. If real life was a movie, Vince would've pegged them both for main characters.

"Wh-what?" Grace stuttered.

"Your mother and I met in a sleepy hollow. She left flowers for the forlorn and unfavored, in an era when the meaning of flowers had long been forgotten. She was so kind and strong, but also pretty and frail. Like a songbird in a cage. Only the cage was wide open. She was too busy looking at me to think about escaping." President Arvis shut his eyes, reliving his story in his mind. "I'll never forget the magical nights we spent together. I'll never forgive myself for the countless nights I've missed with you."

"But how do you... If you..." Grace shivered as if she'd been caught in a downpour. "If you're my father, why haven't I ever seen you before?"

President Arvis took her hands in his. "I didn't know your name. I didn't even know you existed. All this time, your mother and that *aphedron*"—it was a curse—"of a man, James MacGillivray, hid you away. As if that could protect you from fate."

Frustration snarled in his throat. "If James hadn't tried to run... If Orion hadn't found your business card on him... I still wouldn't know." He squeezed her hands. "Once I learned about you, I sent you dreams every evening. I knew you'd find your way home to me." His grip tightened into shackles. "Now, finally, you're in my grasp."

His confession dragged Grace off her feet. Tears rained down her cheeks. If he hadn't been bracing her, she would've melted into a puddle.

"Wh-what am I? What are *we?*"

President Arvis had been waiting for those questions. He released her.

He snapped.

Electricity arced between his fingers.

Thunder snarled through Ponce City Market. The earth quaked, shaken to its core. Vince was thrown to his knees.

"I am Zeus—lord of the sky, ruler of Olympus, and king of the gods." A gust tore through the debate hall. A carnation drifted into Zeus' palm. He tucked it behind Grace's ear. "And you, Grace Batya, are my princess."

Vince lost himself in Zeus' incredible presence. He couldn't move. He could barely breathe. He was a single drop in an endless ocean, drowning, helpless and weary, beneath the unfeeling gaze of a million stars. His bones, each nerve, and the very blood in his veins surrendered in unison.

Before the emperor of everything, he was nothing and no one.

Vince seethed at his own body's betrayal. He didn't give a shit what Zeus was king of. No king he cared about would call a grown-ass woman his princess, feed teens to minotaurs, or laugh about destroying a city. No god he recognized answered prayers with violence and deception.

Zeus circled Grace, a predatory spark in his eyes.

"I have many mortal sons and daughters. Kings and queens. Heroes and beautiful brides. You've even met a couple of them—I'm amazed that Akheilos is still splashing around. But you, dear Grace. You're special. You've inherited so much of my power. With some chisel and polish you could be molded into a goddess worthy of Olympus."

Grace stood spellbound.

"Fifty years ago, I awoke in a barren Olympus above a world I barely recognized. My kingdom was gone. Concrete and pollution replaced my cities and temples. Indifference and apathy replaced law and order." Zeus' phrases swirled around him in a twister.

"Now greedy corporations threaten to starve society. Fat, corrupt governments threaten my authority. Villains threaten my children with daggers and guns." He glared at Vince.

Vince felt as if he was being crushed beneath the weight of the sky.

Zeus shook his head. "Modern technology is nothing more than a weapon of war. Mankind has built drones with more precision than an Oracle of Delphi, bombs that make candles of dragon fire, and nuclear weapons capable of eradicating the race of men, maybe even Olympus, in a minute. And so, in an era that should have enjoyed eternal paradise under my benevolent rule, humanity has fallen so far it cannot be saved from itself."

Gently, he brushed Grace's cheek. "We must save them. Help me. Rise to meet your destiny, and you and I will be together forever."

He offered her his hand.

"I love you, Grace."

Zeus' proclamation wrenched in Vince's gut, reopening wounds, drawing blood. When he saw Zeus—how he looked at Grace like a lost lamb who needed him—he saw Nancy's stepfather. This wasn't right. This wasn't love.

Love was cooking healthy meals or staying up all night with a teen who couldn't sleep. Love was forgiving him for his mistakes. Love was a kiss in the rain.

This wasn't love—it was manipulation. Pressure. *Domination.*

Zeus wasn't a god. He was a monster.

"You... you love me?" Grace repeated, testing the words on her own tongue. "But I'm part of the problem you want to fix. And so is my mom!"

She backed away from Zeus. "She's cursed, isn't she? By your wife. Just like Lamia!" Her voice echoed through the auditorium, gaining intensity until it became a shout. "Why didn't you do something? Why didn't you save her?"

Grace was indeed special. She dreamed of moving people—of being the protagonist in her own story. Vince wished he could show her that she already was. With her in the room, how could Zeus pay any attention to him?

Keeping the phone Charlie had lent him hidden in his pocket, Vince signed into his *Haunt Hunt* account. He started a live stream. He had no active viewers. He never did. But Sun Tzu browsed frequently. Brooks and Roy knew his login info. Tori would surely think to check it, too. No matter what happened here, there would be witnesses. Grace would be a star.

"Sometimes sacrifices must be made for the greater good," Zeus lamented. "As the Gold Age and the Silver Age of man ended, so too, shall the Iron Age. Perhaps, in the next iteration, we will move past metals."

"*Sacrifices?*"

A railing behind Zeus bent with a crank.

"One of many. Today, Atlanta will burn. Your half-brother in

Russia will take the blame. Tomorrow, our war will reset the world."

"You can't save people by killing them!"

A stage light crashed into the ground.

"That's exactly how I'll save humanity. There will be no war in the meadows of asphodel. No corporations. No government. No villains."

"You're not trying to save people. You're trying to wipe out your competition. You're afraid."

The metal of the debate hall rattled around Grace. Stage rigging ripped from the rafters, shaping into sharp points, surrounding Zeus. Ponce City Market shook with fury, ready to defend itself. President Arvis' eagle fell from the sky.

"I'll never help you!" she cried.

Zeus snatched her wrist.

In an instant, everything went still.

"Who said you had a choice?"

The sheer dismay in Grace's eyes lit a wildfire in Vince's chest. It burned away every thought except for one.

"Let go of her!" Vince shouted.

His body was his again. He drew his revolver.

Beyond his iron-sighted barrel, Vince no longer saw Zeus. Instead, he saw the hydra's hungering teeth, Lamia's empty eye sockets, and Asterius' sharpened horns. He saw every monster he'd failed to slay when it mattered.

He'd blamed Roy for the loss of his childhood. But Roy didn't force him into anything. He'd chosen this life, from the very beginning.

Here and now, Grace chose to challenge the king of the gods.

Vince chose to fight with her.

He pulled his trigger.

Zeus held out his palm.

The bullet crumpled mid-air.

With a mighty sweep of his hand, the god sent the revolver spinning across the floor.

A thundercrack split Vince's head in two.

Zeus rounded on him with all the fury of Olympus. "Wretched rat! If you'd stayed in your place, I might have let you live."

This was it. Death had finally caught up to Vince, only five years late.

Reality rippled and fragmented like a movie stream with a poor connection. Grace and Zeus blurred. Disoriented, confused, and breathless, Vince clung to the only thing still in focus—a bright red thread.

The red thread entangled him, Grace, and Zeus. When he touched it, it began to fray.

He followed the thread, leaving his body behind.

A passive observer, Vince watched as he was struck by lightning.

Other-Vince collapsed, singed and seizing. Grace screamed.

Vince felt her raw agony and despair as though they were his own.

Zeus carried her off to heaven in golden chains.

And then there was peace.

Other-Vince awoke in a bed of moss and flowers, on a blessed island, surrounded by honey and bliss. Nancy's mother smiled in the distance. The nightmares were over forever.

For a moment, Vince was tempted. An end would be a relief.

But there was another thread stretching before him—so long he couldn't see what it connected with or where it finished. It lured him through danger, heartache, and pain. It dared him to survive.

Vince realized, with a jolt of wonder, that he could choose which thread was real. Just like he'd chosen the seven of clubs the only time he'd defeated Roy at cards.

He returned to the present. He smirked at Zeus.

"This rat might surprise you."

Somewhere beneath them, a flame burst to life.

An explosion rocked Ponce City Market. Chaos reigned as the building crumbled. Black smoke smothered the debate hall. A hole opened in the floor, swallowing Vince and Grace.

Vince wasn't sure where they would land, but he was sure of one thing: Zeus, lord of the sky, ruler of Olympus, and king of the gods, would remember the name Vincent Lenoir.

CHAPTER FORTY-FIVE

Faceless figures watched Tori. Silk flowed around them in shadowy mantles. After dark, clothing stores were creepier than haunted houses. She didn't even like them when they were open. As she crept under clothing racks and between mannequins, she did her best to ignore the unease growing like kudzu in her gut.

This clothing store was creepy, but it was safer than the main hall of Ponce City Market. Here, she had allies. The mannequins guarded her from Orion's watchful eyes. He'd have to get past them to get a decent shot on her.

He didn't need to. Not while Procyon was on the prowl.

Tearing down the mezzanine had given Vince and Grace a chance to escape. Tori was less fortunate.

Orion's fall left him disoriented and sore. Debris buried Sirius in a grave of concrete and steel. He wouldn't be getting up any time soon with a bullet in his head. Two out of three was pretty good. But it wasn't good enough.

Procyon, the smallest threat, was more than big enough to keep Tori busy. He'd lunged at her with a recklessness only an immortal could muster. He'd hounded her until she'd retreated into the nearest store.

She surveyed her surroundings. Dresses, pants, skirts, and shoes. Empty cash registers. Shelves of perfume. None of that would help her. She was beginning to think she might be in trouble when a blotch of black caught her eye.

She inched closer. Blending in against the ebony-stained floorboards, a foothold trap secured by a chain awaited its next victim —her.

Tori dragged a mannequin over the trap.

Procyon announced his arrival with a low-bellied snarl.

"Who wants a treat?" Tori shouted.

The hound barreled towards her.

Tori held her ground until she could count his teeth and smell his fur. She lobbed a shelf's worth of perfume bottles at its face. Then she dove behind the counter.

Through a cloud of amaranth, Procyon hit the mannequin.

The mannequin collapsed. Its head rolled across the floor.

Snap! The trap shut on Procyon's paw. It locked him in place.

Howling in pain, the hound thrashed. He couldn't break free.

One down, two to go.

An arrow shattered a link in Procyon's chain.

Orion waved from the clothing store's entrance. He'd been enjoying the show right up until the animal abuse. Even after the animal abuse, an ugly smirk stained his lips.

His tail between his legs, Procyon limped to his master.

Orion comforted his dog with a pat.

"If you keep running from me, this won't be much of a date."

Tori was getting real tired of fighting an archer without a ranged weapon of her own. At this distance, her newfound power would be useless. She shouldn't have given up on guns so easily. She should've practiced and practiced and practiced until her nerves steeled and her hands steadied. Now she had no choice but to run. Again.

Smack talk was her only ammunition. "I thought you liked a good chase!" she shot back as she fled into the main hall.

By now, it was clear that the secret service wasn't coming.

Tori was alone and exposed. She had to hide. But where? Most of Ponce City Market's famous shops and restaurants were sealed away behind metal grates. She had three options: what was left of the mezzanine, the food court, and the bar Orion had busted with his grenade.

She made a beeline for the bar. It had lots of furniture to hide behind. Plus, she'd already triggered a trap inside. There was one less to worry about.

As soon as she set foot in the bar, the stench of rotten eggs overpowered her. Did something die in the explosion? Like, a month or two ago?

When she squinted into the bar, she counted three dead somethings. A gas stove, a gas griddle, and a gas fryer. The steel appliances had been ripped from the wall by the blast.

Tori had a plan.

She dug a large frying pan out of the wreckage. Wielding it as a shield, she sprinted towards the food court.

"You're making me dinner? How romantic!" Orion followed her so casually that a bystander might think he actually was on a date.

The size of Orion's ego never ceased to amaze Tori. She wasn't the same scared little girl hiding in a corner of the Winecoff Hotel. She'd outsmarted him at Mimosa Hall. She'd gotten him good in their last fight, too. Without the help of Director Webb, he would've been done for. Yet he still treated her as if she was a kitten batting at yarn.

Soon, Tori would cut that ego down to size. Right now, she needed it.

"If I make you dinner, will you keep those grenades of yours to yourself?"

For the first course: Tex-Mex. She leapt over the counter of a taco stand. She ducked out of view. She cranked on its grill without lighting it.

"The grenades, maybe." Orion flexed his fingers.

For the second course, Tori raided a Szechuan stir fry booth. A golden dragon coiled through its rafters. That dragon deserved some fire. She twisted burners on the booth's enormous cooking range until the whole place hissed like a snake.

Orion's patience wavered. He couldn't see her, and if he couldn't see her, he couldn't appreciate the way she rushed around, flustered and breathing hard, all because of him.

Heavy footsteps thudded towards her.

Tori couldn't risk him catching on to her plan. She headed back into the food court.

The second her toe emerged from cover, Orion launched an arrow at her.

She readied her frying pan.

With a metallic BANG the arrow collided with steel.

The impact hurt her wrist and stopped her heart. But her heart recovered.

"Is that all you've got?" She willed her voice to stay steady despite her erratic pulse. "Maybe you *do* need those grenades."

An arrow sank into her ankle.

Agony blasted through Tori with all the fury of one of Orion's grenades. Her leg buckled. She dropped her frying pan to catch herself on the counter of a bakery. She couldn't fall. If she hit the ground, she was as good as dead.

Orion was done fooling around. He notched another arrow.

Streaking blood across the glass display, Tori hauled herself over the bakery counter. She snapped the arrow's shaft. Her breath caught in her throat. Merely touching her wound stung. And since she didn't want to bleed out, she had to leave the rest alone. Where was Brooks to patch her up with his disapproving sighs and gentle hands? Where was Roy to distract her with his dazzling smile?

Huddled behind the counter, she picked up the pieces of her composure. She tested her ankle. It held her weight, but each pound of pressure shocked electricity through her body. No more running.

This bakery would be Tori's last stop on her culinary tour of Ponce City Market.

Orion fired at her again. His shot smashed into the cash register, scattering change like shrapnel.

She'd pushed him too far. But she had to push him just a little further.

A pastry warmer cast a shadow across her. Ripping its fuel line out of the wall, she wheeled it to her. She crouched behind it and struggled to her feet. She had a new and improved shield.

"An arrow to the ankle? I'm not Achilles. You're never going to finish me like that. No wonder you're compensating with explosives."

The third time was the charm.

At last, Orion pulled out a grenade. "I was going easy on you, my dear Queen. For old time's sake. But you're right. You deserve to go out with a bang."

Finally—Orion took the bait. Tori had been dangerously close to running out of grenade-themed taunts. Her shopping mall bomb was armed. He would be the ignition.

But he was too close.

Using the pastry warmer as a walker, she limped away from the bakery. She had to get out of here.

King Orion claimed the food court as his kingdom. He leapt up onto a table.

Sirius burst from the rubble. Fur had sprouted over his gash, uninterrupted, as if he'd never been shot.

An uneven thump, schlick, thump haunted Tori's footsteps. Procyon was after revenge.

Canis Major loomed up ahead. Canis Minor approached from the side. Behind her, Orion Treyvon stood at the apex of their triangle.

Tori squeezed her eyes shut. She was cornered. That was okay.

Escaping had never been part of the plan.

Once Orion tossed that grenade, all the gas building up in Ponce City Market would rise on wings of fire. Tori engineered software. Typed words into a keyboard. She never studied math or chemistry—her understanding of the physical world was as theoretical as her understanding of monsters and magic.

She didn't know how big the explosion would be. She didn't know if it would be enough to kill her enemies. She didn't know if she had a chance of surviving. But she did know that this food court was far, far away from the party and crowds upstairs. All those innocent people would surely be fine. They wouldn't be fine if she failed to defeat Orion here and now.

Orion was the Greatest Hunter Ever to Live, and he intended to prove it. What other hunter could kill a city?

Through Roy, Brooks, Vince, Artemis, and most of all, Orion, Tori finally understood why she'd shredded that photo of James. Why she'd chased an assassin. Why she risked death again and again for strangers.

All her life, she'd lived at the mercy of others. Bullies, teachers, and bosses convinced her that their way was the only way. That she had to go to college and get a good job. Shut her mouth. Blend into the background. Even Artemis tried to tell her what to do.

Meanwhile, she convinced herself that her family was too broke. She was too dull. She read too much and looked too plain. She had no power to deny them.

But power had nothing to do with money, or good looks, or even supernatural abilities. True power was defining success for herself. It was having a purpose.

Purpose. After twenty-four years, she'd found hers. She could see it. In a burst of blue skies, golden gods, and bloody crimson, the gray of her office building melted away forever. She was the fox, the owl, the bear, and the lion—a predator of predators. Including Orion. She, not him, would be the Greatest Hunter Ever to Live.

Even if it killed her.

Orion pulled the pin of his grenade. He threw it in front of her.

It bounced on the floor.

Nothing.

For a heartbeat, Tori thought she had died. But the heartbeats continued. She realized that the grenade had died, not her. It was a dud.

Screw this. Her luck was insane. From now on, she was going to make her own.

Orion had lowered his bow.

Sirius and Procyon blocked her path forward, not back.

Deep in the savannah, lioness stalked through the tall grass. She was wounded and starving, but her fangs were sharp and her claws ready. A water buffalo ventured away from his herd. He was too proud to check for danger.

Tori lunged at Orion with supernatural speed. She buried her dagger in his chest. If he had a heart, she had pierced it.

Satisfying shock flashed across his handsome face.

Blood dripped down her blade, not silver, but red.

He was mortal after all. Just like her. That meant he could die just like her, too.

In the broken bar, an exposed wire sparked.

Flames devoured everything.

CHAPTER FORTY-SIX

Vincent Lenoir felt as if he'd been hit by a Porsche 918 Spyder. Slowly, carefully he traced his fingers down his chest. No broken bones. Everything was still there. He'd survived Zeus' wrath.

Somehow, he'd ended up six feet under. Dust buried him head to toe. Bricks piled high in cairns around him. Faint light filtered through smoke, cracks in a mausoleum. He couldn't make out much else.

He patted the earth around him, mapping his surroundings. His fingers brushed something soft and warm.

"Sorry!" he blurted automatically.

A hand grasped his.

"Vince? Is that you? Thank goodness! I thought I'd lost you in the blast."

Grace wiped away tears with her sleeve.

"Where are we?" he groaned, rubbing his temple.

She pointed down the hall.

Beyond it, Ponce City Market's shopping mall burned. Most of the building had collapsed. Sulfur, ash, and smog entombed the ruins. The great beast coughed and choked as flames feasted on its corpse.

Vince and Grace had landed on the second floor.

Muffled sirens wailed outside. Red and blue bounced off shattered windows.

Now that his grand stage had literally crumbled, Zeus the President of the United States would have no choice but to retreat. He had damage to control. Meanwhile, Ponce City Market was being evacuated. Soon all those innocent people from the roof would be safe at home. There could be no genocide without innocent people. He'd have to start his war some other way.

Vincent Lenoir: 1, Zeus: 0.

Okay fine, the score was actually Random Explosion: 1, Vince and Zeus: 0.

Vince was pretty sure he'd caused a spark, but he was equally sure that sparks couldn't wipe out two million square foot buildings. Tori must've done something. Hopefully. If Orion had done something, he didn't want to think about it.

"Come on," Grace helped him to his feet. "We should evacuate too!"

Together they fled into a parking deck.

Vince had survived, but the power hadn't.

Lit only by faint green and red emergency LEDs, the parking deck's long, low ceiling stretched into the abyss. Concrete columns stood in rows. Cars neatly filled more parking spaces than Vince could count. A laughably small fire extinguisher waited for duty on the wall.

Vince and Grace had barely made it inside when the familiar clack of hooves on pavement sent them scrambling for cover. They crouched behind an SUV.

Narcissus and Asterius emerged from a stairwell nearby.

"Look on the bright side, Asterius. At least Zeus is no longer pissed at *you!*" Narcissus reached to pat the minotaur's shoulder.

When he caught a whiff of musk mingled with ichor, he quickly withdrew his hand.

"For now," Asterius sighed. "When this is over, you know his wrath will turn on us."

Narcissus smiled—a bitter smile that didn't suit his beautiful face. It was the smile of a man who knew he didn't have much longer to live.

"I once heard that men originally had four arms, four legs, and a head with two faces. Zeus split us apart so that we'd search for our other halves our whole lives. You think he'll split us into quarters?"

Asterius blew air from his nostrils.

"I don't know. But just once, I would have liked to walk free in the sun."

This time, Narcissus patted his shoulder.

"Sun is bad for your skin. These days, it's fashionable to fake it."

Another snort. "Then shall we go out in style?"

Abruptly the minotaur smashed his horns—the sharp one, and the one the elevator had sheared down to a nub—into the SUV in front of Vince and Grace.

The monster hunters scattered to avoid being crushed.

Narcissus sulked as he watched Vince go. "Apparently I'm no longer your type." He glanced at Grace. "And I know better than to touch something that doesn't belong to me." He drew the most ridiculously fancy handgun ever and leveled it at Vince. "Guess we're doing this the"—he licked his lips—"hard way."

Grace raised her arms over her head. Steel beams ripped free from the concrete columns, carving deep cracks into the ceiling. They swirled around Vince to shield him.

Narcissus couldn't get a clear shot.

Vince had pistol envy. His revolver was gone, but he didn't need it anymore. He had a new weapon. But first, he had to create an opportunity to use it.

Asterius swatted the steel beams protecting Vince aside with the mild annoyance of a bull swatting a mosquito. "You have something of mine. I can smell it."

Oh yeah. The minotaur's missing horn stuck out of Vince's bag.

Vince had been planning on carving a new booze mug out of it. But lately, Asterius seemed more man than cow. Maybe sixty-forty instead of fifty-fifty. And not even Vince was metal enough to drink from another man's body part.

"Then what are you waiting for, MoMo? Come and take it from me."

A BANG rang in Vince's ears. Then a second. Then a third.

One by one, Narcissus shot the emergency LEDs above. By the time he'd emptied his magazine, the parking deck was pitch black.

"I learned this trick from you, Princess!"

Great. More darkness.

Vince couldn't see.

And Asterius could track him by scent.

Vince chucked the bull's broken horn down the tunnel.

Before it hit the ground, Asterius was upon him.

The minotaur hauled the monster hunter onto his shoulders.

No matter how much Vince squirmed, he couldn't break free. He was screwed. He was also impressed that this dude could overhead press so much weight with only one arm.

Asterius slammed him into the floor.

Vince landed hard on his back. Pain shocked down his spine.

A hoof gouged a Vince's-head-sized hole into the pavement, mere inches from his face.

Vince snatched the fire extinguisher off the wall, sprayed, and prayed that the stale foam would clog Asterius' nostrils.

Roaring, the minotaur lashed out blindly.

His foot caught Vince in the chest and sent him tumbling down the road.

Somewhere nearby, Narcissus finished reloading. He fired.

A bullet bit into concrete.

Grace cried out.

The rollercoaster of sounds screeched to a halt with the hard click of a gun jamming.

Narcissus grumbled about performance issues.

And then there was light.

Electricity arced over the battlefield in a terrifying display of power.

Grace stood before Narcissus with her hand closed in a fist. Her abilities had crushed the barrel of his ridiculously fancy handgun. A little late—liquid oozed from a gunshot wound in her side—but soon enough to end the fight.

Metal massed above her in angry clouds of black and silver, blocking out the sky.

Before Grace's power, Narcissus was nothing.

A single drop in an endless ocean.

Narcissus, Asterius, and Vince watched Grace breathlessly. She commanded all the air in the room. She could kill them with a flick of a finger.

Lightning flashed.

For one paralyzing moment, it looked like she would.

But she was not her father.

At the thought of becoming a killer, she wavered. A tear streaked down her cheek.

She let go.

The metal clattered lifelessly onto the ground.

Narcissus thudded to his knees. "I... I never asked for mercy!" he hissed bitterly.

Asterius took advantage of the distraction. Lowering his mighty head, he charged at Grace from behind.

His horn would pierce that naïve heart.

Time slowed.

Thousands of threads spiderwebbed in every direction,

weaving throughout the battlefield.

It was so dark, yet Vince could see every fiber of every cord.

He pulled one.

An ominous rumbling shook the earth.

The concrete columns Grace had damaged toppled to the ground.

The roof, the ceiling, and all the floors above caved in. In a wave of destruction that could rival the mighty Mount Rainier itself, cars, debris, and, eventually, fire, erupted through the parking deck.

The landslide swept away both heroes and villains.

* * *

When Vince came to, there was light.

In the ombre glow of the failing sun, Grace was a divine descending from heaven. She straddled him. He'd broken her fall. Such a gentleman.

She eased off and helped him up.

"Finally."

A solemn voice drew Vince and Grace's attention into the remains of the parking deck.

There, Asterius lay motionless in a single ray of sunlight. His missing horn impaled him through the chest. Silver ichor pooled beneath him, catching the blues, reds, and golds of sunset. He would rest forever in endless fields of color.

"Finally... I am free."

As he died, a shadow eclipsed the sun.

Grace gasped. "Vince, was that...?"

Vince seized her hand. Together, they climbed to the top of the ruined parking deck. At the summit, almost four stories high, they had a view of the Atlanta skyline.

A thick, orange fog hung in the air.

Death and destruction painted downtown, Nancy Kingfisher's mural come to life.

Copper-tinted flames swallowed Ponce City Market. In their insatiable hunger, they devoured the neighboring buildings. They gutted apartment complexes with impossible speed. They gnawed skyscrapers down to their bones. They clawed at the sky.

Above the burning horizon, a monstrous, beautiful bird unfurled her wings—the phoenix in all her glory.

Below, the ambulances, fire trucks, and the attendees of the presidential debate, struggled to survive. They were trapped by the living holocaust. And soon, Grace and Vince would be, too.

As though hunting fresh prey, fire stalked up the ruined parking deck. It blocked the way down. The deadliest monster of all, it encircled Vince and Grace. They couldn't escape.

Grace slumped against Vince's back. She'd been through so much today. She had no tears left to cry. Not even for fear of certain death.

He hugged her close.

Here, tangled with Grace under a smoldering sky, with all the city laid out before them... Here, Vince felt something he'd never felt before. He'd lost. The fight was over. And if the fight was over, there would be no more monsters. There was only peace. And Grace. And longing.

His future was now—these last precious moments, burning down the wick of a candle.

"Grace," he breathed.

She met his eyes.

"Grace. No matter what happens, I want you to know..."

Vince had once compared Grace to a swan—delicate, small, and pure. But she was none of those things. She was iron and steel, holding him steady whenever he faltered. She was a spark across the night sky that chased back the darkness. Not pure, but as bright as a supernova.

"...I'm a fucking coward..."

To him, she would always be special.

He traced the line of her cheek.

"...and I should have done this ages ago." He crashed his lips against hers. Into his kiss—into each heartbeat, each electric touch, each labored breath—he poured a lifetime of doubt and desire.

And she let him. She kissed back. She threw her arms around his shoulders, pressing against him, loosening her hair.

The disaster raging around them was lost to the storm, silenced by thundering hearts, magnetic skin, and searing lips. From now on, there'd be no more nightmares. Vince would dream only of Grace. Of his goddess. Who burned him to his soul, lightning in his hands.

And like lightning, their time together passed in a flash.

They parted, breathless, panting for air.

The phoenix's fire had grown so ferocious and tall that Vince could no longer see the sun. Heat pricked at his skin. It sucked the oxygen from the sky.

"Vince," Grace whispered.

Gentle fingers found his.

"Vince, I... I don't want to die."

A black arrow answered her prayer.

It sank into something within the flames—the fire extinguisher Vince had used against Asterius.

The fire extinguisher exploded. Its foam inside cleared a path through blaze.

"Vince! Grace! Thank God, Gandhi, and Mercy!"

Tori towered above them on the edge of Skyline Park, war-painted in blood, looking for all the world like the queen of the hunt. She wielded Orion's compound bow as if it'd been made for her.

"Come on. We can still stop this. But I'm going to need your help."

CHAPTER FORTY-SEVEN

Atlanta burned. The phoenix danced before the sunset. She breathed life into her prophecy of destruction, one beat of her wings, one wave of fire, one terrible second at a time.

There weren't any bodies in the streets. Not yet. Tori, Vince, and Grace still had time.

If the monster hunters slayed the phoenix, the nightmare would end. Her wildfire hadn't spread beyond the bounds of the Great Atlanta Fire of 1917. It was horrible, devastating, and tragic. But it was not beyond the power of men to fight. Firefighters, with their helicopters, bulldozers, and firetrucks, could dispel the magical blaze. The witnesses from the presidential debate would survive.

Vince had captured a confession from "President Arvis" on *Haunt Hunt*. The disaster, and its witnesses, would reach a natural conclusion—*Presidential Arvis lit a fire to ignite a war*. His treachery would make history. Not even Zeus would be above the consequences. He'd be condemned as a traitor, unwelcome everywhere in the world except, perhaps, Olympus.

Together, Tori and Vince hauled Grace from the parking deck onto the boardwalk of Skyline Park.

The amusement park had lost its magic. Its slide had slipped off the building. Its mini golf course had collapsed through a hole in the floor. Its carnival games rested in pieces in a graveyard of toys. The swing ride groaned and screeched, dying on its side, as it tried, and failed, to move.

Only its rollercoaster remained. It towered above the chaos. But it was far beneath the phoenix.

Tori gripped Orion's bow tightly. It was all she'd been able to find of her fated enemy—and his hounds—after she awoke inside the ruined food court.

She'd understood this weapon from the moment she touched it. She'd felt the flex in its limbs, the pull of the bowstring, and the tension of each draw, deep in her bones. Whenever she shot, her aim was true. The Great Huntress called on a thousand generations of the greatest predators ever to live—humanity.

But her supernatural talent wasn't enough to pierce the sky.

She peered up at the phoenix, as helpless as an intern against James.

"I can't reach her from here."

Vince exchanged glances with Grace.

A quiet, knowing agreement passed between them.

It was difficult to detect beneath all the soot and dust, but Tori knew that look well. It was the same look that she and Luke had shared when they first set foot on their college campus. They were prepared to take on the world together.

"You can't, but we can." Vince pointed at the rollercoaster. "Grace will get you to the top of that thing. And I'll... I'm not exactly sure how, but I'll make sure you don't miss."

With a push and a pull, Grace summoned one of the rollercoaster's carts.

Adrenaline and anticipation twisted Tori's chest as she hopped inside.

"Hey."

Vince squeezed her shoulder.

"Thank you, Tori. For everything."

Tori managed a smile.

"Don't you mean good luck?"

With that, the rollercoaster began to climb.

As Tori inched closer and closer to the glorious, infamous Helen of Troy, she wished she'd also stolen Orion's sunglasses.

The rollercoaster's cart reached the climax of its track.

The phoenix's awesome power baptized her in white light and searing heat.

If Tori got any closer, she'd burn. Like the Winecoff Hotel. Like Mimosa Hall. Like Roswell's mill.

I was. I am. I always will be.

The phoenix's words turned in her mind. Today, the cycle of tragedy would be broken.

Closing one eye, Tori drew her bow. She held her breath.

The past was gone. She would never again be afraid to speak up. She wouldn't waste another heartbeat of her life stifled in gray. She wouldn't let Luke's death kill her. She mattered. She'd *always* mattered.

She buried her arrow in the phoenix's wing.

The present was a wildfire of fear and hope. Tori had been forced, by danger and change, to connect to others—Brooks, Grace, Vince, Roy, and even Artemis. She connected with the darker yet stronger parts of herself.

Another arrow pierced the phoenix's neck.

The great bird sang of suffering. But she was still alive.

And the future, oh the future. Tori's future was so brilliant it likened the mighty phoenix to a candle before the Sun and Moon.

Roy waited for her at the Roswell Mill Club, all honey and saffron, a dare in his eyes.

In that future, she might never know what monster had killed Luke. But the what, or how, or why were no longer important to her. He lived on in her "when."

She accepted that she'd see Luke again whenever she looked in a mirror. Her twin echoed in all her footsteps. She would carry him with her forever—on her journey, she'd live enough for both of them.

She notched her final arrow.

Before she let go, dark clouds shrouded her target.

Lightning forked the sky, the tongue of a dragon, accompanied by such a terrible snarl of thunder it quaked in Tori's soul.

A bolt of electricity struck the rollercoaster.

The ride's steel rails lurched.

Tori's cart rolled forward. Weightless, she plummeted down the harrowing hill.

At the bottom of the curve, she met Vince's eyes.

She'd fallen from heaven, but she'd rise again.

The tracks arched upwards—to another peak.

The rollercoaster's momentum pinned her against her seat. She'd be trapped on the wildest ride on earth until she crashed.

Her luck was terrible.

But Vince's wasn't.

Just as Tori reached that intense, dizzying peak, the tracks before her collapsed.

Her cart launched from its rails. She rocketed into the air.

Tori had never imagined flying before. If she'd tried, Roy would've been in the picture, holding her steady, lifting her into the stars. In reality, the only stars she saw were the ones spinning in her own head as the loss of gravity robbed her of her sense of balance.

But she also saw the phoenix.

And then she saw a peregrine falcon, spinning in free fall at two hundred miles an hour, its eyes never leaving its prey.

The world rushed around Tori, yet her focus was clear.

She fired. Her last arrow pierced the phoenix's heart.

Below them, the flames died.

All the fury of the faded inferno erupted around the phoenix instead, a funeral pyre of copper, violet, and blue. The burst of color faded to black. Her beautiful feathers, vibrant eyes, and heavenly wings crumbled to ash.

A whisper of a breeze bore her dying words across the sky.

"Thank you."

And then it was over.

Tori dropped.

Without wings of her own, no owl, no eagle, nor falcon could save her.

Grace's magnetism couldn't overpower gravity. Vince's luck had run out.

The wind tore at Tori's face, wide eyes, and wild hair. Her body screamed for help, yet her voice could not. She spiraled helplessly towards an eternal terminus. Luke waited beneath the bottom, in Hades, or the meadows of asphodel, or heaven or hell.

She was doomed.

She was satisfied.

In this summer snow of cinders and dust, she'd kept her promise.

It was a shame she couldn't keep her promise to Roy.

As if summoned by her wish, a silhouette eclipsed the failing sun.

Tori saw an angel.

Wreathed in dusk sunlight, crowned in amber and gold, Roy Angelus reached out to her. He smiled, saffron and honey. His lips mouthed her name. He caught her in his arms. The wings of his snake-entwined rod slowed their descent to a gentle, easy drift.

There was nothing gentle or easy about the way Tori threw herself around him. She buried her face in his chest. His warmth sparked new fire through her system. If she'd been taller, she might have kissed him.

She was alive. And so was he.

"I'm happy to see you, too," he whispered.

He didn't seem happy. Relieved, definitely. Affectionate, maybe. But not happy.

Resignation flickered in those once-daring eyes. When he landed in Skyline Park, he did so stiffly. He drew short, shallow breaths, pacing himself to keep calm. He'd lost the glowing confidence that made him so divine.

Brooks emerged from the remains of a stairwell, as grim as a ghost.

"Since when could you fucking fly!?" Vince greeted them. His words were harsh, but his eyes were soft with tears.

Roy didn't respond. He only stared at that burning horizon.

Tori followed his gaze.

"Roy." She was afraid to ask. "What's wrong?"

A siren she'd never heard before screeched through Atlanta, bouncing between skyscrapers, booming and absolute.

It was an eerie, monotone sound. Somber. Ominous. A black music of mourning.

Roy's fingers found her hand. He squeezed it tight.

"Sometimes Fate tests us, Tori. Our choices don't actually make a difference."

CHAPTER FORTY-EIGHT

Vincent Lenoir didn't know how to feel anymore.

Before Zeus, he'd felt powerless. Like a fly trapped beneath a jar, throwing himself over and over against the glass prison of fate until he'd somehow escaped through the tiniest gap. Before Grace, he'd felt naked. As if her lightning burned away his layers of guilt, shame, and doubt. There'd been nothing left but desire. Before Tori, he'd felt hope—the courage to dream of a future full of daylight. Together they triumphed over the monsters who lurked in the dark.

But before Roy and Brooks, reunited with the men who'd molded him into who he was, Vince felt empty. He'd already thought every thought. He'd felt every feeling. He'd spent every emotion and now he was broke.

Relieved, yet cold, he shivered.

"Sometimes Fate tests us, Tori. Our choices don't actually make a difference."

Roy's solemn statement totally killed the mood. What was left of it, anyway.

Tori's wide eyes bounced between Roy and Brooks, their

expressions as grim as the reaper on his pale horse. "Don't make a difference? You can't possibly mean..."

She collapsed to her knees.

Grace tugged on Vince's sleeve. "What's that siren? Wh-what's going on?"

"It's the Minuteman." Brooks held up his phone, showing off a map of Missouri. Red circles marked all the missile silos in the state. He quoted Narcissus' IOU-list. "Destination: anywhere. Only now its destination is Atlanta."

"I've seen that map before! In Channel 4's labyrinth, inside the —oh. *Oh*."

The subsequent silence was deafening—and infuriating.

"I don't understand. Teacher"—Vince nudged Brooks—"can you explain to the rest of the class?"

"Before I explain, I need you to know something." Brooks grasped his shoulders. "You three—Grace Batya, Victoria Jaecar, and Vincent Lenoir—are incredible. What you did here was the stuff of epic legends."

His grip loosened. His eyes fell.

"Mercy and I tried to change your destiny. We tried so very, very hard. But we've failed. I fear your legend will be a tragedy."

"The Minuteman, named after colonial soldiers, is a type of ICBM—a nuclear missile. The Minuteman launch sites all over the Midwest were decommissioned after the Cold War," Roy explained, his eyes still pinned on that burned horizon. "But one has been brought back to life alongside the other monsters. It's on its way here. To ignite President Arvis' revolution."

He clenched his snake-entwined staff. Frustration slithered in his tone.

"How ironic. The gods will end this era not with magic, nor divine right, but human technology."

Denial swept Vince off Ponce City Market, out of Atlanta, into the past.

Rain tapped away at the roof, the tick of an invisible clock, counting the seconds until the end of the world. Vince was fourteen again, back in those West Virginia woods, helpless beneath the monster who'd stolen his future. Spearfinger—Lamia—would haunt him forever.

"You... You're shitting me, aren't you?" Vince stuttered. "Why would Zeus use an ICBM? After going through all that trouble with the phoenix?"

"Plan A, Plan B," Roy sighed. "Zeus would rather be king of a charcoal Atlanta than a radioactive crater in the ground. But he'd destroy it all to reclaim his throne."

Denial collapsed into anger.

Lamia screamed into the uncaring sky, lamenting her fate, singing of suffering. After she'd caused so much of her own.

"If you two knew all this... Where the fuck have you been all this time? If you'd told us earlier, we could've done something about it!"

Anger collapsed into bargaining.

Vince would trade himself for Nancy's mother, if he could. She'd been so decisive—so unafraid. He'd always been afraid.

"Maybe we can still do something! I don't understand it, but I've got an in with Lady Luck. Tori is a badass with that bow. And Grace is a goddamned demigoddess. Among the three of us... Maybe, just maybe..."

"What can we do against a nuclear weapon? Zeus himself is afraid of them," Grace recalled softly.

Depression dragged Vince to the ground alongside Tori.

He replayed Nancy's mother's death over and over again in his mind. Thwack. Pop. Crunch. *Rip.* He clutched his head. He covered his ears. But the sounds wouldn't stop.

Capturing President Arvis's confession on *Haunt Hunt* no longer had meaning—a bullet wouldn't fit back in its chamber once it'd been fired. Nothing Tori, Vince, and Grace had done today would matter.

They were going to die. They were all going to die.

Was this the future Nancy had painted?

Roy steadied Vince with a hand on the shoulder. A lifeline.

"We can't allow Zeus to destroy our ancestors' future," Roy stated gently but firmly. "So we have to keep fighting, no matter how hopeless it seems."

He drew Vince's revolver from a holster at his hip. It was a miracle that he'd somehow found it in all the wreckage. He spun it so that its handle was near Vince.

"We don't have a choice."

Vince had seen—no, lived—this scene before. On the night of the day he'd met Roy and Brooks, Roy had offered him the very same gun in the very same way.

"Come with us," Roy had said. "There's no going back now. Even if we drop you off at your high school and never bother you again... Even if you never see anything strange for the rest of your days... You'll always know that evil is real. That people are suffering. That you are *needed*. Come with us. Help us save them."

And Vince had refused him.

Back then, he was just a kid. An angry, abandoned kid. No one needed him.

It wasn't until Lamia kidnapped him and murdered Nancy's mother that he'd chosen to fight with Brooks and Roy. And it wasn't even really a choice. Vince had needed them. Without them, the monsters in his nightmares would've devoured him long ago.

Either way, he'd chosen this life.

Why couldn't he make that same choice again?

Time was running out. The Minuteman could arrive at any second.

"Vince." Roy hadn't expected him to hesitate. "Fate has terrible power. You cannot escape it by wealth or war. No fort will keep it out, no ships outrun it."

Roy had a way with words. But Vince knew these words. Under the weight of these words, all things stopped.

"What..." Vince choked. "What did you just say!?"

Vince remembered now. That night in the rain. Lamia's speech.

Roy had been there to comfort him in an instant.

"It's a quote from Sophocles," Roy replied too quickly.

Too quickly indeed.

"It's also a quote from fucking Lamia," Vince seized Roy by the wrist.

"A quote that she spouted off while Nancy's mother was *still alive!*"

At the time, he'd been too blinded by horror and grief to see. When Roy shot Lamia, he'd been standing right next to her. He could've shot her sooner. Soon enough to save Vince's childhood.

"You could've saved her, couldn't you?"

"You know Lamia's name..." Roy whispered. He didn't deny it.

Vince's heart broke. By the time it beat again, his fingers were at Roy's throat.

"You could've saved her, but you didn't even try! Jesus, Roy. You... You let her die!"

Roy stared back at him, unsmiling, unyielding. He made no move to break free.

Meanwhile, Brooks couldn't look at them.

Vince needed no other confirmation.

Tears rained down, tapping away at the ground between them, the tick of an invisible clock. He bled from the soul he wasn't even sure existed.

"But... But why? Roy, you know what that did to Nancy. You of all people know what that did to me!"

His hands slipped. He begged.

"So... Please. At least tell me *why!*"

Roy searched Vince's eyes for his answer.

"I needed an in with Lady Luck. And..."

One by one, the words dropped. Like the swing of an executioner's ax, they gutted Vince.

"...if I'd saved Nancy's mother, would you have joined me?"

No. *No.*

After five long years, Roy had finally told the truth.

Yet Vince didn't want to hear it. He wanted Roy to tell him that he was wrong—that he'd made a mistake, that he couldn't get a clear shot in all that rain, even if Vince wouldn't believe it. He wanted Brooks to call him childish.

Forget feelings. Forget denial, anger, bargaining and depression.

Vince sobbed and prayed for nothing—for nothing could remove the wine-bronze dagger twisting in his chest. Nothing could ease his pain.

After killing Lamia, Roy'd hugged Vince close. He'd kept him safe and warm. He'd shielded him from that terrible rain. But he'd caused the rain.

Through all those late-night card games—each and every last one—Vince had been getting played.

At the raceway, they'd foresaw a future Roy, not Nancy, had painted.

Beneath the mighty Mount Rainier, they'd explored the mysteries of the universe, the collective knowledge of civilization, and the meaning of life.

Roy had been honest about one thing: there wasn't a point to living.

Let the Minuteman come. Vince's world had already been destroyed by betrayal.

Vince regarded Roy darkly. Speechless.

He'd trusted Roy like a father. Loved him.

And in turn, Roy had manipulated him. Maybe Tori and Grace, too. They never did figure out who'd left that business card on James' desk.

Vincent Lenoir would never have a father.

Love and manipulation couldn't coexist.

So when Vince looked at Roy's handsome face, he saw the hydra's hungering teeth, Lamia's empty eye sockets, Asterius' sharpened horns, and, most of all, Zeus. He saw every monster he'd failed to slay when it mattered.

Roy was a monster.

A monster who deserved to share a grave with Nancy's mother.

Vince would never know who pulled his trigger—whether it was him, Lady Luck, or perhaps Roy himself. All he knew was the crack of his bullet. A hole in the heart Roy couldn't have. The splatter of blood on the boardwalk.

His revolver fired, hitting Roy square in the chest.

In the ombre glow of the failing sun, Roy's blood glittered like drops of mercury. Only instead of red or silver, they were gold.

Not blood. *Ichor.*

Time surged forward all at once.

Radiant light burst through Atlanta, so bright and hot that Vince half believed a star had been born on the surface of the earth.

Every window on every block shattered.

The air hummed, so charged with energy that Vince couldn't speak for fear of burning his tongue.

Ponce City Market trembled. Every brick and nail of the shopping mall crumbled—except for where the monster hunters stood. The great beast bowed before its master.

Roy was gone.

His strawberry blonde hair flowed in fields of gold. Saffron and honey glowed on hallowed skin. Wherever he touched the ground, purple flowers bloomed. Every inch of his body had been masterfully sculpted to inspire youth, beauty, and awe.

The grand wings on the staff in his hands grew until the late phoenix seemed small by comparison. Another pair curled from his brow, and a third from his ankles. White feathers formed a royal mantle around him. For he was the king of angels.

"Mercury!" Grace gasped.

Tori's fingers carved tense trails into the ground. "Not Mercury. Hermes."

Brooks exhaled as if he'd been holding his breath for a decade. "Shepherd of the Crossroads. God of messages, commerce, and... deception."

And a predator of humanity.

Vince didn't care about any of those titles.

"Vince." Roy, or Hermes, guided Vince's hand to the bullet hole on his chest. Already, the wound had started to fade. The god had barely felt it.

Beneath Vince's fingers, pulsed a thump, thump, *thump.*

Proof that Hermes had a heart. That he wasn't calm.

He was afraid.

He was trying to tell Vince something important.

I'm not a monster. I'm still here. Listen.

But Vince would never listen to Roy again.

Because Roy was not Roy Angelus, Mercy, or Mercury, or Hermes.

He was a fucking liar.

CHAPTER FORTY-NINE

Twenty-six years, nine months, and eighteen days ago, Brooks Wyman met Hermes on the edge of a battlefield, laying in a pool of blood. Brooks had seen him once before, in his own home—or rather *her* home—holding the hands of his children.

His precious Jewel had smiled; she'd always loved strawberries. Young Darl had openly stared. He was a smart kid. He'd never trust a stranger, even if that stranger offered sweets and flowers and gold. Cash, Dewey, and Vardaman followed along as if they were eager to go. Hermes led them away. Forever.

Ever since that day, every day, Brooks had wanted to die. He'd enlisted as a soldier. He walked battlefield to battlefield. But as he'd failed as a father, he failed as a martyr. Fate would neither forgive him nor free him from his suffering.

This time, Hermes had come for Brooks' brothers in arms, not him.

And as the glowing god disappeared over the horizon, Brooks couldn't help but reach out to him. "Mercy!" he cried. "Mercy!" For the lost, for those left behind. "Mercury!" he begged and pleaded, desperate for the end of his lonely road.

But God was neither good, nor evil, but something altogether worse—indifferent.

Hermes didn't turn back. And so Brooks followed him.

He'd followed him ever since.

But then Hermes found Vince. Then Tori. And then Grace.

Day by day, word by word, Brooks watched these children perform a miracle. They carved away at Hermes' indifference, like the caress of wind on a mountainside, until what seemed impossible finally happened.

No one—not Brooks, not Mercy, nor the Fates themselves—could've predicted that Hermes could change so much so quickly.

But Time did. Time had brought them together.

Once Brooks saw Hermes touch Vince—a distant, detached divine humbled before a mere mortal he'd wronged—he couldn't breathe.

Something was coming. Something greater than the Minuteman and all the gods of Olympus.

Change.

* * *

Hermes had always been faster than the other gods.

After a thousand years of nothing, when he'd awoken in a world he barely recognized, he'd been enamored, not afraid. Immortality had its drawbacks—repetition, monotony, and boredom. The Classical era had dulled the brilliance within him.

But now, a new horizon had risen. It promised a new mystery, a new danger, and, above all, a new humanity.

Within seconds, Hermes had embraced the new Earth. He touched her face. He explored her curves, her mountains, her cities. He held her pulse in his hands.

The gods of Olympus drew their power from the universe. Like a dam in a river, they redirected the flow of reality, amplified it, and roared with its strength.

With every flicker of a candle, Apollo's light shone brighter. Whenever the guillotine of a slaughterhouse fell, or a young girl murdered her abuser, Artemis the huntress triumphed. Whenever a dictator rose to power or a CEO raised his salary, King Zeus' dominion grew.

But none of them had benefited half as much from the passage of time as Hermes, god of messages, commerce, and deception.

Two millennia ago, the world ran on stamped silver dekadrachm, wax tablets, and family alliances. Now the world ran on ideas—plastic cards and printed paper, boardroom meetings and lobbyist groups, and electricity that sparked words anywhere in an instant.

Hermes had always been a talented thief—so talented he could steal light from the sun—and in a world that ran on ideas, he could have anything he wanted. Except control over his own future.

For no Olympian had any control over the threads of Fate. Not even Zeus, who commanded the Moirae to weave them into tapestries.

They could see them. Read them. Lament them. But never touch them.

Brooks Wyman had been so quick to point that out.

Whereas his father chose companions who filled his cup and kissed his feet, Hermes preferred ones that could hold his fleeting attention. Brooks approached him with the quiet resolve of a man who knew what he believed in. He who longed for Death was unafraid of Progress—he spoke his mind, often, and without holding back. Hermes had enjoyed the novelty.

Brooks spoke of a theoretical God unlike the gods who sat upon the twelve thrones of Olympus, who was neither born of Titans, nor of nature, who'd always been and always would be. Of omnipotence above omniscience. Of a divine unbound by destiny.

He claimed that Fate, not Zeus, was master of the universe.

It wasn't until Hermes met Vincent Lenoir that he'd understood what Brooks had meant.

Nancy Kingfisher had predicted that the end of this era would arrive on the back of a midnight horse.

When Hermes saw that prophecy, he saw his own future. He saw his power returned to silver, wax, and blood. This new Earth that he'd come to love, that loved him back, would die—along with his voice. He'd be his father's herald. A glorified servant. Nothing more.

So when Hermes saw Vincent defeat the guardian of the Underworld with an impossible stroke of luck, the god of cunning saw an opportunity like none before it. An opportunity to become more than just a god. An opportunity to pull the threads of Fate and become the puppeteer.

Thus, Hermes claimed Vincent as his own. One by one, he'd tracked down the other twelve stars named by Oracles of Apollon. All in the name of self-interest.

Now on the roof of Ponce City Market, his ruined temple, Vincent wept at his feet.

Hermes didn't feel Vincent's bullet, but he felt the pain in his tears, the betrayal in his eyes, and the hate in his voice. When Hermes reached out, Vincent pulled away.

Grace Batya, Hermes' half-sister, threw her arms around Vincent. She hugged him, as if she could transfer her strength through warmth.

Hermes pitied Grace. She reminded him of his dear friend Callisto; Zeus hadn't bothered to protect her from Hera's wrath, either. If she survived her ascent to godhood, she would never be the same.

Victoria Jaecar stood strong and serene. Not unlike her brother had been as he crossed into the afterlife. But Hermes knew she was anything but serene on the inside. If they'd been alone, he'd have carried her to Olympus. Shown, not told, the reason behind his lies. He still might. But first, he had to reclaim Vincent.

"Vince." He needed to explain. He could explain anything. He could still repair the link he'd so purposefully broken.

But Vincent wouldn't listen.

"Vince, we need to get out of here!" Grace begged.

Vince squeezed her hands. He wouldn't budge.

Hermes could sense the Minuteman's approach. As a first in his long existence, he'd run out of time. He gripped his staff—the Caduceus—in his fingers. With it, he could evacuate them all to somewhere safe. They could untangle their emotions far beyond the heat of copper-stained flames.

An ax knocked the Caduceus from Hermes' grasp.

Sirius caught the Caduceus mid-air between his teeth. Knowing full and well the grave sin he'd committed, the hound fled into the darkness. Meanwhile, his master laughed.

Orion Treyvon towered over the ruins of the shopping mall. His bones were broken. His wounds fed a river of red. Hermes smelled the Styx on his skin. He'd barely survived his last encounter with Tori, and he wouldn't survive much longer.

Procyon waited at his heels.

"If I'm going down, you're going down with me!" Orion choked through blood and bile.

Before he could waste one more word, Hermes was upon him.

Hermes flew to Orion. He lifted him by the neck.

"You're not going down, Orion. You're going to live forever."

Hermes was not his father. He couldn't grant a body eternal youth. But by his authority as Shepherd of the Crossroads, Orion would never cross into the afterlife—or the stars—again. And by his authority as lord of hares, the giant began to shift.

A long ear stretched from his dark curls. Then a second. Satin fur softened his skin. Whiskers grew from his nose. The final touch —a fluffy tail.

Hermes dropped Orion the Rabbit into the dirt.

"You, Orion Treyvon, will join Lepus."

Procyon stood, sniffing the air.

"No matter how far you run, your hounds will find you..."

The mastiff stalked towards Orion.

"No matter how many times you die, you'll be reborn anew..."

Snarling, he opened his ravenous jaws.

"Prey in the Eternal Hunt."

Procyon lunged. Orion bolted.

Brooks, Vincent, Tori, and Grace watched, their expressions mixed with awe and horror, as the villain fulfilled his destiny once and for all.

Hermes' heart clawed against his ribcage. The ragged breath he didn't need to breath scratched at his throat. Unease pricked in his veins. He'd never been angry before, yet he knew this transcended anger. This was fear. *Desperation.*

He didn't have time to chase down Sirius. It was too late to fly his allies to safety, two at a time. If he winked into Hades, he could survive. He might be able to take someone with him. But who?

He had to save Vince. But Vince might abandon him.

He couldn't leave Tori behind.

His father would never forgive him for losing Grace.

After all these years, how could he be the one to finally end Brooks' suffering?

He couldn't choose.

"Roy?"

A hand steadied him. A lifeline.

Tori peered up at him. She was worried.

Right then and there, Hermes realized that this wasn't anger, fear, or desperation tearing at his soul. It was concern. Sincere, genuine concern.

For mortals.

For four little drops in an endless ocean.

He was no longer ruled by self-interest alone.

There was another choice.

"Grace," he breathed. "Grace, our father doesn't care about anyone except himself. If you walk the path to Olympus, walk it on your own two feet, with your eyes clear, and your heart steady. Heaven isn't the only place where you belong."

Brooks looked at him with the misery and strife of the two long decades between them. He knew what was coming.

"Brooks," Hemes continued. "Your past is the past. You deserve a future. All this time, we've both been in your way."

His fingers curled around Tori's hand. He pulled it to his lips. "Tori. I'm afraid I'll have to miss our dinner. You've come so far, yet you'll go much farther. So far that Lucien Anestis Jaecar will hear of your legends, all the way in the meadows of asphodel."

She didn't understand. She didn't want to let him go.

Hermes turned to the last of his flock.

"And Vincent Lenoir. *Vince.* I manipulated you. But know that you've also manipulated me. If our paths hadn't crossed at the edge of existence, nothing would've ever changed."

He would've liked to embrace his wayward son, but he'd lost that privilege. Instead, he turned his eyes to the horizon.

"This changed world—my world—starts and ends with you."

Anger, fear, desperation, and concern were fleeting before the most magnificent change of all—love. Hermes was satisfied. In terms of love, even Zeus was a pauper at his feet.

"Thousands of years ago I taught mankind their many tongues. I helped Prometheus steal fire to keep you warm. I gave you writing, learning, enterprise, and philosophy. But my greatest gift to humanity, by far, will be the four of you."

With that, Hermes took to the sky.

The Caduceus was a part of him—he snatched it away from Sirius within seconds. Seconds he would've needed to escape. But he no longer needed to escape.

On six great wings, Hermes rose to meet the Minuteman.

Miles in the sky, the nuclear warhead whistled through the air. Deadly silent, it soared faster than the speed of sound. The herald of Olympus was also faster than the speed of sound. He brought the full might of messages, commerce, and deception to bear. He seized the future in his bare hands. He pushed back.

A detonator clicked. White heat seared through his fingers, his bones, his holy ichor.

He was terrified. He was exhilarated.

For he would be the first man, monster, or deity to know what it meant to be a God.

CHAPTER FIFTY

The sun didn't rise for four days—anywhere on Earth. According to Brooks, the mourning Apollo had refused to lend Helios his light. The stock market crashed. Tianyi declared bankruptcy. The salamanders of the Woolworth Building retired from duty; the great temple to commerce burned to the ground.

Tori turned off her television. She dropped the remote to the floor. She didn't need any more news.

Roy had been right—this was the Information Age. Millions of tablets, laptops, and cellphones had captured his final moments. Humanity had proof of the supernatural. The world gazed upon its savior with eyes wide open. Some worshiped him as an angel. Some argued he was a government conspiracy.

Others embraced the deep longing for magic that'd always tugged at their souls. They knew him for the martyr he was. They searched for answers. They demanded the truth.

The only people who knew the whole truth—Grace, Vince, Brooks, and Tori— sat silent in the one room of her once-abandoned Atlanta apartment. They piled into her plain loveseat, along her lonely two-seat dining set, and atop her unmade bed. They'd been here since the disaster at Ponce City Market. Not fighting. Not mourning. Simply existing. They hadn't had the courage to return to their rental in Roswell. Tori might never set foot in Roswell again.

This was Victory. Undeniably so.

Sun Tzu, one of Vince's two video channel followers, turned out to be another alias for "Charlie" Charles Chenlong Li. He leveraged what was left of his great wealth to send Vince's final episode of *Haunt Hunt* straight to the top of the charts.

Vince and Grace headlined as heroes. President Arvis starred as the villain.

Zeus had no choice but to abandon the identity he'd so carefully crafted.

It would take him time to try again.

Next time, humanity would be better prepared.

The chaos that followed the grand treason of a sitting president burned through the world like a fever. Now that mankind had learned the symptoms of Zeus' infection, it could fight back.

But victory's price had been high. This was no happy ending.

Losing Roy was different from losing Luke. Tori had known Luke since the day she was born. She'd only just begun to know Roy. His absence left an aching hole, not in her soul, not in that rushing River Styx, but in the back of her mind. She'd started a romance novel she could never finish. She'd glimpsed secret knowledge that she would never understand.

Someday, when that river of memories dried up, Tori would see Luke again. But Roy? She didn't know.

She did know a thing or two about grief.

And she knew that right now, grief threatened to take Brooks and Vince from her, too.

Brooks no longer spoke. He ate, drank, walked, and slept, but he'd become a hollow empty shell of a man, wandering lost through purgatory.

Vince hadn't stopped drinking since the sun fell below that burned horizon.

He flipped his flask upside down. Not a drop.

Grumbling under his breath, he stumbled towards the kitchenette.

A crash.

Everyone flinched.

Glass snowed across white tile.

Vince had accidentally knocked a picture frame off the counter.

With trembling hands, he handed it to Tori.

Luke smiled up at her at their college graduation. The cracks crisscrossing his face couldn't conceal how happy he'd been—how much he'd loved her. Tori hadn't seen this photograph since the night he passed. She'd set it upside down. Hidden that smile in the dark.

It hurt to see it. But it filled her with hope.

For Luke could still reach her, even now. And so could Roy.

Roy would be with her whenever she touched a freckle on her lip. Whenever she heard Vince laugh or Brooks sigh. Whenever she stood strong and serene against a monster in the hungering darkness. As long as her odyssey continued, she could feel him. She could cross that unknown distance, across grief, across death, across all of creation.

So she couldn't let this be a happy ending. Or a sad one.

It had to be a new beginning.

"Sorry," Vince mumbled.

"Never apologize for things that aren't your fault."

"It was definitely my fault. It was always my fault."

Those quiet, fatalistic words didn't suit Vincent Lenoir. Where was the man who'd defeated her in every spar? Where was the gun-toting ever-smoking bad boy with a roaring muscle car who'd charmed Lady Luck to his side?

"So that's it, then?" she challenged.

"That's what?"

"The great Vincent Lenoir, after finally hitting it big, after facing down the king of Olympus himself, getting the girl, and saving the world... defeated by one lie."

Vince was drowning in liquor. In betrayal. In loss.

Tori couldn't begin to know the depths of what he was feeling. But she understood him. And he was strong enough to keep fighting, even when he was afraid, even when he lost the fight every time he closed his eyes.

She had to channel a little bit of Roy to drag him back to the surface.

From there, he'd swim on his own.

"What about buying that muscle car? Putting Charlie in his place? Grace's mom, the Headless Horseman, and Nancy Kingfisher?"

Slowly, Vince sobered. "I don't—"

"Nothing that happened in these past three months or the five years before them, was your fault... or Grace's... or Brooks'... or mine...."

Tori slung Orion's bow over her shoulder. She headed for the door.

"...so we clearly haven't gone far enough."

"Where are you going?" Brooks' voice was full of rust and cobwebs. But he couldn't stay silent when one of his children was leaving home.

"To hunt."

"Hunt what?" Grace whispered, wary yet excited.

"Apollo. Artemis. Zeus. *Answers.* There are monsters out there."

This was bigger than Tori. It was bigger than Atlanta, the death of a loved one, and all the gods of Olympus.

"Evil is real. People are suffering. We're still needed."

They were not lost without their shepherd. They'd only just been found.

Grace Batya was a princess of heaven, who filled the sky with love and life, not cold, unfeeling stars. Brooks Wyman was a stone-faced guardian who'd weathered the worst of Time. Who shielded others, no matter how he himself was broken. Vincent Lenoir was a surprise improvisation in the script of the universe. And Tori was the Greatest Hunter to Ever Live.

Finally, they knew who they were.

That knowledge was power. Hermes' power.

Zeus was still out there. Ten more Olympians ruled from wine-bronze thrones. A million monsters swarmed at their feet.

Grace, Vince, Brooks, and Tori were four mere mortals capable of challenging them all.

"Aren't y'all coming?"

Tori offered Vince her hand. It was salvation. It was also an invitation.

Twenty-four hours ago, maybe even twenty-four minutes ago, Vince would've backed away. Vince of Now grabbed her hand like a rope.

"Wouldn't miss it for the world."

RIZE publishes great stories and great writing across genres written by People of Color and other underrepresented groups.

Our team consists of:

Lisa Diane Kastner, Founder and Executive Editor
Joelle Mitchell, Licensing and Strategy Lead
Cody Sisco, Acquisition Editor, RIZE
Benjamin White, Acquisition Editor, Running Wild
Peter A. Wright, Acquisition Editor, Running Wild
Resa Alboher, Editor
Angela Andrews, Editor
Sandra Bush, Editor
Ashley Crantas, Editor
Rebecca Dimyan, Editor
Abigail Efird, Editor
Aimee Hardy, Editor
Henry L. Herz, Editor
Cecilia Kennedy, Editor
Barbara Lockwood, Editor
AE Williams, Editor
Scott Schultz, Editor
Rod Gilley, Editor

Evangeline Estropia, Product Manager
Kimberly Ligutan, Product Manager
Pulp Art Studios, Cover Design
Standout Books, Interior Design
Polgarus Studios, Interior Design

Learn more about us and our stories at www.runningwildpublishing.com

www.runningwildpublishing.com, www.facebook.com/ runningwildpress, on Twitter @lisadkastner @RunWildBooks @RizeRwp

www.ingramcontent.com/pod-product-compliance
Lightning Source LLC
Chambersburg PA
CBHW072302020726
47501CB00002B/352